Christie Barlow is the number ... author of twenty-four roma... iconic Love Heart Lane Series ... and *The Story Shop*. She lives ... quaint village in the heart of Staffordshire with her two dogs.

Her writing career came as a lovely surprise when Christie decided to write a book to teach her children a valuable life lesson and show them that they are capable of achieving their dreams.

Christie writes about love, life, friendships and the importance of community spirit. She loves to hear from her readers and you can get in touch via X, Facebook and Instagram.

facebook.com/ChristieJBarlow

x.com/ChristieJBarlow

bookbub.com/authors/christie-barlow

instagram.com/christie_barlow

Also by Christie Barlow

The Love Heart Lane Series

Love Heart Lane

Foxglove Farm

Clover Cottage

Starcross Manor

The Lake House

Primrose Park

Heartcross Castle

The New Doctor at Peony Practice

New Beginnings at the Old Bakehouse

The Hidden Secrets of Bumblebee Cottage

A Summer Surprise at the Little Blue Boathouse

A Winter Wedding at Starcross Manor

The Library on Love Heart Lane

The Vintage Flower Van on Love Heart Lane

The Puffin Island Series

A Postcard from Puffin Island

The Lighthouse Daughters of Puffin Island

The Story Shop

The Café on the Coast

No. 17 Curiosity Lane

Standalones

Kitty's Countryside Dream

The Cosy Canal Boat Dream

A Home at Honeysuckle Farm

THE CAFÉ ON THE COAST

CHRISTIE BARLOW

One More Chapter
a division of HarperCollins*Publishers* Ltd
1 London Bridge Street
London SE1 9GF
www.harpercollins.co.uk
HarperCollins*Publishers*
Macken House, 39/40 Mayor Street Upper,
Dublin 1, D01 C9W8, Ireland

This paperback edition 2026
1
First published in Great Britain in ebook format
by HarperCollins*Publishers* 2025
Copyright © Christie Barlow 2025
Christie Barlow asserts the moral right to
be identified as the author of this work
A catalogue record of this book is available from the British Library

ISBN: 978-0-00-870807-8

This novel is entirely a work of fiction. The names, characters and incidents portrayed in it are the work of the author's imagination. Any resemblance to actual persons, living or dead, events or localities is entirely coincidental.

Printed and bound in the UK using 100% Renewable Electricity
by CPI Group (UK) Ltd

For Cooper – my newest four-legged sidekick, bringing so much joy to me and Nellie. Your cuddles are the absolute best!

Puffin Island

COCKLE BAY COVE

CAUSEWAY

The Clockmaker's Cottage

Puffin Island Farm

B&B

ANCHOR

Rainbow Cottages

Nautical Nook

SEA'S END

Cosy Nook

CASTAWAY COVE

LIGHTHOUSE LANE

Cliff Top Garage

POST OFFICE

PUFFIN

THE CLIFFS

Cliff Top Cottage

Post Office

Puffin

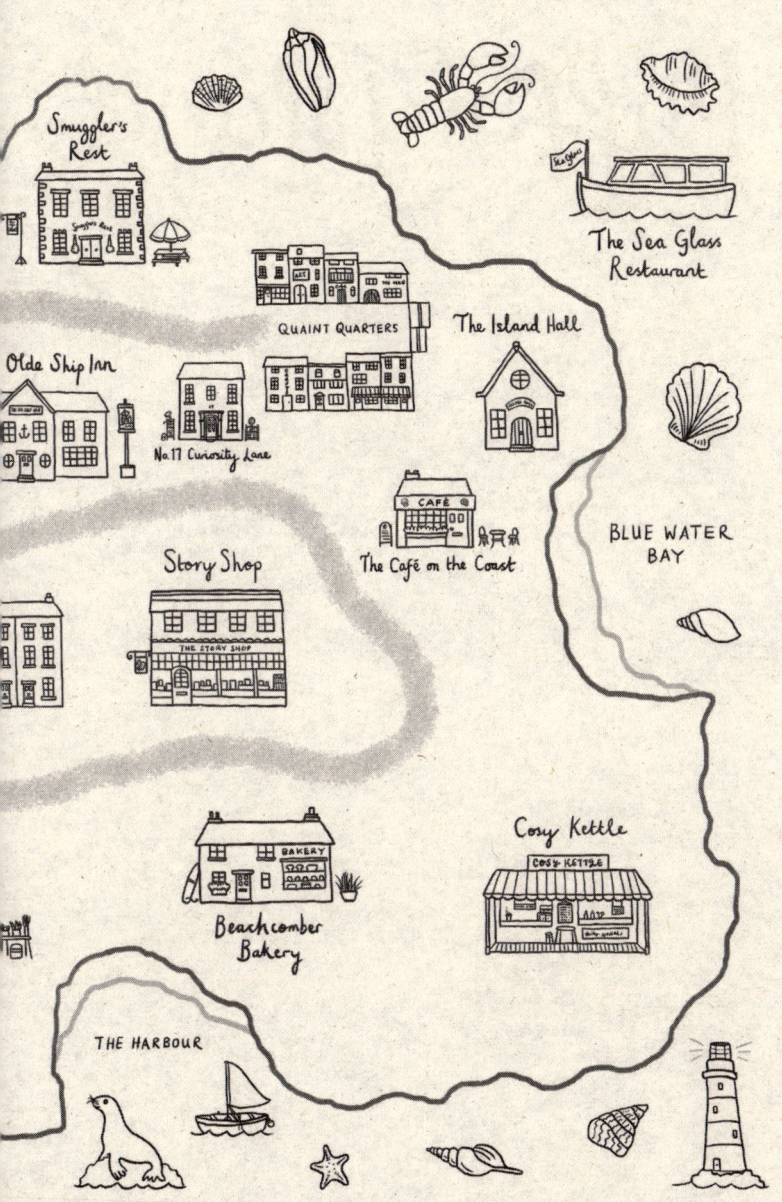

Smuggler's Rest

The Sea Glass Restaurant

QUAINT QUARTERS

The Island Hall

Olde Ship Inn

No. 17 Curiosity Lane

BLUE WATER BAY

Story Shop

THE STORY SHOP

The Café on the Coast

CAFÉ

Cosy Kettle

COSY KETTLE

Beachcomber Bakery

BAKERY

THE HARBOUR

The Royal Women Family Information

Name	Year of Birth	In Power (Year)	Age at Coronation	Year of Death	Age at Death
Queen Eleanor	1873	1913	40	1963	90
Queen Matilda	1893	1963	70	1973	80
Queen Anne	1930	1973	43	1983	53
Queen Charlotte	1953	1983	30	–	72 (current)

The Rose Women Family Tree

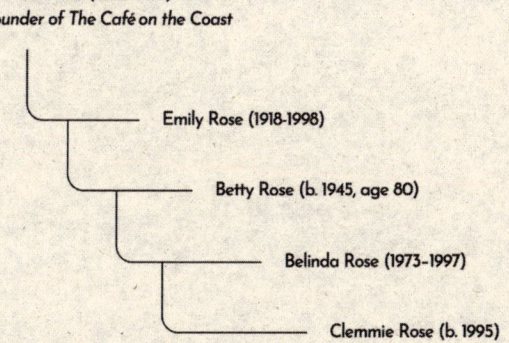

Beatrice Rose (1895-1985)
Founder of The Café on the Coast

Emily Rose (1918-1998)

Betty Rose (b. 1945, age 80)

Belinda Rose (1973-1997)

Clemmie Rose (b. 1995)

Prologue

Eldenbridge Palace, 2nd July 1918

The steady ticking of the clock echoed in the quiet private chamber of Eldenbridge Palace, amplifying the tension in the room. Henry, Earl of Aberford, stood before the Queen, the weight of his title and lineage pressing heavily on him. Today, he would shed that title for good.

The Queen, poised and unyielding, sat across from him. She was known for her strength and composure, but today, he caught a flicker of something else in her cool gaze, a trace of disappointment that made his stomach tighten with guilt.

'Henry'—her voice was precise, each syllable layered with authority—'I trust that you've come to your senses. Alexandra has been more than patient and I expected your return from Puffin Island to bring with it a renewed sense of duty. It is about time an announcement was made.'

Henry swallowed. His time out on Puffin Island had

offered a fleeting reprieve, a taste of the life he secretly longed for. In the quiet simplicity of island life, he'd found solace, free from the weight of titles and expectations. But he couldn't explain that to the Queen. She wouldn't understand.

'Your Majesty,' he began, steadying his voice, 'I've made my decision.'

The Queen's gaze sharpened, her lips thinning as she took in his words. 'What decision, Henry?'

'I intend to end my courtship with Alexandra.' The words hung in the air for a moment before he forced himself to continue. 'The engagement... I cannot marry her. It would not be right. For myself *or* Alexandra.'

Queen Eleanor's face remained composed, but he saw the faint clenching of her hands. 'You've been seeing the princess for months. What's changed?' She paused, her eyes hardening. 'What happened on that island?'

Henry tensed, suppressing another pang of guilt. 'It's me. I've changed. I'm not the man Alexandra deserves and so I cannot go through with this.'

A heavy silence settled between them. The Queen's gaze bored into him, sharp and unreadable. 'You're making a grave mistake, Henry. Do you fully understand the consequences for the family? This could bring scandal upon us all.'

'I do,' he murmured, his voice barely above a whisper.

She studied him, her tone cooling even further as she continued. 'Then why? What could you possibly want that this life, this family, cannot give you?'

Henry's heart clenched, but he kept his voice even. He knew exactly what this life could not give him, but he couldn't tell Her Majesty the truth. There was too much at risk. 'I want a different life, ma'am. A life of my own choosing, away from all this.'

For a moment, her expression softened, then her face steeled again. 'And Alexandra? You think you can simply discard her after all this time? She's been good to you, loyal. She deserves more.'

'I'll take full responsibility and ensure it's clear that she is at no fault for this change in circumstances,' he said, his voice firm. 'And…' He hesitated. 'I think it's best if I quietly disappear so Alexandra can get on with her life. If that means walking away from my title, then so be it. I have cousins who can inherit it.'

'And where will you disappear to?'

He didn't answer; he didn't need to. They both already knew the answer.

The Queen regarded him in silence for some time, and he felt the finality of her gaze. 'I'm sorry to tell you, Henry, but it is not possible for you to relinquish your hereditary title.'

'Then what do you suggest?'

'If you are hellbent on going through with this then I propose that you set your title aside and leave it for your heirs, should you have any, to take up the mantle in time. Move into the next stage of your life as simply Henry Aberford.'

Henry thought about it for a moment and nodded.

'You've made your choice, Henry, but understand this: when you walk away from this titled world, you leave it for ever.'

He nodded again, accepting the terms he had expected. 'I understand.'

He turned to leave, the burden of his choice still settling on his shoulders, when the Queen's voice, now soft, called after him.

'Henry,' she murmured, her tone carrying a trace of a motherly warmth he'd rarely received from his own mother. 'It is my firm belief that you are making a mistake, but I will not stand in your way for your new life. I have always been very fond of you, and though it may not be the done thing, once in a while…'

He nodded, grateful for her kindness.

And with that he left, the life he had always known fading behind him. Ahead lay the freedom he craved. His heart might be weighed down with both relief and an aching regret, but there was no turning back now.

Chapter One

Present Day

Clemmie Rose had just placed the finishing touches on a gloriously fluffy Victoria sponge when she turned her back for a second. The Café on the Coast, her pride and joy, was due to open for business in a little over an hour and with the door open to let in the morning sun, chaos waddled straight into the café.

A squawk pierced the air.

Clemmie spun around just in time to see it. A puffin, bold as brass, was teetering precariously on the counter. Its beady eyes gleamed with mischief as it surveyed the room, its gaze locking onto the sponge like a pirate spotting treasure.

'Don't you dare!' Clemmie shrieked, waving a spatula in the air like a sword.

The puffin cocked its head as if to say, 'Try me', and then plunged its orange beak directly into the centre of the cake.

'Noooo!' Clemmie lunged forward, but it was too late. The bird emerged triumphant, crumbs and cream smeared across its smug little face. She shooed it away as it gave an indignant squawk before flapping its wings and landing on the end of the counter, sending a fine mist of powdered sugar into the air.

'Granny! There's a bloody puffin in the cake,' Clemmie bellowed, her voice echoing through the cosy café. 'Granny! We have a situation!'

From the back of the café came the shuffling of slippers and the sound of a teacup rattling on its saucer. Betty appeared in the doorway, still wearing her floral housecoat, a bemused expression on her face.

'What on earth are you hollering about?' she asked, squinting over her spectacles. 'You sound like someone set fire to the scones.'

Clemmie pointed at the puffin, who was now strutting by the door as if it owned the place. 'That feathery demon just destroyed my Victoria sponge!'

Betty leaned against the doorframe, taking a leisurely sip of her tea. 'Well, that's what you get for leaving it unattended. Puffins are opportunists, you know.'

'I turned my back for five seconds!' Clemmie protested, grabbing a tea towel and attempting to shoo the bird away up the path. The puffin hopped onto a nearby chair, leaving a trail of crumbs in its wake. 'It's a health hazard.'

Betty chuckled, setting her cup down. 'He's got good taste. That sponge looked divine.'

'It *was* divine,' Clemmie grumbled, swiping at the counter with a damp cloth. 'It was for an order this afternoon and now I have to start over again and I won't have time to practise for The Royal Baking Competition. I was going to try out the café's layered mousse-cake tower, as I've not baked it for a while.'

Betty ambled over, her slippered feet shuffling against the tiles. She reached out a wrinkled hand, and to Clemmie's astonishment, the puffin hopped right onto her arm like an obedient parrot.

'Well, aren't you a handsome fellow?' Betty cooed, stroking the bird's head. The puffin squawked appreciatively, nuzzling her with its beak.

'What do you mean, he's a handsome fellow? All puffins look the same! Why does he like you so much?' Clemmie demanded, throwing her arms in the air. 'I'm the one who bakes the cakes!'

Betty smirked. 'You're also the one who shouts and waves spatulas around. Puffins appreciate a calm demeanour.'

Clemmie muttered to herself about traitorous birds and grandmothers who should be retiring, as she stared at the wreckage of her sponge cake, its once perfect layers now a battlefield of cream and jam.

'Right,' she said, tying her apron tighter. 'If that puffin thinks it's beaten me, it's got another think coming. I'll bake a new cake, and it'll be even better. Fluffier, taller, more … victorious!'

'That's the spirit,' Betty said, carrying the puffin to the door and putting it outside. 'But maybe keep the door shut this time, hmm?'

Clemmie glared at her. 'I don't need advice from someone who lets puffins sit on their arm like a pirate.'

Betty gave her a wink and was just about to shuffle back into the kitchen when she said, 'I've been thinking…'

'You do know it's dangerous when you think…' teased Clemmie.

'I think you should reconsider baking the layered mousse-cake tower.'

'Why?' Clemmie asked, feeling a little surprised. 'It's going to look sensational, and I need to stand out from the crowd. There's a lot at stake for the winner. They get their own cookbook published and let's not forget the invitation to the royal garden party. Can you imagine? It would put our café on the coast firmly on the map!'

'Oh, I can imagine,' Betty replied with a knowing smile, 'and that's exactly why I'm suggesting you bake something with real meaning to this place, something tied to its history. Everyone loves a good backstory.' Betty picked up the invitation from where Clemmie had placed it behind the clock on the shelf and took it out of its royal crested envelope. She read it out loud.

👑 *ROYAL INVITATION* 👑

Her Royal Highness cordially invites Clemmie Rose to take part in the prestigious Royal Baking Competition, an exclusive event celebrating heritage, tradition and the art of fine baking.

This esteemed competition will take place aboard The Royal Yacht, which shall be docked at Blue Harbour Bay, Puffin Island, on the 1st of August.

As one of only ten exceptional bakers, each nominated by

esteemed figures in the industry, you are invited to present a
cherished family recipe, steeped in heritage and uniquely your
own. Your creation will be a testament to your roots, history
and passion for the craft.

Your presence would be an honour, and we eagerly
anticipate witnessing the culinary story you choose to share.

Kindly confirm your attendance at your earliest
convenience.

With regal regards,
The Royal Baking Committee

'I think your great-great-grandmother's story deserves to be shouted from the rooftops,' Betty said with conviction. 'It would be such an honour for her because if it weren't for Beatrice Rose, we wouldn't have our beloved Café on the Coast.'

Clemmie smiled wistfully as her thoughts drifted back to the remarkable tale of her great-great-grandmother.

'Go on, you tell it,' Betty said as though reading her mind. She nudged Clemmie's elbow.

'Oh no, you start,' Clemmie replied with a grin. 'You always do, after all.'

Betty rolled her eyes affectionately but launched in without hesitation. 'All right, then. Beatrice Rose – your great-great-grandmother – wasn't just any woman. She had grit, heart and a stubborn streak wide enough to stretch across the entire island.'

Clemmie nodded. 'She needed it. Because when the war came, Puffin Island wasn't spared. The bombs fell, and…'

Betty picked up the thread seamlessly, her voice lowering. 'They took everything. Her home. Her parents. Her whole world, in one terrible night.'

Clemmie exhaled. 'Anyone else might have crumbled. But not Beatrice. No, she found that old pink cottage down by the shore – falling apart, windows shattered, barely standing – and she saw something the rest of the island didn't.'

'Possibility,' Betty said, her eyes bright with pride. 'She rolled up her sleeves, and the whole community joined her. They rebuilt it, brick by brick, board by board, turning it into more than just a café. It became a refuge. A place to gather, to grieve, to heal.'

Clemmie smiled. 'And to eat.'

Betty chuckled. 'Oh, did they ever eat! And every Christmas, she'd host a feast, filling every plate and every heart with warmth. That's when she first made the torte. Her famous clementine torte.'

Clemmie leaned back, crossing her arms. 'And you know what they say…'

Betty lifted a brow at Clemmie's deviation from the usual spiel. 'What do they say?'

'That it wouldn't be Christmas on Puffin Island without a slice of Beatrice's torte.'

Betty rested a hand over Clemmie's. 'So, don't you see? It's not just a recipe. It's your family's history. A piece of the island's heart.'

Clemmie swallowed, the weight of her granny's words settling deep.

Betty stood, brushing flour from her hands. 'And let's

not forget, your name wasn't chosen by accident, Clementine. Beatrice always said clementines carried warmth, resilience and a touch of sweetness. Just like her torte. And just like you.'

Betty gave Clemmie a quick hug and then shuffled out of the room, humming a tune as she went, leaving Clemmie to think about her words.

With the puffin banished and the café door firmly closed, Clemmie got to work making another Victoria sponge. She measured flour and sugar with a determination that would put to shame a general preparing for battle. The eggs were cracked with precision, the butter whipped into submission, and the batter folded with a vengeance. She was just sliding the new sponge layers into the oven when the bell above the café door jingled. Clemmie groaned. 'We're not open yet!' she called, brushing a strand of flour-dusted hair out of her face.

The door creaked open anyway, and in walked Amelia, her best friend, the owner of the local bookshop. She was grinning. 'Just here for my breakfast croissant.'

Clemmie smiled at her best friend. 'I've already bagged one up for you, freshly baked this morning.'

'Perfect, thank you,' she said, looking at the counter. 'What are you baking?'

'Another Victoria sponge, thanks to my early-morning puffin invasion, but it's given me time to think.'

'About? And what puffin invasion?' asked Amelia, pulling out a chair after grabbing her croissant from the bag.

Clemmie explained the saga of the unexpected cake

thief, leaving Amelia smiling at the story. 'And what is it you're thinking about?' asked Amelia.

'The Royal Baking Competition. Granny has given me something to think about and I think she could be possibly right.' Clemmie explained about the traditional torte and the backstory, and asked for Amelia's opinion.

'I'm with Betty. Just think how wonderful it would be to honour your great-great-grandmother – and the media is going to love the story. Now tell me again the story of how you found out you'd made the cut?' Amelia asked, leaning forward with a grin.

Clemmie rolled her eyes playfully. 'But you've heard it a dozen times already!'

'I know, but tell me anyway. It's nice to see how happy it makes you.'

'So, it was two weeks ago, just another morning at the café,' Clemmie began in an overly serious tone, which set Amelia off giggling. 'I was about to unlock the door when I noticed this envelope on the mat – thick, expensive paper, the royal crest embossed on the front. My heart just about stopped. I picked it up, hands shaking, and when I opened it'—she paused for dramatic effect—'there it was: the official invitation. I'd been chosen as one of this year's contestants for The Royal Baking Competition.'

Amelia let out a squeal and asked 'And then?', even though she already knew what happened next.

'Granny took one look at the letter and burst into tears. Proper, joyful, full-on crying. I think she might be more excited about it than I am.' Clemmie chuckled, shaking her head. 'But honestly, I'm still trying to wrap my head around how it even happened. I had to be nominated by someone, but I have no idea who it could have been. Did someone come into the café and secretly taste my baking? Was it a regular? Or maybe'—she leaned in conspiratorially—'an undercover judge?'

Amelia gasped, delighted by the mystery. 'Ooh, I love that idea. Like a baking detective, scouting out the best of the best!'

'Exactly!' Clemmie laughed. 'And now, with the competition being held right here on Puffin Island, the pressure is even higher. The whole town is buzzing about it. I can't let them down.'

Amelia reached for Clemmie's hand and gave it a reassuring squeeze. 'You won't. You're going to make us all proud. Now tell me about the best bit – the prizes!'

'The winner will get an invitation to the royal garden party, where their winning dessert will be baked by the royal kitchen for all the guests, and they'll also get to publish their very own cookbook.'

Amelia cheered then added, 'You'll be amazing and the island will be out in full force, cheering you every step of the way. Have you had a look at your competition?'

Clemmie grabbed the latest copy of *Knead to Know* magazine from the shelf. She tapped the article and spun the magazine towards Amelia. 'This is Fiona Fairweather – my biggest competition.'

**Fiona Fairweather: The 'Queen of Cup Cakes'
Declares Victory Before the First Whisk.**

In an exclusive (and gloriously self-assured) interview with Knead to Know, self-proclaimed baking royalty Fiona

Fairweather has made her ambitions for the upcoming Royal Baking Competition crystal clear: she's already won it. Or at least, in her mind.

Fiona, a full-time baker and Instagram and TikTok personality, is no stranger to controversy or confidence. Her rise to fame began when her meticulously sculpted croquembouche (shaped like the Eiffel Tower, complete with edible sparklers) won The Glorious Bake competition in Chelsea last year. Since then, she's been running her luxury patisserie in Kensington, churning out cakes with price tags high enough to make even billionaires wince.

'Yikes! She's not shy, is she? Full of self-importance,' exclaimed Amelia.

Clemmie added, 'Look at this part: "*I'm not worried about the competition at all*", Fiona Fairweather declared during our interview at her shop, Fairweather's Fancies. "*Let's be honest, darling, how could anyone compete with me?*"

'Apparently, she won another competition last year by sculpting a life-sized giraffe out of marzipan. It's impressive but I'm determined to win. I will not be beaten!' declared Clemmie.

'You'll show her!' Amelia stated, kissing her friend on the cheek. 'I need to get back to the bookshop but you have a good day. And who wants to eat a marzipan giraffe anyway? The brass neck of that woman!'

Clemmie laughed as Amelia disappeared through the door. By the time Betty reappeared, the café smelled of victory … or at least of vanilla sponge. Clemmie carefully lifted the new cake layers from the oven, inspecting them with the critical eye of a seasoned baker.

'Perfect,' she declared, placing them on the counter to cool.

Betty nodded approvingly. 'Well done, and not a puffin in sight.'

'Don't jinx it,' Clemmie warned, glancing suspiciously at the door.

As she began assembling the cake, spreading a generous layer of jam and cream between the sponges, Betty pulled up a stool and began flipping through the café's book of homemade recipes. She sneakily left it open at the page of Clemmie's great-great-grandmother's torte before switching on the kettle.

'I know what you're doing!' Clemmie chided.

'It's your choice. Whatever you decide, this café already has its winner.'

Clemmie smiled. Her granny always had a way of making her feel like she could conquer the world.

As Clemmie placed the finishing touches on the new Victoria sponge, Betty leaned over and said, 'You might want to shut the window.'

Clemmie turned and her heart sank. There, perched on the windowsill, was the puffin, its beady eyes fixed on the cake.

'Oh no you don't!' Clemmie shouted, grabbing a rolling pin and racing towards the window.

The puffin squawked indignantly and flapped away, leaving a single feather behind.

Betty laughed. 'You've got a nemesis now, Clemmie! The Puffin of Doom!'

Clemmie groaned, wiping her hands on her apron. 'If

that bird shows up at the competition, I'm quitting baking for ever.'

But as she looked at the cake – the product of her determination and her love for her craft – she knew she wouldn't quit. Not for a puffin, Fiona Fairweather or anything else.

'Bring it on,' she muttered, squaring her shoulders.

Chapter Two

Clemmie had been curled up on the garden chair all evening. She loved this time of year, the lighter nights, the soft rustle of flowers swaying in the breeze and the soothing sound of the sea murmuring in the distance. On her lap lay the handwritten recipe book from her great-great-grandmother – open at the page of the famous torte – the book's well-worn edges a testament to its history. In her hand, she held her iPad. For the past ten minutes she had been scrolling through Fiona Fairweather's TikTok account. Clemmie had never seen anything quite like it. Fiona was a master of promotion, each reel dripping with glamour and carefully curated, a far cry from the quiet, messy charm of Clemmie's Café on the Coast. The stark contrast made Clemmie's stomach twist with nervous energy.

As Fiona's latest video began to play, the screen filled with her poised smile before her voice purred, 'For The Royal Baking Competition I'll be presenting my family's signature Pearlescent Pistachio Opera Cake, an eight-layer masterpiece that's not only technically flawless but also artistic enough to belong in a museum. Can any of the other competitors in the baking competition say that about their sponge?'

Clemmie wondered how easy it would even be to serve an eight-layer cake at the royal garden party. She felt a wave of self-doubt wash over her, but she couldn't stop watching. Fiona continued, answering a question from an unseen interviewer. 'The key to winning is not just baking, it's branding. People eat with their eyes first. My cakes don't just taste divine; they make people feel important for eating them. It's a skill, and not everyone has it.'

The final clip was the most cutting. With a dazzling smile, Fiona offered her competitors a parting comment. 'Practice makes perfect, but in my case, perfection is innate. Good luck to the rest of the competitors in The Royal Baking Competition. I do hope someone manages to bake a cake that doesn't look like it came out of a children's birthday party. I'd hate to win by too large a margin; it would feel unsporting.'

Clemmie stared at the screen, her mind racing. The self-assured confidence and sharp jabs from Fiona Fairweather were intimidating. Could she compete with someone like that?

The next morning, Clemmie woke with a start, her heart racing and her thoughts tumbling over one another in a chaotic whirl. The early-morning light filtered through her bedroom curtains, but instead of feeling the usual calm that accompanied the golden glow, she felt worried. The memories of Fiona Fairweather's TikTok from the night before looped in her mind like an unwanted reel, each dismissive comment and smug smile chipping away at her confidence.

'An eight-layer masterpiece that belongs in a museum,' Fiona's voice echoed. 'Can any of the other competitors in the baking competition say that about their sponge?'

Feeling disheartened, Clemmie started to spiral. What was she thinking, accepting her invitation to compete in a competition like this? She wasn't some celebrity baker with a high-profile following or a line-up of glamorous cakes on display in a Kensington patisserie. She was just Clemmie, with a cosy café by the coast.

This was a high-stakes competition so she needed to put her best foot forward. To that end, Clemmie had been thinking about what her granny had said. She agreed with her that the torte was the best option; a recipe close to her heart and one that was a firm favourite with the café's customers.

She threw on her dressing gown and padded downstairs into the kitchen, where Betty was already bustling around, humming to herself as she prepared breakfast. The smell of freshly brewed coffee filled the air, but even that comforting aroma couldn't soothe Clemmie's nerves.

'What's the matter with you? You look like you have the weight of the world on your shoulders,' Betty asked, turning to face her with a raised eyebrow.

Clemmie slumped into a chair at the kitchen table, clutching her mug of coffee like it was a lifeline. 'Granny, I don't think I'm good enough.'

'Good enough for what?' asked Betty.

'The Royal Baking Competition.'

'Don't be daft, they selected you. Why the sudden doubt?'

Clemmie sighed. 'Fiona Fairweather's presenting a cake with *eight* layers. Eight! And the way she talks, it's like she's already won. I don't stand a chance against someone like that.'

Betty swiped the flour from her hands, her expression both firm and kind. 'Now you listen to me. Someone who has to shout about their achievements from the rooftops is not a winner. A winner is someone who quietly does the work, puts their heart into it and lets their results speak for themselves.'

'But she's so polished, so confident,' Clemmie protested.

Betty shook her head. 'Confidence isn't about showing off. It's about believing in what you do and why you're doing it. You think your great-great-grandmother had time to boast about her torte when she was baking it for the people who helped rebuild this island after the war? No, she simply baked it quietly with love and gratitude. That's what made it special and it's why people still talk about it today.'

Clemmie bit her lip, her granny's words tugging at her heart.

'Fiona might have fancy cakes and a silver tongue,' Betty continued, 'but you have something she'll never have: roots.

You've got a recipe with a story, a café with history, and a community standing behind you. Let her talk all she wants. You focus on baking from the heart, and trust me, that'll be enough.'

Clemmie looked up at her granny, the flicker of doubt in her chest slowly giving way to a small, tentative spark of determination. 'You really think so?'

'I *know* so,' Betty replied.

'I've decided to go with the torte.'

'I think you've made an excellent choice.' Betty gave Clemmie a hug. 'Now drink your coffee, and let's get to work. You've got a torte to perfect and I need to get these deliveries out before we open.'

Clemmie smiled, the panic beginning to loosen its grip. She still had doubts, but her granny's words settled her. She needed to focus on what mattered most: honouring her great-great-grandmother's legacy and putting The Café on the Coast on the map.

An hour later Clemmie heard the roar of an engine. Mid-whisk, her hand hovering over a bowl of rich chocolate ganache, she stared and narrowed her eyes at the deep blue sports car that had parked just outside the café. It was the kind of car that made you think of glossy magazine covers or the hero of a spy film, not a sleepy little island town that had more puffins than people.

Wiping her hands on her pinny, Clemmie hurried outside. 'I'm sorry, you can't park there. There are numerous carparks on the...' The words died on her lips as she stared, her mouth slightly agape. She now wasn't sure what was more surprising: the sleek, ridiculously impractical sports car gleaming in the sunlight, or the man stepping out of it.

Oliver Lockwood.

For a moment, time seemed to stop. He stood there, a vision of gorgeousness and easy confidence, his dark hair slightly tousled as though styled by a careless breeze. He wore a crisp white shirt with the sleeves rolled up just enough to make her stomach flutter, exuding a casual elegance that looked effortless and yet infuriatingly deliberate. His eyes, that familiar shade of hazel, locked onto hers, and she saw his smile widen.

'Well,' he said, leaning one arm casually on the car door. 'If it isn't Clementine Rose. And this must be the reason you turned me down, The Café on the Coast.' He glanced over the pink cottage that had been transformed into the café at the bottom of Lighthouse Lane. The corners of his mouth lifted into that grin, the one that used to make her feel like she'd swallowed a whole tray of espresso shots. Now, it made her feel … well, exactly the same, even though she wanted to be annoyed. Definitely annoyed. He hadn't fought for her. It was all his way or no way.

Clemmie folded her arms, hoping it would disguise the fact that her heart was pounding. 'Like I said, you can't park there,' she shot back.

His grin widened. All she could think about was the last time she saw him, three years ago, slipping into a black cab outside her hotel room after their last argument that still echoed in her mind.

'You'd give up the chance to see the world for… what? Puffin Island? A little café on the coast?' Oliver's frustration had flared, his voice uncharacteristically sharp.

'It's not just a café', Clemmie had countered, her tone equally fiery. 'It's my life. My home, and there's no other place I'd rather be.'

Oliver, most probably used to getting his own way, had been stunned. For all his sophistication, he couldn't seem to understand why Clemmie would choose a small island over the vast, thrilling adventure he was offering her. She, meanwhile, couldn't understand why he couldn't see the value in staying rooted in the place she loved.

She'd stood at the window watching him go, the cab disappearing at the bottom of the road into the London night. Her heart ached, the pain sharp and immediate, because she knew the best week of her life had just ended. She wished she had thought about it more, about him, about them, before falling headlong into a whirlwind week of passion.

But what haunted her more than the loss was the memory of how he had made her feel, as though she were the only woman in the world. That magic was shattered weeks later when a glossy tabloid photo surfaced showing Oliver, dashing as ever, arm-in-arm with a stunning model at a glamorous event. The sight of his familiar smile aimed at someone else had gutted her, leaving her with a bitter truth … she had been unforgettable to him for just one fleeting moment, while he had become unforgettable to her for ever.

'And how are you?'

'What are you doing here?' Clemmie avoided his question.

'I was passing through and I thought to myself: why don't I call in on my favourite baker?'

'Three years after you left without a backward glance?'

'It does seem like only yesterday, doesn't it?'

Her cheeks flushed as she remembered the raw passion and chemistry between them before he'd smashed her heart into smithereens.

'Is that a Ferrari?'

Clemmie spun around to see her granny standing a few feet away. Apparently, she'd finished the deliveries.

'It's an Aston Martin,' Oliver said smoothly, flashing her a polite smile.

'It's very shiny,' she replied. 'And very impractical for these roads.'

Clemmie couldn't help but smirk at that. Oliver, however, looked entirely unfazed.

'Where can I park it, then?' he asked, turning back to Clemmie.

'Down the lane, near the harbour,' she replied, gesturing vaguely.

'Perfect,' he said, climbing back into the car. The engine purred to life, and with a wave, he drove off, leaving Clemmie standing there wondering if she was actually dreaming.

'Isn't he a sight for sore eyes? He looks like he has everything going for him,' remarked Betty before turning back into the café.

'He's a food journalist, in fact more like a food presenter these days,' replied Clemmie.

'What's his name?' asked Betty.

'Oliver Lockwood.'

Betty straightened, her face lighting up with recognition. 'Oliver Lockwood? Well, now, I've heard that name somewhere recently. That's him? I wish I'd known. I could have introduced myself.'

'What do you mean, "That's him"?'

'He's presenting The Royal Baking Competition special.'

Clemmie's stomach dropped. She stared at Betty, dread creeping over her like a tide. 'Are you sure?'

'Yes, it's all over social media and I was going to ask whether you'd heard of him. By the way, Sam is going to set up a huge screen on the jetty outside The Sea Glass Restaurant so everyone in the village can sit on the beach and watch it live.'

Clemmie didn't answer. Her mind was racing. This couldn't be happening. Oliver Lockwood was going to present The Royal Baking Competition?

Clemmie's hands trembled as she pulled her phone from her pocket, her fingers fumbling to unlock it. A few taps and a search later, the headline stared back at her in bold black text:

Oliver Lockwood Confirmed as Host for This Year's Royal Baking Competition, to be held aboard the Royal Yacht at Puffin Island

Her heart sank. 'Shit,' she muttered, her pulse pounding as she scanned the article until her eye caught on a single sentence that made the whole situation irrevocably worse: *Oliver will accompany the winner of The Royal Baking Competition to this year's Royal Garden Party.* Double shit.

'Do you think he's married? I didn't see a ring. The looks, the career and the car…' Betty chuckled softly. 'You should get in there!'

Clemmie barely heard her. All she could think about was that the man she had tried so hard to forget was now back in her orbit, and all those long-suppressed feelings were quickly rising to the surface.

The realisation hit harder than the headline and was an even more unwelcome surprise.

Chapter Three

The Olde Ship Inn was bustling but Clemmie and Amelia had managed to snag a cosy booth near the window, their table already laden with a plate of fish and chips and two glasses of wine. Clemmie was sipping her Sauvignon Blanc when the door creaked open and she flinched, already bracing herself for the worst.

Amelia picked up her wine glass, her gaze fixed on Clemmie. 'Why do you keep jumping every time the door opens?'

'I don't.'

'You totally do,' Amelia retorted, her grin widening. 'Are you avoiding someone? Or has some mysterious stranger swept you off your feet?' She gasped theatrically. 'Oh my God, is it the guy from the cheese counter at the market? I *knew* there was chemistry between you two!'

Clemmie rolled her eyes, though she couldn't suppress a laugh. 'Don't be ridiculous. It's not the cheese guy.'

'So, it *is* someone,' Amelia said, leaning forward eagerly. 'Go on, I'm listening.'

Clemmie hesitated, her cheeks flushing. 'It's … complicated.'

'Oh, this is going to be good.'

Clemmie sighed, taking a fortifying sip of wine before muttering, 'It's Oliver.'

'Oliver? Oliver who?'

Clemmie gave her a knowing look.

'Oh my God, as in *the* Oliver? Tall, dark and devastatingly handsome Oliver? Great sex Oliver? A week of passion Oliver? "He's the one" Oliver?'

'Okay, let's not go overboard. But yes, that Oliver,' Clemmie confirmed, her body erupting in goosebumps at the very thought of being wrapped up in his arms once more.

'Wait, why do you think he's going to show up tonight? Why on earth would he be here, on Puffin Island?'

'Because it turns out he's presenting The Royal Baking Competition.'

Amelia's eyes widened. 'No way.'

'Yes way, and I saw him today, driving his Aston Martin down the cobbles of Lighthouse Lane.'

'And did he see you?'

'Oh yes, but he forgot to mention he was presenting the competition and made some quip about how he was just here to see his favourite baker. It's only taken him three years…' she grumbled.

'And how do you feel about that?'

'I'm not entirely—'

The door creaked open, cutting her off. A gust of cool air

swept through the pub, along with a man who could have stepped straight out of an expensive cologne ad.

Oliver Lockwood.

Amelia's jaw dropped. 'That's him, isn't it?'

Clemmie froze. He was there, all six feet of irritating perfection, his dark hair slightly tousled and his crisp shirt casually unbuttoned at the collar. And, of course, he wasn't alone. Clemmie sank a little lower in her seat, wishing she had a superpower to disappear from the planet. 'Don't say anything or bring any attention to ourselves,' she whispered.

On his arm was a woman who seemed to embody the very essence of chic. She wore a crisp, tailored tweed coat over a simple yet stylish dress, her silk scarf knotted elegantly at her neck. Her ankle boots were impeccably clean, practical yet stylish, and a leather satchel hung from her shoulder. Her hair was neatly pinned back, framing her face in soft waves, and her delicate pink lipstick added a touch of warmth to her otherwise polished appearance.

Of course he had a woman on his arm. He was Oliver Lockwood, after all … charming, confident and magnetic, with women falling all over him. Clemmie knew this all too well. She had been one of those women once, for a brief but intense week. She cast her mind back to the food market where they'd met. Their conversation began with shortbread but quickly spiralled into discussions of coffee, culinary travels and life. By the end of the night, they were sitting at a nearby café, sharing stories over wine and pastries. Dinner led to Clemmie's hotel room, where they gave in to an undeniable chemistry. For Clemmie, it was unlike anything she'd experienced … a whirlwind of passion and connection that left her breathless. It was a fleeting romance that ended as quickly as it had begun, leaving her as little more than just another name in his long list of conquests, a fact she tried hard to bury. Yet seeing him again, looking just as handsome as ever, stirred feelings she had long ago pushed aside.

'Stop staring,' Clemmie ordered, as she noticed Amelia's wide-eyed gaze.

'I can't help it,' Amelia admitted, unable to look away. 'He's absolutely stunning.'

Clemmie rolled her eyes. 'You are not helping.'

Amelia nudged her, still watching Oliver with awe. 'I can't believe your Oliver Lockwood is in our pub.'

Clemmie's voice grew sharper. 'He was only ever mine for a week. He didn't want me. Never chose me.'

Amelia raised an eyebrow, an unspoken challenge in her gaze. 'But you can say the same about you, right? You never chose him either. He asked you to travel the world and you turned him down.'

Clemmie glared at her friend, her emotions flickering between frustration and lingering hurt. 'Whose side are you on? And he's obviously with someone else now,' she muttered, her eyes flicking to the woman on Oliver's arm. 'Oh, blooming hell. Could my night get any worse?'

'Has the guy from the cheese counter walked in?' Amelia teased, looking towards the door.

'It's her,' Clemmie said in a hushed whisper.

'It's who?'

'Fiona Fairweather – the competition! The woman in the article I showed you, who thinks she's already won The

Royal Baking Competition and her cookbook will be flying off the shelves in no time…'

'Not in my bookshop they won't.'

Clemmie smiled. 'And you can just picture her at the garden party swanning about like she herself is royalty.'

'You don't feel intimidated, do you?' Amelia raised an eyebrow.

'I did until Granny gave me a good talking to.'

'In my opinion, she's all tweed and tarts and you … you are the icing on the cake.'

'And that's why you are my friend.'

'Do you think they're actually together?' asked Amelia.

Clemmie shrugged. They watched Oliver and Fiona glide towards the bar, turning more than a few heads in the process.

Clemmie focused hard on her wine, willing herself not to look. But Oliver's laugh, a low, familiar rumble, drifted across the room, making her stomach flip.

'Okay, I hate to say it,' Amelia said, leaning in, 'but he's ridiculously hot. Like, unfairly hot. Why the hell didn't you travel the world with him?'

Clemmie shot her a glare. 'Because I have a business, and family is more important. And if he'd really cared about me, he would've come to find me long before now. He's only here now because of his job. I hope he doesn't see me.' Clemmie's eyes drifted back towards the bar. Oliver was leaning casually against it, sharing something that made Fiona laugh. As he looked around the pub, Clemmie looked away, making sure she didn't make eye contact. Her stomach sank. Of course, it wasn't enough that Oliver had shown up out of nowhere with someone new. No, he had to bring *her* … a woman whose entire brand revolved around being infuriatingly perfect.

'Out of everyone in the competition I guess he was bound to know her. They both live in Kensington so probably occupy the same circles.'

'I suppose we should have realised that she was going to be coming to the island at some point. After all, the baking competition is happening here.'

'It never crossed my mind that Oliver could be covering the event. I thought he'd still be swanning around on the other side of the world.'

'So you admit you've thought about him then?' teased Amelia, with a smirk on her face.

'Possibly, from time to time… Okay, more than I'd like to admit.'

Three years ago she'd stalked his social media on a daily basis but as soon as she saw a photo of him with another woman she willed herself to be strong and stop looking. Still, there was no denying that he had flashed through her mind from time to time … and still did. At that moment, Oliver and Fiona moved away from the bar, their drinks in hand, and made their way to a table near the centre of the room, close enough for Clemmie to see them but far enough to make eavesdropping impossible.

Clemmie kept her eyes firmly on her glass, whilst Amelia gave her a running commentary. 'He's now leaning back in his chair, looking maddeningly at ease. Fiona is scrolling through her phone, seemingly oblivious to anything beyond her Instagram feed.'

'She's probably posting something about how rustic and

charming this place is, while secretly wishing for a Michelin-starred soufflé.'

Clemmie stole one last glance at Oliver, who was now leaning forward, his expression thoughtful as Fiona gestured animatedly. For a moment, Clemmie felt a pang of something she didn't want to name.

Jealousy? Regret?

She pushed the thought aside, determined not to let him affect her. What did it matter that he was here? She'd managed just fine without him for over three years, so surely she could put up with his presence for a few days.

'Come on,' she said, standing abruptly. 'Let's get out of here. We can grab a hot chocolate from the Cosy Kettle.'

'Sounds like a plan.'

As they turned to walk out Clemmie could feel Oliver's eyes on her, so she turned and stared him down. The intensity in his hazel gaze made her stomach do unwelcome flips – which became worse when he winked at her.

Outside, she erupted. 'He had the audacity to wink at me! The cheek!'

'What if he actually agreed to present this competition because he knew you were a competitor and it gave him the opportunity to come to Puffin Island?' wondered Amelia.

'Don't be ridiculous.' Clemmie brushed off the suggestion, annoyed that Oliver Lockwood was already firmly under her skin when he'd been back in her life for less than a day.

Chapter Four

The sun had barely peeked over the horizon when Clemmie unlocked the door to The Café on the Coast. The little bell above the door jingled in the quiet morning air as she stepped inside. The café wasn't due to open for another couple of hours but with the baking competition fast approaching, Clemmie wanted to start practising. As soon as she walked into the kitchen, she turned on the oven, tied her pinny around her waist and tucked her hair into a loose bun. She took her great-great-grandmother's recipe book down from the shelf and lay it on the counter. The handwritten book with illustrations was essentially the café's recipe bible, holding secret recipes that had been passed down through the family's generations, each one sprinkled with love. Clemmie carefully turned the flour-smudged pages.

The torte recipe was circled in faded ink, with little notes scrawled in the margins.

Add a touch of vanilla here!

Be gentle when folding; no overmixing, no matter how tempting!

Clemmie smiled. It was magical knowing that her great-great-grandmother had taken the time to document everything that she'd once baked in The Café on the Coast, and being able to see the notes in Beatrice's very own handwriting.

'Let's go,' Clemmie murmured to herself, rolling up her sleeves while staring at the list of ingredients. 'No mistakes. No disasters.'

She switched on the radio before rummaging through the cupboards, pulling out the flour, sugar, eggs and chocolate. It was all going to plan until she noticed the pesky puffin was back eyeing up the ingredients through the open window. She quickly leaned forward to shut the window and knocked the bag of flour that was teetering on the edge of the counter. She lunged, hands outstretched, but it was too late.

The bag tipped over, spilling an avalanche of flour.

'Damn.' Clemmie blinked through a cloud of white powder. Two minutes ago, her kitchen was spotless, and now it looked like a snowstorm had passed through. She stood there for a moment, locking eyes with the puffin as it stared back at her, unblinking. With a sharp clap of her hands, the puffin startled and took off, its wings flapping noisily. 'Clemmie, one; Puffin, one,' she muttered, thinking back to the little thief's audacious dive straight into her Victoria sponge. She shook her head. 'Brilliant start, Clemmie,' she said dryly, brushing flour from her face, only to leave streaks of white across her cheeks. 'Let's try that again.'

Brightening the moment, one of her favourite tunes came on the radio. Clemmie grabbed a wooden spoon from the counter. 'You're just too good to be true…' she sang into the spoon, enthusiastically. She began to twirl around the kitchen, ignoring the flour on the floor as she shimmied to the music and belted out the chorus. 'Can't take my eyes off of you!'

Her hips swayed, and she threw in a few dramatic spins, nearly colliding with the open fridge door. Laughing at her own antics, Clemmie grabbed a mixing bowl and used it as a makeshift drum, tapping out the rhythm to the beat. She was mid-twirl, the wooden spoon held up to her mouth, when she spun around – and froze.

Oliver Lockwood was leaning against the kitchen doorway, his arms crossed, a wickedly amused grin plastered across his face. 'Can't take your eyes off me, huh?'

Clemmie's heart jumped into her throat. 'What the—?'

She stared.

'Don't stop now,' he said with a laugh. 'You're not a bad singer or dancer.'

She felt a blush rise in her cheeks. 'What are you doing here? How did you even get in? We don't open for another couple of hours.'

'The door was unlocked,' he said with a casual shrug, his grin never wavering. 'I knocked, but apparently you were too busy channelling your inner pop star to notice.'

'You could've announced yourself or, oh, I don't know, waited outside like a normal person until we opened?'

'But then where would the fun have been in that? I'd have missed the performance,' Oliver said, his eyes sparkling with mischief. 'Seriously, Clem, that was a showstopper.'

Her pulsed raced at the way he said 'Clem', but she glared at him, determined not to back down. 'If you've finished mocking me, I've got a torte to bake.'

'Is that what you're baking for the competition?' He tried to peer over her shoulder towards the counter.

'I'm not divulging that to you, as no doubt you'll run straight back to the opposition, your girlfriend, and share the information.' Damn, she couldn't believe that had slipped right out of her mouth.

Oliver cocked an eyebrow. 'I'm sensing a little bit of jealousy.'

'I'm absolutely not jealous,' she protested, but she wasn't even convincing herself.

'And for your information, Fiona's not a girlfriend, just a long-standing family friend.'

'Who you've probably been intimate with at some point.'

Oliver remained silent.

'I rest my case.'

He was watching her closely. 'I did miss you, you know, after our week of—'

'Great sex.' Double damn, more words slipped out that were not intended. She could kick herself.

He grinned. 'Well, I was going to say "exploring London", but I like your version better.'

'You're insufferable,' she muttered.

'And yet, here I am,' he quipped, stepping closer. 'You know, that week wasn't just about sightseeing or, apparently, great sex. I actually liked spending time with you.'

Clemmie bit her tongue for a moment. She knew women were drawn to him. His confidence, sharp intellect and magnetic presence made him irresistible. But for all his allure, Oliver was a man married to his work. His relationships were fleeting, his love affairs whirlwind, and he liked it that way … uncomplicated, with the world as his playground.

Her pulse was racing but thankfully her poker face didn't give anything away. 'Well, too bad you liked your career more.'

'Touché.'

Stalemate.

Clemmie watched as Oliver walked over to the recipe book, and then it hit her, a faint but unmistakable whiff of his aftershave, a blend of cedar and citrus, so achingly familiar. That scent had clung to her clothes after their time together, lingering long after she'd left London. It brought back memories of lazy mornings, tangled sheets and the way he'd leaned close to whisper something ridiculous in her ear just to make her laugh.

'Is this the legendary torte, the one you spoke about in London?' he said, looking at the page in the book. 'Wasn't it your great-great-grandmother's recipe? Beatrice? Dating back to just after the war.'

She was surprised he'd remembered.

'Maybe,' Clemmie said, turning back to her ingredients in an attempt to regain her composure. 'It's sure to be a hit … if I can manage to bake it without destroying the kitchen first.'

Oliver glanced at the flour-strewn counter and the streaks on her face. 'It's going well so far, I see.'

'Don't you have somewhere else to be?' she asked, grabbing a clean bowl and a whisk.

'Nope.' He leaned against the counter, clearly settling in for the long haul. 'I thought I'd come and see you as I was up. I was woken early by the sound of the gulls and what I thought were cows outside my window.'

'That'll be the puffins mooing.'

He nodded. 'Anyway, I thought I'd walk out and see what Puffin Island is all about. After all, I've heard so many things about this place.'

'When I told you about my wonderful hometown you thought it couldn't possibly be how I described it. In fact, you said something along the lines of "places like that only exist in fairytales".'

Their eyes met and, for a moment, the unspoken memory hung between them. Clemmie wondered if he remembered exactly where that conversation had taken place. They'd been lying in bed in his Kensington apartment, the late-morning sun spilling through the curtains, the hum of the city filtering in through the open window. They'd just shared the kind of languid, unhurried sex that left her grinning and a little breathless.

She'd got up to make coffee, carefully crafting the foam into a swirled heart that had earned an approving smile from him. They'd spent the next hour in bed, sipping coffee, legs tangled together, as he asked her questions about Puffin Island. It had been the first time he'd shown more than a passing interest in her world, and the memory still lingered, golden and bittersweet.

'Are you going to make me a coffee?' he asked.

He'd remembered.

'I assume you still have high coffee standards.'

'Very high.'

Clemmie turned towards the coffee machine. As she ground the beans, she couldn't resist sneaking a glance at him over her shoulder. He was casually leaning his elbow against the counter, giving her that very same look that got her into bed in the first place. The machine hissed and steamed, and Clemmie poured the coffee once it was ready and slid it towards him. 'Freshly brewed. No frills.'

He peered into the mug with exaggerated disappointment, raising an eyebrow. 'No coffee art?'

'It's coffee,' she said flatly, caught off guard.

'Exactly,' he said with mock-seriousness. 'I was hoping for one of those hearts.'

She grabbed a spoon and leaned over the counter, swirling the foam into a heart, then looked at him before breaking it in two.

'I'm getting the impression you aren't happy to see me.' He looked down at the mug and blew on it before swirling the foam into a heart shape once more, a grin spreading across his face. 'That's more like it. The pieces are back together. I know you want to smile, Clemmie, I can see it in your eyes.' He gave her that lopsided grin that had always melted her heart.

Damn. Her heart was telling her to smile but thankfully her head kicked in and she resisted the impulse.

'Those dimples of yours were always very cute.'

She remembered him kissing them every time she smiled. 'I have baking to be getting on with. Are you going to leave?'

He held up his coffee mug. 'Maybe after I finish my coffee.'

The way he was looking at her, things were about to get a whole lot more complicated…

Chapter Five

Clemmie cracked the eggs into the bowl, but as she whisked, she couldn't help stealing a glance at Oliver out of the corner of her eye. He looked entirely too comfortable, his shirt sleeves rolled up, his grin softening into something that made her stomach flip in a way she didn't want to admit.

'That coffee will be cold by now, and you're distracting.'

'Distracting? Me?' He placed a hand on his chest in mock offence. 'I'm just standing here, watching you at work.'

'This kitchen's got a strict "no spectators" policy, especially when I'm practising for the competition.'

Oliver didn't budge. Instead, he picked up a stray spoon and examined it as if it held the secrets of the universe. 'You know, if you need a taste-tester, I'm available.'

'Absolutely not,' Clemmie said, grabbing the spoon out of his hand. 'This is serious business.'

'Serious business covered in flour,' he said, brushing a

speck off her cheek. The gesture was so unexpected that Clemmie froze, her breath catching for a split second before she turned away, pretending to focus on melting the chocolate.

But even the chocolate wouldn't cooperate. The double boiler she'd set up started emitting a suspiciously pungent smell.

'No, no, no!' she said, yanking the pot off the heat. A plume of smoke rose, and the once luxurious chocolate had transformed into a burnt, lumpy mess.

'I don't mind burnt chocolate and it's a shame to let it go to waste,' Oliver said as he delved in with the spoon.

'I've got flour everywhere, burnt chocolate, and you're just standing there like it's comedy hour. You have to leave so I can concentrate.'

'I love it when you get cross, you get this little dimple right here.' His hand touched her cheeks as their eyes met.

He was inches away from her and suddenly every bit of her wanted to grab him and kiss him, to fall back in his arms just like before. But, thankfully, her head overruled her heart and she remained composed.

'But you're right. I'm not sure burnt chocolate torte would win the competition.'

'You don't say,' she said, her tone laced with sarcasm. 'If you think you can do better, be my guest.'

Oliver's grin widened. 'Oh, I wouldn't dream of interfering with greatness. Besides, watching you is much more fun.'

'You're impossible, you know that?'

'So I've been told.'

For a little while they fell into a companionable silence,

the only sounds the radio and the occasional clatter of utensils. Still leaning against the counter, Oliver watched Clemmie closely.

'How much does this competition mean to you?' he asked.

'What sort of question is that?'

'How much do you want to win?' Oliver pressed.

Clemmie considered his question for a moment before answering. 'I'm not really a competitive person, not like some I can imagine in the competition. I just focus on doing my best and hope that's enough.' She smiled softly. 'But if I could have a cookbook with my name on the front, filled with the delicious recipes that have long been baked here at the café, that would be a dream. I'd especially love to showcase some of the recipes my great-great-grandmother created just after the war, when this place was first up and running.' She paused, glancing around the kitchen. 'We're not about fancy frills here, or celebrities. We're about community … about bringing people together. If I could put the café on the map and honour everything she did by letting the food do the talking, it would mean the world to me. And…' She hesitated. 'I love royalty. I've dreamed of receiving an invitation to a royal garden party since I was a little girl.'

Clemmie had always been obsessed with the royals. Her fascination started as a child, and she could remember sitting cross-legged in front of the television with her granny watching grand royal events unfold. Weddings, jubilees, christenings, she devoured them all, her young mind spinning elaborate fairytales about what it must be like to live in such splendour. She followed the royals on social media now. She loved the way they dressed, always so elegant yet contemporary. Even her baking had been inspired by them, and she'd once attempted a miniature version of the towering cake from a royal wedding, though it ended up leaning so precariously that Granny had dubbed it The Pisa Disaster.

Growing up, she'd imagined the palace gardens like something out of one of her storybooks, sprawling lawns with neat rows of hedges, fountains and bursts of colour from flowerbeds that stretched as far as the eye could see. She pictured herself wandering those gardens in a beautiful dress, nibbling cucumber sandwiches and sipping tea from a dainty china cup and hoping she didn't trip over a corgi. It had seemed like the height of sophistication, a world so far removed from the quaint life of Puffin Island.

And now, here she was, with the chance to actually go there. The royal garden party wasn't just a prize to her, it was the dream she'd carried with her for years. Winning The Royal Baking Competition with her great-great-grandmother's recipe wouldn't just be a victory for the café, it would be a personal triumph, a validation of all the hours she'd spent whisking, kneading and tweaking recipes until they were just right. She could already imagine it, stepping onto the perfectly manicured lawns in a dress she'd agonised over for weeks, standing among dignitaries and celebrities, with a sense of pride that she had earned her place there.

'My granny has this old shawl and a brooch that belonged to Beatrice, the founder of the café. We always pretended the brooch was made of real diamonds,' Clemmie said with a fond smile. 'As a child, I'd drape the shawl around my shoulders, clip on the brooch and pair them with Beatrice's tiara. Goodness knows why she even had one, but I adored it. I'd prance up and down the kitchen wearing my regalia and Granny's heels, feeling like a queen.' Her voice softened, the memory vivid in her mind. 'She'd just chuckle and keep baking, right here, whilst I ruled my imaginary kingdom in a kitchen full of love and laughter.' Clemmie paused, her hands stilling over the mixing bowl. 'It's not just about the torte or the prize. It's about proving I can do it. That I'm good enough.'

'You've got nothing to prove,' Oliver said quietly. 'It sounds like this kitchen has a lot of wonderful history.'

'It does, good family memories that I want to pass on to my children.'

Their eyes locked.

'It must be good to have your life worked out and know what you want. I always admired that about you.'

Clemmie noticed his smile falter, the easy charm slipping for just a moment. 'Says you, jetting off all around the world, a different girl in every country, living the time of your—'

She stopped abruptly, her words catching in her throat as a familiar song began playing softly on the radio.

Oliver looked at the radio then back at her, a playful glint returning to his eyes. 'It's our song.'

'We knew each other for a week. We didn't have a song,' said Clemmie, knowing that wasn't quite the whole truth.

'Don't try and deny what we had for that week. Come on,' he said, holding out a hand.

Clemmie frowned. 'What are you doing?'

'Dance with me. Let's pretend we're at the royal garden party.'

'Are you insane? And do they even dance at royal garden parties? It's not *Bridgerton*, you know.'

He laughed. 'You didn't object when we spent most nights dancing around my kitchen.'

'That was then, this is now.'

His hand was still stretched towards her, his gaze steady as it moved between her face and her hand. His eyes seemed to plead with her. 'Come on, just like old times.'

Yet again, her heart and head were in a tennis match. There was a small part of her that wanted to say yes, yet she knew she needed to keep her distance from him. But before she knew it, it was game, set and match to Oliver as he made the choice for her and took her hand. Nervous, she could feel herself lightly shaking, her pulse racing.

He spun her in a dramatic circle and she laughed, nearly tripping over the bag of flour still on the floor before Oliver caught her. They twirled around the kitchen, the torte momentarily forgotten as the song played out and he pulled her in close. She could feel him looking at her, and as she gazed upwards, she found their lips were centimetres apart.

There it was … that look. The one he used to give her in London when they'd stayed up late talking, laughing, just before they ripped each other's clothes off. Every inch of her erupted in goosebumps. Oliver's hazel eyes stayed locked onto hers, and Clemmie felt it – the sexual chemistry was still fizzing between them. She should step back, say something, break whatever this was. But her feet stayed planted, and she swallowed.

His hand lifted, fingers brushing her cheek then

skimming down to her jaw. A barely-there touch, but it sent a shiver through her all the same.

'We shouldn't…' Her voice was barely a whisper.

'I know,' he murmured, his thumb grazing the corner of her mouth.

But neither of them moved. His face dipped towards hers, her lips parted … just one more second and—

The café door slammed open and Betty's cheerful voice rang out. 'Morning, sweetheart! Smells like chocolate—oh my stars, what's happened in here?'

Clemmie practically jumped out of her skin and she pushed Oliver away, smoothing down her pinny.

Betty stood in the doorway, her hands on her hips, surveying the flour-coated kitchen with a look of amused dismay.

'I … uh…' Clemmie stammered, glancing at Oliver, who looked entirely too entertained by the whole situation. Betty's eyes narrowed slightly as she took in the man standing in her café kitchen. 'You're the guy with the Ferrari,' she said, her tone both curious and suspicious.

'Aston Martin, actually,' Oliver corrected smoothly, his grin widening as Betty folded her arms across her chest.

Clemmie knew full well that Betty didn't like anyone in her kitchen who shouldn't be there, so she jumped in hastily. 'Granny, this is Oliver,' she said. 'The presenter of The Royal Baking Competition.'

Betty's expression didn't waver, though her gaze flickered between the man and her granddaughter. 'Yes, I know, and that's all very well, but what are you doing in my kitchen? We aren't open yet,' she said bluntly.

Oliver, unfazed by the stern tone, stepped forward

slightly and extended a hand. 'Betty, it's an honour to meet you. And I must say, this kitchen is as charming as the café itself. You've done a remarkable job creating such an inviting space. It feels like stepping back into a time when people truly cherished good food and good company.'

Betty blinked, clearly caught off guard by the unexpected compliment. Her arms loosened, and a faint pink crept into her cheeks. 'Well, I've always believed that a café should be like a second home for folks,' she said, her voice softening. 'Someplace they can come to for a hearty meal or a slice of cake and leave their troubles behind, if only for a short while.'

'You've absolutely nailed it,' Oliver continued, gesturing around the room. 'I've been to countless cafés and bistros all over the world, in London, Paris, New York … but I can tell you, this place has something special. The charm, the care, the history. It's like the heart of Puffin Island beats right here in this kitchen.'

Betty's face brightened at his words, her bashful smile showing through as she tried to suppress her delight. 'Well, I suppose we do our best. People around here know quality when they taste it.'

'They certainly do,' Oliver agreed, his eyes glinting with genuine appreciation. 'And I imagine that's why this café has become such a beloved staple in the community. You've made it more than just a place to eat … it's a part of people's lives.'

Clemmie mouthed at Oliver, 'Over the top, what are you doing?' She watched as her granny all but melted under Oliver's praise, her sharp edges softening completely. Betty adjusted her apron and brushed a stray lock of hair from her face, clearly lapping up every word.

Oliver winked at Clemmie, who immediately rolled her eyes.

'Well, you've got a way with words, I'll give you that,' Betty said, her eyes twinkling. 'I can see why you're a presenter.'

Oliver chuckled. 'It's not just presenting, Betty, I'm also a food journalist. I've spent years travelling the world, tasting, writing, learning the incredible stories behind the dishes people create. And I can see there are plenty of stories right here in this café. It's a treasure trove of tradition and heart.'

Betty preened herself at the compliment, but before she could respond, Oliver added with a charming grin, 'Speaking of food, though, I must admit, I'm feeling a bit peckish.'

'Well, we're not open yet,' Clemmie cut in quickly, hoping to put a stop to whatever he was about to suggest.

Betty waved her off dismissively. 'Nonsense,' she declared. 'If you're hungry, I'll whip you up something myself. A proper full English. It's nothing fancy, mind you, but it'll stick to your ribs.'

'Granny!' Clemmie exclaimed, her mouth falling open in disbelief.

Looking like the cat who got the cream, Oliver shot Clemmie a mischievous glance before turning back to Betty. 'That sounds absolutely perfect,' he said. 'You've already convinced me this is the best café on the island so I can't wait to taste the proof.'

Betty beamed, clearly thrilled at the chance to show off

her culinary skills. She bustled around the kitchen, taking the sausages and bacon out of the fridge. 'Black pudding?' she asked.

'My favourite, Betty! You are a superstar!'

Clemmie stood frozen, her mouth agape as Oliver sat down at the kitchen table, his grin growing wider by the second.

'Why are you trying to get Granny on side?' Clemmie muttered, shooting him a glare.

'What can I say?' Oliver replied, his tone maddeningly self-satisfied. 'I've always had a way of charming the locals.'

Clemmie shook her head in disbelief as she watched Betty throw herself into preparing the impromptu meal. Oliver had managed to waltz into their lives and, in mere minutes, win over the toughest critic on Puffin Island.

'Don't look so cross, Clemmie,' Oliver added in a low voice meant just for her. 'Your granny is wonderful.'

As Betty hummed a tune and began to sizzle the sausages, she looked over at Clemmie, 'Would you set the table and make Oliver a drink?'

'Another coffee with one of those swirly hearts would be great!' he replied, clearly enjoying every second of Clemmie's discomfort.

'Tell us all about the Royal Yacht. Will the island's residents get a tour?' Betty looked over her shoulder as Clemmie placed cutlery on the table in front of Oliver.

'I'm not sure, Betty, but I can always ask the question.'

'Our Clemmie's going to win that competition, you mark my words. She's been baking since she could hold a whisk, haven't you?'

'Granny!'

'Little Clemmie OBE.'

'Granny!' Clemmie repeated.

'OBE?' queried Oliver. 'Have you got an OBE?'

'OBE … Order of the Baking Empire. Mark my words, one day.' Betty looked pleased with herself.

'I see what you did there, very clever,' said Oliver.

'Here you go,' said Betty, putting the plate of food down in front of him with a flourish. 'You'll want to get that on your social media. It's the best full English breakfast you'll taste for miles.'

'I'm in no doubt. How much do I owe you?' he asked.

'It's on the house,' declared Betty.

'That's very kind of you, thank you.'

'Now about this flour everywhere,' she said, turning to Clemmie. 'What happened? You looked a little flushed when I came in. Are you feeling okay? I know it's my day off, but I don't mind stepping in.'

'I thought the same,' Oliver added.

Clemmie shot him a warning look. He smiled, tucking into his breakfast as if he belonged there. And, annoyingly, it felt like he did. Clemmie could bloody kick herself for letting him in for that one moment as they danced. If she wasn't careful, Oliver Lockwood would more than likely break her heart for a second time.

Chapter Six

The afternoon sun glinted off the turquoise waves at Blue Water Bay. Clemmie was sprawled on a pastel chequered picnic blanket, her floppy sun hat shielding her face from the sun as she sipped from her water bottle. Next to her, Amelia was stretched out with a paperback novel, pretending to read but mainly staring at the waves. Dilly, their other best friend and owner of the Puffin Island lighthouse, who was having a couple of hours free time from her twins, was carefully assembling an elaborate cheese board for their picnic.

'This,' Amelia sighed, gesturing vaguely at the scenery with her book, 'is what Sunday afternoons are made for. Sunshine, snacks and absolutely no drama.'

Clemmie smiled and watched her friends, knowing the news she was about to share would bring all the drama. 'You mean, aside from the fact that I nearly kissed Oliver Lockwood in my kitchen yesterday?'

Amelia dropped her book and Dilly froze mid-grape-placement, their eyes wide and locked on Clemmie.

'Say that again,' they chorused.

'It wasn't intentional! He let himself into the café before opening and caught me mid-flour disaster, then…'

'Then?' pressed Amelia.

'I let him get under my skin and we danced to our old song.'

'Wait, wait, wait,' Amelia interrupted, waving her hand frantically. 'Back up. You danced? Like, actual dancing? With music?'

'Yes, with music,' Clemmie admitted. 'The radio was on, and … oh, it's too embarrassing!'

'Please tell me it was something cheesy. Like Whitney Houston,' chipped in Dilly.

'No!' Clemmie laughed. 'Anyway, we were just about to kiss when Granny walked in and ruined the moment … which, looking back, could have possibly done me a favour.'

'Oh my, this is brilliant! I told you he'd come back for you.'

'Although you did tell us that you would never go anywhere near that man even if he was the last man on earth,' Dilly added.

'I know, and I could kick myself, but it just happened. I was totally stupid.'

'It's clear you two have unfinished business,' said Dilly.

'I'm not proud of myself for almost giving into temptation so easily, and it definitely can't happen again. I need to focus on the competition and not get distracted because the last thing I need is Fiona Fairweather taking the crown.'

'Who is Fiona Fairweather?' Dilly leaned over, grabbed a grape and popped it into her mouth.

'I don't even know why I keep this in my bag, but…' Clemmie muttered, guiltily fishing out the magazine she'd taken to carrying around with her. 'I've read the article so many times I could probably recite it verbatim.' She turned to the article and tapped the page as she handed the magazine to Dilly. 'Fiona Fairweather is my competition.'

'In more ways than one,' Amelia teased. 'She turned up at the pub with Oliver the other night.'

'Apparently she's a friend of the family,' shared Clemmie.

'Never mind Fiona, what was it like to almost kiss him again after all this time?' asked Amelia.

'The blooming butterflies were back, fluttering around my stomach at a hundred knots.'

Dilly and Amelia exchanged glances.

'I know what you're thinking.' Clemmie propped herself up on her elbows, staring out at the glittering water as the tide inched closer to their spot on the shore. She could hear the faint cries of gulls overhead, their calls mingling with the chatter of children playing farther down the beach. She looked back towards her friends. 'I can't let it happen again. Kissing him would be…' She trailed off, pressing her lips together.

'Thrilling?' Dilly suggested.

'A mistake,' Clemmie corrected. 'I need to have more self-worth. He's going to be gone as soon as the competition is over, and after the way he treated me, he doesn't deserve another chance.'

Amelia drew a heart in the sand with the tip of a piece of driftwood, then idly scuffed it out. 'You don't know that,' she said softly.

'Yes, I do,' Clemmie replied. 'If he ever truly cared for me, he wouldn't have just disappeared from my life like he did. He's here to present the competition, not to win me back.' Clemmie sat up fully, brushing sand from her hands and shaking her head as if to clear it. 'I've got to keep my head in the game. Winning this competition would mean a lot to me, and to my granny. It could also mean big things for the café and to put all my great-great-grandmother's recipes in a book would mean a great deal to us all.'

'Not to mention you'd have a chance of mingling at the palace. Can you imagine?' added Dilly. Something in the distance caught her eye and she pointed towards the road. 'Is that a camera crew?'

All three of them turned to look. Sure enough, a van emblazoned with the logo for 'Fiona Fairweather Fanciable Fancies' had parked near the beach and a flurry of crew members wielding cameras, booms and clipboards was piling out onto the sand.

And then Clemmie saw him. Oliver stepped out of the van, handsome in a casual white shirt and navy chinos that were somehow both relaxed and tailored to perfection.

'Oh, great,' exclaimed Clemmie.

'Who's that?' said Dilly.

'*That* is Oliver Lockwood,' confirmed Amelia.

Dilly stared. 'I think you should reconsider getting it on with him!'

'Dilly!' exclaimed Clemmie.

'I take it that must be Fiona Fairweather?' Dilly observed.

Fiona stepped out of the van adorned in a flamboyant floral bikini, a wide-brimmed straw hat and sunglasses so massive they nearly concealed her entire face. She strutted across the sand with the flair of a runway model, utterly oblivious to how incongruous she appeared amidst the rugged beauty of Blue Water Bay.

'It most certainly is,' Clemmie replied.

'What is she doing?'

'Probably making her latest TikTok or a feature for her YouTube channel.'

They all watched as the cameras set up in a semi-circle around Fiona.

'She's garnering quite a bit of attention.' Amelia nodded to a group of fishermen who were gawping in her direction.

'That's what she wants: to generate publicity. But what she fails to understand is that this competition is not about how great your body looks, or how much attention you attract, it's about how well you can bake.'

'Hear, hear,' encouraged Amelia.

They watched in disbelief as what looked like a film set of a kitchen was unloaded from the van, followed by utensils, bowls and trays of cupcakes. It was as if the sandy shore of Blue Water Bay had been transformed into the set of a whimsical baking show. Fiona Fairweather, flamboyant as ever, was pretending to bake on the beach, most likely for her social media followers. She flourished a mixing bowl and wooden spoon dramatically as she spoke to the camera, narrating her 'beach baking tips' with exaggerated enthusiasm.

Oliver was now standing next to her in the make-believe kitchen.

'She's all over him. Look at her,' observed Amelia. 'But he's looking a little uncomfortable.'

'Hey, what have I missed? What's going on?' Their friend Verity, the local vet's assistant, slipped onto the picnic blanket. 'Who's that?'

'That is Fiona Fairweather, Clem's competition for the baking competition, and that'—Amelia pointed—'is Oliver Lockwood, Clem's ex-boyfriend.'

'Was that the guy from London you mentioned?'

'Yes,' they all chorused.

Just at that moment Oliver's phone rang and he walked towards the edge of the sea to answer the call.

Meanwhile, Fiona, ever the consummate show-woman, carried on addressing the camera, whisking furiously at a bowl that likely contained nothing more than air. Her dramatic gestures and sing-song voice were delighting a growing crowd of onlookers, who had begun congregating near the jetty, likely half out of curiosity and half in disbelief at the bizarre spectacle unfolding.

The *pièce de résistance*, however, came when Fiona turned to the oven – a painted cardboard contraption that appeared to be held together with duct tape and wishful thinking – gave a theatrical gasp and flung open the door, revealing a tray of perfectly iced cupcakes. A few of the children watching actually clapped, while their parents exchanged amused glances. Fiona, basking in the attention, held up the cupcakes like they were sacred artefacts.

'Aren't these just divine?' she cooed, turning to the camera. 'Fresh from my pop-up beachside bakery, right here at Blue Water Bay!'

She waved the tray tantalisingly, turning in a half-circle to show her masterpiece to everyone, including a seagull that had begun circling above with keen interest.

As Fiona sashayed towards the edge of the sea, preparing for her grand finale shot, things began to unravel. A mischievous boy sprinted past her, causing her to wobble on her impractically high wedge sandals. The tray tilted ominously, and a single cupcake tumbled off, landing in the sand with a sad *plop*.

Clemmie, Amelia, Verity and Dilly leaned forward on their beach towels like a quartet of judges waiting to see what would happen next.

'I know we shouldn't laugh, but…' Amelia snorted.

'She's lucky it wasn't all of them,' Clemmie said, shaking her head.

'Give it a minute,' Dilly added. 'There's still time for disaster.'

Pretending the slip hadn't happened, Fiona recovered her balance and soldiered on towards the end of the jetty, where a small fishing boat was moored. She held the tray in one hand, placed one hand on her hip and struck a pose.

'I just don't get it,' admitted Clemmie.

'She's not just a baker, she's a brand – or so she believes. By being photographed in a bikini at a picturesque seaside location, she's crafting an image of herself as a glamorous, multi-dimensional lifestyle guru,' Verity chipped in.

'It's also a chance to steal the spotlight,' added Amelia. 'Fiona knows that the baking competition is the talk of the town, and by doing something so outlandishly off-topic, she ensures that she becomes the focus of any conversation about the contest. She may hope her unconventional approach will intimidate more traditional competitors like you, making you feel you can't compete with her star power.' Amelia pointed. 'All those children have gathered to watch and are recording on their phones. They probably don't have a clue who she is but she's creating a buzz.'

'This is the essence of creativity,' Fiona proclaimed to the camera. She waded into the water. 'Taking inspiration from the sea, the sand and the—'

Before she could finish her sentence, a gull swooped down, aiming straight for the cupcakes. Fiona screamed, swatting at the bird with her whisk, but it was determined. The crowd erupted in laughter as the bird's persistence caused the entire tray to flip over, sending cupcakes flying like sugary cannonballs.

'No!' Fiona shrieked, grabbing at the tray. Floundering, as a wave took her off her feet. She lost her balance.

'She's going in,' Verity confirmed, her eyes wide.

And in she went. Fiona tumbled backwards into the water, flailing like an overturned starfish.

'She's gone under,' exclaimed Clemmie.

There was a moment of stunned silence.

Then Fiona's hat floated to the surface, followed by Fiona herself, sputtering and shrieking as she emerged from the water.

The girls stifled their laughter as Fiona began to shout to Oliver, who was still standing a little further up. 'What is that saying on the *Great British Bake Off*?' asked Dilly.

'No one likes a soggy bottom!' Clemmie answered with a smile.

Fiona's enormous sunglasses had gone askew, making her look like a half-drowned bug, and her straw hat floated nearby like a tiny, defeated raft.

Fiona flailed again, trying to steady herself.

On the shore, Clemmie, Amelia and Dilly were in hysterics. 'This will be on TikTok for all the wrong reasons. It's better than reality TV,' Clemmie managed between bouts of laughter.

Oliver, finally off the phone, turned around just in time to see Fiona wading out of the water, her once-pristine cupcakes a soggy, bird-pecked mess floating in the water below.

'Fiona?' he called out, looking puzzled.

With as much flair as she could manage, which, in her current state, wasn't much, Fiona splashed through the shallows. With an exaggerated huff, kicking up water as she went, she stormed past the spectators without so much as a glance. Her ruined hat dangled from her fingers.

Clemmie, Amelia, Verity and Dilly exchanged wide-eyed looks, biting back laughter as Fiona flung herself into the van and slammed the door shut. Just when they thought the drama couldn't get any better, a low rumble filled the air, drawing the attention of everyone on the beach.

'What's that?' Amelia asked, craning her neck.

Clemmie turned towards the cobbled road leading down to Blue Water Bay, her brow furrowing. 'Sounds like … engines?'

A convoy of brightly coloured news vans rumbled urgently towards the bay, their satellite dishes glinting in the sunlight. As they came to a halt, doors flew open, releasing a bustling swarm of reporters and camera crews into the scene.

'This just keeps getting better,' Dilly murmured.

'What the hell is going on now?' Verity muttered, shading her eyes.

But before anyone could speculate, the attention on the beach shifted again and a collective gasp rose from the crowd as eyes turned to the horizon. Clemmie followed their gaze, squinting against the glare of the midday sun, and froze.

Far out on the water, something was approaching. At first, it was just a glimmer, but as it drew closer, its silhouette became clear: it was a yacht. No, not just any yacht … *the* yacht.

'Wait a second,' Dilly said, her voice rising. 'Is that what I think it is?'

Clemmie's heart raced as she took in the sight. The Royal Yacht was a marvel, gliding across the water with the elegance of a swan. Its gleaming white hull caught the sunlight, making it seem almost ethereal, while its gold-trimmed masts stood tall like sentinels of grandeur. Flags bearing the unmistakable royal insignia fluttered from the mast-tops. The yacht seemed to defy logic, both impossibly massive and exquisitely graceful, a floating masterpiece that drew gasps from everyone gathered on the beach.

'It's Her Majesty's Royal Yacht,' Amelia whispered, her tone reverent.

'No way,' Clemmie breathed, her heart thudding in her chest.

'Yes way,' Dilly said, practically bouncing with excitement.

Clemmie picked up her phone and placed a call. 'Granny! Get to the bay! Quick!'

The yacht moved closer, and the buzz on the beach grew louder. Spectators surged towards the shoreline, their phones raised like tiny periscopes, snapping photos and recording videos. Children clambered onto shoulders for a better view, while reporters jostled for position, their microphones and cameras aimed at the approaching spectacle.

Clemmie looked over towards Oliver, who caught her eye. He smiled and waved a hand towards the boat, like he was showing off the Royal Yacht in all its glory.

'You're one of the ten bakers, Clemmie. You're going to be on *that*!' exclaimed Verity.

'Yes!' Dilly chimed in. 'You're going to bake in the royal kitchen on a yacht. A Royal Yacht! This is insane!'

Before Clemmie could respond, a nearby reporter's voice caught her attention.

'The Royal Yacht is just about to dock at Puffin Island,' the woman said, speaking animatedly into her microphone. 'It's here to host the annual Royal Baking Competition, where ten lucky bakers will have the opportunity of a lifetime to showcase their skills.'

Clemmie's knees felt weak. The Royal Baking Competition. This wasn't just any stage … it was *the* stage. And she was going to be on it.

Just then, Betty came hurrying down Lighthouse Lane. She puffed slightly as she joined the growing crowd, pressing her hands to her hips to catch her breath.

'Good heavens, what on earth is going on here?' she exclaimed, her voice carrying over the chatter of the onlookers. Her eyes widened as she caught sight of the Royal Yacht gliding towards the dock, its gleaming hull and towering masts a spectacle. 'In all my years on this island, I've never seen anything like this!'

Clemmie turned to her, barely able to suppress her own excitement. 'I can't believe I'm going to be baking on that yacht.'

As the yacht slowed to a majestic stop at the dock, its horn sounded a deep, resonant note that echoed across the bay. The crowd erupted into cheers and applause, their excitement reaching a fever pitch.

Clemmie could hardly believe her eyes. Every detail of the yacht, from its polished wood decks to its ornate gold fixtures, spoke of prestige and history. It was a symbol of excellence, and it was now the backdrop for her greatest challenge yet.

'Clemmie! There you are! Come on…' Oliver's voice broke through the din, and Clemmie turned to see him striding towards her with a grin full of excitement.

'Me?' she asked, pointing at herself. 'Come where?'

'They want to talk to one of the bakers,' Oliver said, signalling for her to follow him towards the gathered news crews.

'But … look at me.'

'You look beautiful,' Oliver said, reaching for her hand. 'Just be yourself and you'll be grand.'

Amelia gave her a gentle shove. 'Go on … go get 'em, Clemmie!'

Clemmie took a deep breath and stepped forward, her

nerves jangling like a set of wind chimes in a storm. The crowd parted slightly as she made her way towards the cameras, their curious gazes following her every step.

The reporter turned to face her, her polished smile bright and welcoming.

'This is contestant Clemmie Rose,' announced Oliver, his voice brimming with enthusiasm. 'Puffin Island is her home.'

The reporter extended her hand in greeting but didn't give Clemmie much time to react before shifting into professional mode. She counted down briskly, 'One … two…' and then turned her attention to the camera.

'We are live from Puffin Island,' she began, her tone vibrant and engaging, 'where the Royal Yacht has just docked, ahead of the filming of the annual Royal Baking Competition, a beloved tradition begun by the Royal Family many decades ago.'

The camera panned briefly to capture the yacht in all its glory, the sunlight glinting off its polished wood and gleaming brass fixtures. The reporter continued, 'This magnificent vessel will serve as the ultimate stage for ten incredibly talented bakers, each of whom will have the chance to showcase their skills in the royal kitchen.'

Clemmie swallowed hard as the microphone was thrust towards her, the reporter's smile encouraging yet firm.

'We're here with Clemmie Rose, one of the ten talented bakers nominated to compete in this year's competition,' she said, her voice smooth and professional. 'Clemmie, how does it feel to know you'll be baking on the Royal Yacht?'

Clemmie glanced towards it, its grandeur almost surreal, and found her voice. 'It's … it's an incredible opportunity,' she said, her words shaky at first but gaining strength. 'It's … humbling. But this competition is more than just a chance to bake. It's a way to honour tradition and push ourselves to recreate something extraordinary from our heritage.'

'The recipe you have chosen, are you able to tell us anything about it?'

'All I'm going to share at the moment is it's a recipe that was created by my great-great-grandmother and is a firm favourite at our café on the coast.'

The reporter's smile widened. 'And what are you most excited about as you prepare for the competition?'

Clemmie paused, choosing her words carefully. 'To honour my family's baking heritage alongside such a talented group of bakers. I can't wait to see what we all create.'

The crowd that had gathered broke into a round of supportive cheers and Clemmie could see her friends were practically jumping up and down, clapping enthusiastically from their spot on the beach.

'Thank you for talking to us today,' the reporter said, giving her a nod of approval. 'Best of luck to you in the competition!'

As the interview ended, Oliver gave her hand a squeeze. 'That was perfect,' he said. 'You're a natural on TV, which bodes well, given it's a televised competition.'

Clemmie glanced back at her friends, who were grinning and waving like proud parents. She couldn't help but smile. The Royal Yacht, the competition, the chance to bake in the kitchen of her dreams … it was all happening and she was determined to make the most of every single moment.

'You were brilliant,' exclaimed Betty as Clemmie rejoined them.

'I bet Fiona is kicking herself for falling into the water. That could have been her talking to the press instead,' said Verity.

Dilly held out her phone. 'Instead she's all over the socials for the wrong reason. Someone uploaded the video of her cupcakes being stolen by the seagull, followed by her unexpected swim in the sea.' The caption read: *'From cupcakes to cup-flops, when baking dreams take a dive!'*

They all watched the video. 'I'm beginning to feel a little bit sorry for her,' said Betty, though her wicked grin said otherwise.

'You do not, Granny!' replied Clemmie.

'Hopefully you have more finesse than Fiona. Her balancing skills certainly need some work!' She gestured towards the sea, where Fiona had just been floundering.

Everyone laughed.

Clemmie turned her attention back to the Royal Yacht, her thoughts on the prize ahead of her, and the challenge that lay in her hands.

Chapter Seven

The few days leading up to the baking competition felt electric as Puffin Island found itself thrust into the spotlight of a royal event that had captivated the nation. The buzz of excitement was real in every corner of Puffin Island as preparations for The Royal Baking Competition moved into full swing. The island, usually tranquil and serene, had been transformed. The quaint streets were adorned with banners and flags in royal colours, and signs with Clemmie's face and the words *Go Clemmie!* were proudly displayed in shop windows, the local businesses eager to support their homegrown baker.

Despite the prestige of the event, it felt personal to the islanders, who saw Clemmie as one of their own, someone who had spent years perfecting her craft and had finally made it to the grand stage. The entire community had rallied behind her, eager to show the world the warmth, charm and talent that Puffin Island had to offer. The local newspaper had dedicated entire sections to her journey, profiling her as the pride of the island.

The past week had been a blur of chocolate, butter and sugar whilst Clemmie spent time perfecting the torte recipe.

The layers had to be light, yet sturdy. The ganache needed to be velvety smooth and with a slight bitterness to balance the richness of the cake. The clementines added extra oomph and the gold leaf was the final flourish, a touch of elegance that would make the cake look as regal as it tasted.

Clemmie had made countless versions of the cake, adjusting every detail until it was just right. Now, as she carefully boxed up the latest version of her torte, a wave of satisfaction swept through her. For the first time, she felt confident, knowing that this cake might actually stand a chance in the competition.

As she closed the cake box, she felt pride.

'Are you ready?' Betty's voice broke through Clemmie's thoughts, and she turned to see her grandmother standing in the doorway. Betty's smile was encouraging. 'Is that it, the latest torte?' She pointed to the box.

Clemmie nodded. 'Taste it. Be honest, tell me what you think.' She pushed the box towards her.

Betty opened it, her eyes twinkling with delight as she took in the sight of the torte. Her gaze lingered on the glossy layers, the subtle sheen of the ganache, and the delicate finish of the gold leaf that adorned the top along with the slice of clementine. 'This looks outstanding,' she said, her voice full of admiration. She carefully leaned closer, inhaling the rich aroma of the torte. Taking a knife, she cut off a slice and tasted.

There was silence. Clemmie's heart raced as she waited for her granny to speak. She was relieved when a smile broke on Betty's face.

'The balance of the flavours is absolutely perfect. You've captured the essence of the recipe, but with a touch of modern elegance.' She pointed to the gold leaf. 'It's like a work of art and a slice of history all rolled into one. It's made with pure love.'

Clemmie exhaled a breath, 'You think so?' she asked. Her granny's approval meant everything, and the pressure of the upcoming competition was starting to feel almost overwhelming.

Betty smiled. 'Oh, my dear, I *know* so. It has winner written all over it,' she said, her confidence bubbling up with every word. She glanced at Clemmie, her eyes radiating that unmistakable sparkle of belief. 'And I'm not just saying that because I'm your granny. You've nailed it, Clemmie. This is no ordinary cake. It's got that special something, a real wow factor. I've been baking for years, but there's something about this one … it has a real chance to stand out, to make a statement. Honestly, if I were a judge, you'd have my vote already.'

Clemmie exhaled. 'That's the only vote I need.'

'But I suggest…' She looked at the clock. 'You go and get yourself ready. You have to be at the bay in forty minutes. I can't even begin to tell you how jealous I am that you get a tour of the yacht ahead of the competition.'

Twenty minutes later, Clemmie stepped out of the shower and wrapped herself in a fluffy towel as steam swirled around the bathroom. Her skin was flushed from the hot water, and her stomach was churning with nerves.

Towelling her hair dry, she padded to her bedroom and opened her wardrobe, surveying her options. She needed something that struck the right balance – professional yet approachable, polished but still her.

As her fingers skimmed over the hangers, she paused, her breath catching. Then, she smiled. There it was, the perfect outfit. A soft cornflower-blue dress she had worn on her very first date with Oliver. A simple yet elegant piece, it was fitted at the waist with a flared skirt that grazed her knees, the fabric delicate and light. The neckline, just modest enough, was accented by tiny embroidered flowers that caught the light. Would he notice? Would he remember? She traced the embroidery with her finger. Maybe this was foolish. She wasn't looking for a way back to him – she couldn't, not after everything that had happened. She had spent too long trying to block thoughts of him from her memory, to accept that some things were better left in the past. But still … there was a niggle in the back of her mind. Had it meant as much to him as it had to her? If he remembered, if his gaze lingered on the dress even for a second, then she would have her answer. Not one that would change anything – not one she could afford to let change anything – but proof that, once, it had been real. That she hadn't imagined it. That she hadn't been the only one who had fallen, who had believed, who had hoped. It wasn't about rekindling anything. It was merely about knowing it had mattered. She exhaled, smoothing a hand over the fabric. It was just a dress. Just a memory. Maybe this was foolish, but she needed to remind him of what they had, of what he chose to walk away from, what he was missing.

She stepped into the dress, pairing it with pearl drop earrings that had once belonged to her great-great-grandmother before being passed down through the women in the family. They felt like a little token of luck. Her hair, naturally wavy, was pinned back on one side with a silver clip, leaving the rest to tumble over her shoulders in soft waves. As she buttoned the tiny button on the back of the dress, she wondered how Oliver might react. The first time he'd seen her in it he'd complimented the dress, made her twirl to show it off, then kissed her neck.

The memory of that night in London came flooding back. Oliver had taken her to L'Étoile Privée, a swanky members-only restaurant tucked away in Mayfair where the mere sight of its frosted-glass doors whispered wealth and exclusivity. No reservations were needed because the guest list was handpicked, and you didn't just walk in, you glided. Inside, it was all polished marble, gleaming chandeliers and waiters who could probably command more respect than CEOs. Clemmie had nearly tripped over her own feet on the plush carpet, glancing at Oliver like he'd dragged her into a movie set.

'Don't look so scared,' he'd whispered. His hand was reassuring in the small of her back. 'Just act like you belong.'

'Easier said than done,' she'd mouthed, before staring at the menu. The cheapest bottle of wine was £200, and that was a vintage she didn't even recognise. 'This is absurd! It's way out of my price range.'

'You deserve to be spoiled.'

After the waiter poured the wine, there were the oysters. Clemmie had never tried them before, and when they arrived, glossy, raw and perched delicately on a bed of crushed ice, she'd eyed them suspiciously.

'They're an acquired taste but I can't believe you've never even tried one, living where you do, by the sea,' Oliver had said, his grin wicked as he demonstrated how to eat one with maddening elegance.

'I don't mean to appear rude, but they do look like something the cat coughed up.' She'd thought she'd whispered but as a passing waiter stifled his laugher Clemmie knew she hadn't been as quiet as she'd intended.

Trying to mimic Oliver's confidence she'd picked up the oyster and slid it into her mouth. The briny explosion was unlike anything she'd tasted before and she'd gagged, not dramatically, but enough for Oliver to chuckle.

'Swallow, Clemmie,' he'd teased, his eyes alight with amusement.

She'd managed it, coughing delicately into her napkin before fixing him with a mock glare. 'If I die from food poisoning, you're footing the funeral bill.'

By the time they'd finished their decadent meal, including a dessert so intricate it looked like it belonged in an art gallery, Clemmie had been giddy … though whether that was from the wine or Oliver's presence, she wasn't sure. But when they'd got back to his sleek London apartment, the tension simmering between them all evening had boiled over. Her blue dress had barely made it past the door before it was unceremoniously discarded on the hallway floor.

Now, as she adjusted the same dress and tried to tamp down the flicker of old feelings, she couldn't help but wonder: had it meant as much to him as it had to her?

Forty minutes later, Clemmie stepped out of the café to an eruption of cheers that caught her completely off guard. Her eyes widened as she looked around, stunned to see all her friends gathered at the gate, waving and clapping like she'd already won the competition.

'What are you lot doing here?' Clemmie called out. 'I'm only going for a tour of the yacht! You do know I haven't won yet, don't you?'

'You *will*,' declared Amelia with a grin, linking her arm through Clemmie's as the group set off down the lane towards Blue Water Bay. 'The bay's already packed. Everyone's turned out to see the contestants walk onto the yacht. Even the press is there!'

'The bay is *actually* packed?' Clemmie asked, her voice tinged with disbelief.

'Absolutely heaving,' said Verity, gesturing animatedly. 'It's like a festival down there. Oh, and speaking of excitement, as we were walking up the lane, something dawned on me. Remember last year? Madam Zelda?'

'What about her?' Clemmie asked, narrowing her eyes suspiciously at the mischievous expressions on Verity's and Amelia's faces.

'The psychic night at The Olde Ship Inn!' Verity exclaimed, her eyes sparkling. 'Madam Zelda said you were going to meet someone connected to royalty, and there'd be a garden party involved. Does *that* ring any bells?'

Betty, bustling to keep up with their pace, chimed in, 'She said it quite dramatically, too, like it was meant to be important!'

Clemmie rolled her eyes, though a smile tugged at her

lips. 'We all know Madam Zelda's readings are pure entertainment. It's just a comedy act, nothing more.'

'I wouldn't be so sure,' Verity said, wagging her finger. 'She told Amelia she had a big secret, remember? And Amelia *was* hiding the biggest secret of all … being a published author!'

Amelia blushed, but her grin gave her away. 'Okay, okay, she got one thing right. But still, predicting royalty and a garden party is a bit of a stretch.'

Verity looked smug. 'I'm just saying, I think there's more to it. You're going to win this competition, Clemmie. I can feel it. And after you win, you'll be invited to that garden party. Maybe even meet the man of your dreams.'

The only man that was constantly creeping back into Clemmie's mind since he reappeared was Oliver. Ever since his arrival on the island, he had seemed to occupy most of her thoughts at all hours … when she woke up, when she went to bed, and nearly every moment in between. She shook her head, fighting to clear the memory of his smile and wit from her mind.

'Madam Zelda said something else, though, didn't she?' Verity added, her brow furrowing as if she were trying to solve a particularly tricky puzzle. 'What was it? Something about … oh! "A past scandal makes the present stronger."'

'I remember that!' Dilly said, her eyes lighting up. 'What do you think it means? Some juicy bit of island gossip from years ago that's about to resurface?'

'I've no idea what she could've been on about,' Betty said briskly. 'But if we stand here debating psychic riddles much longer, Clemmie will miss the tour of the yacht! And we want to hear all about it.'

The group quickened their pace, their laughter and chatter filling the air as they headed towards the bay. The excitement was infectious, and Clemmie felt a swell of gratitude for her friends' unwavering support. Whatever the day and the competition might bring, she knew she wouldn't be facing it alone. They were living every step with her.

The beach at Blue Water Bay was a hive of activity, buzzing with a mixture of excitement and awe that hung in the salty sea air. Clemmie couldn't believe it, the sight of it all, the families with picnic blankets that had evidently staked out their spots early, happy people watching and taking it all in.

'I actually feel like royalty,' Clemmie said. 'But all we're doing is having a tour of the yacht! You'd think actual royalty was arriving with this crowd. And how did they all find out about it? I only got my email invite this morning.'

Amelia, standing beside her with a knowing smile, nudged Clemmie playfully. 'It's been all over the news and social media, that's how. The *whole world* is watching this baking competition. You've gone from being our local café queen to a national sensation overnight.'

'Don't forget,' chimed in Verity, 'the cookbook that comes out after this will probably go straight to the top of the charts. Everyone will want to try recipes from the contestant who baked on a Royal Yacht! I hope you know what recipes you're going to include.'

Clemmie's cheeks flushed, a mixture of nerves and excitement swirling in her chest. She wasn't sure what felt more surreal: the sight of the glittering Royal Yacht anchored in the bay, the sheer number of people who had turned out, or the idea that her great-great-grandmother's recipes might soon grace kitchen tables around the world.

In the distance, Her Majesty's Royal Yacht shimmered under the midday sun, its sleek white hull and golden accents cutting a regal figure against the sparkling blue of the sea. The royal ensign fluttered gently at the bow, a symbol of heritage and prestige that added to the yacht's aura. Clemmie knew she would be stepping aboard very soon, walking the same decks that had hosted dignitaries and even the Queen herself.

'This feels bigger than I imagined,' Clemmie murmured, glancing at Betty, whose proud smile offered a comforting anchor in the whirlwind of attention.

Betty gave her a reassuring pat on the shoulder. 'It *is* big, love. And you deserve every bit of it. Now stop fretting, hold your head high and enjoy every moment. This is your time to shine.'

'Was it you who nominated me?' Clemmie asked, the thought popping into her head.

Betty shook her head. 'I wish it was but no, it wasn't me.'

'Then who?'

'Your guess is as good as mine.'

The press was out in full force, their presence unmistakable as television cameras stood on sturdy tripods, their lenses glinting in the sun. Reporters darted about, some holding microphones emblazoned with logos of national networks, while others jotted furiously in notepads, their focus unwavering as they captured every moment of the spectacle.

For Puffin Island, a place known for its quaint charm,

hosting such a majestic vessel was like having a piece of a fairytale docked at its shores. Uniformed officials patrolled the area, their presence lending an air of importance to the proceedings. A temporary stage had been erected on the beach, adorned with banners that bore the competition's emblem: a golden whisk encircled by a crown.

For Clemmie, standing with her friends near the edge of the crowd, the scene felt surreal. She glanced at Betty, Verity, Amelia and Dilly, all of whom shared her excitement.

'This is it!' Betty said, her excitement bubbling over. Her eyes sparkled like a child's at Christmas, her enthusiasm infectious. 'You get to see inside the Royal Yacht. Your great-great-grandmother would have loved this, being a royal fan through and through.'

'How you feeling?' Amelia asked, as they all huddled in a group on the sand.

'Nervous, excited,' Clemmie admitted, noticing the other contestants lining up at the side of the stage. 'What if I get seasick?'

Dilly laughed. 'The yacht isn't sailing the high seas! You're overthinking it.' She nodded in the direction of the path. 'And there he is, the man himself. Oh, and he's searching the crowd for … you.'

Clemmie's gaze followed Dilly's nod, and the moment her eyes met Oliver's, her heart annoyingly skipped a beat. Dressed in a perfectly tailored navy-blue suit with a crisp white shirt and a subtle paisley tie, he looked every inch the polished host of a royal event. The suit hugged his broad shoulders, the kind of fit that spoke of custom tailoring and attention to detail. He looked utterly gorgeous.

As soon as he spotted her, a smile spread across his face,

warm and genuine, as though she were the only person on the crowded beach. He raised a hand in a casual wave before gesturing for her to join the other contestants. Clemmie's cheeks flushed, and she barely heard Dilly's teasing remarks as her feet carried her forward.

As she approached, the scent of his aftershave reached her, that sophisticated blend of cedarwood and citrus, fresh and grounding all at once. She couldn't help but notice the way his eyes crinkled slightly at the corners as he smiled at her, or how the sunlight caught the faint stubble on his jawline, giving him a rugged yet refined look.

'Clemmie,' he greeted her.

For a moment, Clemmie was acutely aware of how close he was as they stood side by side. Her pulse quickened, and she prayed it wasn't outwardly obvious. 'Hi,' she managed, her voice sounding steadier than she felt.

'You need to join the others.' He gestured towards the group gathered near the stage, his hand lightly brushing her arm as he guided her. The touch was fleeting but sent a spark racing through her, leaving her momentarily flustered.

As they walked, the din of the crowd seemed to fade into the background. Clemmie could feel her nerves ebbing, replaced by a flicker of something else – excitement, anticipation and maybe just a hint of hope. This was it, her chance not just to win but to represent her café, her family and her little island in front of the world.

A voice crackled to life over the yacht's Tannoy system, cutting through the chatter of the assembled crowd. 'Will all competitors please gather next to Mr Oliver Lockwood, who is now standing on the jetty?'

A collective cheer erupted from the beach.

Taking a deep breath Clemmie looked around at the crowd gathered along the beach. Familiar faces beamed back at her. Sam waved flags from The Sea Glass Restaurant. Becca from the Cosy Kettle shouted, 'Go Clemmie!' Ralph from the boat house was waving and Cora and Dan from The Olde Ship Inn had brought out all the staff with them. The support of her community wrapped around her like an invisible shield as she gave them a thumbs-up and followed the other contestants towards the jetty, where a gangplank stretched between the luxury yacht and the shore. It swayed gently with the movement of the water.

Oliver had moved towards the end of the gangplank and as Clemmie approached, he looked up, his gaze locking onto hers. He smiled, not the polished smile he wore for the cameras, but a softer, more familiar one as he leaned in towards her and whispered, 'I recognise that dress.'

Clemmie felt a strange mix of triumph and uncertainty. Had she achieved what she'd intended, forcing him to see exactly what he had walked away from? The dress had been a deliberate choice, a nod to the past, a reminder of everything they had been, everything they could have been. But now, standing before him, with his eyes tracing the fabric, she wasn't sure if she had won or if she had just opened an old wound in herself.

Did he regret it? Did he miss her?

She saw Fiona watching him carefully and for a moment Clemmie thought she saw a fleeting look of jealousy as Fiona narrowed her eyes at them both and moved towards Oliver, planting a kiss on his cheek. Her hand lingered on his chest as though she was marking her territory. 'You did right nominating me for this competition,' she murmured. 'Kensington will well and truly be put on the map.'

Clemmie was sure the words were for her benefit, a means of reinforcing Fiona and Oliver's shared history, but right in this moment, when she was here flying the flag for Puffin Island, it didn't matter. She was just thankful to be here.

As the competitors filed onto the yacht in a single line, there was a nervous energy in the air, making Clemmie feel like she was a soldier heading off to battle. The crowd lining the beach waved enthusiastically, cheering and shouting words of encouragement like family sending off loved ones with hope and pride. Clemmie smiled at the absurdity of it all, going to culinary war armed with piping bags and spatulas.

The gangplank creaked gently under her feet as she stepped onto the Royal Yacht, and she gasped as the stateliness of the vessel unfolded before her. Polished teak decking shone underfoot, and white railings gleamed in the sunlight. Polished brass fixtures, perfectly coiled ropes and staff dressed in immaculate navy uniforms spoke of a timeless elegance that felt almost surreal.

Inside, the yacht was even more breathtaking. The main reception area boasted a sweeping staircase with a polished mahogany banister, leading up to a glittering chandelier that cast delicate patterns across the plush carpeting. Rich tapestries adorned the walls, and golden-framed paintings of historic royal events hung between ornate sconces. Clemmie's eyes widened as they passed a grand dining hall with a table set for around twenty, complete with crystal glassware and embroidered napkins folded into elaborate shapes.

The tour led them down into the kitchens, which were nothing short of culinary heaven. Stainless steel counters stretched endlessly, lined with every piece of equipment a baker or chef could dream of. Gleaming ovens, rows of copper pots hanging from hooks, and state-of-the-art mixers made Clemmie's heart skip a beat. She ran her fingers over the edge of a prep table, marvelling at how pristine it all was.

The TV crew were filming as Oliver spoke. 'Welcome to one of the kitchens on Her Majesty's Royal Yacht. This is where the competition will take place.' Oliver gestured around the room, his voice carrying a note of reverence. 'This kitchen isn't just a space for cooking; it's a piece of history. The Royal Yacht has played host to countless dignitaries, heads of state and even royalty from across the globe. This kitchen has witnessed culinary feats that have left their mark in gastronomic history. Now, it's your turn to leave yours.' Clemmie's eyes roved over the room, taking in every detail. Each workstation was a marvel of modern design, seamlessly blending the heritage of the past with the innovations of the present.

Oliver continued, walking slowly between the stations as the film crew panned their cameras to capture the room's splendour. 'This Royal Kitchen on the yacht is one of several strategically placed on board. The yacht is not just a royal vessel, it is a floating palace designed for grand state affairs and high-profile events. As such, multiple kitchens are necessary to accommodate the enormous scale of royal dinners, which often involve several courses served at precise times across multiple dining rooms. Some kitchens specialise in preparing delicate desserts, others in cooking fine meats or seafood, while a few are dedicated to catering to dietary restrictions or creating bespoke menus for each guest.

'These separate kitchens make for an efficient operation, with chefs working in tandem but never overcrowding one area. The meals prepared aboard are designed to dazzle and impress – meticulously crafted to reflect not only culinary excellence but the importance of the occasion, every dish a work of art, a statement of diplomacy on a plate.'

Clemmie could imagine the scene he described. The chefs, clad in pristine white uniforms, sweating under the pressure of serving perfection to the most powerful people in the world. She pictured a head chef, an imposing figure with a sharp eye and sharper tongue, orchestrating the team like a maestro conducting an orchestra.

Oliver moved through the group and paused by Clemmie, catching her gaze. 'Clemmie, you're standing where the patissier would stand.' He pointed to the workstation's pristine marble surface. 'This slab here? Imported Carrara marble, chosen specifically for its cool surface, perfect for working with delicate pastries and tempering chocolate. Some of the finest desserts ever served on this yacht were made right here. Can you imagine the pressure?'

Clemmie smiled nervously, her fingers brushing the cool, smooth marble. She could indeed imagine it … all too vividly.

'But this kitchen isn't just functional,' Oliver added. 'It was designed to impress. Notice the intricate woodwork along the cabinets?' He pointed towards a row of custom-built cabinets with gilded edges. 'That's hand-carved mahogany, and it's been polished to perfection for decades. Even the taps over the sinks are gold-plated, a testament to the craftsmanship of the time.'

A ripple of awe swept through the contestants as they absorbed the opulence around them. One of them, a young man named Jacob, raised his hand tentatively. 'Is it just competitions, or do they host other kinds of culinary events here, too?'

Oliver smiled. 'Sometimes the Royal Family want to entertain their guests with more than conversation, and this room transforms into a theatre of gastronomy, with chefs preparing dishes in front of an audience of enraptured guests.'

The mention of theatre suddenly clicked with Clemmie. She noticed, for the first time, the subtle design of the room. In front of the workstations was a wide open space, where rows of elegant chairs were now arranged for the audience. Above the kitchen area, a series of arched windows let in soft natural light, casting a glow that made the room feel both grand and inviting. The walls, painted a deep royal blue, were decorated with paintings of historical maritime scenes, lending the space a regal charm.

'During the golden years of the yacht,' Oliver continued, stepping towards the centre of the room, 'this very space would have been filled with the aroma of freshly baked bread, spiced tarts and caramelising sugar. Guests would sit where the audience is now, sipping champagne and nibbling on hors d'oeuvres while watching the chefs create culinary magic.' He gestured to a corner where an antique gramophone stood on display. 'Music would play softly in the background, adding to the ambiance. This was more than cooking; it was performance art.'

Clemmie's eyes flickered towards the chairs, already imagining the spectators watching when the baking competition began. The quiet murmur of anticipation reminded her of the grandeur Oliver had described. She took another deep breath, steeling herself. If the chefs of the past could thrive under such pressure, so could she.

Oliver's voice rose again, pulling her back to the present. 'Now, I trust you all filled out your forms carefully. You've told the organisers not just what you're baking, but the story behind it, how it has been passed down through generations and what tools and ingredients you'll need to bring your family recipe to life. Everything will be ready for you on the day and waiting at your workstation or on your individual shelf. Every ingredient will be chosen with the utmost care, from flour that holds a royal seal of approval to chocolate that's been handpicked for its unique flavour. It will all be here, ready for you to work your magic.'

Clemmie's hands rested on the edge of her station as she glanced at the equipment. The stand mixer, with its sleek metallic finish, seemed to gleam with an almost otherworldly promise. The knives in their holder appeared razor-sharp, their polished blades catching the light in an almost intimidating way. Every detail in the kitchen from the brass fixtures to the immaculate countertops was designed to inspire, but also to remind them of the standards they were expected to uphold.

'And one last thing,' Oliver added, his tone suddenly serious. 'This kitchen is steeped in tradition. While you're here, I encourage you to think of the chefs who came before you. They worked not just for glory, but to honour their craft. Let that inspire you.'

Clemmie couldn't take her eyes off Oliver as he spoke, his words weaving a tapestry of culinary history that enthralled the room. He was damn good at his job, commanding attention effortlessly.

She thought about the last time she'd seen him in London. In that moment, she felt a pang of recognition. This was a man who loved his work, who lived for it in the same way she lived for her café on Puffin Island. He spoke with a passion that was as undeniable as it was inspiring, and for the first time, she let herself truly see it. Clemmie realised the last day they'd spent together she hadn't considered how he might be feeling.

She remembered that last night in London vividly, though she'd tried to bury it. The way his eyes had searched hers, filled with hope and something that looked like desperation, when he'd told her he wanted her to come with him on his travels. She hadn't hesitated when she had said no, unable to even consider leaving behind her life on Puffin Island. Now, standing here, watching him command the room with the same passion that had scared her off, she felt the sting of regret. Not because she had stayed – she still loved her café and her life by the coast – but because she had never really understood the depth of his love for his work. She had seen his request to leave her home as a threat to her happiness, not as an invitation into his.

The thought wouldn't leave her head, as she stood there, her hands brushing absently over the cool marble of the countertop. She had told herself for years that if he had cared enough, he would have written, called, found her. But had she really given him the chance? She hadn't called him either. She hadn't written. She had let those seven days of passion fade into a bittersweet memory, convincing herself it was better that way. But now, watching him, she wondered if she had been wrong. He was so alive in this space, so utterly in his element, and she couldn't help but admire him. More than that, she envied him, the way he had poured himself into his work, the way he had built a life that reflected who he was. As she stood there, caught in the spell of his voice and the energy that seemed to radiate from him, she couldn't escape the question that had begun to form in her mind … had she given up something too precious too easily? She was beginning to think about what could have been. She'd buried her feelings deep for the past three years, hidden them under the daily rituals of her life, but they were there all the same. In this moment, they were rising to the surface, undeniable and raw.

Oliver caught her eye, his gaze lingering for just a moment before he turned back to the room. It was as if he could read her thoughts, though he didn't say a word. Clemmie felt her cheeks flush, her heartbeat quicken. She looked away, focusing on her hands, but the feeling remained. She wasn't sure what she was feeling – admiration, regret, longing? – but she knew she couldn't ignore it much longer. Watching him now, she realised that the past wasn't as far behind her as she had thought.

The oven positioned right in front of her looked like it had been lifted straight from a professional culinary dream. Its digital display blinked invitingly, and the chrome knobs felt sturdy and precise as she gave one an experimental twist. Behind her, a line of tall silver fridges hummed softly, their interiors stocked with ingredients meticulously organised and labelled. Everything about the set-up exuded precision, luxury and the quiet promise of culinary perfection.

Clemmie inhaled deeply, trying to absorb the gravity of where she stood. This was no ordinary kitchen; it was grand, and a little bit intimidating. She had practised tirelessly, but now that she was here, with the competition looming, the reality of it all was a little overwhelming. Clemmie adjusted the stand mixer's bowl, double-checked the oven's settings, and glanced back at the fridges, mentally mapping out where everything she needed was stored.

Then, out of the corner of her eye, she saw movement. Turning to her left, she felt her stomach sink as Fiona Fairweather sauntered into view and positioned herself at the adjacent station. Fiona gave her a slow, deliberate smile, which managed to be smug, sharp and brimming with unspoken superiority.

Damn. Of all the competitors, why did it have to be Fiona on the workstation next to her? Clemmie could feel the pressure mounting as the woman began fiddling with her own equipment like a queen surveying her domain. Fiona's presence alone was enough to make Clemmie's nerves skyrocket, and now she knew she'd be stationed beside her on live TV for at least two hours. Fiona glanced her way again, her smile widening as if to say, *This will be easy*.

Clemmie breathed in, trying to regain her equilibrium. She wasn't going to let Fiona's smugness or the looming pressure of the competition ruin this moment. This was her chance to prove herself, to put The Café on the Coast on the map, honour her heritage, and maybe, just maybe, win an invitation to the royal garden party.

But she couldn't shake the feeling that Fiona was going to find a way to make this even harder than it already was.

Chapter Eight

Oliver's voice rang out again, rich and commanding, pulling Clemmie's attention back to him. 'In about an hour, there will be a press conference in the royal dining salon, a chance for the media to meet you all. They'll want to hear about your inspirations, your aspirations and your story – what brought you here. This is an opportunity for each of you to make an impression, not just as contestants but as the culinary stars you're aspiring to be. So, use this time wisely to gather your thoughts and, of course, enjoy the tour of the Royal Yacht.' His words carried a note of encouragement, but also a challenge, as if daring them to seize the moment and shine.

Clemmie's heart sank a little at the mention of the press. Public speaking was not her strength, and the thought of being scrutinised by strangers with cameras and questions in front of the other contestants made her nervous. Puffin Island and her café were her heart, her soul, but how did she articulate that in a way that wouldn't sound small or provincial compared to the grand ambitions of the others?

Clemmie trailed behind the group of competitors as their guide, a sharply dressed man with a clipboard and an air of quiet authority, led them along the gleaming main deck. Everything about the Royal Yacht radiated luxury, from the velvet ropes cordoning off restricted areas to the polished brass fittings and the discreet staff who moved gracefully in tailored uniforms. The afternoon sun spilled through the tall windows, casting golden light across the plush carpeting, and Clemmie found herself both captivated and feeling slightly out of place amidst the opulence.

'Everyone keep close, please,' the guide called, his tone crisp as he waved his clipboard for emphasis.

The film crew followed the tour, filming the competitors as they went from room to room. They first passed through the main salon, a sweeping room with velvet cushions, polished wood floors and rich golden curtains framing the windows and their views of the ocean. The chandeliers overhead sparkled like stars, their soft light casting a glow over the room. The guide pointed out the Royal Family's favourite seating areas, and Clemmie could imagine them lounging there, the quiet rhythm of the sea as their soundtrack. As they moved on, the dining room loomed ahead, a long table dressed in pristine linen, set with fine china and silverware that gleamed under the soft lighting. The yacht's history hung in the air, and Clemmie was captivated, but it was Oliver, walking just behind her, that kept drawing her attention. Every few moments, she could feel his gaze on her, making her pulse quicken, aware of the subtle tension that crackled between them both. When they entered the ballroom, Clemmie couldn't stop stealing sidelong glances at him, noticing the way his eyes seemed to linger on her as well, the weight of his stare both thrilling and unnerving. As they went through to the next room, the guide announced the tour was complete and they had forty-five minutes until the press conference. As Clemmie went to walk over to the trestle table set out with tea and coffee Oliver quickly grabbed her hand.

'What are you doing?'

'Let's go and take a proper break and pretend we're royalty for half an hour, before someone misses us.' He led her away from the group and they slipped down the corridor into another room. Clemmie laughed softly, her nerves easing as she took in the opulent surroundings. The room was smaller than the grand hallways they had just left but no less stunning. Rich tapestries adorned the walls, and an intricately carved table stood in the centre, set with crystal glasses and fine china as though awaiting a feast.

'Royalty, huh?' she teased, arching an eyebrow. 'You've really leaned into the whole "man of grandeur" thing, haven't you?'

He stepped closer, his eyes skimming her from head to toe before lingering on her dress. A flicker of something unspoken passed between them, and his voice dropped. 'That dress, Clemmie. It's not fair. You know it brings back way too many memories.'

The way he looked at her, intense, playful, and entirely too knowing, made her heart stutter. 'That week in London is burned into my brain. And seeing you in this now...'

He shook his head, the grin turning softer, almost nostalgic. 'Let's just say it's a good thing we're not by ourselves.'

'But we are,' she countered, though her voice betrayed her with its slight tremor.

Her eyes didn't leave his, knowing something deeper was bubbling to the surface.

For a moment, the world seemed to shrink, the magnificence of the room fading into the background as the space between them narrowed. His hand still lingered lightly on her arm, and she was acutely aware of his touch, the way it sent a ripple of something electric through her.

'I should probably get back to the group,' she said softly, though her feet remained rooted to the spot.

'Probably,' he murmured, his voice low and filled with suggestion.

For a moment, it felt like they were back in London, where time had seemed to stretch and compress at the same time around them, where every stolen glance and brush of hands had felt like the most natural thing in the world. Clemmie knew she should pull away and rejoin the others, but with Oliver's gaze holding hers she couldn't bring herself to break the spell.

'I've been thinking about you,' Oliver said, his voice softening, his usual confidence giving way to something raw and unguarded. It was a rare vulnerability that stopped Clemmie in her tracks, her pulse quickening. 'The other morning in the kitchen—'

'We can't go back to where we were. We've had our chance,' Clemmie interrupted, though the words felt like a betrayal of her own heart. Why had she said that out loud? Because if she were honest with herself, she wanted nothing more than to go back, if not to London three years ago, then at least to yesterday morning, to see what would have happened if Betty hadn't interrupted them.

Oliver tilted his head, studying her as though trying to decipher the truth behind her words. 'But we almost…' he said quietly, stepping closer, his eyes holding hers with an intensity that made her stomach flip. 'And it took me right back to my apartment in London. That week with you … it was the best week of my life. It felt…' He hesitated, his voice full of emotion. 'It felt right. I've not had those feelings since.'

Clemmie's heart raced faster at his confession, her heart warring with her head. 'It's just going to complicate things,' she said, her voice trembling despite her attempt to sound resolute. 'I let my heart overrule my head. Anyway, this isn't the place to have this conversation.' She glanced around, hoping the surroundings of the yacht would remind her of where she was and why she needed to stay grounded.

'But I want this conversation. I can't think about anything else.'

'What is there to say? You made your choice.'

'I chose you, Clemmie. I asked you to come with me, I practically begged you,' said Oliver, his voice laced with frustration.

Clemmie tried to ignore the knot forming in her chest.

'I remember,' she said quietly, her mind flashing back to that night in London.

Oliver's gaze softened, but there was an edge to his words now. 'You didn't want it then. You didn't want any part of it. I get it, I do. But damn, Clemmie, I needed you. I wanted you to travel the world with me, be there with me … to share *everything* with me. My life, my passion. You know how much I love my work. You knew that from the start.'

Clemmie met his eyes, feeling the weight of his words. 'I couldn't leave. I belong here on Puffin Island, with my business, my granny. I wanted to share all that with you but it was never going to be enough for you,' she murmured. 'How could it, when you were so used to jetting off around the world every other week?'

Oliver looked away for a moment, gathering his thoughts. 'I wasn't trying to take you away from your world, Clemmie. I just wanted to share something that I loved with someone I cared about. I wouldn't have wanted you to give up your whole life. We could have at least had a conversation. Found a middle ground that satisfied us both.' He let out a deep breath, frustration giving way to something more vulnerable. 'I thought … I thought if I asked, if I showed you how much it meant to me, that you'd see I wanted to make it work. I guess I was wrong.'

Clemmie's heart skipped a beat, the tenderness in his voice pulling at her in ways she hadn't expected. 'Oliver, you weren't wrong. I just…' She paused, unsure how to finish. 'I have my dreams too, and they're so far removed from yours.'

'I know, I get that now,' he interrupted, but there was no anger in his tone. 'My job is a part of me. I love travel and I want to see what makes the world go around, but… It's never been just about the food or the stories or the travel. It's about *connection*. About bringing the best parts of life together and sharing it with people you care about and I wanted to do that with you.'

Clemmie swallowed a lump in her throat. She had always known he loved his work, but hearing it from him now, seeing the emotion behind his words, made it feel different – real in a way it hadn't before. 'I didn't know you felt like that,' she admitted softly.

'With you, I felt it, Clemmie. After things ended between us… The food tasted flat without you. The stories fell short without you. I just kept thinking, *Maybe next time.*'

He glanced up, searching her eyes, his voice barely above a whisper. 'I wanted you to be a part of it. To be a part of *me.*'

Clemmie swallowed, the reality of his words sinking in. 'I hear you.' She took hold of his hands. 'But for me, right this second, I need to stay focused. Winning this competition could change everything for me.'

Oliver's expression softened, but his gaze didn't waver. 'What about after the competition?'

Her stomach clenched at his question. She forced herself to smile, a hollow attempt to deflect. 'Nothing will have changed. You'll still be travelling the world, and me? I'll be pouring my heart into my café. My cookbook will be selling all over the world, and hopefully that will mean that tourists will flock to Puffin Island to try the recipes I've made famous.' She hesitated, the words catching in her throat as she added, 'My dream is to pass the business down to the next generation … to my children. I need to secure the best possible future for the café for them.'

Oliver's smile returned, playful but tinged with something deeper. 'For that, you'll need a husband …

unless you're telling me you've got married since we last met. That would be a stab to the heart.'

'No marriage,' she said softly.

'Phew,' Oliver said with an exaggerated sigh of relief, placing a hand over his heart. 'I'm glad to hear that.'

His teasing tone broke through her defences, and she found herself laughing despite the tension between them. 'And why would you care?' she asked, curiosity getting the better of her.

Oliver's grin faded, replaced by a sincerity that took her off guard. 'Because you matter, Clemmie,' he said simply. 'You always have.'

The air between them shifted, charged and electric, as if the weight of everything unsaid in the past three years hung in the space separating them. Clemmie opened her mouth to respond but found herself at a loss for words. She wanted to believe him, to let herself get swept up in the moment, but the practical part of her, the one that had built her life brick by brick on Puffin Island, held her back.

'You don't make this easy,' she whispered, her voice barely audible.

'I'm not trying to make it easy,' he replied, his eyes darkening as he took a small step closer. 'I'm trying to make it real.'

For a moment, she thought he might kiss her, and she didn't trust herself to resist if he did. But instead he reached up, brushing a stray strand of hair from her face, his fingers lingering just a moment too long.

'This conversation isn't over,' he said, his voice low and filled with promise.

Clemmie nodded, her heart hammering in her chest as

she tried to regain her composure. 'It's not,' she agreed, though she wasn't sure whether the words were meant as a challenge or an invitation.

She'd always thought she had everything figured out, but hearing Oliver open up like this made her second-guess so much of what she'd believed. She exhaled slowly, her thoughts tangled in a mess of confusion. She wasn't sure how she'd ended up here, stuck between her past and her future, but one thing was clear, he had made her see things differently. She found herself questioning whether she'd misread the situation back then.

'But in the meantime,' Oliver said, pausing to glance at his watch before shooting her a mischievous grin, 'let's have some fun before anyone notices we're missing. Come on.' His voice was low, conspiratorial, and it lit a spark of excitement deep inside her.

'Oliver!' she started, though even she wasn't sure whether she was protesting or encouraging him.

'Trust me,' he said, his eyes gleaming with a boyish daring that she found impossible to resist.

Clemmie's heart pounded as she followed him down the corridor, his hand firm around hers. She could still hear the hum of the contestant's voices in the distance. Her pulse quickened at the thrill of sneaking away, and the way Oliver's fingers laced with hers sent a ripple of something electric through her.

He led her swiftly down the corridor to a door marked 'Private'. Without hesitation, he pushed it open, revealing a room that seemed untouched by time. Clemmie stepped inside and gave a tiny gasp.

The walls were adorned with framed photographs,

mostly black and white, that told the story of the yacht's history. Images of elegantly dressed queens and kings and princes and princesses, sipping champagne at banquets, lined one wall, while another featured candid snapshots of famous actors lounging on deckchairs, their laughter frozen in time. There were also shots of dignitaries, heads bowed or in the midst of solemn handshakes beneath glittering chandeliers.

'Wow,' Clemmie murmured. Her eyes darted from frame to frame, soaking in the glamour and history of it all. 'The stories these walls could tell…'

As she moved further into the room, one particular photograph caught her attention and made her pause. It was smaller than the others, tucked in a quiet corner, but something about it pulled her in to take a closer look.

It showed two men, one in pristine chef's whites, his focus completely on the mixing bowl he cradled in one arm, the other figure tall and commanding, dressed in full military uniform. The second man's posture was formal, but he leaned slightly forward, peering into the mixing bowl with what looked like genuine interest. His hat was tilted at just the right angle to reveal a sharp, clean-cut profile. His jawline was strong; he had a neatly trimmed moustache and an expression of quiet authority mixed with curiosity. He looked young, possibly in his very early twenties.

Clemmie stared, the image somehow familiar to her though she was sure she'd never seen it before. She felt like she knew him, which of course was impossible.

'Who's he?' she asked softly, gesturing to the uniformed figure without tearing her gaze away.

Oliver came to stand behind her, leaning in as he studied

the photograph, his proximity sending a flush across her skin. 'Let's see,' he murmured, reading the engraving beneath the frame. '"Henry, Earl of Aberford." If I remember correctly, there was some sort of scandal involving him.'

'Scandal? What sort of scandal?'

Oliver was thoughtful as he studied the photograph. 'From what I remember, he dated the Queen's daughter, Princess Alexandra, and they were just about to announce their engagement when he did something unthinkable ... he walked away. Gave up his title, his privileges, all of it. Rumours about him have circled through the decades, but it's believed he wanted a life out of the public eye.'

Clemmie looked back towards the photograph. 'Why would someone give all that up? The wealth, the status. Who would walk away from such a privileged life?'

Oliver gave her a knowing look. 'Someone who valued something more. Someone who wanted to find love on their own terms, without the weight of tradition or expectation.'

He took a step closer to her. 'I think love ... real love ... has the power to turn a person's whole world upside down. It's not about titles or appearances. It's about finding that one person who makes everything else fade away.'

'Do you think he found someone else?'

'We'll never know for sure, but my guess is he did.'

Clemmie turned to face him, her heart skittering at the intensity in his gaze.

'If I was a royal, I would give up everything for love. I think when it's real, it's the most magical thing in the world.'

She swallowed, the weight of his words settling over

her. She knew what he was doing, subtly reminding her of what they'd had in London. If she was being truthful, she hadn't come close to feeling that way with anyone else since. Not even once. But was love enough? They couldn't work it out then and there was nothing different about their circumstances now.

Clemmie turned back to the photograph, her voice quiet but firm. 'What Henry had … the courage to walk away for love … it's admirable.'

After a moment Oliver moved towards a polished mahogany sideboard at the far end of the room. 'And here's the crown jewels,' he said, gesturing to an elaborate display of whisky bottles. Each was nestled in a velvet-lined compartment, labelled in gilded lettering. 'Apparently these are all from royal reserves.'

Clemmie arched an eyebrow, folding her arms. 'You're not seriously suggesting—'

'Oh, but I am,' he interrupted, his grin wicked. He picked up a crystal tumbler, holding it to the light. The intricate cuts in the glass refracted the glow of the overhead chandelier, scattering prisms across the walls. 'Come on. One sip. Who's going to know?'

She glanced nervously at the door, her pulse quickening. 'What if we get caught?'

Oliver leaned in closer, his voice dropping to a low murmur. 'You never asked that when we joined the mile-high club.'

Clemmie supressed a smile, the memory of that impulsive, thrilling night flooding back. He'd whisked her away to Paris in a private jet, the ultimate romantic gesture. She could still picture his teasing smirk as they boarded the sleek plane, champagne already waiting on ice.

The city had been everything she'd dreamed of and more. They'd started the evening with a stroll along the Seine, her heels clicking against cobblestones as the Eiffel Tower shimmered in the distance. Then there was the shopping spree, a whirlwind tour of Parisian boutiques where Oliver had insisted she choose an outfit for that evening. She'd tried to protest, but he'd silenced her objections with a kiss that made her forget everything.

He'd picked out a dress for her, a sleek black number that clung to her curves and sparkled subtly under the lights. He said he'd bought it because she'd told him that when she put it on, she felt like she'd stepped into another life.

The opera had been the evening's entertainment. Their private box was draped in rich crimson velvet, gilded with gold filigree. Below them, the orchestra sounded, strings and woodwinds weaving a melody that was utterly romantic. Oliver had barely looked at the stage, his gaze fixed on her as though she were the most captivating thing in the room.

Back in the present, Clemmie rolled her eyes, 'You've officially lost it,' she replied.

'Have I?' he asked, pouring a generous measure of amber liquid into the tumbler. The aroma of aged whisky wafted between them as he held the glass out. 'Come on. We'll toast to rebellion.'

Clemmie hesitated, glancing again at the door. Finally, she snatched the glass from his hand. 'If we get caught, I'm blaming you,' she said, her tone half-serious, half-playful.

'Fair enough.' Oliver poured himself a glass, his movements unhurried and deliberate. He raised it in a toast, his eyes locking onto hers. 'To mischief.'

'To mischief,' she echoed, clinking her glass against his before taking a sip. Clemmie's face immediately contorted. 'Ugh, how do people drink this stuff?' The whisky burned her throat but left a honeyed aftertaste that lingered. She glanced at Oliver, who was savouring his drink with an exaggerated air of sophistication. The moment felt like an echo of Paris, a reminder of that heady, carefree day when anything seemed possible.

Oliver laughed, his eyes crinkling at the corners. 'You're not supposed to chug it like cider, Clemmie.'

She rolled her eyes, setting the glass down. 'You're incorrigible.'

'And you love it,' he said with a grin, leaning against the sideboard. His eyes softened as they met hers. 'You know, this room reminds me of us.'

She tilted her head. 'How so?'

'All these memories, these moments frozen in time. They're still here, still alive, even if the people in them have passed on.' He paused, his voice dipping lower. 'We had our moment, Clemmie. But maybe you're right. Maybe it does have to stay in the past.'

She stared at him, disappointed with herself that she had even planted that thought in his head.

Before she could reply, they heard someone approaching.

'Oliver? Where are you?' Fiona's unmistakable voice rang out, sharp and impatient.

Clemmie's eyes widened in alarm. Oliver shot her a look, holding a finger to his lips.

'You're going to get us both in so much trouble,' she mouthed.

Oliver grinned, looking entirely unrepentant. 'Worth it.'

Clemmie rolled her eyes but couldn't help the smile on her face. 'Come on, we'd better get back before they send a search party.' Just as she was about to slip out of the room she took one last look at the photograph of Henry, Earl of Aberford. That was by far her favourite photo of them all on the wall. There was just something about it.

'Come on, the coast is clear,' said Oliver, peeping around the door.

As they slipped out of the private room and rejoined the group, Clemmie felt her heart racing. The air between her and Oliver still crackled with unspoken tension. Every stolen glance, every mischievous smile, seemed to pull her deeper into the gravitational pull of whatever was brewing between them. It was dangerous, exhilarating and undeniably real.

Fiona turned sharply as they approached, her scowl barely masked by a quick, saccharine smile. Before Clemmie could process the look, Fiona slipped her arm through Oliver's, her fingers resting possessively on his chest. The gesture was deliberate, and it sent an icy jolt through Clemmie.

For the first time, a thought pierced through her emotions: *Was there still something between them? Were Oliver and Fiona … together? Now?*

Immediately there was a dull ache in Clemmie's stomach. She tried to shake it off, telling herself she had no claim over him. They'd had a whirlwind romance in London and Paris, yes, but that had been three years ago. A lifetime in the world of relationships. Yet the thought of him with someone else, especially someone as sharp and smug as Fiona, made her chest tighten. Clemmie headed towards the table of coffee cups but her eyes discreetly followed the way Fiona leaned in, laughing at something Oliver said.

I'm not going to be just an option for Oliver Lockwood. If he wanted her … truly wanted her … he'd have to prove it. The days of her waiting around, hoping someone would choose her, were long gone. She had built a life she loved, a business she was proud of, and a sense of independence she cherished.

As the competitors stood chatting Clemmie plastered on a polite smile, determined to focus on anything but Oliver. But deep down, her heart burned with the awareness of the spark between them … one she wasn't ready to extinguish just yet.

Chapter Nine

The grand ballroom of the Royal Yacht hummed with excitement. The ten bakers, including Clemmie, sat behind a long polished table at the front of the room, the perfect picture of professionalism despite Clemmie's pounding heart and fluttering nerves. Velvet drapes adorned the windows, their rich colours adding a regal flair to the already opulent space. Journalists and photographers lingered to capture the moment and scribble in their notepads.

Oliver stepped up to the podium, commanding the room with his natural confidence and charm. The TV crew started filming and the soft camera lighting seemed to settle on him like a spotlight, emphasising his crisp suit and easy smile.

'Ladies and gentlemen,' Oliver began, 'welcome to the press conference for the annual Royal Baking Competition, held on Her Majesty's Royal Yacht, this year moored at the beautiful Puffin Island.' He paused. Clemmie noticed some journalists recording from their phones whilst others stood at the side of the room, their cameras clicking softly in the background. 'What began as a private contest among the talented chefs of the royal household has grown into one of the most prestigious and anticipated baking events in the country. It's a celebration of skill, creativity and tradition. For those of you wondering how these ten extraordinary bakers came to be seated here, let me explain.' He gestured towards the contestants seated behind him. 'The process is both rigorous and remarkable. The road to the competition began with a nomination, the contestant put forward by someone who believed in their talent – a friend, a mentor, a former teacher, a customer, someone who had witnessed their skill first hand. The application form, completed by the nominator, details why they think the baker deserves to be considered. Was it their natural flair for pastry, an innovative approach to flavours, or a family recipe that told a story, generations in the making?

'Once submitted, each nomination was reviewed by a panel of esteemed culinary experts – renowned pastry chefs, food writers and industry professionals – who carefully deliberated over which bakers had the passion, technique and creativity to take on the challenge. Only those with the most compelling stories and undeniable talent secured a coveted place in the competition, where precision scales, blowtorches and the finest ingredients awaited their arrival.'

He continued, 'This competition isn't just about baking. It's about telling a story … your story. Through every whisk, every fold and every bake, these ten individuals bring something deeply personal to the table. And that's what makes this event so unique. Each creation is a blend of history, passion and the kind of creativity that can only come from the heart.'

Clemmie found herself holding her breath. The thought of her great-great-grandmother's recipe, the torte she had chosen to bake, filled her mind. It was more than a dessert, it was a piece of her family's legacy.

'But that's not all,' Oliver said, his tone shifting, 'Puffin Island has welcomed us with open arms, and we felt it only right to extend that same hospitality. So, for the first time, we've invited some of the residents of Puffin Island to join us here today, to have their own tour of the yacht and sit in on the press conference. I can confirm they have just finished their tour and here they are.'

Clemmie's head shot up. Sure enough, the double doors at the back of the room opened, and a wave of familiar faces began to pour in, Amelia, Dilly and Betty leading the way, each holding a cup of tea. Excitement was written all over their faces. Clemmie beamed at them. She knew her granny would be beside herself to have a tour of the yacht, and for them to be able to share this incredible moment with her made her heart swell with happiness. Betty caught her eye and gave a small, proud wave. Amelia and Dilly were whispering animatedly to each other. Clemmie felt a lump rise in her throat. She hadn't expected this. The sight of them, their unwavering support, was overwhelming.

A wave of applause swept through the room, and Clemmie caught her grandmother's eye again, now brimming with emotional tears. She knew exactly what she was thinking: *if only your great-great-grandmother could see you now.*

The press conference kicked into full swing and Oliver fielded questions with ease, standing confidently at the podium. The reporters then turned their attention to the bakers and a journalist near the front stood and addressed Fiona, seated primly at the far end of the table.

'Ms Fairweather,' the reporter began, 'you've been very vocal about your confidence in winning this competition. Could you elaborate on what gives you such an edge?'

Fiona's perfectly rehearsed smile spread across her face, as if she had been waiting for this exact question. She straightened her shoulders and delivered her answer with theatrical precision, her voice dripping with practised charm. 'Of course,' she said, flicking a loose curl over her shoulder. 'It all comes down to preparation and passion. You see, I've spent years honing my craft, ensuring that every bake I create is nothing short of perfection. My bakery, Fairweather Fancies, is frequented by some of the most discerning customers in the world.'

Clemmie could almost feel the collective eyeroll of her friends watching from the floor as Fiona paused, letting the weight of her words settle, before adding with a coy smile, 'And while I'm not at liberty to name names, let's just say royalty has been known to indulge in a Fairweather Fancy or two.'

A murmur ran through the audience, a few journalists scribbling furiously, and Clemmie locked eyes with her granny, who wore a look of thinly veiled amusement, shaking her head slightly at Fiona's audacity.

Oblivious to the scepticism, Fiona pressed on. 'I've put my heart and soul into this competition. My bake will be something truly special. In fact,' she said, her voice taking on a conspiratorial tone, 'I've already prepared the recipes for the winning cookbook. They're ready to go to print the moment I'm announced as the winner. That's how confident I am in my abilities.'

Clemmie struggled to keep her expression neutral, though inwardly she was rolling her eyes. Fiona spoke with such certainty, such arrogance, as though the contest was a mere formality before her inevitable crowning. It was hard to take her seriously, though the reporters seemed captivated by her bravado.

'I'm not just here to compete,' Fiona continued, glancing briefly at her fellow bakers with an air of superiority. 'I'm here to set a standard. This competition deserves nothing less than the very best, and I intend to deliver exactly that.'

The journalist nodded, jotting down her remarks, and Clemmie could feel the subtle tension in the room, the other bakers exchanging quiet glances that ranged from amused to mildly irritated.

Then, it was her turn. 'Ms Rose,' a reporter called from near the back of the room, his voice crisp and inquisitive.

Clemmie's heart skipped a beat as she felt all eyes fall on her.

'Tell us, Clemmie, what will be inspiring your bake for this year's competition?'

'It's an original family recipe,' she began, her voice gaining strength as she spoke, 'belonging to my great-great-grandmother Beatrice. She first recorded this recipe in 1917, in her notebook, and it's been a favourite in The Café on the Coast ever since. Entering it into this competition allows me to honour her legacy.'

A soft murmur of approval rippled through the room,

and Clemmie could see Oliver's smile looked more genuine than it had been moments earlier.

'A family recipe with a story,' he commented, his gaze flickering towards her in a way that made Clemmie's heart skip. 'I like that.'

The reporters moved on to the next baker and in what felt like no time at all the press conference was wrapped up with Oliver's smooth, polished closing remarks. He spoke about the upcoming challenges, the high expectations for the contestants and the honour of having the winner's creation showcased at the royal garden party. 'The winner's masterpiece will not only be served to every guest,' he reminded the assembled press, 'but will also grace the pages of the winner's own cookbook, released shortly after the competition.'

As the bakers began to disperse, Amelia and Dilly were the first to rush over to Clemmie.

'This is so exciting!' Amelia exclaimed, her eyes sparkling. 'You were incredible, Clemmie! Absolutely incredible and I can't believe we got to see inside the Royal Yacht!'

'You had them all eating out of the palm of your hand!' Dilly added with a grin.

Clemmie smiled. 'Thanks, you two. I was so nervous up there.'

'Well, you didn't show it,' Betty said, joining them. Her tone was full of pride, though her expression shifted as she nodded discreetly towards the far end of the room. 'Unlike some.'

Clemmie followed Betty's gaze and spotted Fiona near the door, her expression thunderous. She had cornered

Oliver and they appeared to be deep in a heated discussion. Even from a distance, Clemmie could see the flush on her face and the sharp tilt of her chin.

Intrigued, Clemmie tried not to stare, but she couldn't tear her eyes away. Fiona looked positively fuming, her perfectly composed facade slipping as she gestured wildly. Oliver, on the other hand, was shaking his head, his stance defensive. He crossed his arms, then ran a hand through his hair in frustration. At one point, he threw his arms up in the air, his exasperation clear.

'What do you think they're talking about?' Amelia whispered, leaning closer to Clemmie.

'No idea,' Clemmie replied. 'But it doesn't look like a friendly conversation.'

Fiona stepped closer to Oliver, her voice rising just enough for snippets to carry through the door. Clemmie caught phrases like 'unfair advantage' and 'undermining my reputation', though the context was unclear. Oliver's reply was too quiet to hear, but his expression was firm.

Then, as suddenly as it had begun, the argument ended. Oliver shook his head one last time and turned away, leaving Fiona standing there with her mouth agape. By the time he re-entered the room, his expression had transformed into an easy, friendly smile. He strode towards a group of journalists, shaking hands and making polite conversation as though nothing had happened.

Fiona, however, didn't recover as quickly. She remained by the door for a moment, her face dark with frustration. Clemmie watched as Fiona smoothed her hair and plastered a brittle smile on her face before heading in the opposite direction.

'What on earth was that about?' Dilly murmured, her brows raised.

'Whatever it was, she didn't win,' Betty said with a chuckle. 'Oliver walked away, and she's still fuming.'

Clemmie felt a flicker of satisfaction. Fiona's confidence had been unshakeable all day, and seeing her composure crack was oddly reassuring. Still, she was curious what they had been arguing at. Was it related to the competition, or was there something more personal at play?

'Do you think it has to do with the competition?' Amelia asked, as though reading Clemmie's thoughts.

'Maybe,' Clemmie said, keeping her voice low.

'Well, whatever it is,' Betty said firmly, 'you've got more important things to focus on. You've got a competition to win.'

'Clemmie!' They were interrupted by a reporter. 'I'd love to know more about the history of The Café on the Coast. Would you like to take part in an interview and discuss what's it like living on such a wonderful island?'

'Of course, and let me introduce you to my granny…' Clemmie and Betty began to chat to the reporter.

Sensing Fiona was watching them closely, Clemmie's mind lingered on the argument she had just witnessed. She couldn't shake the feeling that it'd had something to do with her. A knot of unease settled in her stomach. She knew she'd have to tread carefully. Fiona gave off the distinct vibe of someone who would do whatever it took to come out on top, no matter who got in her way.

Chapter Ten

Clemmie sat at the kitchen table, her hands wrapped around a steaming mug. The aroma of the freshly brewed tea mingled with the faint remnants of baking spices, and the hum of the refrigerator was the only sound in the room. On the table in front of her lay her great-great-grandmother's recipe book and a folded sheet of paper, yellowed at the edges.

To Clemmie, it wasn't just a collection of recipes, it was a journal of love, care and tradition. Beatrice Rose's graceful, looping handwriting filled every page, accompanied by delicate sketches of ingredients, flour sacks, sprigs of rosemary, clusters of berries, and dainty teacups. Clemmie smiled as she turned the pages carefully, her eyes settling on the recipe for Beatrice's signature torte.

But then her gaze shifted to the folded sheet of paper beside the book, and her smile faded. The edges were frayed from being handled too many times, and the ink had bled slightly in places, though the words were still clear.

It was a printed copy of a scathing review that had been published in *The Epicurean Chronicle*, a well-regarded food journal, shortly after Clemmie had gone into partnership with her grandmother.

The headline alone had been enough to send her stomach plummeting:

**The Café on the Coast: Coastal Charm,
But Little Substance**

Clemmie hesitated, but she unfolded the paper anyway. The words hit just as hard now as they had all those years ago.

The Café on the Coast, nestled on the charming seaside of Puffin Island, promises much but delivers little. While the setting is idyllic, the food lacks the finesse one would expect from a café with such a storied history. The lemon drizzle cake, a supposed favourite, was dense and cloyingly sweet, a far cry from the light, airy confections its reputation suggests. The savoury menu fares no better, with over-seasoned soups and limp salads, and scones that could double as paperweights leave much to be desired. It's clear that nostalgia, rather than culinary merit, is the café's strongest selling point. One can only hope that this establishment can either step up its game or gracefully step aside for more capable contenders.

The review had crushed her. Clemmie could still remember the sinking feeling in her chest when she first read it, sitting at the counter with her granny. Her throat had tightened, and tears had stung her eyes as she whispered, 'I've ruined everything.'

Her granny had immediately reached for her hand. 'Don't you dare believe a word of that,' she had said firmly. 'It's one person's opinion and it's not even true. They haven't even had the decency to put their name to it.'

But Clemmie hadn't been able to shake the shame. She had spent weeks obsessing over the review, rereading it late at night, picking apart every line. She'd worried not just about the café's reputation but also about what it said about her. Was she truly not good enough? Had she let her grandmother down? Worse still, had she tarnished her great-great-grandmother's legacy?

It didn't matter that the café's loyal patrons continued to flock through its doors, praising her bakes and chatting happily over cups of tea. The *Chronicle* was influential, with a readership that extended far beyond Puffin Island. For weeks, Clemmie had lived in fear that the review would drive new customers away and that the café's reputation would be irreparably damaged.

But it hadn't. Slowly, she had rebuilt her confidence, pouring her heart into her work. She perfected her great-great-grandmother's recipes and added her own twists to the menu. She worked long hours, sometimes late into the night, determined to prove the reviewer wrong. Over time, the café's reputation only grew stronger, with customers travelling from all over to sample her famous torte and other bakes.

Still, the sting of the review never fully went away. It had been the only bad press the café had ever received, but its words had left scars. Even now, years later, Clemmie couldn't help but feel a flicker of self-doubt when she thought about it.

Her eyes returned to the recipe book, and she traced the smudged page of the torte recipe with her fingertip. This book was a reminder of the women who had come before her, who had poured their love and creativity into their cooking, and now it was Clemmie's turn.

She took a deep breath, folding the review and tucking it under the recipe book. It no longer deserved to take centre stage. She had come a long way since those early days of self-doubt. The café was thriving, her customers were happy and now she was one of ten contestants in The Royal Baking Competition.

As Clemmie sipped her tea her eye was drawn to a notation at the bottom of the torte recipe. A number in brackets: '1705'. She stared at it. It was something she hadn't noticed before. Curious, she browsed carefully through the book, but none of the other recipes had a code like it.

'Granny!' she called, her voice echoing through the café.

Betty appeared in the doorway, a dishcloth slung over her shoulder. 'What is it?'

Clemmie held up the book. 'What's this number? Right here at the bottom of the torte recipe. 1705.'

Betty narrowed her eyes, her glasses perched on the tip of her nose. 'I've not noticed that before. It could be anything. Maybe it's the baking time?'

'No, it's not that,' Clemmie said, turning the book towards her granny. 'None of the other recipes have a number like it. Why would just this one?'

Betty shrugged. 'I have no clue,' she said, heading back into the café to clean the tables.

Clemmie turned back to the book, still staring at the number. Could it be a date? A time? A secret code? Before she could investigate further, she caught a movement outside the window and she nearly jumped out of her skin. Standing just beyond the glass was Oliver, his grin wicked as he peered inside.

'What on earth...' she exclaimed, flinging open the window. 'I nearly knocked my tea all over my great-great-grandmother's recipe book. What are you doing? Do you normally sneak around peeking through windows? There's a name for people like you, you know!'

Oliver leaned casually against the window frame, unbothered by her indignation. 'Good evening to you, too...'

'Oliver!' she scolded. 'You scared me half to death. We do have a front door!'

His eyes twinkled. 'What are you doing tonight?'

'What?' She blinked, caught off guard.

'You heard me.'

Clemmie narrowed her eyes suspiciously. 'Why? What do you have in mind?'

'I can't tell you just yet,' he said, his voice now low. 'But meet me at the harbour at eight. And dress to impress.' He gave her a lopsided grin before disappearing just as quickly as he had appeared, not waiting for an answer.

Clemmie stood frozen for a moment, staring at the empty space he had just occupied. Had she imagined it? The playful invitation, the flicker of something more in his gaze?

Slowly, she closed the window and sat back at the table. She knew she was supposed to be focusing on the contest, on perfecting her recipe and making sure she had every detail memorised. This was what mattered. Or at least, it should have been.

And yet… She hesitated, chewing her bottom lip.

Their conversation on the yacht had been different … real, vulnerable. It had left her wanting to hear more, to understand him in a way she hadn't before. But wasn't that exactly why she shouldn't go? The more she let him in, the more she risked getting hurt. She'd been down that road before and nothing had changed.

Still, she wasn't naïve. She knew the pros and cons of saying yes. Walking away would be the safest option. But as much as she tried to convince herself, she already knew her answer.

She was going.

'Who are you talking to?' Betty appeared in the doorway.

'No one,' Clemmie replied, telling a little white lie.

Betty looked down at the recipe book. 'Maybe it's the number of recipes my mother wrote down in total?' she offered, picking up their earlier conversation.

'I don't think it's that,' Clemmie replied, flipping through the recipe book again. 'There are no other numbers.'

'Then I haven't got a clue,' Betty replied cheerfully. 'But if it's important, you'll figure it out.'

'I hope so. Oh, um … just to let you know, I'm going out tonight.'

'I thought you were going to get a couple of early nights before the competition?'

'I won't be late,' Clemmie replied, knowing she didn't have a clue about how late she would be. As she closed the recipe book, she said '1705' out loud. It didn't help. Something about it continued to nag at her, a tiny itch in the back of her mind. Whatever 1705 meant, she had a feeling it was more important than she realised.

A while later, Clemmie stood in front of the mirror in her bedroom, checking her reflection for what felt like the tenth time. She'd taken Oliver's command to 'dress to impress' to heart, and gone all out. The dress she'd chosen was one of her favourites – a midnight-blue cocktail dress with an asymmetrical hemline that swirled around her knees. Its bodice was sleek and fitted, with delicate lace detailing over her shoulders that gave a hint of elegance without being too formal. She'd paired it with silver strappy heels, a matching clutch and a pair of vintage drop earrings she'd found in No. 17 Curiosity Lane, the antique shop.

Just before eight p.m., Clemmie stepped out of the café, the door clicking softly behind her. The air was cool and carried the faint tang of salt from the sea. The streets of Puffin Island were quiet, the soft whisper of distant waves and the occasional call of a gull the only sounds accompanying her footsteps. As she reached the bottom of Lighthouse Lane, the harbour came into view, the sight before her making her stop in her tracks. It was like stepping into the climactic scene of a James Bond film. The Royal Yacht, bathed in the golden glow of string lights, loomed majestically with an indigo sky haloing it.

And there he was.

Clemmie nearly stumbled at the sight of Oliver leaning casually against a post up ahead. He was a vision in a perfectly tailored tuxedo, the fabric catching the light just enough to hint at its fine quality. His crisp white shirt was a stark contrast to his tanned complexion, and the black bow tie at his neck added a touch of old-Hollywood glamour.

The way he stood, his hand resting lightly in his pocket, his gaze scanning over the water, made Clemmie's heart beat faster. He looked like he belonged to another world. In that moment, he could have been a prince, stepping out of the pages of a fairytale, or a spy ready for his next covert mission.

When his gaze shifted and found hers, his expression softened, then he smiled.

'Wow,' she admired as she walked towards him. 'You clean up well,' she said, her heart hammering in her chest.

His smile broadened, making her stomach flip. 'You're not looking so bad yourself,' he said, his voice teasing.

He stepped closer. The soft scent of his aftershave, woodsy and sophisticated, made her close her eyes for a moment as he kissed her on both cheeks. 'I tried to pull out all the stops,' he said. 'And it was worth it. You look absolutely stunning.'

'Thank you.'

'Ready for an unforgettable evening?'

'Where are you taking me?' Clemmie asked, eyeing him suspiciously. 'Because it seems like we're a little overdressed for a night on Puffin Island. Are you whisking me off to Paris again, or maybe Italy this time?' she teased.

'Not quite. How about dinner on the water instead?' he replied, with that familiar mischievous sparkle in his eyes.

'Get away. We're not going on there,' she said, gesturing to the ship. 'Are you serious?'

'You better believe it,' he said, offering his arm. 'Tonight, we're dining aboard Her Majesty's Royal Yacht.'

'How is that even possible?'

'Because I'm in the know,' he said, clearly enjoying her reaction.

Clemmie raised an eyebrow. 'I take it you have friends in high places … or *royal* places?'

Oliver chuckled. 'Lady Rosalind, a distant cousin of the Queen, is my grandmother's best friend and happens to have a soft spot for me.'

Clemmie shook her head in disbelief. 'Of course she does. You probably charmed her like you charm everyone else.'

'When my grandmother mentioned I was here presenting The Royal Baking Competition, Lady Rosalind insisted that I dine on the yacht and sleep in one of the royal cabins. She used to work on the yacht as a royal caterer.'

'A tour of the yacht is one thing but dinner? You're winding me up.'

'I'm absolutely not,' he replied, smiling at her and holding out his arm.

Clemmie wrapped her arm around his and walked by his side. At the top of the gangplank, they were greeted by a waiter in tails, his white gloves so pristine they practically glowed.

'Good evening, sir, madam,' he said with a bow. 'Welcome aboard.'

Clemmie blinked. 'I actually feel like royalty,' she whispered as they stepped onto the deck, which was a vision of luxury. Lights twinkled overhead, and the sound of a string quartet drifted through the evening air from inside.

'Are we the only ones here?'

'We are.'

'That's insane,' Clemmie murmured, glancing around.

They walked through a set of grand double doors to a magnificent dining hall, but not the one they'd seen on the tour. The walls in this room were panelled in polished mahogany, adorned with gilded mirrors and oil paintings of royal ancestors. Crystal chandeliers sparkled overhead, their light casting a glow over the space.

The waiter showed them to the table. 'Dinner will be served in approximately thirty minutes, but feel free to explore the upper deck and balcony in the meantime. Can I get you any drinks?'

They ordered and he soon returned with their drinks in hand.

'Let's have these on the balcony,' Oliver suggested.

Clemmie followed Oliver up a winding staircase and they entered a hallway lined with doors, each marked with a small brass plaque.

'I want to show you something.'

'I've heard that before.' She grinned playfully.

'Miss Clemmie Rose, you need to remember your manners whilst you sail on the Royal Yacht,' he replied in an exaggeratedly posh voice.

She playfully swiped him as he pushed open a door marked 'Private, Staff Only'.

'Oliver…' Clemmie glanced over her shoulder as if someone might catch them. 'Are we even allowed in here?'

'Relax,' he said, beckoning her inside. 'Lady Rosalind didn't give me that "soft spot" pass for nothing. I thought in your line of work you would love to see this.'

Clemmie stepped into the room, her eyes flitting around. The space before her wasn't just a kitchen, it was a piece of history, perfectly preserved as though its staff might return at any moment.

The walls were lined with cream-coloured tiles and intricately carved wooden panels. A gleaming gold-plated oven stood at the centre of the room like a throne, its polished surface reflecting the soft glow of the hanging brass lights. Beside it, an enormous cast-iron stove loomed, the kind that hinted at decades of elaborate feasts and secret recipes.

'This,' Oliver said, spreading his arms, 'is the historic royal kitchen. It was the first one built on the ship and last used in 1918.'

'1918?' Clemmie whispered, stepping forward in awe. 'Everything looks like they just … left it.'

'They did,' Oliver confirmed, his voice low as if not wanting to disturb the ghosts of chefs past. 'Not because it was abandoned, but because it was sealed. As a tribute.'

She turned to him, brows drawing together. 'A tribute?'

'To Chef Étienne Dupont,' Oliver explained. 'He wasn't just a cook, he was a part of the Royal Family in all but name. His menus, his recipes, even the way he structured meals, became part of their traditions. He ran this kitchen with precision for over a decade, but when the First World War broke out, he enlisted. He never returned from the front and the Royal Family chose to preserve this space in his honour,' Oliver continued. 'By then, cooking operations had already shifted to the smaller galley on the upper deck, which was more practical and easier to modernise over the years. And, to be honest, money played a part, too. The Royal Yacht was a luxury, not a priority. Refitting a kitchen of this scale would have been an enormous expense, and there were always bigger concerns – wars, rebuilding, economic crises – so they left it. Some say out of grief, others because no one could replace Étienne. Either way, it became more than just a room, it became a legacy.'

Clemmie's eyes roamed over the details, taking in every inch of the room. Copper pots and pans, polished to a mirror finish, hung in neat rows above a butcher's block that still bore faint cuts from countless meals prepared for the Royal Family. Along one wall were small storage compartments built into the woodwork, each secured with tiny brass locks.

'What are those?' she asked, pointing to the panels.

'Recipe cabinets,' Oliver explained, moving to open one of the unlocked panels. Inside was a series of small, handwritten notes, still tied with ribbon. 'When the royal chefs were given instructions … like if the Queen had a specific dish in mind for dinner that night, they'd find them here. Once the meal was approved, the notes went back in, locked, and filed away.'

Clemmie ran her hand over one of the compartments, imagining the hidden treasures that might lie within. 'It's so … personal. Meals prepared here weren't just food, they were pieces of history.' She counted quickly. 'There's twenty of these boxes.' She tested another couple of handles, but none of them budged. 'All the rest are locked.' A flicker of curiosity lit her eyes. 'Why lock them? And why are there so many?'

'No idea, maybe it was in proportion to the number of staff that were in the kitchen?'

She moved to the centre of the room where a long wooden butcher's block stood, its surface worn from decades of use but still gleaming as if freshly polished. 'And the gold oven?' she admired, glancing at the imposing centrepiece.

Oliver grinned. 'Pure showmanship. A royal kitchen needs to impress, even if the Queen herself never steps inside. They say it was a gift from a visiting monarch. These,' Oliver said, moving to a nearby wall, 'are ingredient drawers.' He pulled one open, revealing neatly labelled jars of spices and seasonings, each perfectly aligned and untouched. 'Everything needed to make a royal feast at a moment's notice... Though now obviously out of date,' he laughed.

Clemmie turned in a slow circle, marvelling at the sheer opulence and precision of it all. Her gaze fell on a wooden counter where utensils were lined up like soldiers. Even the rolling pins looked regal, carved from fine mahogany and inlaid with gold accents.

'I can't believe this,' she said, her voice tinged with awe. 'Meals for the Queen, actual royalty, were prepared in this room.'

Oliver grinned, leaning against the gold-plated oven. 'I know just how you're feeling. My granny brought me on a tour years ago and Lady Rosalind showed us around areas like this, which the general public doesn't usually get to see. It's still just as fascinating to me as it was that first time.'

'It's all just amazing, but I feel like I shouldn't even be here. Like I'm going to get scolded by a butler in tails.'

'Nonsense,' Oliver said, stepping closer to her. 'If anything, you're exactly the kind of person who should be here.'

Clemmie arched a brow at him. 'Oh? And why's that?'

'Because you actually *care* about the history, about the food, about what it means. You'd probably be one of the few people who'd appreciate the fact that this oven has gold plating, not because it's expensive, but because it was made with expert craftsmanship.'

Her gaze drifted back to the gold oven. 'I wonder what the last dish prepared here was.'

'Maybe a feast for a visiting dignitary, or perhaps a private meal for the Royal Family after a long voyage.'

Clemmie smiled, imagining the bustle of the kitchen in its prime, chefs shouting orders, the clatter of pots and pans, and the tantalising aromas of delicacies being crafted for royalty. 'And that's that man again,' she said, a photograph on the wall catching her eye. 'Who did you say it was? The Earl of Aberford?'

'Yes, the Earl and Chef Étienne Dupont were very good friends. They spent a lot of time together.'

'This is like a dream,' she said, more to herself than to Oliver.

'Well,' he said, stepping towards her with that familiar twinkle in his eye, 'dreams have a way of coming true around you, don't they?'

She turned to him, shaking her head with a laugh. 'You're impossible. I could have been a part of your reality but...'

'You chose life on Puffin Island…' He rolled his eyes playfully. 'I'm kidding. I can see why you chose life on the island over me,' he said teasingly.

'Don't try and turn this around on me,' she protested light-heartedly, then noticed the serious look on Oliver's face.

'I'm not. Come on… There's a royal feast waiting for us.'

Clemmie settled into her seat at the luxurious table dressed in fine linen, her eyes scanning the elaborate place settings of gold-plated knives and forks that shimmered under the glow of crystal chandeliers. A waiter in immaculate white gloves stood nearby, ready to serve the first course, while champagne flutes were already filled with sparkling liquid that fizzed invitingly.

Oliver sat across from her, looking maddeningly handsome in his tuxedo. He smiled as he observed her taking it all in. 'Not bad for a Tuesday night, huh?'

Clemmie chuckled. 'Yep, just your average weeknight dinner.'

The waiter approached, placing an artfully plated starter before them. The dish was a delicate arrangement of smoked salmon rosettes, a dollop of caviar and edible gold leaf, accompanied by a slice of freshly baked brioche. Clemmie's stomach fluttered at the sight, not just from hunger but from the surreality of the moment.

'I feel like I should be taking a picture, not actually eating this work of art,' she whispered across the table, picking up her fork.

'It's something else, isn't it? Imagine living like this all the time,' Oliver said, lifting his glass of champagne.

'And just think, that earl from the photograph gave up

this life.' They toasted, the clink of their glasses echoing softly in the grand room.

The meal was exquisite, each course more elaborate than the last. After the salmon came a rich lobster bisque, followed by a perfectly cooked filet mignon paired with truffle-infused mashed potatoes. For dessert, a tower of macarons sat atop a gilded platter, their pastel colours almost too beautiful to eat.

As the waiter retreated to give them privacy, Clemmie leaned back in her chair, a contented sigh escaping her lips. 'I'm not sure I can move after that.'

'We don't have to. We can sit and listen to the string quartet and have drinks at the bar. I've missed this.'

Clemmie's heart gave a tiny leap. 'What do you mean … this? Fancy dinners on yachts?'

'No,' he said, his gaze locking onto hers. 'You. Your company.'

The words hung between them and Clemmie felt a warmth spread through her, though she tried to play it cool. 'Is that so? We were only together for a week. Did you ever think about me after we parted ways?' she asked, fishing for information.

Oliver leaned forward, resting his elbows on the table. 'All the time,' he admitted, his voice steady. 'Did you?'

Clemmie hesitated, her heart pounding. The truth was, she *had* thought about him – too often, in fact. But she wasn't ready to bare her soul just yet. 'I mean, you were hard to forget,' she said with a teasing smile, deflecting.

He smirked, clearly not fooled. 'You're not going to make this easy for me, are you?'

'Where's the fun in that?'

They both laughed, but the air between them remained charged. Oliver leaned back in his chair, swirling his champagne thoughtfully. 'Puffin Island's special,' he said after a moment. 'I can see why you love it so much.' He hesitated, then added, 'I did a little exploring and took a walk up the cliff path, sat on that old bench outside Clifftop Cottage. Ended up talking to Pete, who told me he and your granny are some of the island's oldest residents. He said plenty of relationships have blossomed from chats on that bench.' He smiled. 'Sometimes it's easier talking to someone who isn't involved in the situation, you know? And Pete … he didn't know me, but he listened. No judgement, just friendliness and a bit of wisdom. I can see why no one would want to give up this place.'

Clemmie raised an eyebrow.

'It's not just the views or the people, it's the sense of belonging. I've spent years travelling, chasing stories, but there's something … different about being here. It feels real.'

Clemmie didn't know what to say, so she stayed quiet for a moment while she sipped her drink and eyed him. 'So, you asked me if I was married but what about you? Is there … someone in your life?' Clemmie immediately noticed the flicker of something in his eyes – hesitation? Maybe even guilt? He glanced down at his glass, swirling the liquid slowly before looking back at her.

'Oh God, not Fiona?' she said, sitting up straight. 'You said she was just a family friend.'

He didn't answer.

Clemmie arched an eyebrow. 'So, it *is* Fiona?'

'No,' he said quickly, leaning forward. 'It's not what you think.'

'And what do I think?' she asked, giving him a sceptical look. 'Enlighten me. Some sort of … situationship, maybe?'

Oliver exhaled, looking slightly uncomfortable. 'Not even that,' he said, his voice softer now. 'It's … complicated. Or, it *was* complicated. I put an end to it once and for all the second I saw you again.'

Clemmie blinked, her pulse quickening. 'Is that what the argument was about between you two earlier?'

He nodded reluctantly, rubbing the back of his neck. 'Kind of. She accused me of having feelings for you and she wasn't happy about it.'

Clemmie's heart skipped a beat at his admission, but she forced herself to remain calm. 'So, what exactly was it? Between you and Fiona, I mean?'

Oliver leaned back in his chair. 'Honestly? I'm not even sure. We've known each other for ever, our families are close friends, and everyone just sort of … expected us to be a couple. It was easy to fall into that idea, even if it didn't feel entirely right.'

'Because?' Clemmie prompted, her voice quiet but steady.

'Because there was this trip to London,' he continued, his gaze turning distant, as if he were replaying a memory in his mind. 'Because I met someone. This girl … she was nothing like Fiona. She was kind, funny, gorgeous, a little chaotic but in the best way. She made me feel alive, taught me what real happiness felt like, even if it was short-lived. She broke my heart, but she also showed me what love could be. After that, I knew Fiona and I would never work. Not in the way people wanted us to. I ended things three years ago, but she never quite let go. Every shared moment since then, family gatherings, get-togethers with mutual friends, she's treated it as an opportunity to try and rewrite our ending. I let it slide, maybe out of guilt, maybe out of habit. But I've made it clear now that there's nothing left to rekindle.'

Clemmie didn't know what to say. The raw honesty in his words left her momentarily speechless. Her eyes stayed fixed on his until he briefly closed them.

'Clemmie,' he said, his voice low and steady, 'whatever it was with Fiona, it doesn't feel like this, and I'm sure I'm not really the love of her life either. I think she's more into using me for my contacts to help her career and bakery than into, you know … me.'

Clemmie tilted her head, intrigued. 'What makes you say that?'

'We've never had deep or personal conversations. We were thrown together by our parents as children and she never went out of her way to remember details about me or my life unless it suited her. For starters, the other day, I mentioned my childhood dog, and she couldn't even remember I had a dog, let alone what its name was.'

'Easy,' Clemmie said, grinning. 'Percy. A scruffy little terrier who loved cheese and hated postmen.'

Oliver's eyebrows lifted in surprise. 'Impressive, but I bet you can't remember why I had two broken teeth when I was nine.'

Clemmie didn't miss a beat. 'Cricket accident. You tripped over your own feet, crashed into the stumps and bam! Down you went.'

He stared at her, half-amused and half-impressed. 'You really did listen during the time we spent together.'

'I did,' Clemmie said with a shrug. 'I wanted to know everything about you. And I mean *everything*.'

Oliver chuckled. 'Oh yeah? Like what?'

'Well,' Clemmie began, holding up a finger, 'your favourite drink is a banana milkshake with chocolate sprinkles because, apparently, you're seven years old at heart.'

He laughed, shaking his head. 'Still true. It's a classic.'

'You can't stand mushrooms, not because you're allergic, but because they feel like tiny sponges from the underworld.'

Oliver pointed at her, grinning. 'That's an exact quote.'

'Your first gig,' Clemmie continued, trying not to laugh, 'was seeing S Club 7 live, and you cried when they didn't do an encore of "Reach".'

His face turned faux serious. 'That was a deeply emotional experience, don't mock it!'

'Oh, I'm not mocking,' she said, her eyes dancing. 'But I *am* wondering why you're not an honorary member by now.'

'Go on,' Oliver challenged, crossing his arms with a smirk. 'What else have you got?'

Clemmie tapped her chin dramatically. 'Your guilty pleasure is eating peanut butter straight from the jar while watching reruns of *Antiques Roadshow*. You secretly like the early work of Taylor Swift but would never admit it and your dream car isn't a flashy sports car, it's an original VW Beetle because you think it has personality.'

Oliver grinned. 'But surely you don't know the ultimate test: my favourite food of all time?'

'Oh, that's easy,' Clemmie said, leaning back. 'Your

grandmother Bunny's treacle tart. You once ate three quarters in one sitting, and your mum had to hide the rest because you were dangerously close to a sugar coma.'

Oliver leaned forward, shaking his head in disbelief. 'You know, most people don't know half those things about me. Fiona couldn't even tell you what my favourite colour is.'

'Green,' Clemmie said immediately. 'But not just any green, the exact shade of the grass on the cricket pitch when the sun hits it just right.'

Oliver blinked, stunned. 'This is getting a little scary. Are you sure you're not secretly writing my unauthorised biography?'

She grinned, lifting her glass. 'I don't need to. I already know the highlights.'

Oliver's laughter softened, and he shook his head. 'It's kind of amazing, you know. You know *me*. I didn't even realise how much I missed being known like that.'

Clemmie felt a flush spread through her chest, but she kept her tone light. 'Well, someone's got to keep track of all your quirks. Otherwise, who else is going to remind you that your guilty pleasure is yelling at contestants on *Bake Off* because they don't temper their chocolate properly?'

'I only yell because I care,' Oliver said, grinning.

'And that,' Clemmie said with mock-seriousness, 'is why I like you.'

Oliver laughed, shaking his head. 'See, that's the thing. Fiona never cared enough to ask about any of this stuff. She doesn't even know the basics, let alone the utterly humiliating details.'

'If she ever wrote your biography, it'd probably be titled

The Fabulous Life of Oliver: A Celebrity Baker's Shortcut to the Stars,' Clemmie said, her tone teasing.

Oliver laughed. 'You're not wrong. She's always been more interested in what I can do for her than who I actually am.'

Clemmie softened, giving him a gentle look. 'Then she's the one missing out.'

They were both grinning, their eyes locked on each other as they sipped their champagne.

'What do you know about me?' Clemmie asked.

Oliver tilted his head, studying her. 'That you are the most beautiful girl in the world,' he said simply.

Clemmie blushed, laughing softly. 'You're deflecting.'

'No,' Oliver said, 'I'm starting with the truth.'

Clemmie rolled her eyes, though her smile undoubtedly betrayed her delight. 'All right, Romeo. Let's hear it. What else can you remember?'

Oliver leaned back slightly, a mischievous grin playing on his lips. 'I know that when you were eight, you tried to turn your bedroom into a rainforest. You hung fake vines, draped mosquito nets from your bunk bed and begged your granny to buy you a parrot.'

Clemmie laughed, covering her mouth. 'Oh, don't remind me. I made poor Granny eat nothing but tropical fruit for a week to set the mood.'

'Oh, and then there was the time you decided you wanted to be an inventor,' Oliver continued. 'You built some contraption out of your granny's egg whisk, rubber bands and a flashlight, claiming it was a robotic kitchen assistant so you didn't have to wash up.'

Clemmie groaned, shaking her head. 'It was supposed to

be a *genius* invention, but it caught fire during the first test run.'

'And nearly took the toaster with it,' Oliver added, laughing.

'All right, all right,' Clemmie said, trying to regain some dignity. 'What else have you got?'

'Well,' Oliver said, his voice softening slightly, 'I know that the only thing you love more than baking is how it makes other people feel. I mean, I heard about that time you stayed up all night baking cakes for the entire village after Dr Sandford's roof collapsed in that storm.'

Clemmie smiled, recalling the memory. 'It was a hard time for the village. That storm caused so much devastation. It just felt like the right thing to do.'

Oliver tilted his head, watching her with a knowing look. 'But I bet you still smiled at every single person who came into the café, didn't you? Then,' he continued, leaning forward slightly, his voice dropping, 'there's Paris.'

Clemmie's breath caught, her fingers tightening slightly around her glass.

'I'll never forget how you looked that night,' he said, his eyes distant as if the memory played vividly in his mind. 'We were walking along the Seine, and you saw that little boutique. Your face lit up like Christmas morning when you saw the dress in the window.'

'It was stunning,' Clemmie murmured, the memory washing over her. 'Then you bought it for me and took me to the opera,' she said, her cheeks flushed. 'I'd never even been to one before.'

'You looked like you belonged there,' Oliver said softly. 'You turned heads the moment we walked in. But you didn't notice because you were too busy staring at the stage, completely enchanted.'

Clemmie bit her lip, smiling at the memory.

'Actually…' Oliver began, reaching into his pocket. He pulled out a small velvet box and placed it on the table between them.

Clemmie looked at it, her brows knitting in confusion. 'What's that?'

Oliver pushed it gently towards her. 'Open it.'

Her fingers trembled slightly as she lifted the lid. Inside lay the most exquisite pair of earrings she'd ever seen, delicate drops of silver and sapphire, sparkling like tiny stars.

'I bought these for you that night,' Oliver said, his voice almost shy now. 'I wanted to give them to you before the opera, but … if I remember rightly, we kind of got distracted … and then we were running late.' He smiled. 'But I kept them. All this time.'

Clemmie's throat tightened as she stared at the earrings, her heart swelling. 'You've kept these for the past three years?'

Oliver nodded. 'I've never stopped thinking about that night or about you.'

For a moment, Clemmie was speechless. She gently ran her fingers over the earrings, her eyes glistening.

'You're full of surprises,' she said softly, looking back up at him.

'I could say the same about you,' Oliver replied.

Clemmie smiled, slipping the earrings back into the box and clutching it close to her heart. 'Thank you.' Lifting her glass again, she said, 'To the big softie behind the tuxedo.

May you always have someone who remembers the important things … like how much you love treacle tart and Percy's love of cheese.'

Oliver clinked his glass with hers, the warmth in his gaze unmistakable. 'Cheers to that.'

For a moment, they sat in comfortable silence, the world outside the Royal Yacht fading into irrelevance. Clemmie couldn't help but think that, in this moment, everything felt exactly as it should, but there was the tiny niggle in the back of her mind.

'The week we spent together in London…' Oliver began, his voice soft but steady, his eyes locked on hers, 'that was the happiest I've ever been. I didn't have to pretend or put on a show. It was just us.'

The way he was looking at her, with so much sincerity, made Clemmie's pulse quicken. But she couldn't let herself get swept away, not yet. She forced herself to ask, 'Then why didn't you get in touch? If it meant so much to you?'

Oliver didn't flinch, and didn't look away. His gaze was unwavering, full of regret. 'Because I thought it would be too difficult. Communicating with someone I couldn't have… Our lives were on two completely different paths.'

Clemmie had told herself the same thing a hundred times since their time in London, but hearing him say it aloud only deepened the pain. She fiddled with the edge of her napkin, her thoughts spinning.

He had meant something to her … *still* meant something to her. She had buried it, ignored it, convinced herself it was a fleeting connection. But now, as she sat across from him, the truth was harder to deny.

'And what's next for you on that path?' she asked, her voice steadier now, though her heartbeat wasn't.

Oliver exhaled, leaning back slightly. 'A year in the States. I've got a job reporting on some of the best chefs in New York, San Francisco and everywhere in between. It's an incredible opportunity, a dream, really.'

Clemmie managed a smile, but inside, a dull ache was beginning to spread through her chest. 'That sounds amazing,' she said, meaning it. She was happy for him, truly, but the thought of him leaving so soon after the baking competition ended made her stomach twist.

'It is,' Oliver said, though his tone carried a touch of hesitation. 'It's everything I've worked for.'

Clemmie nodded, forcing herself to look excited for him. 'You'll be incredible, you're perfect for it. I can already imagine you charming your way into every Michelin-starred kitchen in America.'

He chuckled softly, but there was a sadness in his eyes. 'It'll be an adventure, that's for sure.'

'And a long one,' Clemmie added, trying to keep her tone light.

Oliver nodded, his gaze dropping to the table. 'Yeah. I'll be gone for a while.'

For a moment, neither of them spoke. The only sound Clemmie could hear was her heartbeat pounding in her ears.

She wanted to say something – *anything* – to break the silence, to chase away the looming reality of his departure. But what could she say? That she didn't want him to go? That she hated the idea of him being on the other side of the world, out of reach, when she had only just begun to feel like they were finding their way back to each other?

Instead, she said nothing, her fingers tightening slightly around her champagne flute.

'It's only a year.' He gave her a small, almost shy smile.

'You'll be amazing, and just think of all the opportunities that will open up. You'll be either reporting for the most famous food magazine in the States or presenting a cooking show on TV.' Her voice trembled slightly as she said, 'This is your dream.'

'It is.'

'I'm happy for you,' she said. The words came out steady, but inside, her emotions were swirling like a storm. 'I really am. You deserve this.'

'Can we keep in touch this time?'

Clemmie nodded, a small, almost automatic gesture, but her heart was already breaking in two again. As much as she tried to play it cool, as much as she had pretended his arrival on Puffin Island was no big deal, deep down, she had been thrilled. His presence had awakened a hope she thought she had buried for good, a hope for something more.

But now? Now he was leaving again. The dull ache in her chest intensified as the reality sank in. She understood why he had to go – this opportunity was huge, a career-defining moment for him – and she was proud of him, truly, but that pride was tangled with an ache she couldn't ignore.

She forced a smile, her fingers absently tracing the rim of her glass. 'Of course we can. You'll have to keep me updated on all the fancy Michelin-starred meals and celebrity chefs you meet.'

Oliver grinned, but it didn't quite reach his eyes. 'You'll be the first to know. Though I'll probably bore you with details about every soufflé and scallop.'

She laughed softly and tried to imagine what it would be like to hear his stories from afar, to read his texts or emails, to listen to his voice over the phone, knowing he was on the other side of the world. And worse, knowing he was living an incredible life, meeting new people, making new memories … without her.

The thought unsettled her. As much as she wanted to be supportive, she wasn't sure if she could handle hearing about all the amazing things he'd be doing without her. Would she be happy for him? Or would each story be a reminder of what she couldn't have?

Oliver looked at her for a long moment, his expression unreadable. Then he reached across the table, his fingers brushing against hers. The touch sent a jolt through her, but she didn't pull away.

Oliver stood, holding out a hand. 'Come on,' he said, 'let's go grab a nightcap at the bar. We *are* on the Royal Yacht, after all. Let's make some more memories.'

She smiled, placing her napkin on the table. There was no doubt this night would be a cherished memory, one she'd tell her grandchildren about, but seeing him again like this, having these moments while knowing he was leaving, it felt almost cruel. Every smile and glance only served as a reminder of what they couldn't have. She told herself that keeping her distance would be the smart choice, the sensible thing to do. If she let herself get closer, it would only make saying goodbye harder. Could she really go through that again? They walked towards the bar, her thoughts tumbling over each other. Maybe if she blocked out her real feelings, she could cope. Pretend that this was nothing more than a pleasant evening between old friends, that the weight pressing against her ribs wasn't longing but nostalgia. But even as she tried to convince herself, she knew the truth: her heart had never quite let him go. And here, on the Royal Yacht, the flickering candlelight reflecting in his eyes, the chemistry between them was undeniable. Off the scale.

They sat down at a table and Oliver took hold of Clemmie's hands. 'Are you okay?'

'Of course.' What was the point in telling him how she felt? It wouldn't change anything. The situation remained the same as it always had been: her life was here and his was elsewhere. Being honest with Oliver would only stir up emotions neither of them could afford to entertain. So she swallowed the words, buried them deep and forced herself to meet his gaze with a smile that felt steady, even if she didn't.

Whatever this night was turning into, whether it was a rekindling of something lost, the start of something new or just a fleeting moment in an extraordinary setting, she wasn't ready for it to end just yet.

Chapter Eleven

The kitchen of The Café on the Coast hummed with a lively mix of excitement and nerves on the day of the competition. Sunlight streamed through the windows and the scent of freshly brewed coffee mingled with the aromas of buttered toast, crispy bacon and scrambled eggs. Betty flitted about, placing jars of homemade jam and a pot of golden honey on the table while Clemmie, Amelia and Dilly settled in for a chat.

Clemmie looked at her great-great-grandmother's recipe book. 'I don't think I've ever felt this nervous,' she admitted, glancing at her friends. 'I can't believe it's this evening.'

'By the weekend, you'll be the guest of honour at the royal garden party,' Amelia said, her voice brimming with certainty.

'Assuming I win,' Clemmie replied. 'I'm going to give it my best shot.'

Dilly waved her fork dramatically. 'Oh, you'll win. And when you do, there's only one real dilemma.'

Clemmie raised an eyebrow. 'Which is?'

'What to wear to the royal garden party,' Dilly declared. 'Obviously!'

Amelia laughed. 'You'll need something showstopping. A chance to go shopping!'

Clemmie chuckled despite her nerves. 'I hadn't really thought about it, but you're right … choosing an outfit actually feels as nerve-wracking as the competition itself!'

Amelia tilted her head, studying her friend. 'You look like you haven't slept for days.'

Clemmie gave a half-smile. 'Not sure anyone would sleep well with this evening looming. But … I did have a little adventure, a night to remember, a couple of days ago.'

Dilly's eyes sparkled with curiosity. 'Adventure? On Puffin Island? Do tell!'

Clemmie hesitated, glancing towards the café door to ensure Betty was still busy in the pantry. 'All right,' she said, lowering her voice, 'but you two have to promise not to tell a soul.'

Dilly gasped, placing her fork down with a clatter. 'Is it that juicy? Spill, and don't leave anything out!'

Clemmie leaned in slightly, her cheeks already tinged pink. 'Oliver took me aboard the Royal Yacht.'

Amelia froze mid-sip, nearly choking on her coffee. 'I'm sorry, *what*?'

Clemmie smiled, a dreamy look crossing her face. 'We had dinner on board. Just the two of us. Served by a waiter. There were gold-plated forks, endless champagne, a string quartet and, get this, a kitchen that hasn't been touched since World War One.'

Amelia's jaw dropped. 'You're telling us that you've been off gallivanting on the *Royal Yacht* with Oliver Lockwood?'

Dilly leaned closer, practically vibrating with excitement. 'Forget the kitchen, what about dessert? And by dessert, I mean…' She cocked an eyebrow suggestively.

'Dilly!'

Dilly smirked. 'You totally did. Oh my gosh, you slept with him, didn't you? On the *Royal Yacht* of all places!'

'I did not!' Clemmie protested, her voice an octave higher than usual.

Amelia arched a sceptical eyebrow. 'That pause says otherwise.'

'I didn't pause! And we didn't,' Clemmie clarified, exhaling. 'We just … held each other. Like our lives depended on it. That's all.'

Dilly sighed dramatically, leaning back in her chair. 'That's somehow even more romantic.'

'It really is,' Amelia agreed, taking a sip of her coffee. 'That's the kind of thing people write songs about.'

Clemmie smiled. 'Look, I know how it sounds, but it wasn't just about that night. We talked. Properly talked. He knows how much it hurt when he left without a word, and I know now that it wasn't personal. It was just … him chasing his dream. We've put it to bed.'

Dilly softened. 'Are you sure? Because last time, you were wrecked. I mean, the whole "I'm swearing off men" phase lasted a solid six months.'

'I know,' Clemmie admitted. 'And I don't regret it. But I

understand now that his career, it's part of him, just like the café and the island are part of me. He loves what he does, and I love what I do. It wasn't about me then, and it's not about me now. The timing was wrong before, and it's still wrong.

'He's leaving for a year in the States, flying out right after the competition.'

Amelia reached across the table to squeeze her hand. 'You okay?'

Clemmie hesitated. 'I'm happy for him. It's an amazing opportunity, and he deserves it. But…' She trailed off, searching for the right words. 'There was always a small part of me that thought there was a possibility… But I'm okay with that. It's just circumstances.'

'And you're really at peace with it?' Amelia asked, watching her carefully.

Clemmie hesitated for a moment before nodding. 'Yeah, I am.'

But she wasn't. Not really. Because the truth was, she was putting on a brave face. She didn't want to think about him leaving for a year, because if she had a magic wand, she'd make sure he wasn't going anywhere. But wishing wouldn't change reality, and if she let herself dwell on it, she might not hold it together at all.

Instead, she plastered on a smile and reached across to her bag and pulled out the box. She opened it to show the girls the earrings. 'He bought me these.'

Amelia gasped. 'Look at those, how beautiful.'

'They *are* beautiful. Are you going to keep in touch this time? No disappearing acts?' asked Dilly.

'He asked me that, too,' Clemmie admitted. 'I said yes.

But a part of me isn't sure if I want to hear about all the incredible things he'll be doing over there. It's selfish, but it's how I feel.'

The table fell into a contemplative silence, broken only by the clatter of Betty returning from the pantry, wiping her hands on a tea towel.

'Clemmie,' Betty said, her tone softer than usual. 'I have something for you.'

Betty placed a small box on the table. It was wrapped in delicate tissue paper and tied with a ribbon the colour of the sea. Clemmie looked up at her, puzzled. 'What's this?'

'Go on,' Betty urged. 'Open it.'

Clemmie untied the ribbon, her fingers trembling slightly, and carefully unfolded the tissue paper. Inside was a neatly folded apron, its fabric soft with age but beautifully preserved. The apron was ivory with delicate lace trim around the edges. Across the front, embroidered in gold thread, were the words *The Café on the Coast*, surrounded by subtle patterns of flowers and birds.

Clemmie's eyes widened as she took it from the box, running her fingers over the embroidery. 'This is exquisite. Where did you get this?'

Betty smiled, 'It belonged to your great-great-grandmother Beatrice. She wore it every day of her life. Said it brought her luck in the kitchen. I thought you might want it today, for the competition.'

Clemmie swallowed a lump, close to emotional tears, 'It's beautiful. I can't believe you've kept it all this time.'

'It was a gift from her husband, your great-great-grandfather Arthur. He had it made specially for her by Mrs Pruitt, the seamstress who used to live in the cottage by

Puffin Rock. You know, the little one with the wisteria growing over the doorway.'

Clemmie's eyes widened. 'Of course.'

'Mrs Pruitt was a marvel with a needle. She ran a little sewing shop out of the cottage back in the day. Beatrice told me her husband wanted her to feel loved and cherished every time she wore that apron. And she did.'

Clemmie's hands trembled slightly as she slipped the apron over her head. The fit was perfect, as if it had been made just for her. The fabric settled comfortably against her, and she tied the waistband with care. As she adjusted it, she noticed something stitched on the inside.

Curious, she took off the apron and peered at the stitching. 'Gran, look at this.'

Betty leaned in as Clemmie ran her thumb over the series of tiny embroidered gold numbers. '1705,' Clemmie read aloud, 'The same numbers as in the recipe book.'

Betty's brows knit together. 'I've never noticed that before.' Her eyes widened in surprise. 'Well, now, it's even more of a mystery!' She inspected the stitching closely. 'It's as if this apron and that recipe are connected somehow. Your great-great-grandfather must've known something we don't. I'm sure they will be watching over you today.'

As Betty bustled out of the kitchen, Clemmie turned back to her friends, who were grinning at her like Cheshire cats.

'You have a magical apron and those earrings from Oliver,' Dilly said. 'If that's not ingredients for success, I don't know what is!'

Amelia raised her mug in a toast. 'To Clemmie Rose, Puffin Island's royal baking champion!'

'Hopefully,' added Clemmie as she smoothed down the apron, her mind still very much on the embroidered number 1705. It had to mean something. Whatever it was, she decided, she would try to figure it out … after she won the competition.

'I don't know how you're so calm. How are you going to get through today before the live event starts at six-thirty?' said Dilly.

'I'm working here until after the lunch rush then I have the afternoon off to chill.'

'Sam has gone all out for it. He's arranged for a giant screen to be erected on the jetty outside The Sea Glass Restaurant, angled perfectly so the entire island can gather on the beach and watch the event unfold live,' added Amelia.

'It's actually terrifying,' admitted Clemmie, trying not to think about how many eyes would be on her. It wasn't just the judges she had to impress, now the whole island would be watching. And given it was being televised, who knew how many more eyes would be on her? The whole world, potentially.

'Just try and relax as much as you can for the rest of the day. I've got to get back to the twins, but we'll be out to wave you on to the yacht. You've got this!' Dilly stood up and hugged her friend, followed by Amelia. As soon as they left all Clemmie could think about was how nervous she actually was.

After the lunch rush, Clemmie took a long soak in the bath to try and calm her nerves, before slipping out of the café in the late afternoon. The sun was high in the sky as she walked the narrow path leading to the cliff top. The grassy knoll overlooked the rolling sea, with its endless expanse of shimmering blue stretching out towards the horizon, and the spot held a quiet reverence for Clemmie, as it was where her great-great-grandparents' ashes had been scattered, along with her great-grandparents and her own mother, their love and life forever entwined with Puffin Island. She had never known who her father was, her birth the lasting result of a brief holiday romance. There was nothing missing from her life though, no void she felt the need to fill, but from time to time, when a story about long-lost families reunited appeared on TV or in a newspaper, she would give the situation a fleeting thought before moving on.

As she reached the top of the cliff the wind tugged gently at her hair. She sank to the ground, wrapping her arms around her knees as she watched the waves breaking against the rocks below her.

Taking a deep breath, she began to speak, her voice low but steady. 'Well, everyone,' she said, smiling softly, 'it's a big day for the café. For me. I'm baking the torte tonight, Great-great-granny Beatrice, *your* torte. Can you believe it? And in The Royal Baking Competition! The café still serves the torte using the recipe you wrote all those years ago, and it's still a favourite with everyone. If I win, I get to attend the royal garden party at the palace … and hopefully meet the Queen. I know you would be so excited if you were here.'

Her fingers absently traced the grass beneath her as she continued. 'And you'll never guess what happened this week. Oliver, he's a food journalist and presenter, his granny has friends in royal circles, and he got special permission to take me on an after-hours tour of the Royal Yacht. The actual Royal Yacht! Then he treated me to dinner, champagne, the works. It was like stepping into a different world, like a dream.' She chuckled, shaking her head. 'You'd all have loved it.'

Clemmie leaned back, her gaze lifting to the sky. 'But you know what really has me curious?' she continued, her voice softening. 'That number. Why is "1705" stitched on the apron, and written at the bottom of the torte recipe? What does it mean? Is it a secret code? A special date? Something I'm supposed to figure out?'

As if in answer, a flicker of movement caught her eye. She turned her head towards a nearby rock and gasped softly. Perched on the weathered stone was a puffin, its distinctive black-and-white feathers and bright orange beak vivid against the dull grey of the rock. It stood there, watching her with an air of curious intent.

Clemmie laughed lightly, wiping a hand across her face to clear away an emotional tear that had escaped. 'Well, hello there,' she said, her voice tinged with amusement. 'Don't tell me you've come to steal another cake? I know you puffins all look alike, but I swear you're the same cheeky one who nose-dived into my Victoria sponge.'

The bird tilted its head as if considering her words, and Clemmie found a warmth spreading through her chest. 'Maybe you're here to give me a sign,' she mused aloud.

'Are you? Is 1705 some kind of puffin wisdom I'm supposed to understand?'

For a moment, she sat in silence, staring at the little bird as it fluffed its feathers. The sea breeze carried the scent of salt and Clemmie felt a strange sense of calm wash over her. It was as if the island itself was reassuring her in its own quiet way.

She said softly, 'I hope you're all proud of me. Of the café. Of the life I've tried to build here.'

'Who are you talking to?'

The deep, familiar voice startled her, and she turned quickly to see Oliver standing a few paces behind her, his hands tucked into the pockets of his coat. He was smiling as his eyes met hers.

'I, uh…' Clemmie hesitated, glancing back at the puffin, but the bird was gone. She laughed, a little self-consciously. 'Just my family; their ashes are scattered here. And maybe a puffin. You know, the usual.'

Oliver smiled, stepping closer and lowering himself to the grass beside her. 'Talking to puffins now, are we? I knew there was something strange about this place.'

Clemmie smiled, her heart skipping a beat as he settled in next to her. 'I like to come here when I need to think. Or when I want to feel close to my family.'

He nodded, his gaze sweeping over the view before them. 'It's a beautiful spot. Peaceful.'

They sat in silence, the sounds of the sea and the distant cries of gulls filling the air. Clemmie stole a glance at Oliver, her heart stirring with a mix of emotions.

'How are you feeling about the competition?' he asked after a moment.

'Excited, nervous, scared … you name it. My emotions are all over the place. One minute I'm convinced I'll nail it, and the next, I'm pretty sure I'll set the royal ovens on fire.'

Oliver chuckled. 'Well, for what it's worth, I've come to wish you good luck. Once we're in there, I have to be impartial, but, just for the record, I think you're in with a pretty good chance and I've got everything crossed for you.'

'Thanks,' she said. 'That means a lot.'

'Also – and this is off the record of course – given that I'm meant to be accompanying the winner to the royal garden party, I really need you to win. It can be our last adventure together. Can you imagine the two of us running riot in the palace?'

Clemmie burst out laughing. 'The Queen would have us locked up within five minutes. She'd be shouting, "Off with their heads!" while we're raiding the palace kitchen.'

Oliver joined her laughter, casually leaning back on his hands. 'Honestly, I can picture it. You'd be sneaking eclairs out under your apron, and I'd be caught red-handed trying to smuggle out one of those corgi biscuits they make.'

'It's a good thing you're heading to America. The Queen probably already has us on some kind of watch list.'

'Probably,' he agreed, grinning. 'But seriously, it has been really good to see you again and I'll miss this. I'll miss … you.'

The light-heartedness of the moment shifted and Clemmie swallowed a lump in her throat. 'Right person, wrong time … again.' She couldn't meet his eyes. Instead, she focused on the puffin that had reappeared, its beady eyes fixed on them.

'You know,' she said, changing the subject, her voice

trembling just slightly, 'I think that puffin might be the same one that nose-dived into my Victoria sponge. Or maybe they're all just identical mischievous little thieves.'

Oliver followed her gaze, a soft smile tugging at the corners of his mouth. 'If it's the same one, it's probably here to remind you who the real competition is. Forget the judges; you'll have to keep an eye on that bird.'

Clemmie giggled, grateful for the lighter turn the conversation had taken. She faced Oliver, her smile fading just slightly as she said, 'You've got your adventure waiting for you in America. Big opportunities, amazing chefs, endless possibilities. I'm happy for you, I really am.'

He studied her face, as if trying to read between the lines of her words. 'But?'

'But,' she admitted, her voice quieter now, 'there's a tiny part of me that will miss you, too.'

'Only a tiny part?'

'That's all you're getting.' She bumped her shoulder playfully against his.

'You're wearing the earrings,' he said, reaching his hand to touch one gently, his touch steady. 'Right person, wrong time,' he repeated.

Clemmie blinked back the tears threatening to spill. She forced a wobbly smile, determined not to let him see how much his words affected her. 'Maybe one day we'll get it right,' she said softly.

Oliver's gaze lingered on hers. 'Let's hope so,' he replied, with an unmistakable thread of sincerity that sent a shiver down her spine.

At that moment, the puffin, still perched on its rock, let out a loud, almost comically timed moo, breaking the tension like a cheeky spectator unwilling to be ignored. Both of them turned towards the bird, whose beady eyes glinted with mischief.

Oliver chuckled, the sound rich and grounding. 'Even the bird's rooting for you today.'

Clemmie smiled, grateful for the diversion. 'As long as it doesn't follow me and stick its head right in the middle of my baking.'

'I wouldn't put it past it,' Oliver replied, his eyes crinkling with amusement. Then he stood, brushing off his hands. 'I'll see you at the yacht.'

Before she could respond, his expression softened and he slowly, deliberately, leaned in and brushed a kiss against her cheek.

He pulled back slightly but lingered close, his eyes locked with hers. Time seemed to stretch, the distant crash of the waves and the puffin's intermittent moos fading into the background. Clemmie held her breath as she tilted her head ever so slightly, closing the gap between them. Her lips met his in a kiss that was tender yet firm, a silent acknowledgement of what they both felt but couldn't quite grasp.

Then, just as gently as he'd leaned in, Oliver pulled away. His eyes lingered on hers for a heartbeat longer, as if memorising the moment. He stood up and Clemmie's heart ached as she watched him walk away. She stayed where she was, rooted to the spot on the cliff top. The puffin mooed again as Clemmie wrapped her arms around her knees and tried to focus on the competition.

The kitchen of The Café on the Coast was a whirlwind of movement as Betty bustled around, muttering to herself. Her eyes darted to the clock on the wall before landing on Clemmie, who had just walked through the door.

'Where have you been?' Betty demanded, her tone flustered but tinged with relief. 'I thought I'd have to send out a search party! You've been gone for hours!'

Clemmie offered an apologetic smile, brushing a strand of hair from her face. 'I went up to the rock. I just wanted to touch base with everyone. You know, see if Beatrice had any last-minute tips for me.'

Betty's expression softened instantly, her exasperation melting into affection. She walked over and pulled Clemmie into a hug, her sturdy arms wrapping around her granddaughter in that uniquely comforting way only she could manage.

'Everyone would be so proud of you,' she said. 'And if Beatrice was here, I reckon she'd tell you to trust your instincts and to make sure you use enough butter. She always said that was the key to a good bake!'

Clemmie laughed, the tension in her shoulders easing as she held onto her grandmother. 'Thanks, Granny. I needed to hear that.'

Betty stepped back, giving her a once-over before nodding approvingly. 'Let's get you some dinner before we head down to the bay.'

An hour later Clemmie reached for the worn leather-bound recipe book.

'Ready?' she asked her grandmother.

She glanced at Betty, who smiled, smoothing down her favourite dress, a vibrant floral number she reserved for special occasions. 'Ready as I'll ever be. I didn't get all dolled up for nothing! Do you know how long it took me to find my good handbag?'

Clemmie laughed, and together they made their way out of the café and towards the bay, where Amelia and Dilly were waiting. Betty clutched her ticket to the competition like it was a golden pass to Eldenbridge Palace, her excitement bubbling over as she adjusted her dress for the hundredth time.

Puffin Island was alive with excitement. The cobbled street leading to the bay was a riot of colour and noise, with friends and neighbours lining the road. Homemade banners bearing Clemmie's name fluttered in the breeze, and cheerful shouts of encouragement echoed around them.

'Go get 'em, Clemmie!' shouted Pete, the retired vet and Betty's best friend, waving his cap in the air.

'Make us proud!' called Verity, who was standing next to Sam and the rest of the staff from The Sea Glass Restaurant.

Children ran alongside Clemmie and Betty, waving little flags decorated with her name and puffin doodles. The air was electric with anticipation, and Clemmie smiled, her heart swelling with gratitude for her tiny but mighty community.

Amelia and Dilly fell into step beside her once Clemmie and Betty reached them, their faces beaming with pride. 'Look at this turnout,' Amelia said, glancing around. 'The whole island must be here.'

'I feel so tearful,' Clemmie said, her voice filled with

emotion. 'I'm so glad you all have tickets to come and watch.'

'So are we,' Dilly said. 'You're our Clemmie, and this is *your* moment. Besides, Max is looking forward to setting up on the beach with the twins, catching up with Sam and watching you on the big screen.'

At the end of the lane, they spotted Dilly's partner Max with the twins in their double pushchair. The babies gurgled happily, waving their pudgy fists in the air as if they, too, were cheering her on.

'Aww, look at my favourite people!' Clemmie exclaimed, crouching down to kiss each of the twins on their chubby cheeks.

'Good luck, Clemmie!' Max called with a grin. 'Looks like the whole island's out in force for you.'

'I better not let them down!' she said, standing and brushing a hand over her apron.

As if understanding her words, one of the twins let out an excited squeal, and Clemmie chuckled. 'You two behave for your daddy, okay? Auntie Clemmie's got some baking to do!'

With her friends and family surrounding her, Clemmie felt a surge of determination. The Royal Yacht gleamed just ahead, its grandness a stark reminder of the stakes for tonight. But in that moment, with the laughter and love of her community ringing in her ears, she felt ready to face whatever the day might bring. As she continued to walk and wave, she took in the scene at the harbour. It was more elaborate than she could have imagined. Picnic blankets were spread across the sand, families and friends settling in with drinks and snacks as the excitement built. The TV crews had positioned themselves strategically, their cameras trained on the unfolding event. A towering big screen had been erected on the jetty outside The Sea Glass Restaurant, ensuring that every islander had a perfect view of the spectacle.

Over at The Cosy Kettle, the coffee hut on the beach, Becca was serving chilled glasses of prosecco, a luxury made possible thanks to Sam, who had ensured there was plenty to go around. The air buzzed with anticipation, laughter and the clink of glasses, a party atmosphere sweeping through the crowd.

Up ahead, a red carpet stretched along the gangplank leading up to the Royal Yacht, where the flashes from photographers' cameras went off one after another, capturing every moment in a dazzling flurry of light.

'I'm actually beginning to feel faint, I'm so nervous,' Clemmie muttered to Dilly.

'Stay focused, you've got this. You're going to walk down that carpet like the queen you are and show them what you're made of.'

'Oh my! You're on the big screen!' exclaimed Betty and they all looked over to see the television cameras had captured Clemmie arriving.

Standing at the end of the gangplank to welcome the bakers were the three esteemed judges of The Royal Baking Competition, who were a blend of expertise, charisma and prestige, each bringing unique credentials to the table.

Sir Gregory Whitcomb, a legendary patissier and culinary historian, had spent decades mastering the art of desserts. Known as the Sugar Sculptor, Sir Gregory was a former royal chef who had crafted confections for royal weddings and state banquets, and his discerning palate was said to be able to detect even the slightest misstep in a recipe.

Standing next to him was Margot Hastings, editor-in-chief of *Bakers' Monthly* magazine and a household name in the culinary world. With a sharp eye for innovation and presentation, Margot had spent years championing up-and-coming bakers and curating features on the world's most unique baking trends.

Dominic Hargrove rounded out the trio, the restaurateur and celebrity chef bringing a more contemporary edge to the panel. As the host of a wildly popular TV baking competition, Dominic's charm and wit made him a fan favourite, but his no-nonsense critiques ensured contestants brought their A-game.

Together, the judges represented the perfect mix of tradition, creativity and modernity, making them exceptionally qualified to judge the prestigious baking event.

'I can't believe they're going to judge my baking.' Clemmie stopped and turned to her grandmother, who threw her arms around her.

'What an experience! I wish you all the luck in the world. We have to wait until the bakers are on board until we can go and take our seats, but you need to go now. Try not to be nervous … and good luck!' Betty held her granddaughter's hands before Clemmie turned to hug her friends goodbye.

She set off towards the yacht and saw Oliver was now standing with the judges, looking impossibly dashing in a tailored navy blazer, a microphone in hand as he addressed the gathering crowd. 'Ladies and gentlemen, welcome to the annual Royal Baking Competition. The bakers will be gathering inside very soon and then all those with tickets can make their way to the gangplank.'

His voice carried over the crowd, and Clemmie's heart did a little flip when he caught her eye and smiled broadly. She made her way towards him, feeling both nervous and thrilled.

Taking her first tentative step onto the red carpet, Clemmie soaked up the atmosphere. The buzz of the crowd outside, the glint of cameras flashing and the hum of excited chatter all blended into a surreal symphony. She walked steadily towards the judges, whose faces were even more intimidating in person. These were the culinary legends she'd admired for so long, titans of the baking world who could make or break a career with a single comment.

As she approached, Oliver appeared at her side and introduced her to each of the judges with a warmth that helped ease her nerves. His charm was in full force, and Clemmie noticed how easy he made it all seem. After the final introduction, he leaned in, his voice just low enough for her to hear. 'You ready for this, Clem?'

She gave a small, determined nod, though her heart was racing. 'As ready as I'll ever be,' she replied, managing a shaky smile.

Oliver's grin was laced with encouragement. 'Don't let the cameras put you off. Pretend it's just you in your café, baking up a storm.'

'No pressure, then?' she murmured.

'None at all,' he replied, giving her a reassuring smile.

Fiona stood nearby watching the pair closely. Her perfectly manicured nails tapped rhythmically on a book she was carrying, her sharp eyes narrowing as she took in their exchange. Clemmie could feel her watching them, and dared to glance towards her. Fiona's lips thinned as she adjusted her stance, her attention unwavering.

Clemmie stole a glance back at her cheering supporters. Betty stood front and centre, waving wildly. Amelia and Dilly were clapping and hollering as if they were at a rock concert. Even the twins were waving their tiny fists in unison, coached by Max, who held the pushchair steady.

Clemmie's heart swelled at the sight of them. Their unwavering support was a lifeline, a reminder of why she was here. She straightened her shoulders, her nerves hardening into a steely determination. Just before disappearing inside the yacht, she caught Oliver's gaze one last time. His expression was equal parts confidence and something softer, something that sent her pulse fluttering.

'You've got this,' he mouthed towards her as Clemmie adjusted her apron. A sense of calm settled over her. She wasn't just baking for herself; she was baking for her family, for Puffin Island.

Once inside the yacht, she was guided towards a spacious gathering area set up for the contestants. She paused just inside the doorway, her eyes sweeping over the room, noting the diverse group of competitors, though of course she had seen them all at the press conference. There was a man in his fifties with a neatly trimmed moustache, carefully flipping through what appeared to be handwritten recipes, his hands trembling ever so slightly. Nearby, a young woman with vibrant purple hair was adjusting a headscarf, her lips moving silently as though rehearsing a mantra.

Clemmie took a glass of water from a nearby refreshment table and looked up at the gleaming chandeliers, whose light bounced off the polished gold and mahogany decor. The air buzzed with excitement and nerves, but each competitor was staying focused and keeping themselves to themselves. She spotted Fiona, who was now gushing all over the judges, acting like they were her new best friends. Her high-pitched laughter echoed through the room as she leaned in close to Sir Gregory, hanging on his every word. Clemmie turned away; she wasn't going to let Fiona rattle her. Nothing and no one, not even Fiona Fairweather, was going to stand in her way. Not only did she want to win the competition to put the café on the map, she also wanted one last adventure with Oliver Lockwood.

Chapter Twelve

Moments later Clemmie could almost feel the tense energy in the room and for once even Fiona was looking pensive. All ten competitors had taken their places at the workstations. The judges' table was directly in front of Clemmie's workstation, a pristine white tablecloth embroidered with the royal crest cascading down the front.

Clemmie tried to steady her hands as she adjusted her utensils, taking a moment to try and calm her beating heart. The audience was filing into the room and she immediately spotted her granny among the sea of faces. Betty's eyes glistened with pride, her hands clasped tightly as she sat with Amelia and Dilly, who waved wildly. Despite the nerves churning in her stomach, Clemmie smiled.

Suddenly, a spotlight flicked on, casting a dramatic light over the room. Clemmie blinked under the brightness, her pulse quickening as the hum of excitement rippled all around. A floor manager wearing a headset gestured towards Oliver, who nodded and made his way to centre stage.

The judges were now seated and the cameras were in position, their lenses glinting like watchful eyes. Oliver picked up the microphone and flashed a broad smile that immediately put the room at ease. He waited for the murmurs to die down before speaking.

'Good evening, ladies and gentlemen. Welcome to Her Majesty's Royal Yacht and the annual Royal Baking Competition. The competition will soon begin, but before we dive into a world of whisking, piping and possibly some light pastry drama, we have a few house rules to go over.'

A ripple of laughter spread through the audience.

'Firstly,' he began, holding up a finger, 'we will be live on air, so all mobile phones must be switched off or set to airplane mode. We love a good ringtone, but not while someone's soufflé is trying to rise.'

The audience chuckled again and there was a wave of rustling as everyone switched their phones to silent and tucked them away.

'Secondly, no talking while the bakers are working and the crew are filming. There will be several commercial breaks so we ask that you save any conversation until then.'

Clemmie smiled, her nerves easing as she appreciated the humour Oliver injected into the proceedings.

'Thirdly,' he continued, pacing theatrically across the stage, 'we kindly ask that you remain seated until the interval. Not only because the cameras are rolling, but also because trying to climb over other spectators to reach the bathroom during a tense sponge-cake moment could lead to chaos and no one wants the Queen to see that when she tunes in.

'On a more serious note,' he added, his tone softening just enough to show his sincerity, 'these bakers have worked incredibly hard to be here. Let's support them, celebrate their creativity and, most importantly, enjoy ourselves. Because, really, what could be better than a day dedicated to cake?'

The audience clapped enthusiastically, their spirits high and their smiles wide.

'Now,' Oliver said, gesturing to the bakers, 'let's get ready to bake!'

The lights dimmed over the audience, signalling the start of the competition. Clemmie took a deep breath, the encouraging energy from the crowd and Oliver's presence bolstering her confidence. It was time to show everyone what she could do.

The floor manager started counting down. 'Ten seconds!' he called. 'Nine, eight, seven…'

As the countdown reached 'three, two, one', Oliver stepped forward, microphone in hand. Under the bright lights, he looked perfectly confident as he addressed the camera with ease.

'Ladies and gentlemen, welcome aboard the Royal Yacht for this year's Royal Baking Competition!' he declared.

A woman at the side of the stage held up a card with the word 'applause' and the room instantly burst into cheers and clapping. Clemmie took one last look at her grandmother and her friends, whose enthusiastic cheers rose above the rest.

'We're coming to you this year from the harbour at

Puffin Island, where ten talented bakers are prepped and ready to deliver unique bakes steeped in family history.' Oliver smiled, gesturing to the judges' table. 'Allow me to introduce to you our esteemed panel of judges…'

Oliver's words washed over Clemmie as she focused on taking deep breaths, preparing for the moment the cameras would be on her and her fellow contestants.

As the crowd applauded the judges, Oliver gestured to the row of bakers standing at their stations. 'We have ten remarkable bakers with us today who have travelled from far and wide to showcase their skills and their passion for baking. Let's give them a round of applause!'

He then began introducing each contestant by name, sharing their hometown and a brief snippet about their background. Clemmie barely heard the others' introductions as Oliver drew closer. When he finally reached her, she found herself hoping that her microphone wouldn't pick up the thudding of her heartbeat, as she felt it beating nineteen to the dozen.

'And from right here on Puffin Island, we have Clemmie Rose, co-owner of the beloved Café on the Coast,' he said, his voice steadying her. 'Clemmie, why don't you tell us a little about what you'll be baking today and the story behind it?'

Clemmie cleared her throat, her nerves evident but not overwhelming as she stepped forward. She glanced at the audience, her granny's proud face beaming back at her.

'Thank you, Oliver,' she began. 'Today, I'll be baking a torte that's very close to my heart. It's a family recipe, passed down from my great-great-grandmother, Beatrice, who was the founder of The Café on the Coast. She started baking this torte around 1917 and it's been a favourite of the locals ever since. What makes this torte special isn't just the recipe itself, it's the story behind it. Beatrice's home was bombed in the war and both her parents perished in the blast, but she found solace in opening up the café and creating a place where people could come together, whether it was for celebrations, comfort or simply to share a moment. This torte represents that spirit of connection, community, friends and love.'

She paused, glancing down at her apron before looking back up. 'Wearing my great-great-grandmother's apron today feels like having a piece of her here with me, guiding me through this moment. I hope I can do her proud.'

The judges murmured appreciatively, and Oliver's smile deepened as he nodded. 'Well, Clemmie, I think I speak for everyone here when I say we can't wait to see your creation.'

The cameras panned the audience before swivelling back towards Oliver. 'Before the competition begins the judges have a few pearls of wisdom to share.' Oliver stepped aside to allow the judges to address the contestants. Sir Gregory Whitcomb was the first to rise, his presence commanding yet kind. He folded his hands neatly in front of him and offered a grandfatherly smile.

'Baking,' he began, his voice deep, 'is as much about heart as it is about technique. Each of you has earned your place here today, and now is the time to trust your instincts and let your passion guide you. Remember, a truly memorable bake tells a story … your story.'

Next, Margot Hastings stood, her elegant poise radiating sophistication. 'Presentation is important,' she said, her crisp accent making each word sound deliberate. 'But it's only one layer. Texture, flavour and creativity are what elevate a bake from good to extraordinary. Show us who you are in every bite.'

Finally, Dominic Hargrove rose from his chair, leaning casually against the table as if he were chatting with old friends. 'Don't overthink it,' he said, his grin disarming. 'You've got all the skills you need. Now's the time to enjoy the process. Have fun, take risks and give us something we'll never forget. Oh, and one more thing … don't forget to switch your oven on. It makes all the difference.'

Everyone laughed.

Oliver stepped forward, the room falling silent as he raised his microphone. Behind him, a grand clock mounted on the wall displayed the countdown timer, its gilded hands ready to tick away the precious minutes. 'Bakers, the moment has arrived,' he announced, his voice steady but filled with excitement. 'You have two hours to create something extraordinary. This is your time to shine, to pour your hearts and skills into your bakes. On my count … three … two … one… Let's get baking!'

The room erupted into applause as the contestants reached for their bowls, measuring cups and ingredients. Clemmie took a deep breath, her fingers trembling slightly as she opened her great-great-grandmother's cherished torte recipe. Of course, she knew the recipe off by heart, but Clemmie wasn't leaving anything to chance. The handwritten words on the page seemed to whisper encouragement, reminding her of the countless times Betty had told her, *Add a touch of yourself to every recipe, that's what makes it special.*

Clemmie dared to glance in Fiona's direction, only to find the other woman smirking, her expression practically dripping with condescension. Clemmie briefly closed her eyes, steeling herself. *Focus. For the next two hours, it's just me and the recipe.* After making the sponge, Clemmie placed a pan on the stove, carefully adding double cream, sugar and a tiny pinch of sea salt. As the mixture began to warm, she picked up a bright, fragrant clementine and started zesting it. Fine ribbons of citrus peel curled into the cream, releasing a fresh, tangy aroma that instantly made her think of summer afternoons in the kitchen in The Café on the Coast. Clemmie worked methodically, her focus sharp, but she remained aware of her surroundings. Fiona hovered nearby, too close to be accidental, her presence a prickle at the edge of Clemmie's awareness.

'You're so precise,' Fiona remarked lightly, watching as Clemmie measured out sugar. She laughed, a touch too airily for it to feel natural, before shifting just enough for her elbow to nudge Clemmie's sugar bowl. It didn't tip dramatically, just rocked on its base, but it sent a fine dusting of sugar onto the counter.

'Oops! My fault,' Fiona said quickly, swiping a hand across the surface as if to help, except her 'help' only sent more sugar cascading onto the floor.

Clemmie pressed her lips together. It was nothing catastrophic, but enough to be irritating. 'Don't worry about it,' she murmured, brushing the excess away and swiftly remeasuring the sugar.

She returned her attention to her chocolate mixture, stirring in cubes of butter as the scent of rich cocoa bloomed through the air. The smooth, velvety sheen told her she was on track. Picking up a clementine, she sliced it open and squeezed, the citrus adding a fresh depth of flavour to the chocolate.

Next, Clemmie heard Fiona sigh theatrically. 'Oh dear,' she muttered. Clemmie glanced up in time to see her fumble with a piping bag, a sudden squeeze sending its contents splattering across Clemmie's workstation. Fiona let out a small, flustered laugh. 'I'm so sorry, it seems to have a mind of its own.'

Clemmie wasn't fooled. She ducked her head, choosing not to engage, but the commotion had drawn the attention of the floor manager and even one of the judges. Fiona flashed them an apologetic smile before returning to her own work.

Shaking off the interruption, Clemmie whisked in the cold milk, the mixture turning perfectly smooth and glossy. Almost there. She checked the sponge in the oven, expecting to see it rising, but instead, a jolt of unease shot through her. The oven light was off. Her heart stuttered. The dial, which she was certain had been correctly set, had been turned just slightly. Not off completely, but low enough that the temperature had dropped dangerously.

'Something wrong?' Fiona asked, her voice light, innocent.

Clemmie inhaled. 'No, it's fine.'

She adjusted the oven quickly, knowing she had no choice but to push forward. If Fiona thought she could rattle her, she had another think coming.

With twenty minutes to spare Clemmie's hands were shaking lightly as she piped delicate swirls of cream around the edges of the torte. She garnished it with thin slices of candied clementine peel, which shimmered like tiny jewels, and the finishing touch, an elegant gold leaf.

As she stepped back to survey her work, Clemmie felt a surge of pride. Despite Fiona's discreet sabotage attempts, she had pulled it off. The torte was exactly as her great-great-grandmother had described; smooth, rich and ready to cut like butter.

With five minutes left until the final countdown, Clemmie stood tall, ready to present her creation. The competition wasn't over yet, but Clemmie knew one thing for certain: she wouldn't let anyone, or any sabotage, dim her light.

Chapter Thirteen

When the buzzer sounded, signalling the end of the competition, Clemmie wiped her brow and stepped back from her station. Exhaustion warred with triumph as she admired her chocolate and clementine torte. Beside her, Fiona's eight-layer Pearlescent Pistachio Opera Cake teetered precariously, the pistachio-green layers glinting like gemstones.

Next, each of the ten bakes was plated and carefully carried to a long table near the judges. Each had a name card beside it, ensuring no confusion when the judging began.

Then came the clean-up. A fifteen-minute countdown appeared on the screen above the galley, and with practised efficiency the bakers sprang into action. Mixing bowls were put away, stray smears of ganache were wiped from countertops, piping bags were tossed into bins. The scent of caramelised sugar and toasted nuts still lingered in the air as cloths swiped over stainless steel, leaving everything gleaming as though the chaos of the past two hours had never happened.

As the last few crumbs were brushed away, the show cut to a commercial break. Clemmie exhaled deeply, shoulders back as she glanced towards the audience. Her granny and friends sat in the front row, beaming at her with their fingers crossed in encouragement. A swell of pleasure filled her chest; no matter the outcome, she wasn't alone in this. Her thoughts turned to all her friends who were sitting outside on the beach watching it on the big screen. She hoped she'd done everyone proud.

The stage lights flickered back to full brightness and the murmur of the crowd died down as a hush of anticipation settled over the room.

The ten contestants now stood by their creations. The audience leaned forward in their seats and the cameras zoomed in on each baker's masterpiece. Clemmie stole a glance down the line. Fiona, as always, wore an air of smug confidence, her smirk as sharp as the knife she'd used to trim her cake layers earlier. Clemmie's gaze snapped back to her own torte. She had done her best; now it was up to the judges.

Oliver stepped forward, his usual charm amplified by the dazzling lights. 'Ladies and gentlemen,' he began, his voice resonating through the room, 'the competition is over and the time has come. Our esteemed judges will now begin their tasting journey. Let's see how our bakers have risen to the occasion!'

The crowd burst into polite applause as the three judges stood. Oliver escorted the judges to the first station, and the tension in the room thickened. Each contestant introduced their creation with a mix of pride and trepidation and then the judges tasted, murmured, jotted notes and occasionally exchanged pointed looks that sent ripples of anxiety down the line.

When they reached Clemmie, her pulse quickened. Oliver's encouraging smile was a lifeline as he introduced her. 'And here we have Clemmie Rose, who's drawn on family tradition to create a chocolate and clementine torte. Clemmie, tell us more.' Clemmie clasped her hands to steady them, knowing this was her one chance to connect with the judges. She took a breath. 'I've baked so many things over the years, but I chose this chocolate and clementine torte because it represents everything I love about baking. The richness of the dark chocolate, the brightness of the clementines … it's a balance of bold flavours that somehow still feels comforting. It's the first recipe I truly mastered as a child, standing on a stool beside my granny, zesting clementines and sneaking spoonfuls of melted chocolate when she wasn't looking. I still remember the first time she told me I'd got it just right. Ever since, it's been the bake I turn to when I want to make something special. It's indulgence, nostalgia and tradition all in one.'

Margot leaned in, inspecting the torte with her piercing gaze. 'Clementines, you say? Intriguing. Citrus can be a delicate balance against chocolate. Let's see how you've fared.'

Each judge took a forkful and the room fell silent, the audience holding their collective breath.

Sir Gregory nodded thoughtfully. 'The citrus is subtle yet distinct. It brightens the richness of the chocolate without overwhelming it. A very thoughtful pairing.'

Dominic smiled. 'The pastry is immaculate – crisp and buttery, the perfect foil to the smooth ganache. And the clementine zest on top is a delightful touch.'

Margot set her fork down deliberately. 'I'll admit, I was sceptical … but you've balanced the chocolate and clementines beautifully. Well done.'

Clemmie exhaled, relief washing over her. 'Thank you so much,' she said, her voice trembling with relief.

Oliver, ever the charmer, leaned in. 'Clemmie, it looks like you've impressed our judges. How do you feel?'

'Grateful it's over,' she replied with a nervous laugh, drawing friendly laughter from the audience.

As the judges moved on, Clemmie allowed herself a small smile.

It was Fiona's turn next and the atmosphere shifted. She introduced her creation with dramatic flair. 'I present my signature Pearlescent Pistachio Opera Cake,' she declared, gesturing to the precariously stacked layers. 'It's an eight-layer masterpiece of pistachio sponge, silky buttercream and a mirror glaze, finished with edible pearls.'

Margot arched a sceptical brow. 'Eight layers, you say? Quite ambitious.'

The judges sampled her cake, their reactions more reserved. Sir Gregory commented on the clever use of pistachio, but Margot noted that the layers seemed uneven. Dominic praised the buttercream but remarked that the overall balance was lacking.

Fiona's expression tightened, her smile forced. 'Well,' she said, her tone strained, 'it's a bold creation. Perhaps too bold for some palates.'

After the judges finished their tasting, the contestants

were asked to stay by their workstations whilst the judges disappeared into another room to deliberate.

As soon as they went to the commercial break, a commotion broke out near the open window behind Fiona's station. Clemmie turned just in time to see a puffin … a real, live puffin … flap awkwardly into the room. It swooped low, its trajectory erratic, and nose-dived directly into Fiona's towering opera cake. The audience erupted into hysterical laughter as the puffin's impact sent the precarious layers collapsing in a cascade of buttercream and edible pearls.

Fiona let out a shriek. 'My cake!' she cried, her voice echoing in the kitchen. Her hands flew to her head as she stared at the ruined remains of her once proud creation. Buttercream dripped onto the table in sticky globs, and one of the edible pearls had rolled all the way to the edge of the stage.

The puffin, seemingly unfazed by the chaos, waddled out of the wreckage and perched proudly on the edge of Fiona's station.

'This is sabotage!' Fiona yelled, spinning to face Clemmie. 'You did this! You've been jealous of my cake from the start!'

Clemmie blinked, startled by the accusation. 'Me? Fiona, I didn't summon a puffin to crash through the window and dive-bomb your cake. I wouldn't even know how to do that!'

Fiona's eyes narrowed. 'Convenient, isn't it? A puffin just *happens* to ruin my cake while your torte remains perfectly intact!'

Clemmie raised an eyebrow and pointed to the puffin,

who was now fluffing its feathers as if preparing for its next performance. 'If you're looking for someone to blame, you might want to start with our little friend over there.'

Oliver had wandered over to join them and he bit down a smile before contributing, 'A puffin … on Puffin Island? Honestly, you can't make this stuff up.' He leaned in closer to Clemmie, his voice dropping to a conspiratorial whisper. 'I bet that's the same puffin from the rock earlier. Looks like it's got a taste for drama.'

Clemmie suppressed her smile, 'Well, at least it's consistent,' she whispered back.

But Fiona wasn't ready to let it go. 'My opera cake was a masterpiece, and now it's ruined! This has to be taken into account during the judges' deliberations!'

Oliver shrugged. 'The judges tasted the bakes before the puffin tucked into his afternoon tea so I don't think it makes a difference at this point.' He gestured towards the floor manager. 'What are we doing about getting the puffin out of here?'

The puffin was quickly removed by the security team, and as the judges returned and the cameras began to roll again, Oliver explained the mishap that had gone on during the commercial break.

'If nothing else, it's made for quite the memorable finale!'

There was a ripple of laughter from the audience and even Sir Gregory cracked a rare smile.

Fiona discreetly huffed but as the cameras panned towards her she turned on a smile.

Sir Gregory placed a hand on Oliver's shoulder. 'I think we're ready to announce the winner.'

The grand finale of The Royal Baking Competition had arrived, and the tension in the room was unmistakable. Contestants, audience members and even the camera crew held their breath as the gleaming Golden Whisk Trophy was placed on a pedestal beside the judge's table. The judges sat back, their expressions giving nothing away as they prepared to name their winner.

'Ladies and gentlemen,' Oliver began, his voice brimming with excitement, 'the moment we've all been waiting for is here. Our esteemed judges have deliberated, and now they will each reveal their choice for this year's winner of The Royal Baking Competition. Let's find out whose creation has earned the title *Fit for Royalty*. As a reminder, the winner's creation will be served to guests at the royal garden party, and will be included in a cookbook of their own recipes, which will be published and on the shelves by early autumn.' Oliver nodded towards the judges.

The crowd erupted into anticipatory cheers before settling into a hushed silence. All eyes were on Sir Gregory Whitcomb, the first judge to speak. He stood, adjusting his perfectly tailored jacket, and addressed the room.

'Throughout this competition, we've seen extraordinary talent,' Sir Gregory began, his voice rich and commanding. 'But one creation stood out not only for its technical excellence but also for its elegance and restraint. In my career, I've learned that a dish must be more than delicious, it must tell a story, evoke emotion and leave an indelible impression.' He turned his piercing gaze to Clemmie, who stood beside her chocolate and clementine torte. 'Clemmie, your torte did all of that and more. The clementines brought a regal freshness to the richness of the chocolate, a balance that is both sophisticated and delightful. It is, without a doubt, a dessert worthy of a royal banquet. My vote goes to you.'

The audience burst into applause. Clemmie felt her heart race, emotion surging through her body, and she blinked back tears as she nodded her gratitude. Oliver stepped forward, his grin widening. 'A strong start for Clemmie Rose! Sir Gregory has cast his vote. Now, Margot Hastings, we're eager to hear your thoughts.'

Margot rose gracefully, her sharp eyes softening slightly as she looked at Clemmie. 'This competition is about excellence, and each contestant has shown incredible skill. But Clemmie, your torte had something special, a sense of heart, of legacy. The clementines were a bold choice, and they paid off spectacularly, elevating the dish to something truly memorable. The sponge was the best I've ever tasted, the ganache was smooth as silk, and the citrus brought a brightness that made the whole thing sing. It's the kind of dessert that could grace the table at any royal gathering. My vote is also for Clemmie Rose.'

Another wave of applause erupted. This time louder.

Oliver took the microphone again, his excitement barely contained. 'With two votes, Clemmie Rose is the winner of this year's Royal Baking Competition!'

Clemmie's hands flew to her mouth, her eyes wide with disbelief as the audience roared, Betty's voice ringing out above everyone else's.

'We have our winner, but we also still have one more judge's decision to hear. Dominic, the floor is yours.'

Dominic stood, his charming smile and approachable

demeanour earning a few cheers from the crowd. 'I know you don't need my vote, Clemmie, but you have it. Your torte wasn't just a dessert, it was an experience. The way the clementines complemented the chocolate was inspired, and the precision of your execution was flawless. But what really stood out to me was the sense of tradition and innovation. You honoured the past with so much love, and that's what this competition is about, what makes it so special. If there's one dessert tonight that's fit for royalty, it's yours.'

The room erupted into cheers and applause, the sound nearly deafening, and before she could process her out-and-out victory, Oliver, caught up in the moment, stepped towards her, swept her off her feet and spun her around in an exuberant victory hug.

The crowd roared with laughter and applauded, and Oliver quickly set her down, his face flushing as he realised everyone was watching. 'Well, I think that was unorthodox,' he said, grinning sheepishly. 'But hey, we're making history tonight!'

Betty was on her feet, clapping the loudest of anyone, tears of joy streaming down her face. The audience followed her lead, rising in a standing ovation that filled the hall with thunderous applause.

Clemmie, still dazed, stepped forward to the microphone. Beside her stood the illustrious Golden Whisk Trophy, its elegant handle adorned with the royal crest, encrusted with glimmering diamonds that caught the light like a constellation of stars. The trophy was a symbol of both culinary excellence and regal heritage, a prize fit for

The Royal Baking Competition champion. She took a deep breath and smiled.

'I … I don't know where to begin,' she started, her eyes scanning the cheering crowd. Although emotion threatened to overwhelm her, her voice was steady. 'This means more to me than I can possibly say.' She paused, swallowed the lump in her throat and took a deep breath. 'But I wouldn't be standing here without all the incredible women in my life, particularly my great-great-granny, who opened up the café and passed down her love of baking to all the generations that have followed, and my own granny, Betty Rose, who's been my biggest supporter every step of the way and is the co-owner of The Café on the Coast.'

The audience erupted into applause, but Clemmie wasn't finished. A small, nostalgic smile spread across her face as she continued. 'The Rose women have long been huge fans of the Royal Family. When I was little, Granny and I would sit for hours talking about what it would be like to visit the palace, to have afternoon tea with the Queen herself. My granny had this way of making it all seem so magical.'

The crowd leaned in, captivated by her words. 'And, well,' Clemmie added with a sheepish chuckle, 'I might have taken it a bit too far. I used to dress up in her wedding dress and pretend I was the Queen, sitting in Eldenbridge Palace, eating tiny sandwiches and scones with clotted cream.' Laughter rippled through the audience, and Clemmie's cheeks flushed.

Her voice softened as she glanced towards Betty. 'Those moments, those stories, her love of baking, it's all shaped me into who I am today. This trophy isn't just for me; it's for all the women in my family, and for every cup of tea and slice of cake that's been shared in The Café on the Coast.'

She turned towards the audience, her voice inviting. 'Granny, would you join me up here? This moment is as much yours as it is mine.' Clemmie extended her hand towards Betty. The audience cheered louder as Betty hesitated, clearly emotional, before being coaxed onto the stage. She walked up with a mix of pride and shyness, wiping tears from her cheeks as she reached Clemmie. Clemmie wrapped her in a hug before turning back to the microphone. 'Everyone, this is Betty Rose – my granny and the heart of our family. If it weren't for her and the other strong women in our family, I wouldn't be holding this trophy today.'

The audience rose to their feet in another thunderous standing ovation. Betty waved shyly, dabbing at her tears with a tissue, while Clemmie held the Golden Whisk Trophy aloft, its royal crest glinting in the spotlight. Oliver stepped back to let the moment unfold, his smile wide and genuine.

A moment later, Clemmie turned towards Oliver. 'Can I say something else?'

'Of course.'

The audience went quiet. 'I want to share something I've never spoken about publicly before,' she began, her eyes flicking momentarily to Betty. 'When I first started out in my career, I wasn't sure of myself. I loved baking, but becoming a partner in the café was daunting, especially following in footsteps of my family members, who have all been expert bakers. Then, not long after I became a partner, someone wrote an awful review about me and the café.

They called the menu uninspired and said I'd never measure up to others in the industry.'

The audience let out a collective gasp, and Clemmie offered a small, wry smile.

'Those words hit me hard. I was devastated. I remember sitting in the kitchen that night, reading that review over and over, thinking, "Maybe they're right. Maybe I'll never be a good baker like my great-great-granny or my granny." For weeks, even months, I doubted myself. I doubted everything. I wanted to give up.'

Clemmie paused as her voice faltered. 'But then Granny sat me down. She reminded me that success isn't about being perfect or comparing yourself to others. It's about loving what you do, learning from your mistakes and finding joy in the process. She often says, "The secret ingredient in any recipe is the care you put into it", and it's true.'

She smiled softly, her gaze drifting to the Golden Whisk Trophy for a moment before returning to the audience. 'What I've learned since then is that believing in yourself, truly believing, is half the battle. That review could have crushed me, but it didn't, because I had the best mentor. My granny taught me to bake with my heart and showed me the meaning of resilience, and the people who supported me reminded me of my worth.'

Clemmie's voice grew stronger, more confident. 'Standing here today, holding this incredible trophy, I realise something: self-worth isn't about never failing. It's about knowing you're enough, even when you stumble. It's about having the courage to keep going, to keep learning, to keep dreaming. And it's about surrounding yourself with people who believe in you, even when you can't believe in yourself.'

The audience was utterly silent, hanging on her every word. 'To anyone out there doubting themselves,' Clemmie continued, her eyes shining with unshed tears, 'don't give up. Find your passion, work hard and don't be afraid to lean on those who love you. Because one day, you might surprise yourself. I know I did.'

A tear rolled down her cheek as the crowd erupted into applause once more, louder than ever. Clemmie stepped back from the microphone, holding the Golden Whisk Trophy high, her heart brimming with gratitude. In that moment, she felt her granny's love and lessons resonating within her. This was not just a victory, it was a testament to perseverance, passion and the power of believing in herself.

Chapter Fourteen

The royal crest gleamed magnificently against the opulent navy and gold backdrop of the photo room, the regal setting perfectly befitting the moment. Clemmie stood at the centre, the Golden Whisk Trophy clutched in her hands. Sir Gregory Whitcomb, Margot Hastings and Dominic Hargrove flanked her, their faces lit with pride and satisfaction as they celebrated her remarkable win. Oliver stood nearby, smiling, looking just as mesmerised by Clemmie as everyone else.

The photographer directed them to adjust their poses. 'Let's have one with the judges and the winner,' he called, positioning them with expert precision.

After the photograph, Dominic opened a bottle of champagne with a celebratory *pop!* and poured generous glasses for everyone. 'No royal occasion is complete without a toast,' he declared. Sir Gregory raised his flute and said, 'Here's to Clemmie's triumph and a torte truly worthy of the palace!' Clemmie laughed, happiness blooming in her chest as they toasted her win.

Margot joined in, raising her glass of champagne. 'To Clemmie Rose, whose torte is fit for royalty!' she declared, and the room echoed with cheers.

Each judge offered a few words of praise, and then it was Oliver's turn to step into the frame with Clemmie. 'Let's have the host and the champion together,' the photographer prompted, motioning to them to stand closer. Oliver moved to Clemmie's side, his hand brushing lightly against her waist in an easy, familiar gesture. The unexpected contact made her suddenly aware of the nearness of him, the quiet strength in his stance, the faint trace of his cologne, the way he fitted into her space. She hesitated for half a breath before tilting her head slightly towards him, her cheeks flushing just as the camera clicked.

As the photographer declared, 'Perfect! That's the shot,' Clemmie stepped back, trying to compose herself. Her gaze flicked to Oliver, who offered her an encouraging smile that seemed to hold more than just admiration for her baking skills. Before she could over-analyse the moment, the judges beckoned her back to their side.

Amid the laughter and camaraderie, slices of Clemmie's torte were brought in, presented on fine china. The judges each took a plate then a bite, their delighted expressions reaffirming her success. 'This is even better than I remembered,' Margot said with a satisfied sigh. 'You've truly outdone yourself, Clemmie.'

'Thank you, it all feels so...' Clemmie hesitated when she caught a movement near the door. Fiona and Oliver were deep in conversation. Fiona had that unmistakable sore loser vibe – like she was trying a little too hard to act unbothered.

Clemmie watched from the corner of her eye. What happened next sent a jolt of unease through Clemmie. Fiona's gestures were sharp, while Oliver's usually relaxed demeanour was replaced with one of visible tension. Clemmie noticed his body bristle, and for a fleeting moment, his gaze flicked back towards her, his expression stricken.

Clemmie's stomach twisted as she watched the exchange unfold. Fiona took a step forward, her posture suggesting she was about to head in Clemmie's direction, but Oliver placed a firm hand on her arm and steered her out of sight. Clemmie caught a fragment of their heated conversation as they left: something about 'I'm going to tell her the truth'.

Moments later, Oliver returned without Fiona.

'Is everything okay?' asked Clemmie 'What was that all about?' she asked, trying to keep her tone light.

'Disappointment she didn't win. Let's just leave it at that.'

But she couldn't shake the feeling that there was more to the heated conversation between them. Oliver's earlier expression of anguish flashed through her mind and she wondered what he wasn't telling her. Before she could press further, Oliver gestured towards the door. 'Shall we? There's a crowd on the beach waiting for their champion.'

Clemmie smiled, the thought of the waiting residents of Puffin Island momentarily pushing her concerns aside. As they stepped outside the Royal Yacht and descended the gangway together, the sound of the crowd hit her like a wave. Cheering, clapping and jubilant shouts filled the air as the islanders celebrated her victory. Clemmie felt a swell of pride and gratitude as she walked hand in hand with Oliver, the Golden Whisk Trophy gleaming in the sunlight. For a moment, she truly felt like royalty.

Dilly was the first to reach her, throwing her arms around Clemmie in a fierce hug. 'You did it!' she squealed, with excitement. Amelia wasn't far behind, pressing a paper crown onto Clemmie's head. 'Every champion needs a coronation,' she teased.

Betty was next, throwing her arms around her granddaughter, the happy tears free-falling down her face as she whispered, 'I love you.'

'I love you too, Granny.' The entire island had turned the moment into a party, and Clemmie found herself swept up in the handshakes and pats on the back. A glass of fizz was pressed into her hand.

Sam appeared beside her, grinning. 'This is something Puffin Island will never forget. You were brilliant!'

Max appeared with the twins. 'Clemmie, congratulations!'

For a few minutes Clemmie mingled with the crowd and hugged her friends, who each took the opportunity to hold the trophy. Then Betty appeared at her side. 'I've organised a little party at the café,' she said, her voice quivering with excitement. 'Just a small gathering to celebrate your win. And, of course, you're invited too, Oliver.'

Clemmie turned to gauge Oliver's reaction. He hesitated, his eyes darting back towards the yacht, and Clemmie wondered if he was considering Fiona before he answered. For a moment, it seemed as though he might decline, but then he turned back to Betty with a wide smile. 'How could I say no? That would be lovely, count me in. I'll catch you up.'

Betty clapped her hands together, delighted. 'Wonderful!' As they walked through the crowd towards the café, Clemmie glanced back at Oliver as he headed back to the yacht. She knew he would have some loose ends to tie up with the film crew, but she couldn't help wondering what was going on between him and Fiona. His usual laid-back vibe felt a little off. Something had rattled him and as much as Clemmie wanted to enjoy her win, she couldn't shake the feeling that whatever was happening wasn't finished yet – and it probably had something to do with her.

By the time they reached the café, Clemmie felt the weight of the win hit her, not in a tired way, but in a way that was pure joy. The people she cared about had stood there on the beach, watching her, cheering her on, willing her to win and she had.

Chapter Fifteen

The café was unrecognisable when Clemmie walked through the door. She gave a tiny gasp as she took in the dazzling display that Betty had somehow conjured up in a matter of hours. Strings of bunting crisscrossed the ceiling, gold and silver balloons bobbed gently above each table, and on the back wall a massive banner proclaimed in bold, glittery letters: **WINNER!** But what truly sent Clemmie into a fit of laughter was the life-sized cardboard cutout of the Queen, her gloved hand raised in a cheerful wave.

'Of course, we had to invite Her Majesty,' Betty said with a mischievous grin, giving Clemmie a sly wink.

Clemmie clutched her chest, laughing. 'Granny, you've really outdone yourself.'

The room was filled with familiar faces: Verity and Sam, Dilly, Max and the twins, Amelia and her partner Jack, and Betty's best friend Pete were all there, each holding a glass of champagne and beaming with pride.

'Well done, Clemmie!' Verity cheered, raising her glass. 'We always knew you'd win.'

'You were brilliant,' Amelia added. 'I've never been prouder to say I'm friends with a celebrity baker and soon your cookbook will be gracing the shelves of my book shop!'

Pete nudged Dilly, a sly grin on his face. 'Don't forget us when you're rubbing elbows with royalty.'

The room erupted into laughter, and Clemmie felt happiness spreading through her chest. She turned to Pete, who had a peculiar twinkle in his eye.

'You know,' he began, 'I've been looking after the puffins on this island for my lifetime and never have I come across one quite as ... *sociable* as the one that crashed the competition. I'm half tempted to name him Sir Buttercream.'

The suggestion drew a chorus of laughter.

'Sir Buttercream it is,' Clemmie said, shaking her head in amusement. 'I think he's earned the title.'

The buffet Betty had laid out was nothing short of extravagant. There were finger sandwiches, freshly baked scones, delicate pastries and a towering cake adorned with edible flowers. Champagne flowed freely as everyone toasted Clemmie's victory.

'When and how did you do all this?' Clemmie asked Betty, overwhelmed by the effort that had gone into the celebration.

'Sam helped me,' Betty replied, her eyes sparkling with mischief. 'I couldn't have done it alone as I wasn't going to miss a second of watching you compete.'

'But what if I hadn't won?' she asked playfully, a small knot of uncertainty tugging at her heart.

'Oh, please,' Betty scoffed, waving a hand dismissively. 'There was never a chance of that. You have more talent than all those other bakers combined.'

Clemmie felt a lump form in her throat as her granny's words wrapped around her like a blanket. 'Thank you, Granny. For everything,' she said softly, her voice faltering.

The champagne continued to flow, glasses clinked and the hum of conversation filled the air. Laughter spilled out in bursts from various groups, enveloping Clemmie in a cocoon of happiness.

Soon after, Oliver arrived and, before he could even take in the surroundings, Betty swooped in, wrapping him in a tight hug and pressing a glass of champagne into his hand.

'You're here!' Betty exclaimed, giving him a quick kiss on the cheek before he had a chance to catch his breath. Realising what she had done, she quickly uttered an apology. 'Sorry! It's the champagne. It's gone to my head!'

Everyone around them laughed.

Clemmie smiled as Oliver mingled with her friends, his easy charm making him a favourite among the guests. Despite being swept into conversations and laughter, the two of them kept finding moments to exchange lingering glances. Clemmie felt a flutter in her chest every time their eyes met across the room. Even though he would be heading back to London tonight there was still one last adventure to have together: the royal garden party that was now just a few days away.

All of sudden, she became aware of Oliver standing quietly by the doorway, his glass of champagne untouched.

Their eyes met across the room, and he gave her a subtle nod, a silent invitation to join him.

They slipped into the garden at the front of the café, which was bathed in the soft glow of fairy lights strung up between the trees. The air was cool but pleasant, the distant sound of waves providing a soothing backdrop. Clemmie and Oliver settled into two chairs side by side, letting the sounds of the celebration fade into the background. For a moment, neither of them spoke, content to sit in comfortable silence.

'I'm leaving soon. It's a long drive back to London,' Oliver finally said.

Clemmie's mood slumped a little. It was expected but it didn't make it easier. She didn't want him to go. 'So soon?'

Oliver nodded, looking down at his hands. 'I don't want to go,' he admitted. 'But we still have the royal garden party.' He reached and took hold of her hand and stood up. 'I guess this is it, for now.'

Clemmie nodded, her heart already aching in a way she hadn't anticipated. 'For now,' she replied, trying to muster a smile.

Oliver leaned in, his forehead resting against hers. 'Enjoy the rest of your party, and, just for the record, you are incredible. Don't ever doubt that.'

'I won't.'

He tilted her chin up towards his face and kissed her, a kiss that was soft and tender, but full of unspoken promises. Clemmie melted into him, her hand resting lightly on his chest as her heart beat fast. The kiss ended too soon, but the feeling lingered.

As Oliver pulled back, he smiled. 'See you very soon,' he

said, squeezing her hand one last time before releasing it and walking towards his car, which was parked a little further down the lane.

'You do know you can't park there!' she said, lightening the mood.

He looked back, giving her the most heart-melting smile, before he got into the car and started it up. She watched as he pulled away, the cheers and laughter from inside the café reaching her ears and reminding her that the night wasn't over. But as she turned to rejoin her friends, all she could think about was seeing Oliver again.

Back inside, the celebration continued, but Clemmie couldn't shake the feeling that a piece of her heart had just driven away. Betty bustled over and wrapped her in a loving hug. 'You all right?' she asked, her sharp eyes studying Clemmie's face. 'This is your night.'

'Of course! It's not every day you win a Royal Baking Competition. I need more champagne!' By the time the glass was poured, Sam and Pete had brought out their guitars and started to sing. Amelia and Dilly had their arms around the life-sized cutout of the Queen, and Verity was standing next to Clemmie.

'I saw you outside with Oliver. You okay?'

Clemmie forced a smile and nodded. 'I will be,' she replied. 'Right person, wrong time … again.'

Verity touched her arm. 'If it's meant to be it won't pass you by.'

'I hope you're right.' Whatever was happening between her and Oliver, she wasn't ready to let it go, not yet.

Chapter Sixteen

The next morning, Clemmie woke up with a pounding headache and a dry mouth that felt like she'd been sampling meringue dust all night. She groaned, rolling over in bed. The sunlight was sneaking through the curtains, sharper than it had any right to be. She had the hangover from hell and it wasn't going to go away anytime soon. Thankfully, a comforting sight greeted her on the bedside table: a steaming cup of tea, a packet of headache tablets and a neatly folded copy of the *Puffin Island Gazette*. Beside them, in Granny's neat handwriting, was a note.

Drink this, take these and look at that headline! You deserve a lie-in, so don't even think about coming downstairs. The café is under control!

Last night had been a whirlwind, celebrating her win, toasting with friends and dancing around the café until the early hours. They hadn't crawled into bed until nearly three a.m. She reached for the tea and swallowed the tablets. Picking up the newspaper, she noticed the front-page headline in bold letters:

Clemmie Rose Takes the Crown at the Royal Puffin Island Bake-Off

In a stunning display of culinary mastery, Clemmie Rose has risen to fame, securing victory at the highly anticipated annual Royal Baking Competition, held aboard the Royal Yacht docked in Puffin Island.

Clemmie's winning creation, a decadent chocolate and clementine torte recipe passed down from her great-great-grandmother Beatrice, captured the hearts of both the judges and the audience. The torte, a family recipe dating back to 1917, was hailed as a perfect balance of rich chocolate and refreshing citrus, an elegant treat worthy of royalty. The judges were quick to praise the delicate sponge and velvety texture, with Margot Hastings declaring that Clemmie's sponge was the best she'd ever tasted, the ganache 'smooth as silk', and the citrus bringing 'a brightness that made the whole thing sing. It's the kind of dessert that could grace the table at any royal gathering.'

As Clemmie's victory was announced, the emotion of the moment hit her hard. The sweet taste of success was made even more poignant by the memory of a scathing review that nearly ended her career before it even began. She bravely shared her story in her winner's speech, recalling how the harsh words of an early critic nearly shattered her confidence. 'It's about knowing you're enough, even when you stumble. It's about having the courage to keep going, to keep learning, to keep dreaming. And it's about surrounding yourself with people who believe in you,

*even when you can't believe in yourself,' she said, inspiring
everyone in the room.*

*In the end, Clemmie walked away with the coveted Golden
Whisk Trophy, a recipe fit for royalty, and the honour of a royal
garden party invitation. The moment was made even more
special as Clemmie and her beloved grandmother, Betty (pictured
far right), proudly held the trophy together, smiles wide with joy
and pride.*

As Clemmie flipped through the newspaper and drank
her tea, her heart swelled with pride. This was just
the beginning for her. A cookbook deal was already in the
works, and her dream of becoming a household name in
the culinary world was now one step closer to reality. The
island was buzzing with excitement, but Clemmie knew
one thing for sure: she had baked her way into the hearts of
the world.

Folding up the newspaper Clemmie snuggled back
under the duvet.

Two minutes later, Betty's voice cut through the quiet of
the morning. 'Clemmie!' she shouted, her tone a mixture
of urgency and bubbling excitement. 'Clemmie, you need to
get up!'

Clemmie groaned, still half-buried under her quilt. She
had planned a slow, easy morning after the celebrations of
the night before, but it seemed now Betty had other ideas.
'You said I could have a lie-in!' she shouted, pulling the
duvet over her head.

Her granny's hurried footsteps were soon pounding up
the stairs though, and moments later there was a brisk
knock at her bedroom door. Before Clemmie could respond,

Betty burst in, her face flushed with excitement and a letter clutched in her hand.

'Granny! What's going on?' Clemmie asked, sitting up groggily.

'I'm not sure but I think it's something incredible!' Betty declared breathlessly, waving the letter like it was a winning lottery ticket. 'This is for you!'

Clemmie blinked as Betty thrust the envelope towards her. It was thick, cream-coloured and embossed with gold detailing. Her name was written in elegant, swirling calligraphy on the front:

Miss Clemmie Rose, The Café on the Coast, Puffin Island.

'What is it?' Clemmie asked, her heart starting to race.

'Open it and see!' Betty said, barely able to contain herself. She moved to the window, pulling back the curtains, 'I think it's got something to do with the gleaming black Bentley parked outside.'

Clemmie gasped. 'What?'

'There's a chauffeur!' Betty said, spinning back towards her. 'You need to hurry. No cars can park on the lane for long.'

Clemmie's fingers trembled as she tore open the envelope. Inside, there was a card, and a handwritten note from none other than Oliver. She read aloud:

Dear Clemmie,

I hope you've had a moment to catch your breath after all

*the excitement. I've barely stopped thinking about your torte
or the chaos of that puffin … but mostly about you.*

*This is a personal invitation just for you. I'd love for you
to come to London for a couple of days ahead of the royal
garden party and spend some time with me. A bit of
shopping, champagne and seeing the city sounds like just the
ticket, don't you think? I've arranged for a car to collect you
and take you straight to the Royalwood Cottage, where you'll
be staying as my guest.*

So, pack your bags. London is calling, please say yes!

Oliver x

Clemmie's jaw dropped. 'Royalwood Cottage? I can't
believe this!'

Betty clapped her hands together, practically vibrating
with excitement. 'Oh, Clemmie, this is the opportunity of a
lifetime! You can't say no.'

Clemmie hesitated, the excitement warring with anxiety.
'But … I can't just drop everything and go! What about the
café? I don't even have a dress for the garden party. I can't
show up looking like I just rolled off Puffin Island!'

'You'll get a dress in London,' Betty said firmly. 'You've
got time! There's no better place to shop than the city. As for
the café, don't you worry about that. I can manage.'

Clemmie bit her lip. 'But it's been so busy lately.
What if—'

'No buts!' Betty interrupted, planting her hands on her
hips. 'Clemmie Rose, you've worked so hard for this. You
deserve to go, and I won't let you miss out on this chance
because you're worried about me. I've got Amelia and Pete

to help, and no doubt Dilly will be around if I need her. We'll be fine.'

Clemmie looked at her grandmother, who was practically glowing with pride and determination. She felt a lump form in her throat.

Betty crossed the room to sit beside her. She took Clemmie's hands in hers. 'Listen to me. You've always dreamed of something like this. I remember you as a little girl, twirling around in that wedding dress and pretending you were having tea with the Queen at the palace. Well, now's your chance to not only attend the royal garden party but also stay at Royalwood Cottage.'

Clemmie looked up, her eyes sparkling. 'Okay! I'll go!' she squealed. 'I can't believe this is happening!' she cried, throwing her arms around Betty. 'Thank you, thank you, thank you!'

Betty laughed, hugging her tightly. 'You don't have time to waste. Jump in the shower, pack a bag and get moving! London's waiting for you.'

Clemmie pulled back, her excitement bubbling over. 'Okay, okay! I'm going!' She darted into the bathroom, her heart racing with a mix of nerves and joy.

Clemmie stepped out of the shower feeling refreshed, the excitement of the morning setting her heart racing. She wrapped herself in a towel, her mind whirling as she began chaotically tossing items into her suitcase. Dresses, shoes and her favourite floral scarf tumbled in as she debated what she might need for a few days in London. After finally zipping the bulging suitcase shut, she grabbed her handbag, glanced at herself in the mirror and gave her reflection a grin.

She bounded downstairs, suitcase in hand, her cheeks flushed with excitement. The scent of freshly baked scones wafted through the air as she entered the café to find Amelia and Betty laughing over a pot of tea. Betty looked up and beamed at Clemmie.

'Well, don't you look like a woman ready to take on the world,' Betty said proudly.

'Ready as I'll ever be, but I've got to send an email before I go. I need to send the torte recipe to the royal household, so it can be served at the garden party!'

Five minutes later, the email was sent and Clemmie was standing next to her suitcase. She held out her hand to show it was visibly shaking. 'I'm so nervous!'

Amelia grinned. 'Royalwood Cottage with Oliver. I mean, Clemmie, this is next-level exciting. You have to tell us everything when you get back. Every detail. Every moment and in the meantime, send photos if it's allowed.'

Clemmie laughed, trying to play it cool, though the thought of spending time alone with Oliver in a historic royal setting made her stomach do tiny somersaults. 'I'm not sure there'll be much to tell. It's just a couple of days, shopping, champagne, maybe a little sightseeing … then a royal garden party!'

Amelia nodded towards the life-sized cutout of the Queen, which was still stationed proudly in the corner of the café. 'I think you should put Queenie in the car and take her along for the ride. She deserves a little holiday too.'

They all turned to look at the cutout, her cardboard gaze as regal and impassive as ever, and burst out laughing.

'She's going nowhere!' Betty declared firmly. 'She's staying right here with me. Someone has to keep this place in line while you're gallivanting off to London.'

Clemmie felt a swell of gratitude for the love and support of the people around her. She hugged Betty tightly, then Amelia, before turning towards the door, ready to embrace whatever awaited her in London.

She stepped out onto Lighthouse Lane and glanced at the Bentley, its sleek black body gleaming like a jewel in the light. The chauffeur, a smartly dressed man with a polite smile, stepped forward as Clemmie approached. With practised ease, he reached for her suitcase, lifting it as if it weighed nothing at all. 'Miss Rose,' he said with a nod, his tone courteous and friendly. 'Allow me.'

'Thank you,' Clemmie replied. She turned to glance back at the café, where Betty and Amelia were standing side by side in the doorway, grinning from ear to ear.

'You look like a film star,' Amelia called out, cupping her hands around her mouth. 'Don't forget us little people when you're sipping champagne with royalty!'

Betty, wiped a tear from her cheek and waved her tea towel in the air. 'Don't forget to call when you get there!'

The chauffeur opened the rear door and Clemmie slid into the plush leather seat, sinking into its comfort. The interior smelled faintly of fresh flowers and new car, and the polished wood trim gleamed in the sunlight streaming through the window. As the chauffeur closed the door behind her with a quiet click, Clemmie took one last look at her granny and Amelia, who were now waving enthusiastically. She gave them a final wave through the window as the Bentley began to glide forward, its engine purring softly. The car moved smoothly down Lighthouse Lane, heading towards the causeway that connected Puffin Island to the mainland, and as it picked up speed, Clemmie leaned back in her seat and smiled. This was something extraordinary.

Chapter Seventeen

Clemmie's excitement bubbled over as the Bentley hummed smoothly through the countryside, bringing her closer to London with every passing mile. Soon they were driving up a secluded road lined with ancient trees whose canopies provided dappled shade. With the window open, the fresh air filtered into the car, offering a lovely breeze.

'Are we nearly there?' she finally asked the chauffeur, unable to contain her curiosity.

'We're almost there.'

The car slowed down and turned onto a long, winding driveway flanked by iron gates, each adorned with an intricate crest that Clemmie recognised as the royal insignia. With an almost regal grace, the gates swung open as though by magic, and the Bentley glided forward. Clemmie's heart quickened as they passed into the estate, nestled in the midst of a sprawling expanse of countryside in all its untamed glory. Rolling hills and lush green meadows stretched out before her. The estate was a breathtaking blend of natural beauty and regal elegance.

She caught sight of deer grazing serenely beneath a canopy of ancient oaks, and rabbits darted playfully between bushes, their fluffy white tails flickering like tiny lanterns in the undergrowth.

As the Bentley ascended a gentle hill, Clemmie caught her first glimpse of Royalwood Cottage. Her eyes widened. It was like something out of a storybook. The lodge was an old stone manor, its exterior weathered but timelessly elegant. Ivy climbed its walls in graceful tendrils, and the windows, framed by charming wooden shutters, glowed softly in the waning light. The roof was steep and gabled, with clusters of chimneys poking out like the turrets of a miniature castle. Surrounding the lodge was a perfectly manicured garden bursting with roses, lavender and peonies.

'Oh my goodness,' Clemmie murmured. She could hardly believe her eyes. The lodge radiated history and charm.

The Bentley came to a halt in front of a grand stone archway adorned with ivy and flowers. Clemmie stepped out, the gravel crunching under her feet as she looked up in awe at the ornate wooden door. It was framed by carved stone, its design intricate and regal, with a brass knocker shaped like a lion's head. Her suitcase was gently placed beside her, but she barely noticed, her eyes too busy drinking in the scenery.

'Welcome to Royalwood Cottage, Miss Rose,' the chauffeur said with a slight bow. 'I hope you enjoy your stay.'

Clemmie thanked the chauffeur as she clutched the handle of her suitcase, her fingers trembling slightly as the grand wooden door creaked open. Her heart skipped a beat when she saw who was standing in the doorway.

Oliver.

He looked as handsome as ever, dressed in attire that struck the perfect balance between casual elegance and countryside charm: a tailored tweed jacket with leather elbow patches, a crisp white shirt unbuttoned at the collar, and dark trousers that fit him with the kind of ease that suggested they were made just for him. His boots, polished yet practical, hinted at a man accustomed to striding across grand estates and cobblestone paths alike.

'Welcome to Royalwood Cottage.' He moved towards her and kissed her on both cheeks.

The brief contact sent a jolt through her body.

'You live here?' she asked with awe.

'I wish! No, we're just guests for the next couple of days.'

'For a moment I thought you were going to tell me you were a secret undercover royal.'

He laughed as he picked up her suitcase.

'It's beautiful, like something out of a film.'

'Let's get you inside so I can show your around. My guess is you're probably hungry, and thirsty, too.'

Clemmie nodded and followed him through the front door.

Inside, the cottage was even more breathtaking. The entrance hall was spacious, with polished wooden floors and a grand wooden staircase. A crystal chandelier hung from the ceiling.

The decor was a perfect blend of opulence and homeliness. Plush armchairs upholstered in rich velvets and tapestries were arranged around a fireplace, and shelves lined with antique books hinted at hours of cosy reading. Fresh flowers beautified every available surface, their fragrance mingling with the faint, comforting scent that was seeping through the open window from the surrounding garden.

'Let me show you your room.' Oliver gestured for Clemmie to follow him. She nodded, trailing behind him as they ascended a grand staircase with a polished wooden banister. The corridor at the top was lined with oil paintings of pastoral landscapes, wildlife and foxhunts, each frame gilded and ornate. The soft glow of antique wall sconces lit the hallway, casting a golden tinge over the patterned carpet beneath their feet.

When they reached her room and Oliver pushed open the door, the first thing Clemmie spotted was the four-poster bed that dominated the space, its mahogany frame intricately carved and draped with cream linen trimmed with delicate lace. A velvet quilt in a deep emerald green was folded neatly at the foot of the bed, adding a touch of homely charm. The wallpaper was a soft blush pink with dainty floral patterns, giving the space a nostalgic feel, and heavy velvet curtains framed the tall windows, which offered a breathtaking view of the gardens below.

On the dresser, a crystal vase held freshly cut roses, and Clemmie inhaled their soft fragrance. Next to it, a tray gleamed with delicate macarons in pastel shades, and a bottle of champagne chilling in a silver ice bucket beside two crystal flutes. A delicate china teapot sat nearby, accompanied by a printed card that read, *Welcome to Royalwood Cottage. We hope you enjoy your stay.*

Clemmie crossed the room towards the window. She pushed it open, letting in the afternoon air. Outside, the gardens sprawled as if in a painting, with perfectly manicured hedges, bursts of vibrant foxgloves and a small stone fountain gurgling softly in the centre.

'Wow,' she exclaimed. 'I've never stayed anywhere like this.'

'You have a bathroom through there,' Oliver said, pointing to a door off to the side. 'Clean towels, and all the essentials. I'll wait for you in the sitting room. Take your time, settle in.'

Clemmie turned to him, her cheeks slightly flushed. 'Thank you,' she replied, completely in awe of the space.

Oliver's smile lingered before he closed the door gently behind him.

Clemmie stood in the quiet room, taking it all in. After a moment, she crossed to the bathroom and gasped. It was like something out of an old-world cottage, reminiscent of spaces she'd swooned over on Instagram. The freestanding clawfoot tub sat proudly in the centre of the room, with a gilded mirror hanging above a vintage-style sink. The walls were painted in a soft sage green, with exposed beams overhead that gave it a rustic charm. An old-fashioned perfume pump and a collection of glass jars filled with bath salts and soaps were arranged neatly on a wooden shelf. The tiled floor, with its intricate blue-and-white pattern, added a touch of whimsy to the space.

She couldn't wait to share the moment with Betty. Pulling out her phone, she quickly opened FaceTime and called her granny. Betty's face appeared on the screen almost instantly, her cheeks flushed with excitement.

'Clemmie! There you are! How's it going? What's it like?' Betty asked, her voice bubbling with curiosity.

Clemmie spun the phone around, giving her a virtual tour of the bedroom. 'Look at this, Granny! The bed, the roses, the view… and wait until you see the bathroom.'

She walked into the bathroom, holding her phone steady as she panned the camera around. 'Look at the tub! And the tiles! Oh, and this,' she said, focusing on the dressing table with its silver hairbrushes and mirror.

Betty clapped her hands, her eyes sparkling. 'Oh my goodness, it's beautiful! I can't believe it. You deserve every bit of this!'

'Thank you.'

After hanging up, Clemmie sank onto the plush four-poster bed, which was a masterpiece of comfort, with soft linens that felt like she was sinking into the clouds and a thick quilt she couldn't resist wrapping herself in. She flopped back with a happy sigh, thankful that her hangover had almost disappeared in the excitement. She waggled her feet in the air like a carefree child and giggled at herself, feeling giddy with the sheer luxury of it all. This was a far cry from her cosy yet modest room above the café back home!

She swung her legs over the side of the bed and walked to the window a second time, inhaling the fresh air. A sudden melodic chirping drew her attention to a branch of the tree outside the window, where a robin was delicately perched. Its bright red breast and inquisitive black eyes made her heart skip a beat. It hopped onto the windowsill and looked straight at her. Clemmie froze for a moment, mesmerised by the little bird. A wave of emotion washed over her as she thought of her family. Despite hailing from Puffin Island, each and every one of them had always harboured a soft spot for robins.

'Hello, you little charmer,' she whispered softly, smiling. 'Granny always said you were the messenger of good tidings.'

The robin tilted its head, as if it understood her words. It chirped again, a series of bright, cheerful notes that sounded almost like a conversation. For a few minutes, she watched the robin, feeling a sense of calm and connection that was almost otherworldly. Then, with a final trill, the robin fluttered away, disappearing into the trees.

Clemmie was still smiling as she made her way over to her suitcase, ready to unpack her things and put them in the wardrobe, which was impossible to miss – tall, elegant and covered in intricate carvings.

She opened the door and began hanging up her clothes. Dresses, blouses and skirts found their places among the sturdy hangers, and she carefully arranged her shoes on the bottom shelf.

Just as she was about to close the wardrobe doors, something caught her eye. There, etched into the inner edge of the wooden frame, was a number.

1705

Clemmie froze, her hand still on the door. She leaned in, her brow furrowing as she took a closer look. Her heart kicked up a notch. The numbers were carved neatly, their edges smoothed by time, but they stood out against the dark wood.

'1705,' she murmured, tilting her head as if a different angle might suddenly make sense of it. The number in the recipe book. The number embroidered on her great-great-granny's apron.

Was it just a coincidence? Maybe the year the wardrobe was made? Or was there more to it? It couldn't actually mean anything … could it?

The sound of Oliver shouting up the stairs startled her.

'There's tea and sandwiches when you're ready.'

'Coming!' she shouted back.

She glanced back at the wardrobe one last time before closing the door, the mystery of 1705 lingering in her mind.

She hurried down the stairs to find Oliver was waiting in the living room, and he'd really outdone himself this time. The table was set for a proper afternoon tea, complete with a crisp white cloth and an impressive spread. Tiered trays overflowed with dainty finger sandwiches, golden scones and pastries so pretty they looked almost too good to eat. A silver teapot sat in the middle, and a collection of mismatched china cups added a charming touch.

'Wow,' Clemmie said, her eyes wide with delight. 'This looks incredible! I was suffering from a hangover this morning but now I'm starving.'

He smiled, his boyish charm making her heart skip a beat. 'Only the best for my honoured guest,' he said with a playful bow.

'You've set the bar pretty high, you know. I can't believe I'm sat in Royalwood Cottage. I watched a documentary about this place once.'

'Well, I figured if we got to stay here, we might as well

do it properly,' he replied, pulling out a chair for her. 'Now, my queen, would you care for tea?'

She giggled as she took her seat. 'Why, thank you, your majesty.'

For a while, they devoured the delicious food. Clemmie marvelled at how light and buttery the scones were, and how the strawberry jam tasted like it had just been made that morning. They swapped stories and jokes, the easy banter making her feel very much at home.

'May I present to you, Queen Clementine of Tea-topia,' Oliver said with an exaggerated bow.

Clemmie laughed. 'Oh, stop it! If I'm the queen, then you're the king, King Oliver of Sandwich-land.'

He gave a mock-serious nod. 'Indeed and as your loyal subject, I demand you try the lemon tart. It's fit for royalty.'

As Clemmie took a bite, letting the tangy-sweet flavours melt on her tongue, her gaze wandered to the big bay window. Outside, the lodge's gardens rolled out in a sea of green. The peaceful scene was broken only by the sound of a steady thud of hooves. Two riders trotted across the lawn, their horses moving gracefully, coats gleaming in the sunlight. 'Look how shiny they are.'

Oliver followed her gaze and smiled. 'That's one of the things I love about this place. You never know what or who you might see.'

'What do you mean…? Who was that?'

'The Queen loves her horses and is often seen riding around the estate.'

Clemmie looked back towards the window. 'Granny wouldn't believe me if I told her I've just seen the Queen riding her horse.'

'It happens quite often.'

'Is this place used often? Who else has stayed here that you know?' Clemmie tilted her head curiously. 'These walls feel like they have so many stories to tell.'

Oliver leaned back in his chair, a thoughtful expression crossing his face. 'Royalwood Cottage has always been a place of discretion. Officially, it's been used as a retreat for royal friends or visiting dignitaries. But unofficially...' He paused, his grin turning mischievous. 'Let's just say it's a place for people who couldn't exactly stroll into Eldenbridge Palace without raising eyebrows.'

Clemmie's eyes widened. 'You mean ... secret rendezvous?'

He nodded. 'Something like that. Over the years, it's hosted everyone from artists and writers to ... let's say, more adventurous acquaintances of the royals. The walls here could certainly tell some fascinating stories, but they've always been sworn to secrecy.'

The intrigue sent a shiver of excitement through her. 'Now I'm here,' she said with a whisper, leaning in. 'What's my story going to be?'

Oliver raised his teacup in a toast. 'Whatever it is, I'm sure it'll be unforgettable.'

They clinked their cups together, and Clemmie felt a warmth that wasn't just from the tea.

As the conversation turned to lighter topics, Clemmie questioned Oliver about the number she had seen earlier. 'Does the number 1705 mean anything to you?'

Oliver frowned slightly. '1705? Not off the top of my head. Why?'

She explained how she had noticed the number engraved inside the wardrobe upstairs and how she'd also found it in Beatrice's recipe book and on her lucky apron. 'It's probably nothing,' she said, shrugging. 'But it caught my eye.'

Oliver laughed, 'The furniture here is old, really old. That could just be the year it was made. But if you find a secret passage or a treasure map, do let me know.'

Clemmie grinned. 'You'll be the first to know.'

The sound of hooves on the gravel path could be heard again and Oliver glanced out the window, a knowing smile spreading across his face. 'Speaking of horses, I have a surprise for you.'

Clemmie raised an eyebrow. 'A surprise?'

'I've booked us in for a horseback ride this afternoon,' he announced casually, as though it were the most ordinary thing in the world.

Her jaw dropped. 'A horseback ride? Oliver, the last time I was on anything remotely resembling a horse, it was a donkey on the beach when I was seven and it didn't end well.'

He leaned forward, clearly intrigued. 'Tell me more.'

'The donkey refused to walk along the sand like it was supposed to. Instead, it marched straight into the sea, lay down, and I ended up falling face-first into the water. My granny had to fish me out while the donkey just sat there looking smug.'

Oliver burst into laughter. 'I promise you this won't be anything like that. These horses are well trained, and you'll have me beside you, every canter and stride.'

'Do *not* let my horse canter.'

He held up his hands in surrender. 'Deal. But I guarantee you'll have fun.'

As she finished her tea, Clemmie was suddenly feeling a little nervous. She liked the thought of a romantic horse ride through the countryside together, and only hoped it would be as magical as it sounded, rather than an awkward disaster involving runaway horses, tangled reins or an ungraceful dismount into a muddy puddle.

Chapter Eighteen

Ten minutes later, Clemmie stood in the hallway of the cottage staring at Oliver in disbelief. He was dressed like he'd stepped straight out of an equestrian catalogue, in a tailored riding jacket, spotless white breeches, polished leather boots and a helmet that looked as if it had never seen a speck of dirt.

'You're kidding, right?' she said, gesturing to his outfit. 'Is there a horse-riding fashion show at the end of this I don't know about? And when did you get all the gear?'

Oliver smirked, smoothing the front of his jacket. 'I've ridden my whole life. It's something my grandmother taught me to do. Actually, she used to keep her horse at the stables on this very estate.'

'How do I not know this about you?'

He grinned. 'What did you bring to wear? Because I'm assuming you're not expecting to ride in that?'

Clemmie took off her wide-brimmed hat and gestured to her floral dress. 'I brought this. And about five other versions of it. I didn't exactly pack for a gallop through the countryside. I actually thought…' She paused. 'Well, I hoped that you were joking and there would be a carriage to sit in.'

He rubbed his chin, pretending to think. 'Wearing that, you could ride side-saddle like a Victorian duchess…'

Clemmie shot him a playful death glare but he wasn't done. 'Alas, there is no carriage. We're riding.'

'Really?' she asked, her voice rising an octave in disbelief.

'Really!' Oliver repeated, his lips twitching into a grin.

'Like I said, my suitcase is full of dresses, sandals and about three cardigans.'

He tilted his head, giving her a once-over. 'What about trousers? Any type at all?'

Clemmie scrunched up her face. 'Only my pyjama bottoms.'

'Perfect. They'll have to do.'

Her jaw dropped. 'You can't be serious.'

'Completely serious,' he said, turning her towards the stairs and gently pushing her back up. 'Now go, and for the love of all things royal, make sure they're decent.'

Ten minutes later, Clemmie descended the stairs in a pair of bright pink pyjama bottoms covered in cartoonish red love hearts. She'd paired them with a mismatched yellow hoodie she'd brought for comfort, and her shoes. She knew her face was the picture of resigned amusement as she reached the landing.

Oliver took one look at her and widened his eyes. 'You look ready to conquer the world. Let's pray we don't bump into the Queen.'

Clemmie snorted, waving a hand at him dismissively. 'Don't worry. If I do, I'll tell her you insisted I go out in public like this. That way none of this can be blamed on me.'

At the stables, the scene was nothing short of a comedy waiting to happen. The moment Clemmie laid eyes on her designated horse, a towering steed named Shadow, she froze. The animal was jet black with a glossy coat, standing at least sixteen hands high, and its deep brown eyes seemed to size her up immediately.

'You've got to be joking,' she muttered.

Oliver patted Shadow's neck affectionately. 'He's a gentle giant. Aren't you, boy?'

The horse snorted loudly, making Clemmie jump back. 'Gentle? He looks like he eats people for breakfast.'

It didn't go unnoticed by either of them that the stable hand looked Clemmie up and down in disbelief as he handed her a pair of boots in her size and a riding helmet, which was comically oversized. She slipped it on and it immediately fell over her eyes.

'Perfect,' Oliver said, biting back a laugh. 'You look like a serious equestrian now.'

'Don't start,' she warned, handing the helmet back and swapping it for one that fitted. 'I really can't get on that thing.'

'You'll be fine,' Oliver said reassuringly. He patted the horse's neck. 'Shadow is a sweetheart.'

Clemmie wasn't convinced. 'Sweetheart? He looks like he's plotting my demise.'

After much coaxing from Oliver, Clemmie approached

the horse cautiously. 'How am I supposed to get on this thing?'

'Easy,' Oliver said, grabbing the reins. 'Just put your left foot in the stirrup and swing yourself up and over.'

Clemmie gave him a look. 'Swing myself up? That high? I'm not a gymnast.'

Despite her protests, she attempted to follow his instructions. Her first try involved a lot of awkward hopping, but her foot missed the stirrup entirely. Oliver tried to hold the stirrup steady from the other side while she jumped again, but she couldn't get high enough and fell backwards. They both collapsed into laughter.

'This isn't working,' she gasped, clutching her stomach.

Oliver wiped tears of laughter from his eyes. 'Wait here.'

He returned moments later with a small set of wooden steps. 'Your throne awaits, my lady.'

With the help of the steps, Clemmie finally managed to mount Shadow, though she squealed as the horse shifted under her. 'It's moving! Why is it moving?'

'It's just adjusting,' Oliver said, mounting his own horse, a chestnut beauty named Blaze, with practised ease. He looked entirely too comfortable in the saddle.

Once they were both ready, the stable hands led them out onto the estate grounds and waved them off. Clemmie clutched the reins tightly, her knuckles turning white.

Oliver looked over his shoulder at her. 'See? You're a natural.'

As they began to walk gently along the gravel path, finally Clemmie started to relax.

'What a beautiful place,' she said as she looked out over the estate.

But her peace was short-lived. As she adjusted her position, her foot accidentally nudged Shadow's side and the horse broke into a brisk trot. Clemmie panicked and without thinking she kicked the horse again. 'Oliver!' she screamed, gripping the reins for dear life. 'Make it stop!'

'Pull back on the reins!' he shouted.

'I'm trying!' she shrieked, bouncing wildly in the saddle. Shadow seemed entirely unfazed by her panic, trotting gracefully across the grass while Clemmie flailed. Her body was bouncing up and down as she let out a string of incoherent cries. Suddenly, Shadow veered towards a small lake and history repeated itself as he waded straight in and came to an abrupt halt in the middle. Clemmie found herself perched precariously on the saddle, her boots now submerged as the horse stood motionless.

'You've got to be kidding me,' she groaned.

Oliver had dismounted and tied Blaze to a nearby post. He stood there, doubled over, struggling to contain his laughter. 'It's like the donkey story all over again!' he managed between gasps. 'Count yourself lucky that he hasn't lain down!'

'It's not funny!' Clemmie's voice was full of panic. 'How am I going to get out of here?'

'Stay put. I'm coming to get you.'

Like a knight in shining armour, he stepped straight into the water, wading towards her as if it were the most natural thing in the world. The water swirled around his thighs, darkening his breeches, but he didn't seem remotely bothered.

'Okay, you're going to have to jump,' he said when he reached her.

Clemmie gave him a dubious look. 'Jump? What if you drop me?'

'I won't drop you.'

'You hesitated.'

'I did not! Come on, swing those legs around. I'm not standing here all day.'

Muttering to herself, she pulled her feet from the stirrups, feeling completely ridiculous. Swinging one leg over the saddle, she attempted some level of grace but, naturally, ended up lurching sideways. With an undignified yelp, she fell towards Oliver…

…who caught her effortlessly, strong arms securing her against his chest. Their faces were suddenly inches apart, her hands on his shoulders, his amused gaze locked with hers.

'You know,' he murmured, 'if you wanted to be in my arms again, there were other ways to do it.'

'Don't be cheeky! Just get me to dry land!'

He was still smirking as he turned.

The embarrassing ordeal was finally nearing its end when the sound of approaching hoofbeats sent a new ripple of dread through her. Clemmie turned her head just in time to see a rider coming towards them. As the figure drew closer, her stomach plummeted.

The neatly tied headscarf was a tell-tale sign of a very specific equestrian enthusiast. The very equestrian enthusiast she'd hoped to avoid.

Clemmie blinked rapidly, convinced her eyes were deceiving her.

'Oliver,' she whispered, her voice barely above a breath.

'Hmm?'

'Oliver!' she hissed again, more urgently this time. 'Look!' She nodded furiously towards the approaching figure.

'It's her!' Clemmie squeaked.

'Her who?' Oliver asked, still completely unfazed.

'The Queen, Oliver! The actual Queen!'

Oliver finally turned his full attention to the approaching rider. Much to Clemmie's utter horror, he still didn't seem perturbed.

Clemmie closed her eyes in pure mortification.

'Oh, yes, it's her,' he said with a casual shrug, as if spotting royalty during a chaotic horse-riding debacle was the most normal thing in the world.

Clemmie, however, was anything but calm. 'What do we do? She's coming this way!'

'Relax,' Oliver said, clearly enjoying her flustered state. 'She is human, you know. Just smile and wave.'

'Smile and wave?' she echoed, her voice climbing higher. 'I'm stuck in the middle of a lake in your arms.' Before Oliver could respond, the Queen's voice rang out, clear and unmistakable. 'Lovely day for a ride, isn't it?'

Clemmie froze at the familiar cadence. Her Majesty's presence was magnetic, even from a distance.

Clemmie gawked as the Queen guided her horse closer, a serene smile on her face. The headscarf, a practical yet elegant accessory, complemented her riding jacket perfectly, unlike Clemmie's mismatched loungewear and waterlogged boots.

The Queen stopped her horse a few feet from the lake's edge, her gaze landing on Oliver first. 'Good afternoon, Oliver. I trust everything is under control?'

Oliver bowed his head. 'All under control, Your Majesty,' he replied with a grin.

'You must be Clemmie, Oliver's visitor, staying at the cottage?' the Queen said, her sharp eyes twinkling with amusement as she turned to Clemmie.

Clemmie's heart was pounding as she, too, bowed her head, 'Uh, yes, Your Majesty,' she stammered, utterly mortified.

The Queen chuckled softly. 'What an adventure you're having.'

Clemmie gave a nervous laugh. 'You could say that.'

Oliver placed Clemmie back on dry land and then turned back to the Queen. 'I just need to rescue the horse now.'

The Queen's gaze shifted back to Clemmie, her expression kind. 'Don't let him tease you too much about this, dear. Everyone has their first riding mishap. Mine involved a rather stubborn pony and a hedge.'

Clemmie felt a flicker of relief at the monarch's easy manner, though her cheeks still burned with embarrassment.

By the time Oliver reached Shadow, the Queen had resumed her ride, her voice carrying back to them as she trotted away. 'Enjoy the rest of your day! Do try to get dry before you catch cold.'

Clemmie watched her disappear into the distance, still struggling to process the surreal encounter. 'Did that really just happen?' she asked Oliver.

'It did,' he replied, grinning. 'And you survived it beautifully.'

'Barely.'

As soon as the horse was out of the water it let out a loud neigh, causing Clemmie to jump. 'That horse is mocking me.'

'Do you need help getting back on?'

'Are you kidding me? I'm done with horses for today,' she declared. 'And for any day for that matter.'

Still grinning, Oliver held up his hands in surrender. 'Fair enough. We'll walk back.'

Despite her soggy boots and aching muscles, Clemmie couldn't stop smiling as they strolled towards the stables. The day had been a whirlwind of chaos and laughter, and she couldn't remember the last time she'd felt so alive.

'You know,' she said, nudging Oliver with her elbow, 'this might go down as one of my most embarrassing moments.'

'Or one of your funniest,' he countered, his hazel eyes twinkling.

She laughed, shaking her head. 'I'll let you decide when you're writing my biography.'

As they reached the stables, Clemmie turned back to look at Shadow, who was now contentedly munching on hay. 'Next time, we're sticking to bicycles!'

Chapter Nineteen

As soon as they arrived back at the cottage, Clemmie decided to indulge in some much-needed relaxation and take a bath. After turning on the taps, sending a stream of hot water rushing into the tub, she grabbed a jar of lavender-scented bubble bath and poured in a generous splash, watching as soft, frothy bubbles spread across the surface. The scent was dreamy, floral, fresh, and way better than her pyjama bottoms, which reeked of pond water and were now spinning around in the washing machine in the utility room. She dipped a hand in to check the temperature, then slipped out of the rest of her clothes and stepped into the tub with a happy sigh. The bubbles wrapped around her like a warm hug, and the faint scent of lavender mixed with the fresh air from the open window made it feel like she'd stepped into another time entirely.

On a whim, Clemmie glanced towards the bottle of champagne she'd spotted earlier. 'Why not?' she murmured to herself. Wrapping herself in a plush towel before padding barefoot across the room, she retrieved the champagne and returned to the bath.

With a satisfying *pop*, she uncorked the bottle and poured herself a glass. The bubbles sparkled like tiny diamonds, and she took a long sip, the crisp, effervescent taste adding to the indulgence. She leaned back against the edge of the tub, closed her eyes and allowed herself to fully relax.

Her mind wandered as she soaked, replaying the day's events. The awkward horse ride, the Queen's unexpected appearance and, of course, the lake incident. It was all so ridiculous and yet so wonderfully surreal. The memory of Oliver laughing as he carried her in his arms made her smile.

After a much-needed long, luxurious soak, Clemmie climbed out of the tub and dried herself. Her dress for dinner, a simple yet elegant navy number, was already laid out on the bed. She quickly blow-dried her hair and began applying her make-up, giving herself a more sophisticated look. As she swiped on some lipstick, her phone buzzed with an incoming FaceTime call from Betty.

'Granny!' Clemmie answered, propping the phone on the dressing table.

Betty's face filled the screen, her mischievous grin already in place. 'If it isn't Lady of the Lake herself!' she teased. 'Your text had me giggling!'

Clemmie groaned, but she couldn't help laughing. 'Don't even start. It was mortifying!'

'I mean, meeting the Queen while stuck in a lake and wearing pyjamas? Only you, Clemmie. Only you!'

'It wasn't my fault!' Clemmie protested, though she was

laughing too. She recounted the entire escapade in vivid detail, from Oliver's rescue to the Queen's casual conversation.

By the time she finished, Betty was wiping tears of laughter from her eyes. 'You're a walking sitcom, I swear. But honestly, it sounds like you're having the time of your life. Royalwood looks absolutely beautiful. How did Oliver manage to get you both an invite to stay? I never did ask.'

'I think it's something to do with Lady Rosalind. She's a friend of the Queen's and great family friends with Oliver's grandparents. But Granny, listen, you'll never guess what I've found – the number 1705, right here in my room at the cottage!'

'Really?'

'It's so bizarre, it's engraved in the wood on the inside of the wardrobe.'

'Now that *is* strange.'

'I asked Oliver about it but he thinks it just means when it was made.'

'He's probably right, but what a strange coincidence. Oh, by the way,' Betty said, her tone shifting, 'you'll never guess the latest local news. The Royal Yacht is still moored at Puffin Island and isn't leaving anytime soon.'

'Really? Why?'

'Apparently there's an issue with the engine, so it's going to be here for at least another week.'

'All the tourists will love that. I'll be home in a few days to help out. I bet the café will be heaving.'

'You're not wrong. I've been run off my feet baking the now infamous torte. Everyone wants a slice!'

'That's incredible,' Clemmie said.

'So many people want to meet you… Oh, and I've been looking through all the recipe books from the past and seeing what you could possibly include in your new cookbook. Amelia said she's going to clear a whole shelf for copies of your book in The Story Shop when it's published.'

'That's lovely. Thank you.'

'I want lots of updates!'

'I'll keep you updated on everything!'

After wrapping up the call, Clemmie gave herself one final glance in the mirror. Satisfied, she headed downstairs, the soft rustle of her dress accompanying her footsteps. When she reached the kitchen, the rich aroma of something delicious greeted her.

The kitchen was straight out of another time, full of old-world charm. A big racing-green Aga took centre stage, its cast-iron doors slightly open, letting out a gentle heat. Above it, copper pots and pans hung from a rail, their surfaces catching the light.

To one side, a grand inglenook fireplace dominated the wall, its blackened beams framing an empty hearth. The sturdy farmhouse table in the middle of the room was well-worn, its mismatched chairs only adding to the charm. A vase of fresh wildflowers sat in the centre, bringing a splash of colour.

The pantry door stood ajar, revealing shelves packed with neatly labelled jars of preserves, sacks of flour and tiny glass bottles of spices. Rustic wooden cabinets with wrought-iron handles lined the walls, while the polished stone countertops were scattered with fresh vegetables, a loaf of crusty bread and a well-used wooden chopping board.

Oliver stood at the counter, wearing an apron emblazoned with the words 'King of the Kitchen' and looking entirely at ease.

'King of the kitchen? Did you bring that apron with you?' Clemmie teased, raising an eyebrow.

He grinned and shook his head, gesturing towards the pantry. 'They were hanging in there. There's a "Queen of the Kitchen" one, too! Someone in the royal household clearly has a great sense of humour.'

'It suits you,' Clemmie said, laughing lightly as she leaned against the doorframe. 'You've been busy, I see. Are we eating here? Shall I set the table?'

He nodded towards the door leading off the kitchen. 'We're eating in there and everything is already set.'

Clemmie peeked around the door and stopped in her tracks. The dining table was like something out of a dream, set with fine china with delicate gold patterns, silverware that practically gleamed and crystal glasses that caught the light. A little vase of fresh flowers sat in the middle, clearly picked from the garden, and tall candles flickered softly.

'It's beautiful,' she said, her voice tinged with awe, touched by the effort Oliver had gone to.

'Only the best for you,' he replied with a grin, pouring her a glass of wine. 'Go on, take a seat.' He gestured towards the head of the table. 'I'll bring the food through in a moment.'

'What are we having?' she asked curiously, standing in the doorway.

Oliver wiped his hands on his apron and leaned against the counter. 'A bit of a royal feast, actually. The roasted vegetables are straight from the estate gardens. Carrots, parsnips and the most enormous butternut squash I've ever seen – all grown just beyond the hedgerows. The herbs are from the kitchen garden here, too – rosemary, thyme, sage. And the venison? That comes from the royal grounds as well. Locally sourced, shall we say?' He winked.

Clemmie's eyes widened. 'You're joking. Venison from here?'

'The royals like to live off the land. I'd say it's probably the most well-fed deer in the country, grazing on these immaculate lawns. Don't worry, though, I've kept it simple. Pan-seared with a red wine reduction. For dessert, we have a crumble made from apples grown in the orchard at the back.'

Clemmie clutched her chest dramatically. 'You're spoiling me. Do I need to curtsy before dinner starts?'

Oliver laughed, returning to the stove to check on the food. 'Only if you want to. I think the Queen would approve of this spread though. Now, give me a moment to plate it all up.'

As she waited, Clemmie admired the dining room in more detail. It had the same old-world charm as the kitchen. Wooden beams stretched across the ceiling, and the walls were adorned with portraits and landscapes, many of which, she guessed, were of the Royal Family or the estate. A grand fireplace stood at one end, its mantel lined with ornate brass candlesticks and a large gilded mirror. A Persian rug softened the stone floor, and the heavy oak dining table looked like it had hosted centuries of meals and conversations.

Her eyes wandered around the room, her gaze landing on the large wooden bookcase that stood against the far wall. It was filled with old leather-bound tomes, antique ornaments and framed photographs. Intrigued, Clemmie walked over to examine it more closely. As her fingers brushed against the spines of the books, one in particular caught her attention. It was larger than the others, its leather cover cracked with age and its edges worn smooth from decades of handling. Embossed in faded gold lettering on the spine were the words *Visitors' Book*.

Clemmie pulled it gently from the shelf and was surprised by its weight. She carried it to the table, the scent of fine old paper wafting up as she opened it. The first page bore an elegant inscription in swirling script: *Royalwood Cottage Estate. 1916.* Beneath it, an embossed royal crest added a touch of grandeur.

'This is amazing,' she murmured, running her fingers over the lettering.

Oliver walked into the room. 'What have you found?'

'A visitors' book. Looks like it was created just before the war ended,' she said, flipping to the first entry. The pages were filled with neat handwriting, each line a record of someone who had stayed at the lodge over the decades. The dates, names and occasional notes were meticulously inscribed, and Clemmie could feel the history radiating from the pages. She scanned the first few entries, marvelling at the names. Lords, ladies, barons and diplomats.

Then her eyes stopped on two names, 'Henry, Earl of Aberford,' she read aloud. She paused. 'And Chef Étienne Dupont! The scandal guy and the chef. You said they were friends.'

Oliver nodded, 'Yes, I did.'

'I wonder if they ever worked together to host dinners at

places like this cottage. Can you imagine the meals that must have been created here? In this very kitchen.' Clemmie looked back at the book, her fingers trailing over the elegant script. The thought of those two legendary figures walking through these same rooms, laughing and collaborating, made her feel connected to history in a way she never had before. 'Did he disappear from royal life before or after the chef was killed?'

'I'm not sure.'

Clemmie turned another page. 'To think,' she murmured, 'their names are right here, in this book.' She closed the book gently, resting her hands on its leather cover. 'This place,' she said, looking around the room, 'it's like a time capsule. A gateway to another era.'

Oliver nodded, his gaze steady. 'Now you're part of its story too. Let's eat.' He walked back into the kitchen then appeared moments later, balancing two plates laden with food. The vibrant colours of the roasted vegetables glowed against the white china, the venison glistening under its red wine reduction, sprigs of fresh herbs adding the final touch.

'You've really outdone yourself. You are more than a food journalist, you could be a Michelin star chef,' she said, beaming as he set the plate before her.

'Well, I aim to impress,' Oliver replied, pouring wine for them both and taking the seat opposite her. 'Following the chefs and watching them cook, over the years I've picked up a lot of tips. Now, tuck in before it gets cold.'

Clemmie picked up her knife and fork and took a bite, the flavours bursting on her tongue. The vegetables were perfectly roasted, their natural sweetness heightened by a hint of caramelisation, and the venison was tender and rich, the sauce adding a depth of flavour she hadn't expected.

'This is incredible,' she said, shaking her head. 'I'm going to need the recipe.'

Oliver chuckled. 'I'll write it down for you, though I think it might taste better here, surrounded by all this.' He gestured around the room, its history enveloping them like a comforting embrace. 'Don't you forget to write in the visitors' book before you leave. The current one is in the hallway.'

'I won't.' Her mind lingered on the Earl, wondering what his life was like after he walked away from his title. Did he just become a regular man walking the streets of London, blending in among the bustling crowds? She tried to picture him, perhaps sitting in a small café, unnoticed by the world yet carrying a lifetime of extraordinary memories.

Of course, he would have passed away by now, but she wondered, if he'd reached one hundred, would he have received a birthday card from the Queen? If he had, would she have known it was *him* … the Earl who had once been part of her family's circle, whose name was inked into the very history of Royalwood Cottage? The idea tickled Clemmie, and she let out a soft laugh.

She had a feeling her time at the cottage was going to be interesting, the secrets it held just waiting to be revealed.

Chapter Twenty

After dinner, Clemmie and Oliver retreated to the cosy living room, bottle of wine in hand. Even though it wasn't chilly, Oliver walked over to the grand stone fireplace that dominated the room.

'You're not getting the full experience without this,' he announced, kneeling to arrange the kindling and wood that were stacked neatly by the hearth. With practised ease, he struck a match, and soon a crackling fire was spreading its heat across the room.

Clemmie perched on the arm of a chair, holding her glass of wine and watching him work. 'I didn't have you down for a fire-lighting expert,' she teased.

'Well,' he said, dusting his hands off, 'there's more to me than meets the eye.' He stood, satisfied with his handiwork, 'Now, shall we see who's the better sleuth?'

She raised an eyebrow. 'What are you talking about?'

He stepped over to a nearby shelf and pulled out a

worn, brightly coloured box. 'Cluedo. Or, as we'll call it tonight, Royal Cluedo.'

Clemmie laughed as he set the game on the low table between the sofas. 'Royal Cluedo? What, are we solving who stole the Crown Jewels?'

'Something like that.' Oliver grinned as he began to set up the board, carefully laying out the cards and pieces. 'But to make it more fun, we'll rename the characters after the royals. Colonel Mustard can be Prince Rupert, and Miss Scarlett … maybe Isobel.'

'Oh, I like this already,' Clemmie said, settling into the plush sofa opposite him. 'But what about Professor Plum?'

'Prince Frederick, of course,' Oliver said without hesitation.

'And Reverend Green?'

'Let's make him Prince Henry,' Oliver said with a wink.

They went back and forth, renaming all the characters, their laughter filling the room.

With the fire blazing and the wine flowing, the game took on a life of its own.

'You can't seriously accuse Princess Eloise – aka Mrs White – of hiding a dagger in the ballroom!' Clemmie said, feigning outrage.

Oliver leaned back in his chair, tapping a finger against his temple. 'She's crafty. Don't underestimate her.'

'Crafty? She's one of the most straightforward royals there is!'

'Ah, but that's what makes her the perfect suspect,' Oliver countered, grinning wickedly.

As the game went on, their banter became more playful, filled with dramatic accusations and exaggerated reactions.

Clemmie accused Oliver of cheating when he deduced that Princess Helena had used a candlestick in the conservatory, but he protested his innocence, swearing he was merely blessed with unparalleled deduction skills.

In the final round, Clemmie made a bold guess and was triumphant, solving the mystery and winning the game. She stood and did a mock curtsy, adjusting an imaginary tiara on her head.

'Bow to your Cluedo Queen,' she declared, unable to hide her smug grin.

Oliver clapped slowly, rising from his seat. 'Fine. You win. But I demand a rematch sometime.'

As she reached for her wine glass, a thought struck her. 'Oliver! I almost forgot. I need a dress and a hat for the garden party.'

'That's okay, we have time tomorrow to go shopping. Kingswell has some wonderful boutiques.'

'Kingswell?' she repeated, her eyes lighting up. 'Isn't it very posh there? Am I about to live out a scene from *Pretty Woman*?'

'Minus the opera and the penthouse, perhaps,' he quipped. 'But then, we've already done the opera.'

Clemmie smiled before draining the last of her wine. After the fire had fizzled out and the board game had been tidied away, they climbed the stairs to their rooms, the atmosphere between them shifting as the playful teasing gave way to a quieter, more intimate energy. They reached the top of the staircase and stopped, standing just a few feet apart.

'Goodnight, Clem,' Oliver said softly, his voice holding

tenderness, like he was trying to say more without saying anything at all.

'Goodnight, Oliver,' Clemmie replied, her heart thudding in her chest, faster than it should have. They had talked about the reasons they ended things three years ago, his job, the constant travelling, her café on the coast, and how they just couldn't make it work. And now, he was leaving again very soon. For another year. It was like déjà vu, but this time, it wasn't just the goodbye that stung. It was also the feeling that maybe they hadn't fully let go of each other.

Neither of them moved but the space between them seemed to shrink, the air between them charged. Clemmie's thoughts started to spiral… *He's leaving in a few days. He's still the same guy with the job that takes him all over the world, and you're the same woman who loves her life at the café. Nothing has changed.*

But then, almost without thinking, Clemmie took a half-step closer. Her gaze locked onto his, and for a moment, it felt like everything else faded away. The world seemed to hold its breath, like it was waiting for her to decide, *Should I really do this? Should I really let myself feel this again, knowing how it ends?*

Before she could second-guess herself, before her mind could catch up with her, she leaned in. Her lips brushed against his, a soft, hesitant touch, almost like she was asking permission. She thought about pulling away. She thought about how it had felt the last time they were together, how they both knew the relationship couldn't survive their separate lives. She thought about the café, the one thing she could never leave behind, and how much she'd poured into it.

But then his lips pressed upon hers, and she couldn't stop herself. It wasn't just a kiss, it was a reminder of everything they had once felt, of how easy it had been to get lost in each other. Her mind screamed at her, *This doesn't change anything. He's still leaving. You can't pretend this is for ever.* But her heart wasn't listening. All she could feel was the warmth of him, the familiar taste of him, the way his arms wrapped around her like they had never been apart.

She pulled him closer, telling herself that for now, it didn't matter. For just a few moments, it was enough to pretend that maybe, just maybe, there was something more than just the life they had chosen.

When they finally broke apart, both were breathless, their eyes searching each other's faces. She took his hand, turned and opened her bedroom door. Oliver followed without hesitation, and as the door clicked shut behind them, the rest of the world faded away.

Pulling the curtains shut, she pressed her body against his in the near-darkness and gasped with desire. Still kissing him, she felt an immense tingle through her body. As they started to pull at each other's clothes there was an urgency, electricity sparking between them. She unbuttoned his shirt and ran her hands over his body. His face was in her hair, then he was kissing her neck. He unbuttoned her dress and, as it fell to the floor, he pulled her on to the bed and unhooked her bra. He looked at her with such adoration.

'Are you sure?' he whispered.

Her heart raced, the connection between them

impossible to ignore. *Forget the future*, she told herself, staring back at him. Right now, all she wanted was this, his moment, this connection. She didn't want to wonder what came next or how much time they had left. She just wanted to live for the moment. To feel the thrill of being with him, without second-guessing anything. Her heart overruling her head.

For Clemmie, this night at Royalwood Cottage was shaping up to be one she'd never forget.

'I'm sure,' she whispered before Oliver stole what was left of her breath.

Chapter Twenty-One

Clemmie woke to the soft chorus of birdsong. A contented smile lingered as she lay there, savouring the moment. Oliver had slipped out of bed about ten minutes ago. The events of the past few days had felt like stepping into a fairytale, and she wasn't ready for the spell to break just yet. From her horse-riding escapade to dinner, the discovery of the visitors' book, and of course last night, every moment had been memorable.

After a quick shower, she slipped into a light floral dress, tied her hair back into a loose ponytail, and headed downstairs. The smell of freshly brewed coffee wafted through the cottage, and as she stepped into the kitchen she was greeted by a picturesque scene. Oliver was already there, arranging breakfast on a rustic wooden table beneath the grand old oak tree just outside the door. The garden was a vision of English charm: perfectly manicured lawns, vibrant flowerbeds bursting with colour and a small fountain in the centre that gurgled cheerfully. Butterflies flitted about, and the air was filled with the sweet scent of blooming roses and lavender.

'Good morning!' Oliver smiled as he poured her a cup of coffee. He was wearing a casual linen shirt and trousers, looking every bit the relaxed country gentleman. 'Did you sleep well?' he asked with a mischievous grin before pressing a kiss to her cheek.

'I think you know the answer to that,' Clemmie replied, settling into one of the cushioned chairs. 'This is stunning. Did you do all this?' she asked, gesturing at the spread of croissants, fresh fruit, scrambled eggs and smoked salmon.

'Absolutely. I rose at dawn, milked the cows, churned the butter and baked the croissants from scratch.'

'You're a man of many talents,' Clemmie said, laughing as she helped herself to some fruit.

They ate in a leisurely way, chatting about anything and everything, apart from Oliver's impending departure to the US. There was no point. She couldn't change things, and she didn't want to dwell on it. Oliver leaned back in his chair and gave her a thoughtful look.

'Have you thought about what you would like to wear to the garden party?' he asked, swirling his coffee.

Clemmie groaned. 'I haven't the faintest idea. I've never attended a royal event before and my wardrobe at home is more pinnies and casual stuff, with the odd dress.' She looked down at what she was wearing.

'After breakfast, I'll take you to the best places I know. I'm sure you'll find something.'

'Valmont or Rosewood Street?' she joked.

'Actually, I was thinking more Whitmore Square. This

isn't just any garden party, Clemmie. It's Eldenbridge Palace. You need to look the part.'

Clemmie raised her eyebrows. 'Whitmore Square? That's absurd. I'll end up spending a month's rent on a single dress.'

'Consider it an investment,' Oliver said, before sipping his coffee. 'Plus, you're going to have your first grand royal experience. Why not do it properly?'

After breakfast, a sleek black Bentley pulled up outside the cottage, its polished exterior gleaming in the morning sunlight. The driver stepped out, a tall man in an immaculate suit, and opened the door with a bow. 'Sir, madam, your car is ready.'

'Is this not a little excessive?' she asked, sliding into the luxurious interior, the leather seats cool against her legs. A chilled bottle of champagne sat in a silver ice bucket between them, and two crystal flutes glinted invitingly.

'Excessive is half the fun,' Oliver replied, pouring them each a glass. 'I want your trip to be as memorable as possible.'

They clinked glasses, and the car glided smoothly onto the main road. As they left the tranquillity of the royal residence, the scenery shifted from sprawling parkland to the bustling outskirts of London.

The drive was a tapestry of iconic landmarks. They passed through Ashford Vale, where the River Elen glittered in the light, and soon the spires of Larkminster Cathedral came into view. Edris Tower stood tall, its clockface an unwavering – and literal – reminder of the passage of time. Clemmie leaned closer to the window, catching a glimpse of Valmont Avenue, lined with Union Jacks fluttering in the breeze. Ahead, a royal convoy of black Range Rovers sped towards Eldenbridge Palace, their blue lights flashing discreetly.

'Do you think that's for the Queen?' Clemmie asked, her voice tinged with awe.

'Possibly,' Oliver replied, his gaze following the convoy.

As they entered Whitmore Square, heads began to turn. The Bentley's unmistakable elegance and the way it moved with unhurried grace through the narrow streets made it a spectacle. Clemmie caught sight of people pausing mid-stride, their eyes lingering on the car. It was a world apart from anything she'd ever known.

The shops came into view, each one more opulent than the last. Glittering window displays showcased gowns dripping with sequins, tailored suits that oozed sophistication, and jewellery that sparkled like a thousand stars. Names like Chanel, Dior and Prada were emblazoned on the fronts.

'I feel a little out of place,' she whispered.

Oliver squeezed her hand. 'Well, you shouldn't.'

Each time her gaze found Oliver, she felt a little more drawn in. His quiet confidence, the way he seemed to see through everything, made her wonder if she could ever be part of his world. But then, the image of her grandmother's smiling face and the comforting hum of the café filled her mind. That was her world, her heart's home. She couldn't imagine leaving it behind, not even for a fleeting moment.

The car pulled up outside a boutique that seemed to have stepped straight out of a film. 'I'll return for you both at three p.m.,' the driver said with a respectful nod as he held the door for Clemmie.

Clemmie and Oliver strolled down Rosewood Street, a world of exclusivity and elegance unfolding around them. Oliver flashed her a reassuring smile as they approached the entrance of one of the most luxurious boutiques on the street.

Inside, the air was perfumed with subtle notes of vanilla and jasmine, and dresses, each more exquisite than the last, lined the walls like masterpieces in a gallery. Soft golden light bathed the room, and the plush carpet absorbed every step, creating a cocoon of quiet luxury. A poised personal shopper, immaculately dressed in a tailored suit, approached them with a smile.

'Good morning! How can I help you today?' she asked, her tone perfectly pitched between enthusiasm and professionalism.

Clemmie hesitated, her nerves bubbling to the surface. Sensing her discomfort, Oliver stepped forward. 'We're looking for a very special dress for the royal garden party tomorrow,' he explained, his deep voice resonating with authority.

The personal shopper's eyes lit up with genuine excitement. 'The royal garden party? You've come to the right place!' She turned and gestured towards a colleague in the corner, who appeared almost immediately with a tray bearing two flutes of chilled champagne and a selection of delicate truffles. Clemmie's eyes widened as she accepted the glass, feeling like she'd stepped into a dream. She'd never been treated like this before, never imagined she could feel so … important.

'Please, make yourselves comfortable,' the personal shopper said, directing Oliver to a sumptuous red velvet sofa. He sank into it with casual elegance, his eyes never leaving Clemmie as she was guided towards a rack of dresses.

The dresses were breathtaking. Fabrics shimmered in the light: silks, chiffons and satins in every colour imaginable. The personal shopper began selecting pieces. 'This one would bring out your eyes,' she said, holding up a gown in deep emerald green. 'This one, the embroidery is all hand-stitched.'

Clemmie nodded, still overwhelmed but beginning to appreciate the thrill of the experience.

Behind the privacy of the dressing-room curtain, Clemmie tried on dress after dress. Each time she emerged, Oliver's reaction was the same, his eyes lighting up with approval and delight. 'Stunning,' he said when she stepped out in a sleek navy dress. 'That colour suits you,' he commented.

'It's beautiful but just doesn't feel right,' shared Clemmie.

'What about this one?' the personal shopper asked, appearing with a dress that immediately captured Clemmie's attention. It was a timeless design, a cornflower-blue creation that fell just below the knee. The soft A-line silhouette was complemented by delicate embroidery along the hem and bodice, with subtle beading that caught the light. The fabric moved like liquid silk, shimmering gently as it flowed. The capped sleeves and a modest V-neckline added an air of refinement, making it perfect for the regal yet relaxed setting of a garden party. 'This is part of our latest collection. It's perfectly elegant,' the personal shopper said, her tone brimming with confidence.

'I actually love it!'

Back into the changing room Clemmie went and as she slipped into the dress her heart was pounding. When she turned to face the mirror, she barely recognised herself. The dress hugged her in all the right places, its elegance making her feel a quiet confidence she hadn't known she possessed.

'Are you ready?' called Oliver. 'We're dying to see.'

Taking a deep breath, she stepped out of the dressing room.

Oliver's reaction was immediate and breathtakingly sincere. He stood up, his usual composure momentarily replaced by awe. 'Clemmie…' he said, his voice almost a whisper. 'You look … perfect.'

Clemmie felt a blush creep up her cheeks, but she couldn't stop smiling. 'Do you really think so?' she asked, smoothing the fabric nervously.

'I don't think,' Oliver said, his eyes locking onto hers, 'I know. This is the one.'

The personal shopper clapped her hands together, her excitement genuine. 'It's absolutely divine on you. Shall we look for the perfect accessories?'

They moved to another section of the boutique, where rows of shoes, handbags and hats awaited. Clemmie's nerves had completely disappeared, replaced by a bubbling excitement. 'What do you think of these?' she asked, holding up a pair of strappy silver heels.

The personal shopper tilted her head, considering. 'They're lovely, but I'm thinking…' She pointed to a pair of elegant ivory ballet flats. 'From experience, you don't want to be thinking about your feet in a pair of heels at a royal garden party. These match the dress perfectly.'

Clemmie sat on the nearby sofa and tried them on. They fit like a glove. 'Definitely these,' she said, standing and walking up and down the room just like her granny used to make her do whenever she tried on new school shoes.

Next came the handbag. The personal shopper presented a chic clutch embellished with subtle beading that mirrored the embroidery on her dress.

'This one,' she said confidently. 'It's made for you.'

Finally, the hat. 'A garden party calls for something fabulous, but a royal garden party calls for something extra fabulous,' the personal shopper declared, guiding them to an array of fascinators and wide-brimmed hats. Clemmie tried on a few, but it was Oliver who found the winner, a delicate creation in the same colour as her dress, beautified with a soft spray of feathers and pearls. 'You look like royalty,' he said, grinning.

Clemmie laughed. 'I feel like royalty,' she replied, sipping the last of the champagne and eating truffles from the silver-plated tray.

She changed back into the dress she'd arrived in and they made their way to the counter to pay for everything. Oliver turned to Clemmie. 'I told you this would be fun.'

'Fun doesn't even begin to cover it,' Clemmie replied, her eyes shining. 'I've had a blast and feel a little tipsy with all that champagne. Thank you for this morning.'

He took her hand briefly, his touch reassuring. 'Glad you enjoyed it.'

They watched as the boutique's staff wrapped each item in a beautiful box, lined with fine tissue paper that Clemmie was convinced was edged with gold. The bags were handed to her, and Oliver reached for his wallet.

'It's on me,' he said firmly.

Clemmie's eyes widened. 'Oliver, no. That's too much. I can't let you.'

'Yes, you can.' His tone softened as he reached for her hand. 'When you visit me in America, I'll make sure we go to an event where you can wear it all again. Consider it an investment in our memories.'

Was that an official invitation? He was making his intentions clear. It didn't matter if he was on the other side of the world, he still wanted to see her. She liked that thought.

She hesitated, her gaze flicking to the price total. It was exorbitant, but the way Oliver looked at her, like she was worth every penny, made her heart flutter. Finally, she nodded. 'Thank you,' she whispered, pressing a soft kiss to his cheek.

They stepped outside, the cool air brushing against their faces as Clemmie clutched the boutique's elegant bags. 'I do feel like Julia Roberts in *Pretty Woman*!' They had barely taken a few steps when they almost collided with a striking woman in a tailored coat and towering heels. Her hair was styled in perfect waves, and as she spun round her sharp eyes immediately swept over Clemmie, taking in her bags and her appearance before narrowing slightly.

'Fiona,' Oliver said, his tone polite but edged with tension.

'Oliver,' she replied, her voice smooth as silk but carrying an unmistakable chill. Her gaze flicked back to Clemmie, scrutinising her for a moment before shifting back to the boutique behind them. 'Wow, making bold choices, I see. That Café on the Coast must be doing well despite that bad review of yours.' Clemmie felt suddenly uncomfortable, unsure why Fiona would bring that up. There was an undertone in her words that Clemmie couldn't quite place, but it made her feel exposed in a way she hadn't expected. Fiona's attention returned to Oliver, her smile turning coy. 'I suppose you've always had an eye for the unconventional,' she said lightly, her words dripping with implication.

'Good to see you, Fiona,' Oliver said curtly, his tone leaving no room for further conversation. He placed a steadying hand on Clemmie's back and gently steered her away.

'Lunch?' Oliver suggested. 'We've earned it.'

'Lunch is definitely on me,' Clemmie replied, glancing back over her shoulder to see Fiona disappear at the end of the road. 'What did she mean, despite that bad review of mine?'

Oliver shrugged. 'Probably just because you mentioned it in your winner's speech. Who knows what goes through Fiona's mind? Take no notice of her. I know a gorgeous bistro just down here.'

Despite Oliver's attempt to brush it off, Fiona's comment lingered in Clemmie's thoughts. It felt like Fiona was questioning her worth in a way that left her doubting herself, even though she knew better than to let it get to her. She didn't want to give Fiona the satisfaction of ruining her mood, but the nagging feeling wouldn't go away.

'Sounds just perfect.'

Chapter Twenty-Two

Clemmie was lying in bed, cradling her morning coffee, mentally preparing for the exciting day ahead. Today was the royal garden party, and thinking about entering Eldenbridge Palace made her both nervous and excited. She swung her legs to the floor and wrapped herself in her dressing gown before grabbing her coffee and heading down the stairs. She was about to attend one of the most prestigious events in the country, and she could hardly believe it.

'I woke up to coffee and I wanted to wake up to you.' Clemmie slipped her arms around Oliver's waist and snuggled into him where he was standing by the stove, the smell of freshly brewed coffee and something delicious filling the air.

'Good morning! I thought you might need a little time to wake up before we dive into the day.'

Clemmie smiled back, 'I'm excited … and a little terrified, to be honest.'

'You're going to be brilliant. Just think, the whole of the royal garden party is going to sample your torte!'

'It's scary, isn't it?'

'Have you thought about the recipes you want to showcase in your cookbook?'

'I have! I want to use a lot of the coastal recipes that my great-great-grandmother introduced to The Café on the Coast because we still have those favourites on the menu today.'

'Any thoughts on the title of the cookbook?'

She smiled, 'I thought I'd keep it simple, maybe something like *Cook with Clemmie!* or *The Café on the Coast Cookbook.*'

'Both good ideas. I've made you something light for breakfast,' he said, motioning to the plate on the table. 'Something gentle on the stomach, in case the nerves get the better of you.'

Clemmie looked down at the breakfast he'd prepared: soft scrambled eggs with chives, a few slices of smoked salmon, and a warm croissant, golden and flaky. 'You're a keeper!' she exclaimed happily, but as soon as the words left her mouth, she suddenly felt a twinge of sadness. 'But you'll be gone by the end of the week.' She pulled a sad face.

He met her gaze. 'Let's not dwell on that today. This is your day and I want you to enjoy it from start to finish.' He kissed the top of her head.

'You have spoiled me from the moment I've got here. I will never forget all this.'

Oliver smiled and sat across from her as his phone rang out. He looked at the screen then said, 'Can you excuse me for a second?'

Clemmie nodded and overheard him say, 'Yes, I've been staying at Royalwood Cottage' as he stepped out of the room. Moving to the window, she watched him walk down to the bottom of the garden. As she returned to the table and started to eat her breakfast, she could still see him talking animatedly, raking one hand through his hair. His face looked thunderous and as he hung up the call, he took a moment before walking back.

'Everything okay? That looked a bit heated,' she asked as he re-entered the room.

Oliver hesitated and seemed to be about to share something with her, but they were interrupted as a loud bell rang out, causing Clemmie to jump.

'What is that?'

'The front door.'

'That's louder than a church bell!' she exclaimed. 'Are you expecting someone?'

Clemmie glanced at Oliver, who had a knowing smile on his face. 'It's for you.'

'Me?' she said, puzzled.

She followed Oliver to the door. When he opened it, a stylish woman was standing there, radiating confidence and grace. She immediately put her arms out and hugged Oliver before kissing him on both cheeks.

'It's good to see you, and this must be Clemmie.'

'It is, and Clemmie'—Oliver stepped aside as he introduced them—'this is Seraphina Westlake.'

Clemmie's mouth fell open. She'd heard that name before. 'Aren't you a make-up artist to the stars?'

Seraphina smiled. 'I'm here to prepare you for the royal

garden party. I'll be helping you with your hair, nails and make-up this morning.'

'Really?' She looked towards Oliver. 'Is this your doing?'

'We can't have you meeting Queen Charlotte with bed hair.' He nudged her playfully, making her blush as she swiped his arm.

'Oliver!'

'It's okay, I've known Seraphina since primary school, she knows all my secrets.' Oliver's grin was playful as he looked at her. 'I thought you might appreciate a little pampering.'

Clemmie threw her arms around him and kissed his cheek. 'I can't believe this. Thank you!'

Seraphina smiled. 'Today is all about you. Let's get started.'

'I need a shower first!'

'We have plenty of time. You go and have that shower, and I'll be set up and ready for you when you're done.'

Oliver and Seraphina laughed as Clemmie squealed and raced up the stairs.

'It feels like Christmas!' Clemmie shouted over her shoulder.

A few hours later, Clemmie stood in front of the full-length mirror in her bedroom, taking a deep breath. She looked so different, like she'd stepped into someone else's life. She felt gorgeous, confident – as if she'd been dropped into a dream.

It was hard to believe that just a few days ago she had been in her café, covered in flour, trying to perfect her clementine torte for the competition. Now, here she was, dressed to the nines, about to attend the royal garden party. It felt surreal.

A soft knock at the door broke her thoughts. Seraphina poked her head in, her smile approving. 'Are you ready? It's time.'

Clemmie nodded, smoothing out her dress one last time. She turned and headed for the stairs. At the bottom, Oliver was waiting for her, looking sharp in a grey pinstriped suit and a perfectly fitting waistcoat. A silver pocket watch caught the light, and his shoes shone. He looked every bit the gentleman. When Clemmie appeared, his jaw nearly hit the floor.

For a moment, Oliver seemed unable to speak. His eyes widened, and he stood there frozen, staring at her. Clemmie paused midway down the stairs. Resting her hand on the banister, she smiled.

'Oliver,' she said softly, teasingly. 'Do you have tears in your eyes?'

He blinked rapidly, as if trying to gather himself, and then let out a sheepish laugh. 'I do,' he admitted. 'You look … stunning. Absolutely breathtaking.'

As she took the final steps down the staircase he held out his arm, and she wrapped her hand around it.

Seraphina, ever the perfectionist, stepped forward to adjust a strand of Clemmie's hair then dabbed a touch of gloss on her lips. She stepped back, her critical eye scanning Clemmie from head to toe before nodding with satisfaction. 'You're ready,' she declared. 'Have fun!'

'I can't thank you enough. I would have never looked this good without your help.'

'You are very welcome,' she replied, before turning to

Oliver. 'Good luck in America, but let's speak before you go. And remember, take note of what I said.'

He nodded and briefly looked towards Clemmie, and she saw a flicker in his eyes of something she couldn't identify.

'I'll be off now but have a wonderful day!'

'I'll see you out,' said Oliver.

Clemmie watched them walk towards the door then pulled her phone from her bag, snapping a quick photo of her radiant reflection in the hall's mirror.

Captioning the photo, she wrote:

CLEMMIE

Off to the royal garden party! 👯 Feeling like a princess for the day. Wish me luck! xx

She posted it to her café's social media page and sent it to her friends' WhatsApp group. Within seconds, her phone buzzed.

BETTY

Clemmie! You look absolutely stunning. Like a proper royal! 😍 Enjoy every second, you deserve it. xx

AMELIA

Oh my goodness, Clem, you look amazing!! Can't wait to hear all about it. Make sure you get lots of photos. So proud of you! 💕 Go and bag a prince! Ha ha.

DILLY

Look at our girl!! 😱 You're glowing! Have the best time ever. Also, if Prince Charming is there, don't forget to invite him to the café. 😄 xx

Clemmie laughed at Dilly's message, the familiar banter grounding her in the moment. Oliver was walking back towards her as she slipped her phone back into her clutch.

Her nerves were now giving way to giddy excitement. 'How are we getting to the palace?' she asked.

Oliver grinned. 'Your car awaits,' he said, gesturing towards the driveway where the Bentley was making its way towards them.

'Only the best for today,' Oliver said, opening the door for her. The driver tipped his hat as she climbed in and Oliver joined her in the back. The car purred to life as they drove through the countryside and Clemmie settled back into the plush seat. She couldn't believe it. Here she was, in a Bentley (again!) and on her way to a royal garden party, with Oliver beside her.

After a few miles, Oliver turned to her with a grin. 'Hang tight. We're getting close.'

'Close to what?' she asked looking out of the window.

The car began to slow and then came to a smooth stop.

'Why have we stopped?' Clemmie asked, climbing out the car. Then she gasped with surprise.

Waiting for them was a beautiful horse-drawn carriage, its polished black body gleaming in the sunlight. The horses, sleek and well-groomed, wore braided reins, and a footman stood at attention, his uniform impeccable.

'I don't know what to say.' Clemmie's voice was filled with amazement.

The footman stepped forward, opening the carriage door with a respectful bow. 'Miss Clemmie, sir,' he said, his voice deep and formal.

Clemmie turned to Oliver, her eyes sparkling. 'This is incredible,' she said, her smile wide as she took Oliver's hand and stepped inside the carriage. He climbed in beside her, and the horses began to move. The nerves that had hit her earlier were now replaced by excitement. Not only was she going to the royal garden party, but she was doing it in a way she never could've imagined.

She turned to Oliver, her smile soft. 'Thank you,' she said simply. 'For making this day so special.'

Oliver reached over, taking her hand in his. 'You're welcome.'

Clemmie barely had time to take in the admiring glances and waves from the gathered onlookers. She smiled and lifted a hand in response. The steady clip-clop of the horses' hooves echoed against the grand facades lining the street.

Her grip tightened on her clutch as the enormity of what lay ahead truly settled in. The carriage turned gracefully onto a wider street, where wrought-iron lampposts stood in neat rows along the pavement.

Then, suddenly, it came into view. Eldenbridge Palace.

Clemmie gasped softly, as the famous palace appeared before her. The gilded wrought-iron gates, with their intricate design and regal crests, shimmered in the sunlight, a symbol of timeless elegance. Beyond them, the palace itself stood proud and majestic. The long, sweeping driveway leading to the grand entrance was lined with perfectly clipped hedges, and uniformed guards stood at attention, their red tunics and bearskin hats striking against the stately backdrop.

'It's beautiful,' Clemmie whispered, her voice barely audible over the rumble of the carriage wheels.

Oliver turned to her. 'It is. But not as beautiful as you look right now.'

She glanced at him, her cheeks flushing, and couldn't help but laugh nervously. 'You always know exactly what to say, don't you?'

'Only when I mean it,' he replied.

She playfully bumped her shoulder against his.

As the carriage approached the gates, Clemmie felt a fresh wave of nerves wash over her. She clutched Oliver's arm slightly tighter. 'I can't believe this is happening,' she said softly. 'I keep thinking I'll wake up and realise it was all a dream.'

Oliver reached over, his hand covering hers. 'It's not a dream. This is real and you're here because you deserve to be.'

The carriage slowed as it reached the security gate.

'We need to leave the carriage here.'

Clemmie was helped down and walked alongside Oliver towards the gates, where a uniformed officer stepped forward to greet them. He checked their invitations, then nodded and stepped back, signalling for the gates to be opened. They creaked softly as they swung inward, revealing the full magnificence of the palace grounds. As they walked through the gates, she slipped her hand into Oliver's.

'Queen Charlotte awaits,' said Oliver.

When they emerged into the palace gardens, the scene before them was nothing short of glorious. Ladies in elegant dresses and vibrant hats moved gracefully across the grounds, their laughter mingling with the soft hum of polite conversation. Gentlemen in tailored suits and morning coats nodded and exchanged pleasantries. They followed the path around the side of the palace, walking beside its towering stone walls. It was more stunning than Clemmie had ever imagined. The grounds stretched endlessly, a lush expanse of perfectly manicured lawns interspersed with winding paths, fountains, a rose garden and vibrant flowerbeds. A pavilion on the right provided shade for a few guests, while others strolled at a leisurely pace towards the heart of the garden. To their left, from a grand marquee came the lively sound of a military band. Abba's 'Dancing Queen' drifted across the lawn, bringing a smile to Clemmie's face. It was unexpectedly charming to hear such a cheerful tune in such a formal setting.

'This is … extraordinary,' she murmured, her eyes wide.

'It is,' Oliver agreed. 'Wait until you see the rest. The gardens here are legendary.'

They moved further into the grounds, where a lake added to the tranquil atmosphere. Clemmie marvelled at the sheer scale of it all, the lake's mirrored surface reflecting the deep blue sky, the rose gardens bursting with blooms of every shade. Guests strolled along the pathways, some pausing to admire the flowers, others simply enjoying the serene beauty of their surroundings.

As they approached the marquee, the delicious scent of freshly baked scones and delicate pastries wafted through the air. A long line of elegant tables stretched out beneath the marquee's shelter, each laden with an array of afternoon tea delights. Uniformed attendants moved gracefully among the guests, serving tea, coffee and soft drinks with quiet efficiency.

Clemmie's eyes widened at the sight of the spread. Finger sandwiches, neatly trimmed and filled with cucumber, smoked salmon or egg mayonnaise, sat alongside plates of golden scones with clotted cream and jam. Tiny cakes and pastries, each a work of art, tempted guests with their delicate designs.

'I'm actually speechless,' Clemmie said, her mouth watering as she accepted a small plate from one of the attendants. 'Everything looks so perfect.'

'It's a tradition,' Oliver said with a smile. 'They've been doing this for generations.'

Clemmie quickly scanned the area. 'Oliver, there's no torte. I thought the royal kitchen were baking my torte to be served to all the guests as the garden party? What if they've forgotten or they've changed their mind?'

'Don't worry, they will be doing a special presentation for it later on.'

Clemmie's hands flew straight to her beating chest. 'I wish Granny was here to see all this.'

'Cucumber sandwich?' he asked.

Clemmie laughed. 'Of course!'

Nibbling cucumber sandwiches they strolled towards the main lawn where uniformed attendants were handing out ice-creams. Clemmie took one, its cool sweetness a welcome treat in the afternoon sun. She and Oliver found a shaded bench near the rose garden and sat for a moment, soaking up the atmosphere and watching the ebb and flow of the elegantly dressed crowd.

'What do you think so far?' Oliver asked.

Clemmie smiled, gazing at the lake in the distance where swans glided gracefully across the water. 'It's all just magical. Imagine actually living here.' She looked over towards the palace.

Oliver's expression softened as he pointed towards a lady standing beneath the shade of a nearby tree. She wore an exquisite lavender suit with subtle embroidery along the edges, a matching hat adorned with delicate feathers perched elegantly on her silver hair. Her posture was straight, her every movement poised, as though she had been born to inhabit such a setting. 'Come on.' He grabbed her hand. 'I need to introduce you to Lady Rosalind.'

Lady Rosalind turned, her face lighting up the second she spotted him. She extended her arms towards him and he stepped forward and embraced her tightly, a movement that spoke of years of affection and familiarity.

'My dear boy,' she said, her voice low and melodious, carrying the unmistakable tone of someone used to addressing rooms filled with people. 'It's been far too long.'

'You look as radiant as ever,' Oliver replied with an easy charm that made Clemmie smile.

Lady Rosalind chuckled, then turned her attention to Clemmie. 'This must be Clemmie,' she said. 'I've heard so much about you.'

Clemmie felt her cheeks flush. 'It's lovely to meet you, Lady Rosalind,' she said, offering her hand.

Lady Rosalind waved it away and pulled her into a gentle hug instead, her embrace unexpectedly warm.

'Congratulations on winning The Royal Baking Competition,' she said, stepping back but still holding Clemmie's hands. 'That torte of yours has been the talk of the royal kitchen. We can't wait to taste it.'

Clemmie's blush deepened. 'Oh, thank you. It's all been such a whirlwind.'

'Well, enjoy every moment of it, my dear,' Lady Rosalind said, her smile encouraging.

Before Clemmie could respond, another woman joined them, her presence just as commanding. She wore a classic cream dress with pearls around her neck. Her silver hair was styled perfectly, and her eyes sparkled with delight as she looked at Oliver.

'Ah, Granny,' Oliver said, stepping forward to kiss her cheek. 'I knew you couldn't be far away.'

'Granny?' Clemmie exclaimed, turning to him in surprise. 'You didn't tell me you had family here!'

The woman laughed, her voice rich and full of life. 'This one is as slippery as they come,' she said, her tone affectionate as she gestured towards Oliver. 'Always keeping his royal connections close to his chest.'

Oliver grinned. 'I like to keep a little mystery. Granny, this is Clemmie, and Clemmie, my granny, Bunny.'

Just at that moment, there was a sudden shift in the energy of the crowd and a ripple of anticipation swept through the guests. Guards in traditional uniforms, complete with bearskin hats, marched onto the lawn, forming two long lines that created a clear path through the centre of the gathering. Clemmie's pulse quickened.

'They're coming,' Oliver murmured, his voice calm but tinged with excitement.

The band began to play the national anthem and the Royal Family began to emerge from the palace. Clemmie recognised Queen Charlotte immediately. She was resplendent in a soft pastel ensemble that perfectly complemented her regal bearing and gracious demeanour. She made her way down the line, pausing to speak with guests, her genuine interest evident in every interaction. Beside her were other members of the Royal Family, their elegant attire and approachable manners adding to the magic of the moment.

Clemmie and Oliver moved closer, positioning themselves near the front of the line. As Queen Charlotte approached, Clemmie's nerves surged. The Queen stopped just a few feet away to chat with a couple dressed in matching shades of blue, and Clemmie couldn't help but marvel at how relaxed and personable she seemed.

'I can't believe this is happening,' Clemmie whispered to Oliver, her cheeks flushed. 'I feel so nervous.'

Oliver squeezed her hand gently. 'You're going to be fine,' he murmured. 'It's not like it's the first time you've met her.'

The Queen turned towards them, her gaze alighting on Oliver with recognition. A smile spread across her face as she extended her hand. Oliver bowed slightly, then took her hand, shaking it briefly but with evident respect.

'Your Majesty,' Oliver said, his voice steady.

'Oliver,' the Queen replied, her smile widening. 'It's always a pleasure to see you.' Then, with a playful glint in her eye, she added, 'No doubt Lady Rosalind and your grandmother are sneaking the sherry from the drinks tent. I'm envious.'

Clemmie chuckled, the Queen's unexpected humour catching her off guard.

Oliver grinned. 'I'll be sure to keep an eye on them.'

The Queen's gaze shifted to Clemmie, her expression softening further. Clemmie curtsied.

'Clemmie, we meet again.' The Queen leaned forward. 'No pink heart pyjamas today?' she said with a chuckle.

Immediately put at ease, Clemmie relaxed. 'Not today, Your Majesty.'

'I've heard all about your Café on the Coast on Puffin Island.' The Queen's smile grew as she extended her hand to Clemmie, who quickly but nervously shook it. 'Congratulations, Clemmie, on winning The Royal Baking Competition,' the Queen said. 'Your torte was quite the triumph. My royal bakers are preparing your recipe as we speak. Soon, everyone at the garden party will have the chance to taste it.'

'Thank you, ma'am. I'm truly honoured.'

'I believe a cookbook is in preparation as well?' the Queen continued.

'Yes, ma'am,' Clemmie replied, her voice wobbling slightly from nerves.

'Well, I shall look forward to it,' the Queen said. 'I would like a signed copy, personally.'

Clemmie's heart raced. 'Of course, ma'am. I'd be delighted. Do I … do I just send it to the palace?'

The Queen's smile turned amused as she nodded. 'I'm sure it will reach me,' she said, her tone gentle. 'Congratulations again. I hope you enjoy the rest of the day.'

With that, she moved on, the interaction leaving Clemmie both breathless and starstruck.

Clemmie turned to Oliver, her cheeks glowing. 'Did I make a complete idiot of myself?' she asked, half-dreading his answer.

Oliver laughed, his eyes full of affection. 'Not at all. You were wonderful and she liked you, I could tell.'

Clemmie let out a breath of relief, then followed Oliver's gaze towards the drinks tent. Sure enough, Lady Rosalind and Oliver's grandmother stood huddled together, laughing and gesturing animatedly. They looked as though they were sharing some grand secret, and Clemmie smiled at the sight.

'She's right about them, isn't she?' Clemmie said, nudging Oliver playfully.

He nodded, his expression fond. 'Oh, absolutely. If I had to guess, I'd say they're undoubtedly up to no good.'

'How does your grandmother know the Queen?'

'She was her seamstress for many years,' Oliver said casually, as though it were the most normal thing in the world.

Clemmie blinked, stunned. 'And you only thought to tell me that now?'

Oliver grinned. 'It's not something you drop into everyday conversation.'

Clemmie shook her head, laughing. 'You live in another world.'

Before Oliver could respond, Lady Rosalind's voice cut through the hum of the crowd as she approached them with a smile and a glass of prosecco in each hand.

'Thanks very much,' said Clemmie, taking one of the

glasses. 'This is just an amazing day.' She took a sip and glanced over at the royals before her gaze shifted and she froze.

Walking towards them, amidst the sea of elegance and poise, was someone Clemmie had never expected to see here. Fiona Fairweather.

Clemmie's heart skipped a beat. Fiona was dressed to impress, her outfit striking but somehow too bold for the refined setting. Her hat was an elaborate concoction of bright feathers, and her dress, though undeniably expensive, seemed to scream for attention rather than match the understated elegance of the event.

'What on earth is she doing here?' Clemmie murmured, her voice laced with disbelief. 'How did she get an invite? She didn't even win the competition!'

Fiona was now just a few steps away, her eyes scanning the crowd before landing squarely on Clemmie and Oliver. A sly smile spread across her face as she approached, her confidence unmistakable. Clemmie felt a knot of unease form in her stomach. The day had been perfect, almost too perfect, and now, with Fiona's sudden appearance, she couldn't shake the feeling that something was about to disrupt the magic of it all.

'Clemmie, let me introduce you to someone,' said Lady Rosalind, who had suddenly appeared at Fiona's side. 'My granddaughter Fiona.'

Clemmie's mouth fell open before she hastily shut it. She would have to do everything in her power to stay composed.

Chapter Twenty-Three

Clemmie had excused herself to find the bathroom, needing a moment to gather her thoughts. Five minutes later as she stepped back outside, Oliver was waiting for her. His expression was sheepish, almost guilty, and Clemmie immediately sensed that something was off.

'Why didn't you tell me she would be here?' Clemmie asked. 'Is that not a bit of information I should have known?'

Oliver straightened, meeting her gaze.

'You must have known,' she continued, her voice growing sharper. 'If she's Lady Rosalind's granddaughter, you had to know she'd be here.'

'This is your day. Don't let her being here spoil it.'

Clemmie glanced over her shoulder, her gaze landing on Fiona, who was holding a flute of prosecco and wearing a smirk that could only be described as smug. The glint in Fiona's eyes sent a fresh wave of irritation through Clemmie's chest.

'Why is she looking at me like that? It's like she wants to tell me something, as though she thinks she has some sort of hold over me.'

Oliver followed Clemmie's gaze. 'Come on,' he said softly, taking her hand. 'Let's go for a walk. The gardens here are gorgeous. You don't want to miss them.'

Clemmie hesitated, glancing back towards Fiona, who was still watching them with that infuriatingly self-satisfied expression. 'Whatever it is she's dying to tell me,' Clemmie said, turning back to Oliver with determination in her eyes, 'it's not going to ruin my day.'

They began to walk, stepping out onto the vast expanse of manicured lawns and blooming flowerbeds that stretched as far as the eye could see. The air was fragrant with the scent of roses, and a soft breeze rustled the trees, their branches casting dappled shadows on the ground. But even as Clemmie marvelled at the beauty around her, Fiona remained on her mind. After a few minutes of silence, she couldn't hold back any longer.

'I can't picture you with her,' Clemmie blurted. 'Not even for a quick fling.'

Oliver glanced at her. 'What do you mean?'

'She's not your type,' Clemmie said, her tone more frustrated than she intended. 'She's so … smug. I can't picture you with someone like that at all.'

Oliver's gaze was fixed on the path ahead. 'I told you, our families have known each other for a long time,' he began, his voice measured. 'Lady Rosalind and my grandmother have been friends for decades and I think they both quietly hoped Fiona and I would end up together.'

Clemmie frowned, her steps slowing as she absorbed his words. 'Like some sort of arranged marriage?'

'Not quite,' Oliver replied, 'It was never formal. Just … an unspoken understanding, I suppose. A wish more than anything else… But there's something you need to know,' he shared.

Clemmie's stomach twisted, her mind racing with possibilities. 'What is it?'

Oliver hesitated. 'I invested in her business.'

'You're partners with her in her bakery business?'

'Yes, and if I take my money out, her business would more than likely fold. But between you and me, I want out.'

'And how do you think that will go down?'

'I think it's safe to say she won't be happy. Fiona doesn't like losing. She's always been competitive, which isn't a bad thing in business, so hopefully she can get another backer. Even if I hadn't met you, it would have been something I would have thought about doing. Come on … listen to that…'

Just then, a fanfare sounded. They quickly made their way back to the marquee. Clemmie placed her hands over her heart, overwhelmed by the surreal sight of the royal chefs serving slices of her torte on gleaming plates. They hurried closer, and her heart swelled with pride when she saw the bold, elegant sign beside the table:

Winning Royal Baking Competition Recipe by Clemmie Rose, The Café on the Coast, Puffin Island.

'Go on,' Oliver insisted. 'You need a photo with *your* torte.'

Clemmie allowed herself to be ushered closer, and Oliver eagerly pulled out his phone. She posed beside the sign, then held up a plate with a delicate slice of the torte, its chocolate clementine topping glinting in the sunlight. Oliver captured every angle, laughing when she struck a playful pose holding a fork.

'Perfect,' he said, snapping a final photo. 'These are going straight on social media – or maybe the café's wall of fame? Because after this I bet you have lots of famous people visiting your café.'

Clemmie laughed, her nerves momentarily forgotten as she imagined her little café bustling with customers eager to try the torte that had won royal acclaim. The thought of people flocking to Puffin Island for a slice of her great-great-grandmother's creation filled her with both pride and disbelief.

Before she could respond to Oliver's playful teasing about a wall of fame, a familiar voice interrupted.

'There she is, the woman of the hour!'

Clemmie turned to see Lady Rosalind approaching alongside Oliver's grandmother.

'A masterpiece if ever I saw one,' Lady Rosalind said. 'It's no mean feat to win The Royal Baking Competition. It takes hard work, tradition and a bit of courage, too.'

Clemmie flushed at the praise. 'Thank you.'

Lady Rosalind picked up a plate with a slice of torte, studying it with the precision of someone who truly appreciated the art of baking. She held the fork delicately, like a wand, as though the act of tasting was something sacred. But before she took her first bite, she leaned in closer.

'Over the years, I've sampled many cakes and bakes from the royal kitchen,' she began, her voice tinged with nostalgia. 'There was one chef in particular who was very fond of me. He used to leave me a slice of cake most days in a rather amusing hiding place. You'll never guess where?'

Clemmie tilted her head, intrigued. 'Where?'

Lady Rosalind laughed softly, a rich sound that hinted at countless untold stories. 'The back of a grandfather clock, just outside the kitchens. I'd slide the little panel open, and there it would be, wrapped neatly in a linen napkin. I suppose we thought ourselves quite clever at the time. A secret little ritual, just for us.'

Clemmie couldn't help but laugh, the image of a younger Lady Rosalind sneaking cakes from a clock both endearing and amusing.

Lady Rosalind smiled fondly at the memory before fixing her gaze back on Clemmie. 'Now, tell me about this recipe of yours. How did it come to be?'

As Clemmie explained, Fiona appeared at Lady Rosalind's side.

Clemmie hesitated for a moment before continuing, a wistful smile tugging at her lips as she came to the end of her story. 'In her recipe book, she wrote, "This will be fit for the royals!"'

'That's marvellous,' Lady Rosalind said, clearly delighted. 'Beatrice sounds like quite a woman.'

'I believe she really was,' Clemmie agreed.

Lady Rosalind's smile softened. 'A recipe like that isn't just food, it's history, tradition, love. It carries the spirit of the person who created it and judging by the way the royal chefs are handling it, I'd say your family would be immensely proud.'

Oliver's grandmother reached out, giving Clemmie's hand a reassuring squeeze. 'Your great-great-grandmother would be thrilled to know her recipe is being enjoyed by royalty, and by us,' she added with a smile.

Lady Rosalind finally lifted her fork and took her first bite of the torte. Her expression shifted subtly as she chewed, her brows knitting together ever so slightly. She swallowed, placing her fork down with deliberate care.

'What do you think?' Clemmie asked, her voice laced with nerves.

Lady Rosalind paused for a moment, her gaze thoughtful. 'It's … remarkable,' she said slowly. 'In fact, it tastes exactly like the torte I've tasted many times over the years.' She glanced at Oliver's grandmother, then back at Clemmie. 'I would even go so far as to say it's the *same* recipe.'

Clemmie blinked, taken aback. 'The … same? It can't be.'

Lady Rosalind nodded. 'There's no mistaking it. This torte tastes exactly like the one that's been around in my family for generations, and the Royal Family, too.'

Before Clemmie could process the revelation, Fiona took a sip of prosecco, her smirk as sharp as ever.

'Well, isn't that interesting,' Fiona cut in. 'I wonder how that could be. Tell me, Clemmie, did you cheat? Did you make up that charming little story about your Café on the Coast to win votes?'

Clemmie's cheeks flushed, a mix of shock and indignation bubbling inside her. 'Excuse me?'

Fiona raised an eyebrow. 'It's all very convenient, isn't

it? A torte recipe with royal roots, passed down through generations, suddenly winning The Royal Baking Competition. Almost … *too* convenient.'

'That's enough, Fiona,' Oliver interjected, his tone firm and unyielding. 'You're making baseless accusations, and you know it.'

Fiona's eyes flicked towards him. 'I'm simply pointing out the obvious, Oliver. No need to get defensive, unless … did you give her the recipe?'

Oliver looked bemused. 'What are you implying?'

Clemmie composed herself. 'For the record,' she said, her voice steady despite the fact she felt shaky, 'the recipe has been in my family for generations and I didn't win because of a story, I won because of the torte itself. If you'd like, I can share the recipe with you. Maybe it'll help your bakery.'

Fiona's cheeks coloured slightly, but she quickly masked it with a tight smile. 'How generous of you,' she said coolly.

Lady Rosalind placed a hand on Clemmie's arm, her touch reassuring. 'I'm sure there's some explanation.'

'But I think as there's some doubt about the origin of the recipe, it needs to be brought to the attention of the adjudicators of the competition … because that's grounds for disqualification,' Fiona said sharply. 'Wouldn't that be a scandal for your little café on the coast? You'll be returning home a cheat, not a hero.'

'That's ridiculous. As I said, the recipe has been in my family for generations—'

'Then prove it,' came the reply. 'The competition organisers may have been happy with a signed declaration via email confirming the recipe was original to your family, but given there was no actual fact-checking you should provide proof in order to clear your name. Otherwise, who's to say you or someone from your family didn't merely lift it from an old book or overhear it in someone else's kitchen? Without proof, it's just a nice story, and nice stories don't hold up in competitions.'

Lady Rosalind straightened. 'There must be something,' she said, though a flicker of doubt passed over her face. 'Beatrice must have left a record somewhere.'

Clemmie swallowed hard. She had the tattered recipe in the journal written in her grandmother's hand, but was that enough? Was there a way to prove it belonged to Beatrice first?

Clemmie stared at Fiona before Oliver gently took her hand. He tried to lead her away but Clemmie pulled her hand back. She stiffened and looked Fiona right in the eyes. 'My great-great-grandmother created that recipe herself, and I will not stand here and let you question her integrity – or mine. It's an original recipe, and I can back that up with evidence. Handwritten notes, dated journals and even her original cookbook, with her own annotations in the margins. If you want to take it to the adjudicators, be my guest. But don't for a second think I'll let you rewrite my family's legacy to suit your narrative.'

The words hung in the air like a challenge.

As Clemmie turned and walked away, she could feel herself shaking with anger. Her pulse pounded as she and Oliver wove through the crowd, the laughter and clinking glasses around them a stark contrast to the unease that was swirling in the pit of her stomach. She stole a glance over her shoulder, her mind racing. The torte. Fiona. Lady Rosalind. The Royal Family.

'It can't be the same recipe. It just can't,' she said. 'It was written in my great-great-grandmother's own hand.'

'It'll be similar, that's all and don't let Fiona get to you, she's just a sore loser.'

But Clemmie hesitated, a thread of unease suddenly winding through her. Before the advent of modern technology, most recipes were copied down by hand and then passed from one person to another. But did that mean there was a chance that Beatrice had simply written it out from a book, or borrowed it from a friend? The thought made her feel uneasy. No. It wasn't possible. The recipe was her great-great-grandmother's. It had to be.

Clemmie's gaze snapped back to Fiona. She was on the phone now, her expression unreadable.

'She's calling someone. What if it's about the competition?' A chill crept up Clemmie's spine.

'Forget her and just enjoy this moment,' Oliver urged, but his words barely registered.

A sinking feeling settled deep in Clemmie's stomach.

Something wasn't right.

A scandal was brewing and she was about to be caught right in the middle of it.

Chapter Twenty-Four

C lemmie stared at the delicate slice of torte on her porcelain plate. Beside her, Oliver had already taken a bite, his face melting into a look of pure bliss.

'Oh, this is divine,' he murmured, his voice muffled by the mouthful. 'You've got to try it.'

Clemmie picked up her fork, hesitating for a moment. She broke the torte's glossy surface, the fork gliding effortlessly through its velvety layers. As the first bite melted on her tongue, she let out a quiet gasp.

'This is nearly as good as mine,' she joked.

Before she could savour another bite, a tall man in a pristine white chef's coat approached them. His appearance was impeccable, silver hair neatly combed back, a perfectly trimmed moustache, and an air of authority softened by the faintest twinkle in his eye. He stopped a few feet from them, hands clasped behind his back, and offered a polite smile.

'I believe you are Clemmie Rose, winner of the baking

competition, I trust you are enjoying your torte?' His voice was smooth and polished.

Clemmie and Oliver exchanged a glance before nodding enthusiastically.

The chef's smile widened. 'Allow me to introduce myself. I am Chef Laurent de Vauclaire, the head pastry chef here at the palace.'

Clemmie's eyes grew even wider.

'I had the honour of organising my kitchen to bake your creation today,' he said with a small bow. 'I would love to show you, as the creator of this recipe, where the magic happens.' He gestured towards the palace.

Clemmie's heart leaped. 'You mean the royal kitchen?'

'Precisely,' Laurent said. 'Come, I will introduce you to the team.'

Without hesitation, Clemmie and Oliver followed Laurent through the garden, weaving between elegantly dressed guests and uniformed staff. They entered the palace through a discreet side door and descended a short staircase that opened into a sprawling kitchen.

The royal kitchen was a masterpiece in itself. Gleaming pots and pans hung from racks suspended above pristine marble countertops. Rows of ovens lined one wall, their dials and handles polished to a mirror finish. A team of chefs in immaculate white uniforms moved with precision, each focused on their individual task. The air was filled with the heavenly aroma of freshly baked pastries, caramelised sugar and roasted nuts.

'Welcome to the beating heart of the palace,' Laurent said with a touch of pride.

Clemmie stepped further inside, taking in every detail.

A pastry chef was delicately piping whipped cream onto a row of eclairs, while another was meticulously arranging candied fruits on a towering croquembouche. In the far corner, a sous-chef was stirring a pot of rich, bubbling caramel, the golden liquid catching the light.

'Everyone, may I present the winner of The Royal Baking Competition, Miss Clemmie Rose.' The staff paused briefly to nod and smile before returning to their tasks.

'This is extraordinary,' Clemmie exclaimed.

Laurent led them to a large workstation in the centre of the kitchen, where a freshly baked torte sat cooling on a wire rack. 'This, my friends, is your torte's sibling, prepared first to make sure we got it right.'

As Laurent carried on with a tour of the kitchen, a sudden voice interrupted them. 'Excuse me, Chef Laurent,' said a man dressed in a sharp black suit. He was composed yet authoritative.

Laurent turned to him. 'Ah, Mr Kensington, how may I assist you?'

The man's gaze shifted to Clemmie and Oliver. 'I am Her Majesty's Personal Assistant,' he introduced himself. 'I was asked to escort you to her sitting room where the Queen is waiting.'

Clemmie froze. 'The Queen?' she stammered.

'Indeed,' Mr Kensington said with a polite smile. 'If you would kindly follow me.'

Laurent gave an encouraging nod. 'Go. It is not every day one receives such an invitation.'

With hearts pounding, Clemmie and Oliver followed Mr Kensington out of the kitchen and up a grand staircase. As they walked, Clemmie leaned close to Oliver, her voice a nervous whisper. 'Do you think she's going to question me about the recipe? If she thinks I've stolen it, she might say *off with her head*!'

Oliver gave her a sidelong glance, stifling a grin. 'I hear she prefers scones over executions these days.'

'Very funny,' Clemmie murmured.

The corridors they passed through were lined with portraits of monarchs past, their regal gazes seeming to follow them like disapproving chaperones. Finally, they stopped outside a door guarded by two stoic footmen. Mr Kensington knocked once, and the door was opened to reveal an elegant yet understated sitting room which was the perfect blend of grandness and comfort. The walls were decorated with soft floral wallpaper, and the regal mantelpiece held a collection of framed photographs: smiling children, black-and-white portraits, and the occasional candid shot that hinted at family moments rarely seen by the public. A low coffee table stood between the sofa and the Queen's armchair, its surface draped with an intricately embroidered tablecloth and a tray laden with delicate china cups, a teapot and an assortment of biscuits neatly arranged on a silver plate.

Seated in a comfortable armchair was the Queen herself. The sight of her still took Clemmie's breath away. Her Majesty's kind yet piercing eyes met Clemmie's, and a small smile played on her lips.

Clemmie's instincts took over. She dropped into a deep curtsy while Oliver executed a respectful bow.

'Do come in,' the Queen said, gesturing to the sofa. 'Please, sit.'

Clemmie and Oliver exchanged a quick glance before sitting down opposite her.

'I needed a brief escape from the crowd. Even queens require a moment of peace, and a slice of Chef Laurent's baking never fails to do the trick.' The Queen's tone was friendly and conversational. She turned towards Mr Kensington. 'Would you please pour my guests some tea.'

After Mr Kensington poured the tea, he handed a cup and saucer each to Clemmie and Oliver then bowed towards the Queen.

'That will be all for now. Thank you.'

Mr Kensington exited the room. The door closed with a faint click, leaving the three of them alone.

'I hope the two of you are enjoying the party. These occasions can be a bit … overwhelming, I imagine.'

Oliver, ever the diplomat, smiled warmly. 'It's been a lovely afternoon, Your Majesty. Thank you for inviting us.'

Clemmie nodded in agreement, though her fingers fidgeted with the handle of the teacup. She couldn't help feeling slightly out of place in such regal surroundings.

The Queen set her cup down, offered them a biscuit and reached for one herself. 'I must confess,' she began, her tone light, 'I do like a good cup of tea and a biscuit.' She held up the biscuit with a small smile. 'Shortbread. A classic.'

Clemmie managed a nervous laugh. 'My granny always says a good cup of tea fixes everything.'

The Queen's expression softened again. 'She sounds like a wise woman. It reminds me,' she continued, leaning back in her chair, 'of my own grandmother, Queen Eleanor. Did you know she was quite the baker in her day?'

Oliver and Clemmie exchanged a surprised glance. Clemmie shook her head. 'No, I didn't. That's fascinating.'

'Indeed,' the Queen replied. 'Stories have been passed down in our family about how she learned to bake from the palace chef, a dear friend of hers. Tragically, he was killed during the war, but his lessons stayed with her. She would spend hours in the kitchen, perfecting his recipes. This very torte we've been serving today reminds me of one of those recipes.'

Clemmie glanced towards Oliver whose eyes widened.

'I've even baked something very similar myself.'

'You bake, too?' asked Clemmie.

The Queen smiled. 'Baking has always been a bit of a refuge for me. My mother, Queen Matilda, was much the same. I remember when I was a child, she would invite me into the kitchen to help her. Of course, the staff were always on hand, but she insisted on doing some things herself. She said it was important to stay connected to simple pleasures.'

The Queen paused, her gaze falling to the teapot as she poured herself another cup. 'I can still recall the scent of the kitchen, the feel of dough beneath my fingers. My mother had a particular fondness for making fruit cakes. She would let me stir the mixture and sneak a taste when no one was looking. It was our little secret.'

Her voice carried a note of fond nostalgia, and for a moment, Clemmie felt as though she were peering into a private corner of the Queen's life, one rarely glimpsed by the outside world.

'It sounds wonderful,' Clemmie said softly.

The Queen nodded. 'It was. Those moments taught me that even in the midst of great responsibility, one must find time for simple joys. It's a lesson I've carried with me throughout my reign.'

She reached for another biscuit, her movements unhurried. Then, as if struck by a sudden thought, she turned her attention back to Clemmie. 'Tell me, Clemmie, does your family have any royal connections? Perhaps your great-great-grandmother did?'

Clemmie blinked, caught off guard by the question. 'Oh, no, Your Majesty. My family has always been fascinated by the Royal Family, especially my granny, but we've never moved in those circles.'

The Queen's expression didn't change, but there was a flicker of something in her eyes, a thoughtful intensity. She leaned forward slightly, her tone becoming quieter. 'Have you, by any chance, ever come across the name of the Earl of Aberford?'

The question hung in the air as Clemmie's mind raced. Instinct told her to tread carefully. She nodded. 'I recently saw a photo of him for the first time, and his name is written in the visitors' book at the royal cottage where we're staying. Why do you ask?' she replied, her voice steady despite the flutter of nerves in her chest.

The Queen studied her for a long moment, her expression unreadable. 'Well,' she said, her tone returning to its earlier warmth, 'my great-grandmother was very fond of the Earl, and he told her tales of visiting Puffin Island.'

'What a coincidence.'

'Yes, it is, and I have it on good authority that he loved a good torte.' She glanced at the clock on the mantelpiece and stood gracefully. 'I mustn't keep you from the festivities any longer and I should return to the garden before anyone notices my absence.'

Clemmie and Oliver rose as well, both murmuring their thanks and placing their cups and saucers on a nearby table. The Queen jiggled a bell and Mr Kensington immediately appeared to escort them back to the garden party. The Queen offered a parting smile. 'I do hope you've enjoyed this little interlude. Perhaps we'll have another chance to talk soon.'

As the door closed behind them, Clemmie turned to Oliver, her voice barely above a whisper. 'What was that all about? The Earl of Aberford has been to Puffin Island?'

Oliver shrugged, but his brow was furrowed in thought. 'I'm not sure. But it felt … significant, didn't it?'

Clemmie nodded. The name 'Earl of Aberford' lingered in her thoughts. She had never heard him mentioned by her family, though they were obsessed with royalty. Surely his name would have cropped up before now if it was significant, especially if he had a connection to Puffin Island?

As they stepped back into the sunlight and the lively buzz of the garden party, she couldn't dispel the feeling that this was only the beginning of something much larger. The Queen's words had been kind, but they had left a lingering sense of mystery. Clemmie knew she had some important questions for her granny when she returned home.

'Well,' Oliver said with a grin as they stepped back into the garden. 'That's one way to spend an afternoon.'

'No one back home will believe me when I tell them I've had tea with the Queen. It was so surreal, just like this place. Shall we grab another drink? Then I would love to take a closer look at the rose garden,' said Clemmie.

The sweet scent of roses hung softly in the air, blending with the distant murmur of voices and the music from the band. Clemmie and Oliver strolled down the gravel path, their prosecco glasses catching the light, refracting tiny rainbows onto the ground as they walked.

The rose garden was serene, tucked away from the lively bustle of the main garden party. Rows of perfectly pruned rose bushes stood in disciplined symmetry, their petals ranging from soft blush pinks to deep crimson reds. At the heart of it all, a weathered wooden bench beckoned. As they sat, Clemmie leaned back, exhaling deeply. 'Can we just talk about Lady Rosalind for a moment? The way she kept going on about that recipe... It's almost as if she's convinced that I've copied it from somewhere. Which I have, my great-great-grandmother's recipe book.' She glanced sideways at Oliver.

Oliver swirled his prosecco thoughtfully. 'It's peculiar, isn't it? She was sure she'd tasted your creation before. Do you think...' He hesitated, choosing his words carefully. 'Do you think that's why the Queen invited us for a chat?'

Clemmie's expression grew serious. 'I'm beginning to feel uneasy about all of this. If Lady Rosalind genuinely believes she's familiar with the recipe, it might stir up trouble. And Fiona...' She blew out a breath. 'Fiona will jump at any opportunity to make waves. If Lady Rosalind's suspicions fuel her, I could be in for a very rough ride. What if I'm branded a cheat?'

'Don't be ridiculous.' But just as the words left Oliver's

mouth, Fiona appeared at the edge of the rose garden. Her expression was one of triumphant glee.

Clemmie's stomach lurched as Fiona strode purposefully towards them.

'Oh, God, what does she want now?' Oliver muttered.

'Well, well,' Fiona began, her voice dripping with faux sweetness. 'I hate to interrupt your little idyll, but I thought you should know there's going to be an inquiry into just how original your recipe really is.'

Clemmie's breath caught. 'An inquiry? Are you serious?'

Fiona's smile widened. 'Oh, absolutely. Lady Rosalind's remarks caught the attention of some rather influential ears. It's only right to ensure that everything is above board, don't you think?'

Oliver stood, his tone firm. 'Fiona, this is ridiculous. Clemmie won fair and square. You need to accept that and move on. Bow out with dignity instead of clinging to petty vendettas.'

Fiona's eyes flashed. 'Petty vendettas? Oh, Oliver, you've always been such a white knight, haven't you? But this isn't about pettiness, it's about fairness. And besides,' she added with a sly grin, 'it's a day for secrets to be revealed.'

Clemmie's heart sank. 'What's that supposed to mean?' she asked, looking between them both.

Oliver's face darkened. 'Fiona, don't do this.'

But Fiona was clearly revelling in the moment. 'Oh, come on, Oliver. You can't honestly expect me to keep quiet about *that*.' She turned to Clemmie, her expression a mix of mock sympathy and delight. 'Darling Clemmie, did you ever wonder about that scathing review of your little café?

The one you mentioned in your so-called winning speech, that left you doubting yourself for years?'

Clemmie froze, her blood running cold. 'What are you talking about?'

Fiona's grin turned feral. 'It was Oliver. He wrote it. Every cutting word.'

The world seemed to stand still. Clemmie stared at Oliver, her voice trembling. 'Is that true?'

'Clemmie, I can explain,' Oliver began, stepping towards her.

But she held up a hand, stopping him in his tracks. The betrayal hit her like a tidal wave, and she felt her chest tighten with hurt and fury. Without another word, she turned and walked away, her steps brisk and determined. She didn't look back, but the sound of Oliver's and Fiona's raised voices followed her like an echo.

Chapter Twenty-Five

Clemmie slammed the wardrobe door shut. She was furious. It didn't take her long to pack her suitcase. Royalwood Cottage suddenly felt stifling and alien. She wanted to be gone. Now.

Her phone buzzed. Another message from her granny, no doubt, asking how the garden party was going. She ignored it, zipping up her case, whilst the tears she had been holding back began to blur her vision. She swiped at them angrily.

She couldn't stop replaying the day's events in her mind. It was all too much. She ripped off the dress Oliver had bought her, flinging it onto the bed. One by one, she laid out the ensemble: the hat, the matching bag, the now-worn shoes. 'I don't want any of it,' she muttered to no one in particular, her voice cracking. 'I just want to go home.'

She grabbed her phone, her trembling fingers finding Amelia's number. The phone barely rang before Amelia picked up.

'Clemmie? How's it going? Are you still at the palace?'

That simple question undid her. The tears came freely now, and she sat down heavily on the edge of the bed. 'Amelia, it's all a mess. I can't … I can't even think straight.'

'What do you mean? What's happened? Start from the beginning.' Amelia's voice was calm but concerned.

'There's going to be an investigation,' Clemmie said, her words tumbling out. 'The recipe … the one from Great-great-granny … they're saying it was stolen. Apparently, the recipe has been used in the palace for decades. God, it's just humiliating and Oliver… I never want to see him again. Ever.'

'Wait, hold on,' Amelia said. 'What do you mean stolen? Are they saying Beatrice copied it? That's ludicrous!'

'That's exactly what they're saying,' Clemmie replied. 'But in my eyes, it's impossible. The recipe has been baked in The Café on the Coast for decades. I have no idea how this could have happened, but I'll have to talk with Granny when I get home. If anyone can make sense of this, it's her.'

Amelia's tone softened. 'You'll figure it out and as for Oliver … what exactly happened? Did he say something?'

Clemmie swallowed hard, fresh anger rising to the surface. 'It's what he did. He wrote that bloody review. Remember, the one I mentioned in my winning speech? The one that crucified me in my first week of becoming a partner in the café? He didn't even tell me. It was Fiona who had the great pleasure of revealing the truth. How could he do that?'

Amelia was silent for a moment. 'That … doesn't sound like the Oliver that you know. Are you sure there's no misunderstanding?'

'No, I obviously don't know him at all,' Clemmie said flatly.

A car horn bleeped outside, and Clemmie stood, peering out the window. A black taxi had just pulled up. 'I've got to go, my taxi is here. I'm on my way to the train station.' Clemmie hung up, then grabbed her case.

As she opened the front door, she noticed another taxi pulling up beside hers. Her stomach churned when she saw who stepped out. Oliver. He looked dishevelled and frantic, his tie askew and his hair windblown. His eyes locked onto hers the moment she stepped outside.

'Clemmie,' he called, hurrying towards her.

She didn't slow her pace. 'Don't, Oliver. I have nothing to say to you.'

'Please, just listen to me,' he said, his tone pleading. 'It's not what you think.'

She whirled around, her suitcase wobbling on its wheels. 'Not what I think? You wrote the review, didn't you? Just answer me that.'

He hesitated, and that pause told her everything she needed to know. Still, he nodded. 'Yes, I did. But—'

'Then there's nothing more to talk about,' she said, her voice icy. 'Do you have any idea what you did to me?

'Clemmie, please listen,' he said, stepping closer. 'I didn't know it would cause all this. I didn't mean for… It was a long time ago.'

'And that makes it okay, does it? And you didn't mean for what?' she interrupted, her voice rising. 'For it to blow up in your face? You should have thought about that before you put pen to paper. Cruel words affect people's lives. I bet you felt smug, and for what? A few paragraphs in a magazine? A pat on the back from your editor? I hope it was worth it. You are a coward. You didn't even put your name to it.'

'Because the review was particularly harsh, the editors removed my name to protect me from potential fallout.'

'Very convenient.'

'Please, just give me a chance to explain.'

He reached for her arm, but she pulled away and stared at him, 'That's what Seraphina meant when she said, "Take note of what I said", wasn't it? And that must have been Fiona on that call you took in the garden. She threatened to tell me before the garden party and you discussed it with Seraphina whilst I was getting ready. She told you to tell me, to let it come from you … and you chose not to. I'm done giving you chances,' she said firmly. 'You've made your choices, Oliver. And now I'm making mine.'

With that, she turned and climbed into the taxi. She slammed the door shut, avoiding Oliver's gaze through the window. The driver, sensing the tension, quickly loaded her suitcase.

As the taxi pulled away, Clemmie felt a wave of exhaustion wash over her. The tears threatened to return, but she blinked them back. She needed to stay strong, at least until she was home. Until she could see Granny and try to make sense of it all.

Oliver stood growing smaller in the rear-view mirror with every passing second. For a fleeting moment, she wondered if she'd made a mistake. Should she let him explain? But the anger and betrayal resurfaced, drowning out any lingering doubt.

There was no going back now.

Chapter Twenty-Six

As soon as the taxi pulled up outside the quaint seaside café, Clemmie's eyes were immediately drawn to the Royal Yacht anchored in the distance, its regal silhouette sharply outlined against the late evening sun. A shiver ran down her spine, though not from the coastal breeze. She had envisioned this moment, her triumphant return, imagining herself walking into the café after attending the royal garden party with a story of success and joy that would have the regulars beaming with pride. Instead, the knot in her stomach told a very different story.

Her train ride from London had been a battle against tears, her trembling hands clutching the strap of her bag as if it were the only thing keeping her from falling apart. Somehow, she had managed to hold herself together … until now.

The bell above the café door tinkled softly as she stepped inside, the familiar aroma of freshly baked scones enveloping her. The café was still festooned with Union Jack bunting, and the life-sized cutout of the Queen stood proudly by the counter, her cardboard smile radiating unflappable cheer. It was as though the celebrations of her winning the competition were still going on, a stark contrast to the storm raging in Clemmie's heart.

Before she could say anything, Betty appeared from behind the counter, her face breaking into a concerned smile as she took in Clemmie's tear-streaked face and trembling body. 'Oh, Clemmie,' she murmured, pulling her into a tight embrace.

The dam burst. Clemmie clung to Betty, sobbing uncontrollably. Betty's sturdy arms were a safe haven, and Clemmie allowed herself to crumple completely, her muffled cries soaking into her granny's apron.

'What the hell has gone on?' Betty asked softly. Before Clemmie could summon the strength to reply, the door jingled again, and Amelia burst in, her face alight with worry.

'I saw the taxi arrive. Oh, Clemmie,' Amelia exclaimed, rushing forward to hug her friend. 'Are you all right?'

Between them, they guided Clemmie into the living room. Amelia and Clemmie sat on the sofa, while Betty settled into her armchair, her eyes never leaving Clemmie's face.

'Right,' Betty said firmly, 'start from the beginning.'

Still trembling, Clemmie began to recount the disastrous chain of events that had unfolded at the royal garden party, right down to the moment the Queen herself mentioned the Earl of Aberford. The baking competition had been meant to be the crowning achievement of her career, a chance to showcase her family's cherished recipe in front of royalty and some of the finest culinary minds in the country. Instead, it had descended into chaos.

'Okay, I know the ending to the garden party wasn't brilliant,' Amelia interjected when Clemmie paused, her voice kind but firm, 'but don't let Fiona Fairweather or Oliver take this away from you. You know what she's trying to do. She wants that cookbook in her name. But you were there on your own merit. Someone nominated you. Someone chose you, and decided your baking was worthy of being showcased among the elite, and they weren't wrong.'

Clemmie nodded weakly, though her tears hadn't entirely stopped.

Amelia pressed on. 'If there is an investigation, so what? You've got the evidence. That recipe book dates back decades. Generations. It's as authentic as they come. I'm sure they won't even find grounds for an investigation. At the end of the day, it's a baking competition, not a political scandal.'

Betty snorted at that. 'Honestly, I'm sure what Fiona Fairweather baked wasn't some cherished recipe passed down by her great-great-grandmother either. It was probably something she pinched off the internet and her personal chef whipped up last minute.'

That drew a small, watery smile from Clemmie, and Amelia seized the moment to lighten the mood further.

'As for Oliver,' Amelia said with a dramatic eyeroll, 'he's got a long way to go to redeem himself. If he's even capable of that.'

Betty's expression darkened. 'He's not welcome in my

café, I'll tell you that much. If I see him, I'll chase him out with my rolling pin.'

The image of Betty wielding her rolling pin like a sword sent the three women into a fit of giggles, the tension in the room easing ever so slightly.

As the laughter subsided, Clemmie took a deep breath. 'It doesn't matter as he's off to America. I don't think I'll ever hear from him again. Thank you. Both of you. I don't know what I'd do without you.'

Betty said simply, squeezing her hand, 'We stick together, always.'

Amelia leaned forward. 'You said, the Queen mentioned the Earl of Aberford. Who is he and how does he factor into all of this?'

'The Earl of Aberford.'

Betty froze, the colour draining from her face. 'Say that again?' she said staring.

'The Earl of Aberford,' Clemmie repeated slowly. 'Apparently, there was some kind of scandal. He decided not to use his title and then disappeared from royal life, years ago. Why?'

For a moment, the only sound in the room was the soft ticking of the clock on the wall.

'I've actually heard that name before,' she said.

Clemmie and Amelia exchanged a curious look.

Betty's eyes looked up towards the hatch in the roof in the hallway. 'And I've seen that name before.'

'Where?' asked Clemmie.

'There's a box in the loft with that very name on it. I asked my mother about it and she said it belonged to her mother and it was never to be opened.'

Chapter Twenty-Seven

Betty and Amelia stood at the bottom of the loft ladder, peering upwards into the shadowy space beyond the hatch. The floorboards creaked faintly as Clemmie shuffled about above them, her voice drifting down in muffled bursts.

'What exactly am I looking for again?' Clemmie's voice echoed faintly in the space, the words punctuated by the soft thuds of her shifting boxes and old trunks.

'It's a cardboard box,' Betty called back, cupping her hands around her mouth. 'Should be labelled simply "Earl of Aberford". It's not too big, I don't think. Your great-great-grandmother was very particular about labelling things.'

'If it's so particular, why's it buried under all this?' Clemmie grumbled under her breath. 'Honestly, there's a century's worth of dust up here. I'll be sneezing for days.'

'Do you need some help?' Betty called up, craning her neck.

'No, no. I'm fine. I've just got to… Oh, hang on… What's

this?' Clemmie's voice grew sharper, edged with curiosity. 'It's a suitcase. Feels empty though. Not what we're after.'

'Keep looking,' Betty urged.

The floorboards creaked again as Clemmie moved further into the loft. A thud followed as she tripped and crashed to the ground and muttered, 'Oops. Sorry about that!'

'What was that?' Betty demanded.

'Nothing important,' Clemmie replied quickly. 'I think it was just an old lamp.' There was a pause, then, 'Oh, here we go. There's a box with writing on it. It's … oh…'

'What?' Betty's voice sharpened with anticipation. 'What is it?'

Clemmie's voice dropped into something almost reverent as she picked up the box. 'This must be it.'

Her footsteps grew slower and more deliberate as she approached the hatch. In her hands she held a box, small enough to cradle but heavy enough to make her arms strain slightly.

'I'm coming down.' Carefully, she passed the box down to Betty, who received it as if it were made of porcelain. Clemmie climbed down the ladder slowly. When she reached the floor, the three women stood in a triangle, the box resting between them on an old wooden table. The writing on the lid was faint but legible.

'Why would Great-great-granny have a box labelled "Earl of Aberford"?' Clemmie asked, her voice low.

Betty didn't answer immediately. She was staring at the box as though it might spring open of its own accord. Her lips moved silently, as though debating with herself.

Amelia shifted uncomfortably, taking a step back. 'I should leave. This feels … personal.'

'No,' Betty said firmly, shaking her head. 'Stay.'

'Granny, with all due respect, at some point this box would have been opened. If not by us, then by someone clearing out the loft years from now. If it holds any kind of secrets, surely it should be us who discover them.'

Betty's brow furrowed, her eyes still locked on the box. 'It's not that simple, Clemmie. My mother was adamant. I don't know what's in there, but I do know she believed it shouldn't be disturbed.'

'But why?' Clemmie countered, her voice rising slightly. 'Why would she have a box with such a cryptic label if it wasn't meant to be opened? That doesn't make any sense. Do you think this actually has something to do with the Earl of Aberford, or the scandal that led him to disappear?'

Amelia glanced between them, clearly curious despite her discomfort. 'Maybe it's not as dramatic as you think,' she offered.

Clemmie shook her head. 'No. This feels important. Granny, please. Whatever's in this box, we deserve to know. *You* deserve to know.'

Betty hesitated, her fingers brushing the edge of the box. From her expression she was torn, her conscience warring with her curiosity. Finally, she exhaled heavily. 'You're right,' she said quietly. 'If it's been hidden away all these years, it's time someone knew the truth and if anyone should open it, it should be us.'

They headed towards the living room and placed the box on the coffee table. Betty reached out, her hands trembling slightly as she unfastened the string. Everyone held their breath as Betty opened the lid.

Chapter Twenty-Eight

They all stared at the worn, ribbon-bound bundle of letters in front of them. Betty began to untie the delicate knot that had kept the secrets within hidden for decades. Each envelope bore the same looping handwriting, addressed to *Beatrice Rose, The Café on the Coast, Puffin Island*.

Gently, Betty pulled the first letter from the stack and unfolded it. Her eyes skimmed the neat cursive writing.

'Are they from the Earl of Aberford?' asked Clemmie.

'If his first name is Henry, then I assume so,' replied Betty, her eyes firmly on the words on the page.

One by one, the three women read through the letters.

August 10, 1916

My Dearest Beatrice,

It has been mere days since I left the shores of Puffin Island, yet my thoughts are so fixed upon you that I feel as though I never truly departed. In every quiet moment, I find myself back at your café, watching you as you measure flour, the soft hum of your voice and the sweet smell of sugar filling the air. How I miss those peaceful afternoons in your company. The world feels darkened without your light, and all the fineries of London pale in comparison to the warmth of your laugh.

Do you remember the recipe we discussed? I've enclosed chef's notes for a spiced chocolate cake he adores. He always said that a hint of nutmeg added unexpected depth. I cannot think of a better pairing than your fruit preserves with rich chocolate, two unlikely companions creating something rare and sweet, just as you and I have.

I will be in touch as often as I can. Until then, please hold our secret close.

Yours,
Henry

September 3, 1916

My Darling Beatrice,

Another sleepless night, and again, my thoughts turn to you and our beautiful Puffin Island. How I wish I could walk the windswept paths of its shoreline, breathing in the salty air and talking for hours as we used to do. I carry a heavy heart tonight, as we are surrounded by conflict here, and the weight of my duties feels nearly insurmountable. Yet thoughts of you give me strength; how extraordinary you are, and how blessed I am to know you.

When I think of your café, I am reminded of the night we stayed late after closing, attempting to perfect that dessert together. I swear, I will never forget the taste of your berry preserves combined with the rich, creamy filling we created. Have you managed to recreate it yet? I imagine your hands working away, testing and tasting, perfecting it. Perhaps we will name it something special, so I may carry a part of it with me, even when I am far from Puffin Island.

For now, if I don't survive this war, promise me you will keep the secret safe.

With all my heart,
Henry

October 20, 1916

My Sweet Beatrice,

I find myself writing this from yet another distant place, the thought of you, your café, and our recipe the only things able to fill me with such peace. I wonder if you know how truly remarkable you are. How I miss your laughter, how it seemed to brighten the café and warm my heart in a way that no hearth ever could.

Last week, I dreamed of us baking together. You were laughing as you whisked ingredients in a flurry, a dusting of flour on your nose, your cheeks flushed with joy. In my dream, I tasted the dessert we had created – our secret – the tartness of the berries, the hint of chocolate, and I awoke with such an ache, longing to be in the café again.

When I return, we shall share it together, and I will toast to the remarkable woman who made it.

All my love,
Henry

November 15, 1916

My Beloved Beatrice,

Tonight, I sit here writing by candlelight. I must confess, I have tried to recreate the magic of your kitchen, but my attempts pale in comparison to yours. How I long to be back in that kitchen with you, breathing in the scent of fruit and spice, and hearing your gentle laughter over the clatter of pans. You are my peace, Beatrice, my sanctuary amidst the storm.

As I promised, here is another recipe for you to try, a family favourite from the royal table, yet never shared with anyone beyond. It is a custard with a dash of vanilla and a pinch of cinnamon, delicate but warming. Imagine how lovely it might taste combined with your berry preserves. Perhaps this will be our secret ingredient, a symbol of our trust, and a reminder of all that we share. I entrust it into your hands, knowing you will make it even more splendid than I could ever hope.

Hold our creation close.

All my love,
Henry

December 25, 1916

My Dearest Beatrice,

*Merry Christmas, my love. The snow falls softly here,
How I long to walk through your door this evening, chat
about things that no one else can ever know about.*

*I gift you the enclosed recipe from the royal household for
your beautiful café on the coast. This will be a future success,
of that I am sure. The torte is Chef Étienne's favourite so do
guard it as you would a treasure. I hope you will make it
tonight, and have a very Merry Christmas.*

All my love,
Henry

Clemmie gasped. 'So the recipe wasn't original, it was gifted by the Earl! But the royal chef was killed in the war, so how would people in the royal palace today even remember the recipe?'

'It's probably been passed down through the generations, just as it was in our family,' Betty said simply.

'At least now you have evidence that you haven't stolen the recipe; it was gifted,' said Amelia.

'I'm confused,' stated Clemmie. 'What do you think their relationship was? Do you think they were having an affair?'

Betty was still staring at the letters. 'I'm not sure, but all these letters were sent during the war.'

'When did Great-great-grandad meet Great-great-grandmother?'

'My mother told me they met near the end of the war at a tea dance that the islanders had arranged to keep spirits up. It was love at first sight.'

Betty's eyes softened and her voice was tinged with nostalgia as she painted the scene. 'Picture this. The island's village hall. Inside, the air was alive with laughter, and the faint clink of teacups, and the melodic strains of a small orchestra playing a waltz. Beatrice was in her early twenties and wearing a pale blue dress that shimmered like the sea under the lantern light, or so she told me. Her auburn hair was swept up with delicate combs, and my mother said she had a way of carrying herself that caught everyone's attention.'

Betty's eyes twinkled as she continued. 'Arthur was a young officer. He wasn't much for social gatherings, but his mates had dragged him along, saying he needed to remember what life was like beyond the trenches. He stood at the edge of the dancefloor, feeling out of place, until he saw Beatrice laughing with her friends. She was radiant, her laughter like a melody that outshone even the orchestra, he told me once.'

'Did he go straight up to her?' Clemmie asked.

Betty chuckled. 'Oh no, he hesitated. He was nervous, you see. War had hardened him in some ways, but the idea of asking a beautiful stranger to dance made his palms sweat. But Beatrice, oh, she was bold. She caught him staring and, instead of waiting for him to make a move, she walked straight up to him and said, "Well, are we going to dance or shall we just stand here all night?"'

Clemmie giggled. 'What happened next?'

'He was completely flustered,' Betty said with a laugh.

'But he managed to nod and take her hand. The moment they stepped onto the dance floor, it was as if the rest of the world faded away. They moved in perfect harmony, as though they'd been dancing together their whole lives. My mother told me once that it was in that moment he knew she was the one.'

'How romantic,' said Clemmie.

'By the time the night ended, they had exchanged addresses, and they soon became inseparable. When Arthur proposed, he did so on that very same spot they'd met on Puffin Island, under the light of the same lanterns that had witnessed their first dance. It's stories like these that remind us where we come from, Clemmie. Love, courage, tradition, they're all part of who we are.'

'With such a beautiful story, the Earl had to be just a friend. I wonder how they met, though. Baking somehow seems to be a passion for both of them,' chipped in Amelia. 'Perhaps, during the war, the Earl visited Puffin Island and stumbled into the café by chance? And because of his status, their friendship had to remain under wraps.'

'Maybe we will never know,' added Clemmie.

Betty placed her hand over her heart and let out a nervous laugh. 'For a moment I thought we were going to discover a huge love affair between Beatrice and the Earl.' She gave a soft chuckle, the tension easing from her shoulders. 'There's one more letter,' she stated.

Unlike the other envelopes, this one was sealed with wax. Clemmie carefully broke the seal and unfolded the letter. Her eyes scanned the page, the words jumping out at her with each line.

July 3, 1918

Dearest Beatrice,

This will likely be the last letter I send, though I cannot be certain. Circumstances are evolving faster than I anticipated. As you know I've already formally broken off my proposed engagement to Princess Alexandra. It is only right. I could not continue to live this charade while my heart belonged elsewhere.

I've surrendered my title – I know I do not deserve it, not after the choices I've made – and I've stepped away from public life.

Your secret and my secret will now stay buried together, along with the rest of the letters. They will remain sealed in the box, locked away from prying eyes. To retrieve them now would be too dangerous – too many are still watching. But should you ever need those letters, they are yours. The royal solicitor's address is enclosed below and he will be able to guide you to the letters' location. The code to open the box is our special number; you know the one.

Beatrice, I owe you more than words can say. Your kindness and your friendship have been my light in dark times. Though I must let you go now, I will be with you very soon. You are remarkable, and the world is better for having you in it.

All my love,
Henry

Clemmie's hands shook as she finished reading. Her mind raced with questions and implications. She hadn't expected this, not by a long shot.

Amelia was the first to speak, her voice barely above a whisper. 'He … he broke off an engagement with the Queen's daughter? Then left his aristocratic life behind?'

Clemmie's eyes were wide. 'What are all these secrets and where does Arthur fit in to this? This letter suggests they both have a secret. Is it the same secret? Did your mum ever let anything slip?' asked Clemmie.

Betty shook her head, her brow furrowing in concentration. 'I'm just trying to do the maths,' she murmured. 'My mum, Emily, was born December 1918, which means Clemmie's great-great-granny, Beatrice, must have fallen pregnant around … March 1918.'

Amelia nodded, fascinated. 'So your mum is Emily, Emily's mum is Beatrice, and it's Beatrice who's connected to the Earl. This is all very intriguing. How old were you when you had Clemmie's mum Belinda?'

The moment Amelia spoke Betty's face crumpled, her eyes glistening with unshed tears. 'Oh, I'm so sorry, I didn't mean to upset you.'

Betty took a deep breath, gathering herself. 'It's okay,' she said, but her voice faltered. 'They say time is a healer, but some wounds never really mend, the loss of your own child.'

Betty had sat down to tell Clemmie all about her mother's death when Clemmie was ten years old. It had been a bitter winter's night, the air crisp with frost as Belinda drove across the causeway that connected Puffin

Island to the mainland. She had just finished a late shift at the small hotel in Seas End where she worked. The tide had been low, and the road, though narrow and treacherous, was passable. But that night, a group of boy racers had been tearing across the causeway, engines roaring, music blaring, their cars weaving recklessly in and out of the oncoming lane.

Belinda never stood a chance. They had taken her out in an instant. The impact was so severe that her car had spun out of control, flipped over and hit a tree at the end of the causeway. By the time help arrived, it was too late. She was gone. Belinda was only twenty-four when she was killed, leaving behind Clemmie, who was two years old at the time, too young to understand the enormity of her loss.

It was Betty who had stepped in, raising Clemmie as her own, ensuring that her granddaughter grew up knowing love, even in the shadow of such a tragic loss.

'She was so young,' Betty whispered now, lost in thought. 'A life stolen in an instant.'

Amelia reached for both their hands, squeezing them gently. 'She'd be proud of you, you know,' she said softly. 'And of Clemmie.'

Betty nodded, dabbing at her eyes with a crumpled tissue. 'I hope so, I really do.'

Clemmie reached inside the box, her fingers brushing against brittle edges of time-worn photographs. She gently pulled out a handful, her eyes scanning their faded images.

'This is a photo of the Earl,' she announced.

She turned the photo around in her hands, marvelling at the noble figure staring back at her, his stance proud and assured. The resemblance was undeniable; this was the same man she had seen in framed portraits aboard the yacht.

Her fingers moved through the pile, carefully selecting another image.

'And this,' she breathed, 'this is Chef Étienne Dupont. Oliver told me he was killed in the war, and as a mark of respect for such an excellent chef, his royal kitchen was left untouched.' She glanced up at Amelia and Betty. 'I've been in that kitchen. Oliver showed me around. I've stood right there.' She pointed to the exact spot in the photograph where Chef Étienne stood next to the Earl, captured for ever in a moment of laughter, a towel slung over the chef's shoulder, his crisp uniform pristine.

'They look so handsome,' she mused. She passed the first photograph to Betty while she examined the next.

'Oh, and these were sealed boxes where the Queen could leave messages for the kitchen staff and request her favourite recipes.'

She passed the photograph to Amelia, who peered closely at it.

'Look at the gold combination numbers,' Amelia pointed out. 'They're so intricate.'

Clemmie soon realised that Betty hadn't spoken a word since she had handed her the first photograph. She turned her head, suddenly feeling uneasy.

Betty's face had gone ashen, her hands trembling slightly as she clutched a fragile picture between her fingers. Her breath came in uneven gasps, her lips parting but no sound emerging.

'What is it, Granny?' Clemmie asked.

Without answering, Betty stood and walked towards the dresser. She opened the door and pulled out a dented tin biscuit box.

Clemmie and Amelia exchanged a look but said nothing as Betty returned to the sofa and rested the tin box on her knee. She opened it, revealing an assortment of old photographs, their edges curled with age.

For a moment, she simply stared at them. Then, she reached in and pulled out a single photograph. She held it in front of her, her eyes scanning the image as if seeing it for the first time.

The photo showed a young couple standing outside The Café on the Coast. The woman's face was soft with laughter, her arm wrapped around the man beside her.

Betty's voice, when it came, was barely more than a whisper.

'This is my grandmother and grandfather.' She placed the photo on the table as both Clemmie and Amelia leaned in to look at it.

Then Betty laid the photograph of the Earl and the chef next to it.

'That can't be the Earl,' she murmured, her voice breaking under the weight of her revelation. 'Because ... that is Arthur Rose. My grandfather.'

A stunned silence filled the room.

Clemmie felt her heartbeat quicken, her mind racing to make sense of what she was hearing. She glanced from one photograph to the other.

They were the same man.

The same piercing gaze, the same proud stance.

But that was impossible.

She looked at Betty, who was trembling.

'Does this mean the Earl is my grandfather? No, it can't be.'

But the evidence was undeniable.

The man Clemmie had identified as the Earl, the man whose image was displayed aboard the Royal Yacht, was the same man her granny claimed to be her grandfather.

'I don't know what to say. I've never seen any photographs of my great-great-grandfather when he was young, so I wouldn't have recognised him, but yes, I can see the similarity.'

'There's nothing similar about it, they are the same person,' declared Betty.

Clemmie looked towards Amelia, 'What do you think?'

Amelia nodded. 'I agree with Betty.'

Betty was quiet for a moment. 'Did he actually give up the Queen's daughter for a life on Puffin Island? I don't know what to think. Was he more than just a humble café owner on the coast? Was he … was he secretly a nobleman, an Earl, a man with ties to royalty?

'I've never questioned who I am until now.'

Just then, the front doorbell rang.

Betty was about to stand, but Clemmie was quicker, springing to her feet.

'I'll get it. Amelia, pour Granny a stiff drink. I think she needs it.'

As Clemmie left the room and made her way towards the door, her mind was spinning. The Earl was her great-great-grandfather? It seemed impossible. Unreal. And yet, here they were. What a secret to have buried for all these years. It seemed so surreal.

As she opened the door, she briefly closed her eyes. This was all she needed right at this moment.

Oliver stood on the doorstep, his face drawn with something between regret and urgency.

'Please, let me explain.'

'This really isn't a good time,' Clemmie said, her thoughts still tangled around Granny and the revelation they'd just uncovered.

'Please, Clem,' he said, his voice quieter now. 'I've come all this way. I've been an idiot, and I need to explain. If, after that, you never want to see me again … I'll go. I promise.'

Clemmie studied him for a second, then let out a breath. 'Wait here.' She shut the door and turned back towards the living room.

Betty was putting on her coat.

'Where are you going?' Clemmie asked, concerned.

'I need some air. I need to think.' Betty's voice was firm but distant. 'I'm going for a walk, I won't be long.'

Clemmie and Amelia watched as she disappeared out of the back door.

'To think, it's usually Granny who is the keeper of secrets,' Clemmie murmured. 'I doubt she's ever experienced this kind of shock before.'

'Who was at the front door?' Amelia asked.

'Oliver. He's here to explain. He must have jumped in his car the moment I left.'

Amelia glanced towards the back door, then back at Clemmie. 'You listen to what he has to say. Call me if you need me.' Without another word, she slipped outside after Betty.

Clemmie turned back towards the front door, steadying herself.

She took a deep breath, pulled it open and met Oliver's gaze.

'You have ten minutes,' she told him.

Chapter Twenty-Nine

Oliver sat down on the sofa whilst Clemmie made tea. She wasn't sure why she had even offered him a drink. Maybe it was politeness, maybe a distraction, or maybe, deep down, she wanted to delay hearing whatever he had to say.

She placed the mug in front of him with a firm clink and took a seat opposite, 'Go on then,' she said, 'explain.'

Wrapping his hands around the mug, Oliver took a deep breath. 'I owe you an apology, Clemmie. A huge one. That review … it was cruel. I know that now.'

She shook her head slowly. 'Nice of you to realise, what, years later? Do you have any idea what that did to me?'

He looked down, shame settling on his face. 'I do now and I hate myself for it.'

'Then why did you do it?' she demanded. 'Why write something so scathing when you hadn't even set foot in my café?'

Oliver took a deep breath. 'Fiona.'

Clemmie's eyebrows shot up. 'Fiona? Now why didn't I guess she would be involved somehow?'

He nodded. 'I've already explained that our families always expected us to end up together. Same background, same social circles – it was practically written in the stars, according to them. And for years, I didn't question it. We grew up together, and when you spend that much time with someone, you don't always see them for who they truly are. She was always cutting, always had this edge to her, but I convinced myself it was just ambition. That she was just hungry for success.' He let out a breath. 'But that's not it. She doesn't go about things the right way. I made excuses for her, brushed over the snide comments, ignored the way she put others down. But every time I worked away and came back, I saw her more clearly and I didn't like what I saw.' His gaze met Clemmie's, filled with regret. 'I hate that you've been caught in the crossfire again. She's jealous. Jealous of your kindness, your talent, how hard you work – the list is endless. And she's jealous because she knows how I feel about you.'

Clemmie tilted her head, sceptical. 'Why the bad review?'

'As I told you, I invested when Fiona started her business. It seemed like the natural thing to do. When I became a food journalist, she encouraged me, said I had the perfect voice for the industry: critical and sharp. No sugar-coating.' He looked at her properly now. 'Then, one day, she told me about this café she'd visited on holiday.'

Clemmie's stomach dropped. 'She'd been here?'

Oliver hesitated, then nodded. 'She made it sound like a disaster. She told me the service was dreadful, the coffee was cold, and that she was treated rudely. She said you were arrogant, full of yourself, and that the place didn't deserve the praise it was getting.'

'That's a complete lie.'

'I know that now,' Oliver said quickly. 'But at the time, I believed her. She said she wanted me to write the review as a favour. She was furious about how she'd been treated and wanted to "balance the scales".'

Clemmie scoffed. 'That's pathetic.' Her expression hardened. 'So, you just blindly did what she wanted? Without fact-checking? Without thinking about the people it would hurt?'

Oliver flinched. 'I was young and stupid, and she was always pushing me into things I didn't want to do. I know it's not an excuse.' He sighed, running a hand through his hair. 'And the truth is, she convinced me it would help my career. Fiona told me that being critical, standing apart from the usual flowery, overly positive reviews, would make me stand out. That people respected brutal honesty. Given that it was a trial review for the magazine, and I was offered a permanent job soon after, and my career began taking off, it seemed like what she said was true.'

Clemmie was shaking her head. 'Honesty? There was nothing honest about what you wrote.'

'I know,' Oliver said, his voice quiet. 'I regret it more than anything. Your café was just collateral damage in her twisted games.'

Clemmie swallowed hard. 'That review destroyed my confidence. It made me feel like I wasn't good enough to run this place. I nearly walked away.' Her voice cracked slightly. 'My granny always says, "If you've got nothing good to say, don't say anything at all." Shame you never heard that one.'

Oliver looked stricken. 'Clemmie—'

'No, you don't get to just apologise and expect it to fix everything,' she cut in. 'You made me doubt myself. Every time I stepped behind that counter, I heard your words in my head. I thought I was a fraud, a joke and the worst baker in the world.'

'I wish I could take it back,' Oliver murmured. 'How can I put this right?'

'You can't.' She blinked back angry tears.

'I'm so sorry, Clem. I really am.' He raked a hand through his hair, his eyes glistening with tears. 'The review was a huge mistake, but I can promise you I now have your back completely. Yes, you broke my heart, but I could see how beautiful you are, how driven you are, and how your family means the world to you. All the qualities I'm looking for. Believe me when I say Fiona doesn't mean anything to me, not even as a friend anymore.'

For a moment, silence stretched between them. Then Oliver exhaled and leaned forward slightly. 'On the way here, I contacted my solicitor.'

Clemmie frowned. 'Why?'

'I'm pulling my money from Fiona's business. I don't want to be a part of it anymore.'

Clemmie studied him carefully. 'Are you sure that's what you want?'

'Yes. I don't want any association with her. It may cause a rift between the families for a while, but I have to do what I believe is best.'

Clemmie could see the anguish in his eyes as he

admitted everything, and appreciated what he was doing to put it right. He'd opened up to her and had been completely honest, owning his wrongs, and for that, she admired him. 'What about the competition? She's contacted the officials.'

Oliver shook his head. 'I don't believe you stole the recipe. It's just a coincidence that they're similar.'

Clemmie glanced towards the table, where the stack of letters and old photographs lay scattered. Her expression shifted. 'Well,' she murmured, 'there's been a development.'

Oliver followed her gaze. 'What do you mean?'

Clemmie exhaled, reaching for one of the aged envelopes. 'Unfortunately, on this occasion, Fiona may be right.' She carefully unfolded a fragile letter, the ink slightly faded but the words still legible.

'This letter is from the Earl of Aberford to my great-great-grandmother. They wrote to each other during the war, and in one of these letters, he tells her about Chef Étienne's favourite recipe. He actually gifts it to her, promising it will be a hit for The Café on the Coast.'

Oliver's eyes widened. 'The Earl of Aberford? He knew your great-great-grandmother?'

'It appears so. It's such a shock and we've only found out – literally, just before you rang the doorbell.'

'You're saying that your great-great-grandmother and the Earl were friends? That they wrote to each other?'

Clemmie nodded. 'Yes. And this letter is proof that the recipe came from the Earl himself.'

Oliver let out a low whistle. 'Wow. I suppose, technically, the recipe does belong to the Royal Family if it came from the royal chef.'

Clemmie pursed her lips. 'It's complicated. The Earl was friends with both Chef Étienne and Beatrice, and he willingly gave her the recipe and encouraged her to use it in the café.'

Oliver leaned back, mulling it over. 'Do you know how they met?'

Clemmie shook her head. 'I have no idea but there's more. A lot more.'

Oliver raised both eyebrows.

Chapter Thirty

As soon as Clemmie had shared the revelation, a wave of guilt crashed over her. Should she be sharing this? The letter had made it clear that both the Earl and Beatrice had secrets. If those secrets were to come to light, what then? What if they had the power to shake the monarchy itself? The weight of that possibility settled heavily in the pit of her stomach. But before she could voice her apprehension, Oliver reached for the photograph that was lying on the table.

He narrowed his eyes, his sharp gaze flicking between the picture and the similar photo they had seen on the Royal Yacht of the Earl and Chef Étienne.

'There's no mistaking the Earl.' He turned the photograph over and read the words scrawled on the back in faded ink. *'Beatrice and Arthur, December 1918.* Arthur?' Oliver repeated, his brows knitted in confusion. He glanced up at Clemmie. 'This is Henry.'

She hesitated, feeling torn. 'I'm not sure I should be

sharing this,' she admitted. It was one thing to discover a family secret, it was another to reveal it to someone else. But at the same time, she knew Oliver had connections, resources that could help them uncover the truth. That's what she was telling herself to justify this. It wasn't just reckless curiosity, it was a search for clarity, for answers that had been buried for generations.

'I just… I don't know, Oliver. What if we're opening a door that was meant to stay closed?' she said, her fingers tightening around the edge of the letter.

Oliver gave her a measured look. 'What if we're finally giving history its truth? What is it you know?'

She let out a shaky breath and, with a nod, continued. 'We've just discovered that the man in this photograph, standing beside Chef Étienne on the Royal Yacht, is the same man seen here with Beatrice, my great-great-grandmother. We can only assume that after he ended his engagement, he changed his name to Arthur Rose.' She swallowed hard, barely believing the words coming from her own mouth. 'That means … he is more than likely my great-great-grandfather.'

Their eyes locked on each other. Silence stretched between them, thick with implications neither of them had fully processed yet.

Oliver shook his head slowly. 'No, he can't be…'

Clemmie gave a mirthless laugh. 'Twenty minutes ago, I would have agreed and said it was ludicrous, but…' She trailed off, the reality of it setting in. If this was true, then everything she thought she knew about her family's past was a lie. The Earl – Arthur – had walked away from royalty, from duty, from everything. Why? What had happened that had driven him to erase his past and start anew under a different name? The only explanation was that after falling in love with Beatrice, he followed his heart.

Oliver's expression was unreadable as he studied the photograph again. 'If this is true, then you're part of a story the world was never meant to know.'

She exhaled, knowing full well that they had just uncovered something far bigger than either of them had anticipated. Yet, despite the unease coiling in her stomach, she couldn't ignore the pull. She wanted to know the rest of the story.

Oliver studied the photographs again. 'Arthur Rose,' he murmured, before placing them back on the table.

'We know there was a scandal, and the Earl chose to disappear from public life,' he said slowly, as if piecing together a puzzle. 'But was that because he was having an affair with Beatrice?' He picked up his phone and quickly typed something into the search bar. 'Let's see what we can find on Arthur Rose. Was that just a name that he made up?'

'I doubt you'll find much on the internet. It was a long time ago.'

'You're probably right but leave it with me.' Oliver's tone was confident. 'After all, I do have contacts in the Royal Family.'

Clemmie's expression turned serious. 'Please don't let Fiona get wind of this.'

Oliver met her gaze. 'Of course I won't. Let me see if I can uncover anything first…' He paused for a moment. 'My granny knows everything. How would you feel if we went and spoke to her?'

Clemmie thought for a moment. 'All this was a long

time ago, well before her lifetime. Do you really think that she'd know anything? Maybe we've uncovered all there is to know. Henry fell in love with Beatrice, became Arthur and lived the normal life he craved.'

'Possibly,' replied Oliver. 'But we could try? My granny is travelling to Scotland tomorrow. Maybe we could meet her somewhere or she could stop off here? What do you think?'

'I'm thinking I should check with my granny first.'

'But is there any need? What if we don't uncover anything else, and upset her needlessly?'

Clemmie thought for a second. 'Okay. You're probably right. Thank you. See if she has time.'

Oliver leaned back in his chair, looking thoughtful. 'I noticed the Royal Yacht is still here. Apparently, there's a problem with the engine?'

'Yes, I'd heard the same.'

Oliver finished his tea and placed his mug on the coffee table, 'Are we okay? I really didn't mean to upset you. It was unbelievably thoughtless of me to write that review, and I didn't consider the consequences, especially how it would make you feel.'

Clemmie studied him for a moment before asking, 'When we met in London, did you remember writing it?'

He shook his head firmly. 'Not at all. It was only when Fiona arrived on Puffin Island for the competition and sensed there was history between us that she reminded me. That was when I realised where my priorities truly lay, and it wasn't with my money or reputation. Maybe I should take a leaf out of the Earl's book and give up the life I know for love.'

She hesitated, then asked, 'Do you think you could?'

Oliver's gaze met hers, something unreadable flickering in his eyes, sending a shiver down her spine. 'That depends entirely on your plans,' he said with a slow, teasing grin.

Clemmie let out a soft laugh and swiped at him playfully. 'You are incorrigible.'

'Let me phone Granny and see if there's a chance we can meet up tomorrow.'

Chapter Thirty-One

The next morning Betty and Clemmie sat at their usual table in the café, the comforting aroma of fresh coffee and warm pastries filling the air. The café wasn't officially open yet, but that was one of the perks of being the owner: you could sit in your own establishment before the chaos of the day began.

Clemmie gazed at Betty over the rim of her coffee cup. 'So, where did you walk to yesterday?' she asked.

Betty looked up, stirring a spoon through her tea. 'I went to see Pete.'

Clemmie's brows lifted slightly. 'Did you tell him?'

'Yes, I needed some perspective.' Betty sat back, pushing her cup aside. 'And, well, he gave it to me.'

Of course he had. Pete always did.

'He said it how it is.'

Clemmie tilted her head, waiting. 'And how is it?'

Betty hesitated, choosing her words carefully. 'Does it actually matter if my grandfather was once an earl? He chose love. He walked away from all that pomp and tradition because being with Beatrice meant more to him. Honestly, I still can't get my head around the sacrifices he made to be with her. It doesn't sit right with me that they must have had an affair, but who am I to judge? They stayed together sixty years.'

'That says a lot about the kind of man he was. A decent human being. Okay, it may have started when he was in another relationship, but can you imagine facing the Queen to tell her you were breaking it off with her daughter? That took courage and honour.'

'I'd be petrified,' said Betty. 'What does it really change?' she murmured. 'Knowing it now? I'm still me. The café is still here. My life is exactly the same, except for the fact that I now know the truth.'

Clemmie studied her for a moment before softly saying, 'Maybe it's not about change. Maybe it's about understanding.'

Betty nodded slightly. 'Maybe.'

Clemmie took another sip of coffee before placing her cup down with a determined expression. 'There's something I need to tell you.'

Betty looked up, sensing the shift in her tone. 'What is it?'

Clemmie glanced towards the window as if checking for unseen listeners. 'After you left yesterday … Oliver turned up.'

Betty stilled, her hands folding in her lap. 'Oliver?'

Clemmie nodded. 'He was apologetic. Said he regretted writing that awful review. He explained why he did it, how he felt pressured, how he thought he was doing the right thing at the time.'

Betty's expression remained unreadable. 'And?'

'I told him about the Earl.'

Betty's eyes widened. 'You did what?'

'I know, it just seemed the right thing to do at the time.' Clemmie sat forward, urgency in her voice. 'He's arranged a meeting with his grandmother. She has close connections with the Royal Family. She might have heard things from the past, things that could help piece it all together.'

Betty rubbed a hand over her face, exhaling deeply. 'Clemmie … I don't think there is anything more to piece together. I think we know what happened.'

'But do you not think this is an opportunity to find out more?'

There was a long pause before Betty asked, 'What more could there be?'

'There's been something playing on my mind… Remember the number 1705? Maybe she could shed some light on it. It's in the recipe book, sewn into Beatrice's apron and etched into the wardrobe at Royalwood Cottage. I know the Earl and the chef had been there because their names were in the visitors' book. It's strange to now think I was standing somewhere my great-great-grandfather had visited.' Clemmie hesitated. 'Anyway, it could be a chance to finally make sense of it all. But if you'd rather me not go through with this, I'll call it off.'

Betty considered it for a moment before shaking her head. 'No. Go.'

'Are you sure?'

Betty offered a small smile. 'Yes. I'll keep myself busy here.'

Clemmie smiled back, relieved. 'I'd love for you to come with me.'

Betty shook her head, standing up. 'I trust you. Besides, someone has to make sure the café doesn't fall apart.'

Clemmie chuckled just as the front door swung open, the brass bell jingling overhead.

Amelia strode in, her face pale, her hands gripping a folded newspaper. Without a word, she dropped it onto the table in front of them.

Betty picked it up, smoothing out the front page. The bold headline screamed up at them all.

SCANDAL AT THE ROYAL BAKING COMPETITION

Clemmie felt a sudden churn in her stomach as her grandmother read aloud, '"It appears the winning contestant, Clemmie Rose, may not have submitted a recipe that was dear to her own heritage."'

Clemmie's eyes widened. 'I don't believe this.'

Betty continued, her voice growing sharp. 'The article states that it was brought to light at the royal garden party that the torte you baked in the competition had been sampled by the royal household previously and has been baked in the royal kitchens dating back to the First World War.'

Clemmie reached for the newspaper, scanning the lines in horror.

A source close to the Royals told us, 'This particular torte has a long history within the royal household. It is not merely a well-loved dessert but one with deep roots dating back to wartime. As it appeared in the competition under the guise of a personal creation, questions must be asked.'

Betty's lips pressed into a thin line. 'They're saying you didn't have the right to claim it as your own.'

Clemmie slumped back in her chair. 'This is a joke, right? I've already won, the show was televised live.'

Amelia's voice was tight. 'I wish it were.' She exchanged a glance with Clemmie. 'I suppose they could disqualify you.'

'What will happen to The Café on the Coast if I'm branded a cheat?'

Chapter Thirty-Two

The next afternoon Clemmie kissed her granny on the cheek and stepped outside the café. The crisp sea air wrapped around her as she spotted Oliver's car pulling up. The moment she slid into the passenger seat, she caught the concern in his deep blue eyes.

'I saw the newspaper yesterday,' he said quietly, his brow furrowed. 'I'm really sorry, Clemmie.' He leaned across and kissed her on her cheek.

'It's ridiculous. Sensationalised nonsense.'

'I could have a word with Lady Rosalind,' he offered. 'She has the right contacts to squash bad publicity.'

Clemmie hesitated, 'Would she really help me?' she asked cautiously. 'I mean, given Fiona's her granddaughter...'

Oliver nodded thoughtfully. 'Rosalind has always been a fair woman. Blood ties don't cloud her judgement. If she believes something is right, she'll do it. But we'd have to be honest with her. We'd have to tell her the recipe was gifted from the Earl.'

Clemmie felt a lump rise in her throat. The whole thing was a mess, and yet Oliver's unwavering support soothed some of the sting. He reached over with his left hand, his eyes still on the road, his fingers wrapping around hers. 'We can sort anything, together.'

But they couldn't. The realisation hit her like a wave. Because he was leaving. In just a few days, he'd be gone, flying across the world to chase his career, while she remained rooted on Puffin Island.

'Honestly, this will all come good,' he reassured, his thumb brushing gently over her knuckles. 'You suddenly look very sad.'

'It's just…' She trailed off, unsure how to put it into words.

'Just what?' he prompted, his gaze never wavering.

She swallowed. 'Timing. Again. I was so mad with you at the end of the garden party, yet my time at Royalwood Cottage was so wonderful. I know it sounds daft, and I could never afford somewhere so grand, obviously, but it felt like … we were a proper couple. Living together. Waking up, having breakfast, I had so much fun shopping for my dress…'

'Which is in the boot of the car along with all the accessories. They belong to you.' Oliver smiled, his grip on her hand tightening. 'And I know. I was thinking the same.'

Silence settled between them, thick with unspoken thoughts, the hum of the radio the only sound filling the space. They both knew what was coming. The distance. The uncertainty.

'A year isn't for ever,' Oliver said finally, his voice soft yet firm. 'We can work it out … if we both want to.' He began driving.

Of course she wanted to work it out. But how? She could never leave Puffin Island – it wasn't just where she lived; it was part of her, stitched into her very being. The café, the sea air, the people who felt like family. And Oliver? He thrived on movement, on adventure, on the sheer unpredictability of his life. Even if they tried long-distance for a year, then what? Would she be left waiting again, counting down the days until his next visit, only for him to be off to another continent after America? Would every milestone, every birthday, every bad day when she just needed him, be marked by a video call instead of a touch? Love wasn't the problem. It never had been. But was love enough to bridge an ocean when the real question wasn't just where he was going next, but whether they'd ever stop being two people pulled in different directions?

'You do know I never want to move from Puffin Island,' she said quietly, taking a sidewards glance towards him.

He did the same, before refocusing on the road ahead. 'Yes, I know,' he admitted. 'And I've got to work out how I feel about that. I love my job, I love the travel … and I don't want to let you down by making promises I might not be able to keep. No one can see into the future, but there's one thing I do know.' He paused. 'I want you in my life. We just need to find a way to make that work.'

Warmth spread through her, a flicker of hope among the uncertainty. But doubt still lingered. Love wasn't always enough, was it?

An hour later, Oliver turned into the car park of an

elegant hotel, its sandstone exterior standing proudly against the mountainous terrain.

Inside, the foyer was the epitome of refined luxury. Chandeliers sparkled overhead, casting delicate patterns on the polished marble floor. Elegant flower displays decorated the space, and well-dressed guests chatted as they passed through the reception.

They walked towards the bar, where Bunny sat waiting for them on a leather chesterfield. She was the embodiment of old-world elegance. Dressed in a perfectly tailored twin set, a string of pearls resting at her collar, she exuded a presence that demanded attention. Her sharp blue eyes flickered up as they approached, then she smiled and stood up. Oliver kissed her on both cheeks. 'Granny,' he said and reintroduced her to Clemmie before they all sat down.

'This is all very cloak-and-dagger,' she remarked, picking up her teacup and taking a sip. 'Accosting me on my way to Scotland like this. Now, tell me what's going on.'

Clemmie swallowed, stealing a glance at Oliver, who nodded encouragingly. She took a deep breath and began to explain, her fingers tracing the edges of the old photographs she had carefully laid out on the polished wooden table. 'We have evidence that the Earl didn't simply vanish without a trace. He withdrew from public life entirely, assumed the name Arthur Rose, and settled down somewhere far from the prying eyes of society – Puffin Island, in fact. Arthur Rose was my great-great-grandfather.'

Bunny sat back in her chair, her fingers interlaced as she absorbed Clemmie's words. A flicker of something, perhaps recognition or unease, passed across her face before she shared the next bit of information. 'Étienne was a distant cousin of mine by marriage,' she admitted, 'and I grew up hearing the rumours around the Earl's disappearance.'

Clemmie tilted her head, curiosity gleaming in her eyes. 'What kind of rumours?'

Bunny exhaled, as if bracing herself. 'You have to understand, these stories have been passed down through generations. No one really knows what's true and what's simply embellishment. But from what I heard, the Earl lived by the coast for some time. Some even claimed he worked on a cruise ship, though that could just be whispers distorted over the years. People love a mystery, don't they?' She gave a small, knowing smile before continuing. 'But there was always something about the way his name would come up in hushed tones, especially among those who had connections to the royal staff. It was as though those who knew anything concrete didn't dare say it outright.'

Clemmie exchanged a glance with Oliver, then reached for another photograph. 'Look at this,' she said, sliding it towards Bunny. 'This is a photograph of him with Beatrice. And this one'—she placed a second image beside the first—'is of him with Étienne. There's no mistaking it. The Earl and Arthur Rose were the same person.'

Bunny studied the images, nodding slowly. 'That does seem clear,' she murmured. 'But what else do you have?'

Clemmie hesitated for a fraction of a second before reaching into her bag and pulling out a battered old recipe book. 'This,' she said, flipping open to a specific page, 'has a number written in it: 1705. The same number is sewn into an apron we found, and etched on the wardrobe door at

Royalwood Cottage. But, to our knowledge, Beatrice had never been there. And yet…'

Bunny's brow furrowed.

'There were a number of letters, too, and one of them suggested that the Earl and my great-great-grandmother both had secrets.'

'Interesting,' replied Bunny.

'Then there's this, too.' Clemmie retrieved another photograph from her collection and placed it before Bunny. 'This is a picture of the kitchen on the Royal Yacht that was left untouched following Étienne's death.'

Bunny picked up the photograph and studied it closely. 'Now that is interesting,' she said, tapping the image with her index finger. 'Did Beatrice ever work on the Royal Yacht?'

Clemmie shook her head. 'Not that we know of. Why?'

Bunny leaned back, a twinkle of intrigue in her eyes. 'You see the recipe cabinets,' she said, pointing to them in the photo. 'The rumours I've heard suggest that these compartments were used to pass secret messages between the staff. Not recipes – notes. Love notes. Many an affair was conducted onboard back in the day.'

Oliver let out a low whistle. 'Does that change anything?'

'It does indeed,' Bunny agreed. 'Now, what was the number you found again?'

'1705,' Clemmie replied.

Bunny's expression sharpened. Without hesitation, she pulled out her phone and dialled a number. A moment later, someone answered Bunny's call. 'Wilf, it's me,' she said without preamble. 'Go to the drawing room and check the family tree chart,' she instructed.

Clemmie exchanged a curious glance with Oliver, mouthing, 'Who's Wilf?'

Oliver whispered, 'My grandfather.'

Bunny continued speaking into the phone. 'I need you to check something for me. Étienne Dupont, his date of birth. Can you confirm it?'

There was a brief pause and then Bunny looked very pleased with herself. 'I knew it,' she murmured. 'Seventeenth of May.' She hung up the phone and turned back to Clemmie and Oliver. 'My gut instinct was right. That number – 1705 – is Étienne's birthday.'

Clemmie's mouth fell open. 'Then that means…'

Bunny picked up the photograph of the royal compartment in the kitchen of the Royal Yacht. 'My guess? One of those boxes holds all the answers,' she said confidently. 'And the combination to open it is 1705.'

Chapter Thirty-Three

As Clemmie and Oliver sped away from the grand hotel, there was non-stop chatter about the possibilities of what they were going to find.

'Even if the Royal Yacht is still there, how exactly do we get on board?'

Without taking his eyes off the road, Oliver gave her a smile. 'I've got that covered.' As they approached the causeway leading to the island, he dialled a number, adopting a polished yet urgent tone. 'Yes, hello, this is Oliver Lockwood, I believe I may have dropped a rather sentimental cufflink during my last visit aboard the yacht... Yes, quite, a family heirloom. Any chance I could come aboard for a quick look?' There was a pause, then a polite but hesitant response on the other end. Oliver leaned into his charm. 'I'd be ever so grateful. Wouldn't want to trouble anyone, of course, but perhaps just a quick check? Your officer on duty could assist?' There was another pause before Oliver ended the call with a satisfied nod. 'We're in,' he said, throwing Clemmie a triumphant glance. 'Now let's just hope they don't ask too many questions.'

When they arrived back on Puffin Island, they headed straight for Blue Water Bay and parked the car. 'I'm actually shaking.' Clemmie held out her hand to demonstrate.

'My heart is beating fast. Are you ready?'

Clemmie looked towards the Royal Yacht. 'Do you believe in fate?'

'I do.'

'Because I think that yacht was stalled for a reason.'

'I think you may be right. Come on. Let's see if we can actually get back to the kitchen.'

'How are we going to know which box it is? Because there were quite a few.'

'We'll have to try them all.'

'I feel like I'm on a secret mission and you're my wingman.'

'I like the sound of that,' replied Oliver as he locked the car and they hurried towards the yacht.

Clemmie's heart hammered against her ribcage as her heels clicked on the polished wood of the gangplank. Oliver, of course, was the picture of calm, hands tucked into the pockets of his tailored coat, his stride easy, his gaze sweeping ahead.

As they approached the security checkpoint, a uniformed guard straightened, stepping forward to block their path. His name badge read *H. Merrick, Chief of Post*. The friendly smile on his face told Clemmie that he and Oliver had met before.

'Oliver,' Merrick greeted, nodding slightly. 'Good to see

you again. How are you? I hear you're off to America. Lady Rosalind was telling us all about your next adventure.'

'Yes, I leave Friday. Merrick is a friend of my grandmother's – and, of course, Lady Rosalind's,' Oliver added for Clemmie's benefit. 'Our paths have crossed many times over the years. When I was a little boy, he used to let me run riot around the Royalwood Cottage gardens. Once, I even managed to capsize a rowing boat on the royal lake, after sneaking out past my bedtime. Merrick fished me out and got me back in bed before anyone even noticed I was missing.'

Clemmie laughed. She knew exactly what Oliver was doing, laying on the charm so no one would suspect they were here for anything more than a lost cufflink.

'Honestly, as a young lad, you kept me on my toes,' Merrick chuckled. 'Thankfully, I'm due to retire soon, so my days of rescuing boys from boats will finally be over. It's just been radioed through that you've lost a cufflink on board the yacht. We've checked thoroughly, but nothing has been found. You're welcome to take another look though.'

'Ah, thank you, Merrick,' Oliver said, feigning relief. 'That cufflink is something of a lucky charm, so I'd rather not leave without it.'

Merrick stepped aside without another word and waved them through.

As soon as they were out of earshot, Oliver grinned. 'Well, that worked, didn't it?'

They hurried down the corridors, their steps muffled by the plush navy carpet beneath them. The walls gleamed with polished mahogany, oil paintings of past monarchs watching them as they wove their way deeper into the ship.

'You do know we'll be caught on CCTV?' Clemmie whispered, glancing over her shoulder.

'Possibly,' Oliver admitted. 'But let's cross that bridge when we get to it.'

She didn't argue, pressing forward until Oliver suddenly stopped in front of a door. He pushed it open.

'Here we are.'

Clemmie slipped inside, 'I don't know how you find your way around. It's like a rabbit warren.'

In front of them was the large, reinforced cabinet with twenty identical gold boxes, each secured with a combination lock. Clemmie's stomach was churning. 'If there *is* something in the box, what's the plan?'

'I'll stuff whatever it is inside my jacket and we get out of here as fast we can before we do get caught.'

Oliver ran a hand along the locked boxes. 'Are you sure you want to uncover whatever we might uncover?'

Clemmie hesitated. 'What more *can* we actually uncover? I think it will just be the confirmation that the Earl became Arthur Rose after falling in love with my great-great-grandmother. So yes, let's get that confirmation. We need to be quick.'

'Then stop talking and start cracking,' Oliver said, moving to the bottom row. 'You take the top, I'll take the bottom.'

Clemmie reached for the first box. She spun the dials quickly. Nothing.

To her left, Oliver was working at a rapid pace, his fingers steady despite the urgency of the moment. She could hear his muttered curses each time a box refused to open. She wasn't doing much better. The tiny dials felt stiff beneath her fingertips, and her hands kept slipping in her haste.

'Damn it,' she murmured, moving to the next one.

Minutes stretched on, as they tried box after box, tripping over their own fingers as frustration mounted.

'I swear to God,' Oliver muttered, 'if this turns out to be some elaborate wild goose chase—'

Click.

Clemmie froze and her breath caught in her throat as the lock mechanism released with a soft metallic snap.

'Oliver,' she whispered, her fingers trembling as the lid of the box swung open.

Inside, neatly stacked beneath a layer of velvet, were loose-leaf pages, the edges curled and yellowed with time.

Oliver exhaled. 'We've got it.'

For a second, neither of them moved.

Clemmie looked up at Oliver, her heart hammering with the adrenaline. 'Now what?'

'Now we run,' ordered Oliver.

Chapter Thirty-Four

Clemmie's heart was still racing as they hurried along the bay.

Oliver kept glancing over at her. 'You all right?' he asked.

'I can't believe it,' said Clemmie, 'I mean, I really *can't* believe the code opened the box.'

'I think it's Betty's choice what she does with these documents. What do you think?'

Clemmie nodded. 'I agree.'

As they approached The Café on the Coast, they saw that Betty was flipping the 'OPEN' sign to 'CLOSED'.

'Granny!' Clemmie called out.

Betty turned, raising an eyebrow as she took in the pair of them, flushed from exertion, eyes alight with urgency.

'What's got you two in a flap?' she asked. 'You look like you've just run from a ghost.' She opened the door wide and they walked into the café.

'Get that door locked,' said Clemmie.

Betty closed the door behind them, her eyes flicking from one to the other.

'What's going on? Has something happened?'

Clemmie took a steadying breath. 'We met with Bunny at the hotel,' she started. 'Granny, she cracked the 1705 code.'

Betty's eyes widened. '*What?*'

Clemmie nodded rapidly. 'She figured it out because of the photograph, the one of the royal recipe cabinets. Chef Étienne is a distant cousin of Bunny's and his birthday was May seventeenth. *Seventeen-zero-five.*'

Betty looked astonished.

'This,' Oliver said, gesturing to the stack of aged papers, 'is what we found inside the box that the code unlocked.'

Betty stared at the documents as if they might combust at any moment. Then, with a deep breath, she shook her head, walked over to the kettle and flicked it on.

'Well,' she said, reaching for the tea caddy, 'if ever there was a time for a cuppa, it's now.'

'Do you want us to leave you to have a look through it all?' asked Clemmie.

'I can leave,' suggested Oliver.

Betty looked at them. 'I think we're all in this together.' She set out three mugs and reached for her glasses. 'Go on, take a look.'

Clemmie took the top document. 'These,' she said, 'are handwritten notes. They look old. Really old. Recipes, mostly.'

'You mean to tell me you've got classified royal recipes?' asked Betty.

Clemmie exhaled a shaky breath. 'Not just recipes. Look

at this.' She pointed to a page filled with flowing script. 'It's not just about food, it's about *who* was served and *when*. It's a log. A detailed history of who dined where, what was prepared.' As Clemmie flipped through the bundle, a small note fell from between the letters. She carefully unfolded it, her eyes scanning the faded ink.

To find what's hidden, listen to the tick of time. Where the past has stood still, beneath the weight of old wood and memories, it rests. The clock keeps it safe.

Betty raised an eyebrow. 'What is this about? It sounds very cryptic, like a riddle. The clock?'

Clemmie's heart skipped a beat. 'The clock… Do you think it has something to do with the old grandfather clock in the hallway?'

'I've no idea,' said Betty, glancing at the door to the hall.

Clemmie's eyes widened as a memory clicked into place. 'Lady Rosalind told us about a grandfather clock. She mentioned how the chef would hide cakes in the clock for her, in a secret compartment no one would suspect. What if that's the same thing here? What if Rosalind and the chef weren't the first people to use the clock as a hiding place?' Her voice lowered with excitement. 'Granny, we need to check it.'

The two women exchanged a look before turning to Oliver. 'What do you think?' asked Clemmie.

'I think you'd best check it.'

Clemmie, Betty and Oliver stood in the hallway, staring at the ancient clock that hadn't ticked or tocked for as long as either woman could remember. It stood there, as solid as the house itself, its brass pendulum no longer swaying, its face worn with age, the hands forever frozen in time. A family heirloom, passed down through generations and never once altered or repaired. Just like the recipes Betty had inherited, the clock had remained in the family, enduring the years without a second thought.

Clemmie stepped closer to the clock. 'Well, there's only one way to find out,' she said. With a gentle twist, she turned the brass knob hidden just below the clock face.

To their surprise, it gave way easily, revealing a small, concealed door. Betty gasped, her hand flying to her chest. 'I can't believe it!'

The door opened. Nestled in the dusty compartment was an old, yellowed document. Her heart skipped a beat. She reached inside and carefully pulled it out, revealing the delicate paper.

'It's a marriage certificate,' she murmured. 'For Beatrice and Arthur! They were married here at the church on Puffin Island!'

Betty blinked back a tear. 'A lovely piece of family history.'

'There's more,' said Clemmie. Right at the back was an old, worn diary.

Back in the living room, Clemmie opened the diary at the first page. 'It's *Beatrice's* diary,' she said reverently.

They all stared at it.

'Do you want to read it?' asked Clemmie, knowing that

they were about to embark on a journey that could potentially uncover a whole lot more secrets, if the letters they'd discovered in the attic were anything to go by.

'My heart is beating that fast,' admitted Betty. 'You flick through and see if there's anything obvious that stands out.'

'Are you sure?' asked Clemmie.

Betty nodded.

Clemmie took a deep breath and began to read some of the entries out loud.

March 5, 1918

The tea dance was like any other. The music, the laughter, the hum of conversation, all familiar. But then, there was him. Arthur Rose. A soldier from Scotland, with eyes like the stormy sea and a smile that disarmed me entirely. He asked me to dance, and my world shifted. I had never believed in love at first sight, but tonight, I know it exists.

March 7, 1918

Arthur leaves tomorrow. The war calls him back, and I am left with nothing but a memory of his touch, the way he whispered my name as we swayed to the music. It is unbearable, this ache in my chest. I never imagined love could bloom so quickly, nor did I know how deeply it would root itself within me.

April 10, 1918

Puffin Island is quiet today. The sea is restless, waves battering the shore, much like my own heart. The café is coming together, but my thoughts stray only to Arthur. His letters are sparse, but I clutch each one as if it were my lifeline. He is fighting, and I am waiting.

May 14, 1918

I have been feeling unwell for weeks. Fatigue, dizziness, a sense of unease I cannot shake. Henry visited today – he always seems to know when I need company. He is troubled, I can tell. He confided in me that he will tell the Queen his relationship with Princess Alexandra is over. I was stunned. To give up all that he has known. But when I saw the sorrow in his eyes, I understood.

May 18, 1918

Henry arrived unannounced tonight. He asked if he could stay the night, and I saw the weight he carried. He told me everything. About Étienne. About the love that would never be accepted by the world he was born into. I watched his hands tremble as he spoke, his voice raw with grief and frustration. They'd spent last night at Royalwood Cottage where they celebrated in private their relationship and Étienne's birthday. Love should not have to be hidden.

Clemmie chipped in, 'I should have noticed the date in the visitors' book at the cottage was the seventeenth of May … 1705.'

June 3, 1918

I am with child. My hands shake even as I write the words. Arthur's child. The realisation fills me with equal parts joy and terror. How will I raise a child alone? Will Arthur return to me? I have told no one, not even Henry.

July 9, 1918

Étienne is dead. Murdered at war, just moments after Henry met with the Queen and decided to step away from public life. I have never seen Henry so broken. He weeps without shame, crumbling before me. I wish I could take his pain, as he has comforted mine. The world is cruel to love, it seems.

August 1, 1918

Henry has taken refuge here. We do not speak much of our grief, but it lingers in the air between us. He knows now about the baby. He held my hand as I cried, whispering reassurances I am too numb to believe. I am lost.

August 20, 1918

The telegram came today. Arthur is dead. My heart has shattered, and there is no mending it. I screamed until my voice broke, until Henry wrapped his arms around me and held me through the storm of my grief. I will never love again. I know that now.

Henry says he understands. That there will never be another Étienne for him, just as there will never be another Arthur for me. He looks at my growing belly and makes a choice. He will take Arthur's name. He will be my family.

September 10, 1918

Henry Aberford is gone. In his place stands Arthur Rose, my Arthur. We will make this work, for the child who will never know their true father, and for the love that could not be but will always remain.

September 13, 1918

Henry and I have set a date. I need to remember to call him Arthur. We will be married before the baby arrives. It is not the love story I once dreamed of, but it is a new kind of love, built on trust and understanding. Puffin Island has always been our sanctuary, and its people our family.

December 14, 1918

Emily is here. My beautiful daughter. When I hold her, I

see Arthur in her eyes, but I also see hope. Henry was there
for her birth, and he held her as if she were his own. In that
moment, I knew we would be all right.

December 20, 1918

Everyone on Puffin Island has embraced us. They know
Henry's truth, the islanders are privy to Henry's secret and
they have accepted it without question. They welcome him as
Arthur Rose, the man who has chosen to stand by my side.
We have found peace, at last, in our quiet corner of the world.
Our family is not conventional, but it is ours, and it is
enough.

The room fell silent as the weight of the words on the
fragile, yellowed pages settled over them like a thick mist.
Betty, Clemmie and Oliver sat around the counter, the diary
resting between them, its secrets laid bare.

Clemmie was the first to speak. She exhaled shakily and
wiped her eyes, 'Henry Aberford … and Étienne.'

Oliver let out a low whistle, running a hand through his
hair. 'And Arthur Rose wasn't Arthur Rose. He was Henry.
He took on the name of the man she loved so her child
would have a father. That's … that's devotion.'

Betty's hands rested on her heart. 'My heart aches for
them both. For the love lost, for the sacrifices made. They
created a life together out of grief and necessity, but also out
of love, in their own way and the world never knew.'

'What do you want to do about this?' asked Clemmie
tentatively. 'Do we share their story?'

'No.' Betty's voice was firm. 'This isn't for the world to

know. It never was. If it was meant to be known, they would have told it themselves. Instead, they chose secrecy, and we need to respect that.'

'Are you sure?' asked Clemmie. 'This is a part of history. This changes things. Who Henry really was, what he sacrificed…'

'What would that do now?' Betty's eyes met hers, steady and unwavering. 'It would turn their love, their choices, their heartbreak into nothing more than a spectacle. This was their life. Not some tale for people to pick apart. They built something here, something safe. It was their truth to keep, and I won't be the one to undo it.'

'I agree,' added Oliver, looking between the pair of them.

Betty closed the diary. 'We let them rest. We protect them, just as they protected each other.'

The three of them sat in silence for a long moment, the weight of Betty's decision settling between them.

Some secrets were never meant to be told.

This one would remain safe, for ever.

Chapter Thirty-Five

The Café on the Coast had been busy all day, the usual stream of tourists and locals keeping Clemmie on her feet from morning until closing. As soon as the doors had shut, she'd been even busier preparing for tonight. Oliver's last night. Their last dinner before he made his way to the airport. In the last half-hour she had swamped the café with candles and placed a jam jar of wildflowers in the centre of the chosen table.

She heard the bell above the door jingle, and Oliver stepped inside. He held out his arms and immediately they hugged each other tight.

'You okay?' he asked.

Clemmie nodded, swallowing a lump, telling herself to enjoy the evening, and that somehow it would all work out.

'I hope your phone is charged because the only break you'll have from me is when I'm on that nine-hour flight. I'll be FaceTiming you from the airport, the bar and just before take-off,' he said, lightening the mood.

'Fully charged,' she replied, pulling away slowly.

'What is that I can smell? What are we eating?'

'Shepherd's pie – and for dessert it had to be clementine torte. Are you having one glass of wine?'

'As much as I would love to share a drink with you, I would be tempted to have more and that would mean missing the flight.'

'I best get you drinking then,' she teased. 'There's water on the table. I won't be a minute.'

Returning to the kitchen, she watched him through the door, her heart tightening in that awful, bittersweet way she'd grown too familiar with. He was leaving. They'd talked about her visiting, of course. But life had a way of filling up faster than you realised. The Café on the Coast had become the new must-visit spot, her days swallowed by tourists, orders and the endless demand for her clementine torte. The cookbook was coming out at the end of the month, an actual book with her name on it. She was thrilled – of course she was – but as she looked at Oliver sitting at the table in her candlelit café, she wondered if success always came with a price.

'This looks and smells amazing, Clemmie,' he said softly as she placed the food on the table. 'Is this going to be in the cookbook?'

She smiled. 'I wanted our last night to be special and yes, it is.'

'I promise there will be others.' He reached across the table and held her hand. Neither of them wanted to let go. 'I want to make it work.'

'I do, too, but I can still be sad you're going.'

'I know, I feel the same.'

'Let's eat,' she said, pulling her hand away.

They ate slowly, lingering over every bite. The conversation ebbed and flowed, light and teasing one moment, quiet and deep the next. But despite the chemistry between them, there was an underlying sadness neither of them could dispel.

'You must be exhausted,' Oliver said, taking a sip of water. 'The café has been non-stop since the competition. I barely got through the door when I popped in earlier. I swear, I saw people queuing outside before you even opened.'

Clemmie laughed. 'It's been madness, but the best kind. And it's only going to get busier. The recipes have been sent to the publisher. It's officially happening. The book will be out in no time.'

Oliver grinned. 'I saw the announcement on social media.'

'Pre-orders are already in the thousands. It's surreal. And we've set up a launch night at the café on publication day. I'll be signing books, and everyone gets a free slice of torte.'

'Free cake? That'll cause a stampede,' Oliver teased.

Clemmie laughed. 'Probably. But it felt like the right way to celebrate.'

'It's perfect. Just like you handled everything after the competition. You were incredible, Clemmie.' His expression softened. 'I'm really proud of you.'

She reached for his hand across the table. 'I couldn't have done it without you.'

They sat in comfortable silence for a moment before Oliver said, 'I'm glad we told Lady Rosalind some of the truth about Henry Aberford.'

'Me too, and I'm grateful that the allegation of cheating was quickly dropped and my name cleared,' Clemmie said. 'No doubt Lady Rosalind and Bunny had something to do with that.'

'Without a doubt,' Oliver agreed. 'I told you Lady Rosalind was a fair person.'

'Dare I ask how it's going with Fiona?'

'It's in the solicitor's hands so hopefully it will all be done and dusted soon. But let's not spoil this night talking about her.'

'Agreed. I'm just glad it's all over and things worked out. I can finally breathe again.'

Oliver lifted his glass. 'To new beginnings.'

She clinked hers against his. 'And to this moment. No matter what happens next.'

They drank, letting the warmth of the evening wrap around them, holding on to every second as if time itself might pause if they wished hard enough.

The last spoonfuls of clementine torte were eaten. Oliver looked at his watch. It was time to leave and Clemmie knew it.

Bracing herself, she briefly closed her eyes. 'Go on. I know you have to go.'

Oliver exhaled. 'I truly get why you could never leave this place, why you love it here. These people, the way they keep each other's secrets and protect the island's own. It's remarkable.'

Her throat tightened. 'Oliver…'

Neither of them wanted that conversation. It was too difficult.

'Damn the timing,' she replied, trying to lighten the mood.

'It's been a hell of a couple of weeks, Clemmie Rose,' he murmured, standing and pulling her into his arms.

The dam broke, and the tears came fast and hot as she clung to him. 'A year is a long time, Oliver.'

'It'll go fast,' he promised. 'This isn't the end.'

He kissed her deeply and she kissed him back just as fiercely, unwilling to let go.

Finally he pulled away, breathing hard, and cupped her face. 'I have one more secret to tell you before I leave.'

She looked up at him. 'What is it?'

'Just in case you still wonder, it was me who nominated you for The Royal Baking Competition. I didn't nominate Fiona, she just assumed I did, and I never put her straight. As they say, "You have to pick your battles." My guess is that Lady Rosalind nominated her.'

She froze. 'What? You nominated me?'

He gave her a lopsided grin. 'I knew you would smash it, though I wasn't aware we'd open a box of secrets! But I'm grateful for this whole experience. It brought us back together.' He pressed his forehead to hers.

She let out a watery laugh. 'You absolute menace!'

He grinned. 'I know.'

Then, after one last lingering kiss, he walked out the door.

She stood in the doorway and watched him climb into

the driver's seat. Her heart felt like it was being wrenched from her chest as he gave one last wave and the car began to roll down the lane, its red taillights disappearing into the night. She wiped her cheeks, whispering to herself, 'This isn't the end. He'll be back soon.'

Chapter Thirty-Six

Clemmie picked up the pen and walked over to the calendar that was hanging on the café wall, a quiet ritual she'd performed every morning since Oliver left for America. Another day ticked off. Eleven more months to go.

'Don't you be all maudlin looking at that calendar. Today is all about celebrating what an amazing granddaughter I have,' Betty ordered.

'I will be celebrating, don't you worry!' replied Clemmie.

Today her cookbook was out in the world, and Betty had gone all out. Bunting hung from the beams, fairy lights twinkled in the windows, and, of course, the life-sized cardboard cutout of the Queen had made a grand reappearance in the corner. The books had arrived in all their glossy-covered glory and were stacked high on the centre table, ready for signing later on. Betty and Clemmie had spent the whole day baking tortes, in between serving the regular customers. Prosecco, cake and books felt like the perfect combination for the evening ahead.

Still, as she checked her phone again, Clemmie's excitement dimmed slightly. No message from Oliver. It wasn't like him. Despite the time difference and his hectic schedule, they'd managed to FaceTime nearly every day. But today, of all days, there was silence. She shook it off. He was probably just caught up in work.

By the time seven o'clock rolled around, the queue outside the café stretched down the street.

'Granny, Amelia, have you seen all the people queuing? It's insane!'

'Isn't it just? And you deserve every bit of this success.' Betty held up one of the cookbooks.

'It's time to open the door. Get that pen ready,' exclaimed Amelia. She flung open the door. 'Please form an orderly queue, collect a copy of the book from the first table and pay at the second table, then make your way to Clemmie, who will sign your book and be ready for any photos. Then do help yourself to a slice of torte!'

Betty was in charge of the payments, whilst Amelia was making sure everything else ran smoothly.

An hour into the book signing, Clemmie had barely had time to catch her breath as she signed book after book, sharing laughs and hugs with familiar faces. The café buzzed with conversation, the pop of prosecco corks punctuating the air. It was everything she had dreamed of, yet there was still that niggle that wouldn't leave her mind. Why had there been no word from Oliver? She took a short bathroom break and once more checked her phone.

'Are you okay?' asked Amelia. 'Can I get you a drink?'

'Just water for me. I know I should be on top of the world but...'

'But what? This is going amazingly well. The press have just arrived to take some photos too.'

'It's Oliver. This is the first day I've not heard anything from him and he always messages. I feel a little anxious, if I'm honest.'

'He's not let you down before so I'm sure there's a good reason. Anything could have happened: he could even have dropped his phone down the toilet, or it's been stolen ... anything. Push it out of your mind and get back to it; the queue is quite long again. Just enjoy this moment.'

'Yes, you're right.' Clemmie went back to the table and put a smile on her face.

She'd just finished having her photo taken with a fan and sat back down when a copy of the cookbook was pushed in front of her and she heard a familiar voice say, 'I believe the shepherd's pie is very good!'

Clemmie looked up and froze.

There, standing in the queue, was Oliver.

He looked tanned and a little travel-weary, but his smile – that smile – was as bright and steady as ever. He was here.

'What are you doing here?'

'You didn't think I would miss this, did you?'

Tears pricked her eyes as she abandoned all decorum, pushing back her chair and launching herself at him. Laughter and applause rippled through the café as he caught her, his arms strong and familiar around her. She clung to him, her heart hammering against his chest.

When he pulled away, he, too, was tearful. 'I can't do it,

Clem. I can't be in America when you're here. Not for a year, not for a day. I love you, and I want my life to be here, with you.'

Her eyes widened, her body trembling. 'But your career, your plans?'

He shook his head. 'I think I need to take a leaf out of the Earl's book. Love is more important. None of it matters if I don't have you.'

'I don't know what to say. Are you sure?'

'I've never been surer of anything in my life.' He grinned, tucking a strand of hair behind her ear. 'You're my home, Clemmie. I don't want to spend another day without you.'

The whole café erupted into cheers as he kissed her, sealing the promise between them.

In that moment, with the scent of warm cake in the air and the sound of their friends celebrating around them, Clemmie knew this was her happy ending. Not in a far-off dream, not in the pages of a book, but right here, in the place she loved, with the man who had just chosen her over the world.

As Oliver pulled her in for another kiss, she knew that the best chapters of their story were still to come.

'I love you, too.'

RECIPES FROM CLEMMIE ROSE'S CAFÉ ON THE COAST

Introduction

Welcome to *The Café on the Coast Cookbook*, a collection of mouthwatering recipes and delicious bakes inspired by the heart and soul of my family's beloved café.

Perched on the rugged shores of Puffin Island, The Café on the Coast has been a cherished retreat for both locals and visitors since 1917, when my great-great-grandmother, Beatrice Rose, first opened its doors. What began as a humble seaside café serving comforting home-cooked meals soon became a haven of warmth, good food and community spirit, a legacy I am proud to carry on today.

From the very first cup of tea poured to the last crumb of cake savoured, this café has been shaped by the remarkable women who came before me. This book is dedicated to them: to Beatrice Rose, whose dream started it all, and to my granny, Betty Rose, the strongest, most incredible woman I have ever known, whom I love with all my heart. Their passion for food, family and resilience has been my greatest inspiration.

Winning The Royal Baking Competition was a moment I

will never forget, putting The Café on the Coast firmly on the map and sharing our little slice of heaven with the world. Now, with this book, I invite you to bring a taste of Puffin Island into your own kitchen. Whether you're craving a comforting seaside supper, a showstopping bake or a simple treat to enjoy with a cup of tea, these recipes are designed to be loved, shared and savoured.

So, preheat your oven, dust off your mixing bowls and let's get baking. After all, good food isn't just about flavour, it's about memories, love and the joy of sharing something truly special.

With love,
Clemmie Rose

Clementine Chocolate Torte

(AWARD-WINNING ROYAL RECIPE)

A rich, indulgent torte with the vibrant flavour of clementines, perfect for special occasions.

INGREDIENTS

- 200g dark chocolate (70% cocoa), chopped
- 175g unsalted butter, cubed, plus extra for greasing
- 200g caster sugar
- 4 large eggs
- 125g ground almonds
- 50g plain flour
- Zest of 3 clementines
- 2 tbsp clementine juice
- ¼ tsp fine sea salt
- Cocoa powder, for dusting

INSTRUCTIONS

STEP 1: **Prepare the tin:** Heat the oven to 180°C/160°C fan/gas 4. Butter and line the base and sides of a 23cm springform or loose-bottomed cake tin with baking parchment.

STEP 2: **Melt the chocolate and butter:** Place the butter and dark chocolate in a small saucepan. Gently heat on low, stirring occasionally, until melted and smooth. Remove from heat and set aside to cool slightly.

STEP 3: **Whisk the eggs and sugar:** Using an electric whisk, beat the eggs and caster sugar together in a large bowl for about 5 minutes until pale, thick and billowy, resembling the consistency of old-fashioned custard.

STEP 4: Combine the chocolate and egg mixture:
Gradually pour the slightly cooled chocolate and butter mixture into the whisked eggs and sugar, folding carefully with a large metal spoon to retain as much air as possible.

STEP 5: Incorporate the dry ingredients: In a separate bowl, mix the ground almonds, plain flour, clementine zest and sea salt. Gently fold this dry mixture into the batter, ensuring an even consistency. Finally, stir in the clementine juice to enhance the citrus flavour.

STEP 6: Bake: Spoon the batter into the prepared tin, smoothing the top. Bake for 35–40 minutes, or until the torte is evenly set with a delicate crust on top. The centre should have a slight wobble.

STEP 7: Cool and finish: Leave the torte to cool in the tin until warm. Carefully release the cake from the tin, peeling away the parchment. Dust generously with cocoa powder before serving.

STEP 8: To Serve: Cut into wedges and enjoy on its own or with a dollop of crème fraîche or whipped cream. The bright clementine notes balance the richness of the chocolate, making every bite unforgettable.

Coastal Berry Pavlova

A light meringue dessert topped with a medley of fresh coastal berries.

INGREDIENTS

- 4 egg whites
- 200g caster sugar
- 1 tsp white vinegar
- 1 tsp cornflour
- 300ml double cream
- 1 tbsp icing sugar
- A mix of fresh berries (blueberries, raspberries and blackberries)
- A drizzle of local honey

INSTRUCTIONS

STEP 1: Preheat the oven to 120°C (100°C fan). Line a baking tray with parchment.

STEP 2: Whisk the egg whites until soft peaks form. Gradually add the sugar, a tablespoon at a time, whisking until stiff peaks form.

STEP 3: Fold in the vinegar and cornflour. Spoon the meringue onto the tray, creating a circular base.

STEP 4: Bake for 1 hour, then turn off the oven and leave the meringue to cool completely inside.

STEP 5: Whip the cream with icing sugar until soft peaks form. Spread over the cooled meringue, top with berries and drizzle with honey.

Hearty Fisherman's Stew

A rich, warming stew inspired by the seaside.

INGREDIENTS

- 2 tbsp olive oil
- 1 onion, finely chopped
- 2 garlic cloves, minced
- 2 carrots, diced
- 1 celery stalk, diced
- 400g tinned chopped tomatoes
- 500ml fish stock
- 200ml white wine
- 300g fresh white fish (e.g., cod or haddock), cut into chunks
- 200g prawns
- 1 tsp smoked paprika
- 1 tsp dried thyme
- Salt and pepper to taste
- Fresh parsley, chopped, to serve

INSTRUCTIONS

STEP 1: Heat olive oil in a large pot. Sauté onion, garlic, carrots and celery until softened.

STEP 2: Stir in tomatoes, fish stock, wine, paprika and thyme. Simmer for 20 minutes.

STEP 3: Add the fish and prawns, cooking gently for 5–7 minutes until tender.

STEP 4: Season with salt and pepper. Serve hot, garnished with parsley.

Sea Salt and Honey Shortbread

A sweet treat with a hint of the ocean.

INGREDIENTS

- 150g unsalted butter, softened
- 75g caster sugar
- 200g plain flour
- 1 tbsp local honey
- A pinch of sea salt flakes

INSTRUCTIONS

STEP 1: Preheat the oven to 160°C (140°C fan). Line a baking tray.

STEP 2: Cream the butter and sugar together until pale and fluffy. Mix in the honey.

STEP 3: Add the flour and a pinch of sea salt, mixing until a dough forms.

STEP 4: Roll out the dough and cut into shapes. Sprinkle with extra sea salt.

STEP 5: Bake for 15–20 minutes, until lightly golden.

Lemon and Lavendar Drizzle Cake

A fragrant, zesty cake perfect for a coastal tea break.

INGREDIENTS

- 200g unsalted butter
- 200g caster sugar
- 4 large eggs
- 200g self-raising flour
- Zest of 2 lemons
- 1 tbsp dried culinary lavender
- Juice of 2 lemons
- 100g icing sugar

INSTRUCTIONS

STEP 1: Preheat the oven to 180°C (160°C fan). Grease and line a loaf tin.

STEP 2: Cream the butter and sugar, then beat in the eggs one at a time.

STEP 3: Fold in the flour, lemon zest and lavender.

STEP 4: Bake for 45 minutes, or until a skewer comes out clean.

STEP 5: Mix lemon juice and icing sugar to create the drizzle. Pour over the warm cake.

Spiced Coastal Crab Bisque

A creamy soup with a hint of spice.

INGREDIENTS

- 2 tbsp butter
- 1 onion, chopped
- 2 garlic cloves, minced
- 2 tbsp plain flour
- 500ml fish stock
- 300ml cream
- 200g fresh crab meat
- 1 tsp cayenne pepper
- Salt and pepper to taste
- Crusty bread, to serve

INSTRUCTIONS

STEP 1: Melt butter in a pot and sauté onion and garlic until softened.

STEP 2: Stir in the flour and cook for 1 minute. Gradually add fish stock, stirring constantly.

STEP 3: Add cream, crab meat and cayenne. Simmer for 10 minutes. Season to taste.

Dark Chocolate and Seaweed Brownies

A unique take on classic brownies, with a hint of savoury.

INGREDIENTS

- 200g dark chocolate
- 150g butter
- 3 large eggs
- 200g caster sugar
- 100g plain flour
- 1 tbsp finely chopped dried seaweed flakes

INSTRUCTIONS

STEP 1: Preheat the oven to 180°C (160°C fan). Line a baking tin.

STEP 2: Melt chocolate and butter together. Whisk eggs and sugar until fluffy, then fold in chocolate mixture.

STEP 3: Add flour and seaweed flakes, mixing until combined.

STEP 4: Bake for 25 minutes. Cool before cutting.

Raspberry and White Chocolate Scones

A fruity twist on the classic.

INGREDIENTS

- 250g self-raising flour
- 50g butter
- 50g sugar
- 150ml milk
- 100g fresh raspberries
- 50g white chocolate chunks

INSTRUCTIONS

STEP 1: Preheat the oven to 200°C (180°C fan). Line a baking tray.

STEP 2: Rub butter into flour until it resembles breadcrumbs. Stir in sugar.

STEP 3: Add milk, raspberries and chocolate chunks. Mix gently to form a dough.

STEP 4: Cut into rounds and bake for 12–15 minutes.

Summer Peach Galette

Rustic and charming, this dessert is perfect for a coastal picnic.

INGREDIENTS

- 1 sheet of ready-made puff pastry
- 4 ripe peaches, sliced
- 2 tbsp brown sugar
- 1 tbsp honey
- 1 egg, beaten

INSTRUCTIONS

STEP 1: Preheat oven to 200°C (180°C fan).

STEP 2: Lay out the pastry, arrange peaches in the centre, and sprinkle with sugar.

STEP 3: Fold edges over, brush with beaten egg, and drizzle with honey.

STEP 4: Bake for 20–25 minutes until golden.

Seaside Shepherd's Pie

(SEAFOOD VERSION)

A coastal twist on a hearty classic.

INGREDIENTS

- 500g white fish, flaked
- 200g prawns
- 500g mashed potatoes
- 1 onion, diced
- 2 tbsp butter
- 300ml milk
- 1 tbsp flour
- 1 tsp mustard
- 100g grated cheese

INSTRUCTIONS

STEP 1: Preheat oven to 180°C (160°C fan).

STEP 2: Sauté onion in butter, add flour, then milk to create a sauce. Stir in mustard and cheese.

STEP 3: Combine fish and prawns, layer with sauce in a baking dish, and top with mash.

STEP 4: Bake for 25 minutes until golden.

Acknowledgments

Writing a book may be a solitary act, but turning it into something worth reading takes a village. I am beyond lucky to have the best one.

To Charlotte Ledger, the captain of One More Chapter, who takes my words and steers them into stories – thank you for believing in me and my books.

To Laura McCallen, my incredible editor, who polishes, tweaks, and shapes my stories into the very best versions of themselves – I am forever grateful for your talent and patience.

To Tony Russell, the eagle-eyed copy editor who ensures my characters don't change names halfway through the book and that my commas are where they should be – thank you for making me look far more competent than I actually am!

To Helen Williams, my go-to at OMC, who ensures everything runs like clockwork – from production to marketing – thank you for your dedication and for making sure my books find their way into the hands of readers.

To my four wonderful children, Emily, Jack, Ruby, and Tilly – thank you for being my greatest joys.

To Nellie and Cooper, my writing partners-in-crime and four-legged besties – thank you for your unwavering loyalty, your warmth at my feet, and for listening to my plot dilemmas without ever rolling your eyes.

To Anita Redfern, my best friend, my rock, and my cheerleader for 32 years (and counting). From the moment we met, you have believed in me, even when I didn't believe in myself. I'd be lost without you.

To Julie Wetherill, my best friend, travel partner, gin-drinking accomplice, and the fastest reader I know! Thank you for your endless support and for devouring my books at record speed. You make this journey all the more special.

Thank you to all the book bloggers, booksellers, and library staff for reviewing and recommending my novels! And of course, a huge shoutout to every reader who picks up this book – thank you. You make this all worthwhile.

This book was inspired by two incredible people. First, my best friend, Anita – because she loves cake (and let's be honest, that's reason enough). And second, my brilliant editor, Laura, whose Instagram is a treasure trove of royal life. Honestly, I'm convinced she's a secret royal!

I really hope you enjoyed *The Café on the Coast*. I had the best time writing Clemmie and Oliver's story. If you enjoyed reading it, I'd love to hear about it – please do tag me on social media!

Warm wishes,
Christie x

Verity Callaway is running away.

The plan is simple: hop in her reliable camper van and cross the Channel, headed for a rendezvous with her best friend in Amsterdam to kick off six months of travel. But when Verity stumbles across a decades-old postcard while preparing her cottage for its temporary tenants, her life takes an unexpected turn, and she finds herself on a ferry to Puffin Island instead.

Verity's childhood was filled with tales of adventures set on the picturesque island, but she'd always thought her beloved granny had made it all up. Now, knowing the stories and the setting were real, Verity is determined to find the postcard's sender and uncover the secrets of her grandmother's past … even if it means setting off a sequence of events that will change not just her own life, but also that of the sleepy island's close-knit community…

AVAILABLE IN PAPERBACK, EBOOK AND AUDIO!

Christie Barlow

The Lighthouse Daughters of Puffin Island

'Full of warmth, fun and feel-good factor'
KATIE FFORDE

Can she weather the storm?

Having narrowly avoided losing everything to her romance scammer ex, artist Delilah Waters is done with men and focused entirely on her quest to buy Puffin Island's magical lighthouse. It's a crucial piece of her own family's history and the perfect space to turn into her home. But then Max Harrington walks through her door.

Her feelings for her former art teacher might have been forbidden at the time, but now he's back, and single, and there's no denying that the attraction is mutual! But when something seems too good to be true, it normally is, and Dilly soon makes a shocking discovery that changes everything…

AVAILABLE IN PAPERBACK, EBOOK AND AUDIO!

Christie Barlow
THE
STORY SHOP
Is there anything more tempting than a good book?

Is there anything more tempting than a good book?

When travel writer Jack Hartwell arrives on Puffin Island amidst a terrible storm, he stumbles into The Story Shop, the island's quaint bookshop.

Seeking refuge, he finds himself immersed in Amelia Brown's enchanting world of books, puffins, and an eccentric group of book club regulars. So when the enigmatic Amelia challenges Jack to read a mysterious novel *The Temptation Bucket List* – and to complete its challenges with her – he can't resist.

But with Jack's time on Puffin Island ticking away, the stakes rise. The final item on the list? To share a secret that no one else knows…

AVAILABLE IN PAPERBACK, EBOOK AND AUDIO!

ONE MORE CHAPTER

YOUR NUMBER ONE STOP
FOR PAGETURNING BOOKS

The author and One More Chapter would like to thank everyone who contributed to the publication of this story...

Analytics
Imogen Wolstencroft

Audio
Fionnuala Barrett
Ciara Briggs

Contracts
Laura Amos
Inigo Vyvyan

Design
Lucy Bennett
Fiona Greenway
Liane Payne
Dean Russell

Digital Sales
Laura Daley
Lydia Grainge
Hannah Lismore

eCommerce
Laura Carpenter
Madeline ODonovan
Charlotte Stevens
Christina Storey
Jo Surman
Rachel Ward

Editorial
Janet Marie Adkins
Rosie Best
Kara Daniel
Charlotte Ledger
Laura McCallen
Jennie Rothwell
Tony Russell
Sofia Salazar Studer
Helen Williams

Harper360
Emily Gerbner
Ariana Juarez
Jean Marie Kelly
emma sullivan
Sophia Wilhelm

International Sales
Peter Borcsok
Ruth Burrow
Bethan Moore
Colleen Simpson

Inventory
Sarah Callaghan
Kirsty Norman

Marketing & Publicity
Chloe Cummings
Grace Edwards
Katie Sadler

Operations
Melissa Okusanya
Hannah Stamp

Production
Denis Manson
Simon Moore
Francesca Tuzzeo

Rights
Ashton Mucha
Alisah Saghir
Zoe Shine
Aisling Smyth
Lucy Vanderbilt

Trade Marketing
Ben Hurd
Eleanor Slater

**The HarperCollins
Distribution Team**

**The HarperCollins
Finance & Royalties
Team**

**The HarperCollins
Legal Team**

**The HarperCollins
Technology Team**

UK Sales
Isabel Coburn
Jay Cochrane
Sabina Lewis
Holly Martin
Harriet Williams
Leah Woods

**And every other
essential link in the
chain from delivery
drivers to booksellers
to librarians and
beyond!**

ONE MORE CHAPTER

One More Chapter is an
award-winning global
division of HarperCollins.

Subscribe to our newsletter to get our
latest eBook deals and stay up to date
with all our new releases!

<u>signup.harpercollins.co.uk/</u>
<u>join/signup-omc</u>

Meet the team at
<u>www.onemorechapter.com</u>

Follow us!

@onemorechapterhc

Do you write unputdownable fiction?
We love to hear from new voices.
Find out how to submit your novel at
<u>www.onemorechapter.com/submissions</u>